THE THORPE HAZELL MYSTERIES

The Thorpe Hazell Mysteries
and More Thrilling Tales
On and Off the Rails

Victor L. Whitechurch

Coachwhip Publications
Landisville, Pennsylvania

CONTENTS

A slight, delicate-looking man, with pale face and refined features, light red hair, and dreamy blue eyes.

Such is a brief description of Thorpe Hazell, book-collector and railway enthusiast, a gentleman of independent means, whose knowledge of book editions and bindings was only equalled by his grasp of railway details.

At least two railway companies habitually sought his expert advice in the bewildering task of altering their time tables, while from time to time he was consulted in cases where his special railway knowledge proved of immense service, and his private note-book of such "cases" would have provided much interesting copy to publishers.

He had one other peculiarity. He was a strong faddist on food and "physical culture." He carried vegetarianism to an extreme, and was continually practising various "exercises" of the strangest description, much to the bewilderment of those who were not personally acquainted with his eccentricities.

With this brief introduction of the man, it is proposed to set forth, for the first time, a selection of railway "cases" in which he played a more or less prominent part.

"I tell you I only paid fivepence each for them."

Harry Brett took the cigar from his customer's hand, looked critically at it, smelt it, and then shook his head decidedly.

"Can't be done!" he said, "must be a fake."

"Unroll it—you're welcome."

The young tobacconist broke the cigar in half, rubbed the leaves between his palms, and examined them carefully.

"Ye—es," he admitted, "it's right enough. Same leaf all through."

"What did I tell you?"

Harry Brett turned round, reached for a box on a shelf, took it down, and selected a cigar, which he compared with the fragments lying on his counter.

"Same brand," he said at length. "But I can't make it out at all. Now, I can't afford to sell these under sixpence each, or sevenpence from a broken box, and even then the profit's a mere nothing. You must have got these over the water Mr. Wilson?"

"No, I didn't."

"You couldn't have bought 'em retail at the price."

"I did, though."

"What, at a shop?"

"Yes."

"Where?"

"In this town."

"In Netherton?"

"Exactly."

"By George! Who was it, Mr. Wilson?"

"Well, at Crane's, if you want to know. There's no secret about it."

Harry Brett brought down his fist on the counter with a bang that made the scales rattle. The mention of Crane's name had evidently upset him.

"It's all very well," he said, "but I tell you it can't be done. Either Crane's a bigger fool than I took him for, or he means having you in the end, and is only running this sort of thing to advertise his business. Why, he hardly knows anything about the trade; he's only been in it six months. You're welcome to buy them, Mr. Wilson, of course. *I* can't do them at the price."

"'Well," returned the customer, "I'm a bit of a judge of a weed, and if he begins palming off inferior stuff he won't impose on me. But till then I'll save my money and deal with him. But, as he makes no reduction in other goods, I'll take a tin of my usual mixture from you."

"Oh, go and get your baccy where you buy your cigars," exclaimed Harry Brett, who had been working himself up into quite a rage. "I don't hold with all this underselling business, nor with those who encourage it. Good morning, sir!"

Mr. Wilson smiled slightly at the young man's outburst of passion, shrugged his shoulders, and walked out of the shop.

Harry Brett leant on the counter with his elbows, gazing angrily at the fragments of the object which had upset him so much. He had been a tobacconist from his boyhood upwards, having begun to work in his father's shop ever since leaving school, and since his father's death, three years previously, he had come into the business. It was not a very large one, but it was well established, and had many old customers. And Harry himself had been calculating for some little time that there was profit enough out of the shop to support two, besides which he had a very distinct notion of the choice of a partner.

But for the last three months certain things had troubled him. His takings had grown distinctly less, and certain customers had become irregular. And it was a curious coincidence that these troubles had begun to date from the time when Peter Crane had opened a rival business in Netherton, with an announcement that during the first week he would give away a "tip-top cigar" with every quarter of a pound of tobacco purchased.

It was galling, inasmuch as this Peter Crane had nothing to recommend him. Netherton knew him as a ne'er-do-well, turning up every now and again at his widowed mother's, who kept a small confectionery shop in the town. He had cleared one window of this shop of its contents, and substituted the fragrant weed in its various forms, and, as often as not, his mother dispensed these goods, for there were intervals during which Peter Crane himself seemed to abandon his new trade.

"Well, Brett," said a quiet voice, suddenly, "you seem wrapped in thought. What is puzzling you? Half a minute, please, before you answer. It is time for my mid-day exercise."

Brett looked up at Thorpe Hazell, who had entered without noise, and now stood before him twirling his arms rapidly round his head and then suddenly thrusting them out in front. Hazell lived at Netherton, but had a little bachelor flat in town, where he spent a good deal of his time. He was a regular customer of Brett, who knew his little eccentricity.

When he had finished Brett told him about the cigar and his suspicions. Hazell leant on the counter and listened attentively.

"I know this young Crane," he remarked, "and I'm afraid he doesn't bear the best of characters. Of course, this affects your trade?"

"It does, sir, to a certain extent."

"Do you suspect anything?"

"Well, sir, I hardly like to say. This particular brand of cigar can be picked up very cheaply in Holland or Belgium, and if they could be got over without the duty I could understand it."

"You think it's a question for the Revenue officials?"

"Oh, *I'm* not going to put them on his track," said Brett scornfully. "There's honour in trade as in other things. Besides which, if there were nothing in it I should pose as a spiteful sort of chap, and it would be all the worse for me."

"I see. You've excited my curiosity, Brett. Well, I want some cigarettes of the usual brand—thank you. If you hear anything about Crane's movements you might let me know. And, by the way, don't talk about the thing. Good morning."

On his way home he called in at Crane's shop. Here he made a trifling purchase. Mrs. Crane served him.

"H'm," he muttered to himself as he regained the street. "That collarette of hers was genuine Brussels lace. I wonder whether Brett's suspicions are correct. It may be a case worth investigating."

Netherton was about twenty-five miles from London, on the Mid-Southern and Eastern Railway, and Thorpe Hazell constantly ran up to town. On this particular evening he was due at a meeting at Kensington.

He had scarcely taken his seat in the train when a young man came in and sat opposite. Hazell glanced at him over his paper, and recognised him as Peter Crane. He remembered Brett's little difficulty for a moment, but dismissed the subject as he resumed his paper.

Now, when the train drew up at the London terminus of the Mid-Southern and Eastern Railway, Hazell did not hurry himself in the least. He was not due at Kensington just yet, so he determined to wait till the departure of the Continental train. There were many things to interest him. The type of engine running, the number of coaches—dozens of details that are only apparent to the enthusiast of railway matters.

He was standing on the platform, taking in these various things, when he suddenly caught sight of Crane going into the Continental booking-office. An impulse seized him, and a moment or two later he was standing close behind the tobacconist, overhearing him ask for a return ticket to Gantes. He began to be interested.

"Now," he reasoned to himself as he went out of the station and took a hansom, "there's evidently a bit of clever smuggling going on here. Let's think. A return ticket. *How* does he get the cigars through? How does he bring them back? Seems to me there's a chance of a railway mystery here. Of course, it may be on the boat, but I shouldn't think so. I'll have a look into this. There's any amount of frontier smuggling on Continental railways, I know. I once saw half a hundredweight of tobacco fixed under a passenger coach on the St. Gothard, and beautifully run through Chiasso. This may be well worth investigating."

Once having made up his mind, Hazell lost no time in making further inquiries as soon as he returned to Netherton, the result being that he ascertained that Crane had a regular date in the month for absenting himself from home.

And so it happened that the next time the latter took a return ticket to Gantes, Thorpe Hazell, disguised in a black wig, and looking very much like a commercial traveller, was already seated in the Continental train, booked through to the same destination. He had his eyes wide open, and had already taken in the fact that Crane's luggage consisted of a fair-sized brown Gladstone, and a very large black kit bag.

Hazell kept well out of Crane's way all the journey, for he knew very well that it was the return trip only that demanded careful scrutiny. So he snatched what sleep he could. They reached Gantes in the small hours of the morning, and Hazell noticed that Crane put the kit bag in the cloak-room, after which he proceeded to an adjacent hotel, a porter carrying his Gladstone.

Hazell, whose luggage was quite small, looked about him, noticed a hotel just opposite, rang up the sleepy night-porter, and took a front room, so that he could command the entrance of Crane's hotel. Instead of undressing, he opened his bag, changed into a tourist's knickerbocker suit, and then lay down on his bed with a determination not to sleep more than a couple of hours.

At daybreak he was at his window, keeping careful watch. An hour or two passed, and then his patience was rewarded. Crane came out of the hotel, smoking a cigar and suspecting nothing.

The next minute Hazell was in the street, following his prey to the station. He lounged into the booking-office in time to hear Crane take a return ticket to Antburg.

Then he inquired of the booking-clerk casually whether one could take a return to Antburg and come back the next day.

"No, monsieur, tickets are only available for one day."

He shrugged his shoulders lazily, for he never believed in taking too much trouble over anything. It was clear that Crane would be back in Gantes that day. The only thing was to find out whether he took his black bag with him. He did.

"Now," said Hazell to himself, as he went back to his hotel, "that young man is precious shrewd. It's pretty clear he's gone over to Antburg to get his goods—there isn't a better place in Northern Europe for getting them—probable out of bond, too. But why does he take this route? It's a roundabout way to get to Antburg. I know. He works the trick on the Mid-Southern and Eastern, and the other line won't do. It's well worth finding out, but I can't do anything yet."

He had his breakfast, strolled round the town, and finally came back to his room. He had jotted down the times of trains returning from Antburg.

Then he settled himself to perform a "nerve-strengthening" exercise, which consisted of lying down on the flat of his back and holding a tumbler of water, filled to the brim, over his head for ten minutes at a time, the object being not to spill a drop of it. He entirely abstracted himself from the object in hand, except at such times as Antburg trains were due, when he got up and carefully watched the street leading from the station.

In the afternoon Crane appeared once more and entered his hotel. Then Hazell paid his bill, went to the station, and waited for the train back to England. He was keen and alert now. If that black bag, which he surmised was in the cloak-room, contained cigars, he was particularly anxious to see how the Customs were evaded.

Exactly in accordance with his surmises, Peter Crane came down to the station in time for the afternoon boat train.

And this is what he did. He took the black bag out of the cloak room and registered it through to London. That meant that until the bag reached London he could not possibly get at it, and then he would have to open it in the presence of the Customs' officials, through registered luggage being examined there, and not at Dovehaven. The brown bag, which appeared to be heavy, he took in the train with him.

Thorpe Hazell began to be mystified. Assuming the bag to be filled with cigars, he could see no way in which they could be brought through free of duty. He watched the luggage being taken on the boat at Ozende, but Crane was absolutely regardless, and had thrown himself on a saloon berth, and was sleeping almost immediately, his brown bag beside him.

At Dovehaven the examination of hand luggage took place, and Hazell had squeezed himself close beside Crane in order that he might see what was in the brown bag. There was nothing suspicious. It contained quite a pile of books and articles of clothing, a pink shirt being rather conspicuous.

As soon as the examination was over Crane turned to the porter who was carrying the bag.

"Put that in the van," he said. "Label it for London. I shan't want it in the carriage with me."

Hazell, still wondering, now went up to the guard's van and watched the luggage being put in, both of Crane's bags being among them. The guard himself was busily engaged helping the porters, as the boat was rather late, and he was anxious to get off.

"Now then, sir, are you going on? Take your seat, please. Right away!"

A shrill whistle, a wave of the green lamp, and the train was off, the next stop being the London terminus.

"Curious," said Hazell to himself as he took a packet of plasmon chocolate, and a flask of milk out of his bag and proceeded to "dine." "Perhaps I'm wrong, after all. Ah!"—as a thought struck him— "well, we'll wait till we get to town."

A couple of hours later that night the train drew up at the London terminus, having, of course, run through Netherton without a stop. Behind the long barrier stood a number of Custom House officials waiting to examine the registered luggage before it was passed through. Hazell watched by the guard's van until Crane's two bags were deposited on the platform. Crane took charge of the brown one himself, and a porter followed him with the black one to the examination counter. Hazell stood a little behind, eagerly awaiting the result.

"Anything to declare, sir? Tobacco, scent, cigars?"

"No—nothing."

"Open your bag, please."

"Certainly."

He unlocked the large black bag and threw it open. Hazell bent forward. And he caught a glimpse of a pink shirt—and books.

The black bag contained the identical articles that he had seen in the brown bag at Dovehaven.

A solution struck him. Glancing round he saw a platform inspector whom he knew. Rushing up to him he exclaimed, in a whisper:

"Jarvis—I'm Mr. Hazell—look here."

"Lor', sir, I shouldn't have known you. I—"

"Hush. Don't let on, man. Quick; you see that fellow in the light overcoat doing up his bag. Get one of those officers to examine the brown bag by his side. Sharp!"

The next moment Jarvis was behind the counter and had spoken a word to the official. Crane had just strapped up his bag and was moving off. Hazell had darted away.

"Sir—one moment."

"What is it?"

"That other bag. I want to see it."

"It's not registered luggage. It was examined at Dovehaven. Here's the chalk mark on it."

"Never mind. Open it, please."

"Oh! very well," cried Crane with a laugh, laying it down on the counter and unstrapping it. "Here you are."

The official looked inside, his face burst into a smile.

"All right, sir!" he exclaimed, "that's soon settled."

Jarvis, who was standing by, smiled too. A minute later Hazell accosted him.

"Well," he asked, "what was inside that bag?"

"Nothing, sir. It was *empty!*"

"Empty was it? Oh! please say nothing about this, Jarvis."

He went into the refreshment-room, ordered a cup of coffee, lit a cigarette, and sat down to think it over. For once in his life he was completely baffled. It had seemed quite simple to him as he came up in the train, and he had thought that the opening of the brown portmanteau would prove the solution of the enigma. Alter a while a plan of action developed in his mind, and he went out of the refreshment-room. Jarvis was still on the platform.

"Jarvis," he said, "I don't want it known that I came up by the boat train to-night."

"Very well, sir."

Jarvis knew of more than one railway mystery in which Thorpe Hazell had been involved, and was to be trusted.

"Thought you'd caught a bit of smuggling, sir?" he asked.

"Oh!" drawled Hazell, "I was a little suspicious, that was all. Capital run up to-night."

"Yes, sir. Bob Nobes is a good driver."

"Ah! The guard was smart with the luggage at Dovehaven."

"John Crane, sir? Yes. He's one of our best guards. Runs this train in regular shifts."

Hazell's eyes sparkled for a moment.

"You—er—didn't see what became of that young man?"

"Yes, sir. Got into the train on No. 2 platform."

"Ah, that's mine, I believe, to Netherton. Goodnight, Jarvis."

He got into the train, a smile of satisfaction on his face. He meant to master this little mystery.

A couple of days later he was buying cigarettes.

"Oh, by-the-way, Brett," he said, "I think I can promise you that your hated rival will shortly shut up shop."

"Indeed, sir! Well, I shouldn't be sorry. I've lost half my trade in cigars."

"Ah! Oh, I say, Brett, there's a fellow named John Crane—something on the line. Know him?"

"Peter's cousin, sir."

"I see. Well, keep your mouth shut, and let me know when Crane goes away from home. I think we might have quite a little bit of fun then."

Three or four weeks later Thorpe Hazell received a note from Brett. In answer to it he wrote:

"Come round to my house to-morrow at about 8 p.m. Bring a great coat."

The tobacconist duly turned up, and found Hazell in his study.

"Sit down, Brett. Have some toast and water. No? Well, then, take one of your own cigarettes."

"Thank you, sir."

"I ordered the dog-cart for 8.30," went on Hazell. "We have quite a drive before us. That's why I mentioned your great coat."

"What are we going to do, sir?"

"You'll see all in good time."

They were soon bowling along the high road in the opposite direction from that of London. Hazell had the reins, and was not disposed to be communicative. After they had gone about seven or eight miles, Hazell turned down a by-road.

"You know where this leads, Brett?"

"Across Pinkney's Common, sir."

"Exactly."

Presently he said:

"There are the lights of the main line signals?"

"Yes, sir."

A couple of red lights stood out in the blackness of the sky.

"And there's the level crossing?"

"Yes, sir."

"All right. We'll put our lamps out."

He drew up to perform the operation.

"Good, and now we're going to drive on the grass across the common. And don't speak above a whisper, please."

They drew nearer the line. On their left, where the road crossed the railway, the bright light of the gatekeeper's-box was discernible. Presently Hazell pulled up.

"We'll tie the cob to this tree," he whispered. "That's right. We shan't have long to wait."

"It's a lonely place," said Brett.

"Quite so. We don't want to go close up to the line. This will do. It's the up-train we want."

Wondering what was going to happen, Brett waited.

Presently Hazell said: "Here she comes. Those are her headlights. Now you watch what happens. Keep your eyes open."

A white light above a green appeared in the distance, and grew brighter every moment. Then there was a roar as the approaching express bore down upon them. The train was running on a slight embankment, and they could see along its whole length.

"Look!" said Brett suddenly, "one of the doors is open—in the last carriage."

"Exactly. The guard's van, Brett. There he stands. Look out! Ah! There's a pretty little smuggling dodge for you."

As the train swept by they could distinctly see the guard silhouetted against the light in his van. He appeared to be leaning out of his door, holding some large and heavy object. The next moment he had dropped this on to the soft turf of the embankment. As the train rushed by the crossing, a green light appeared for a moment, held out of the guard's van, and turned towards the rear of the train.

"Now," exclaimed Hazell, "we'll just wait and see what happens. First of all, we'll get as close as we can to that package—ah!—here it is. A convenient bush to hide us, too. He's coming, Brett!"

A man, carrying a lantern, came with a limping gait from the box at the level-crossing. Every now and then he paused, as if looking for something. Presently he gave a grunt of satisfaction as the light fell on a package lying on the grass.

He was just about to pick it up when Hazell stepped forward and said, very quietly:

"How much do you get for your share in this little transaction, my man?"

"Good Lord!" exclaimed the other, dropping his lantern in his fright. Hazell picked it up and turned it on him.

"Ah, you've a wooden leg, I see. No use to try to run. I suppose you were to keep this little lot till Crane came for them?"

"Don't—don't be hard on me, sir. I don't know nothin' about the contents—I—I—if you split to the company, sir, I'd lose my post."

Hazell laughed.

"Answer my first question, man. How much do you get out of this?"

"Ten bob a time," faltered the delinquent.

"Poor pay for the risk! How long has Crane been running this?"

"Six or seven months, sir."

"I see. Well, I'm afraid he won't find this little lot to-morrow. You can tell him when he comes for them that we've forestalled him. I should advise you to get your half-sovereign out of him before you tell him. And you can also add that if he wants to get them again he'd better call at Somerset House. Good-night—here's your lantern."

"I shall lose my post, sir."

"Not this time. You may think yourself lucky, though. Here, Brett, give me a hand with this parcel."

They carried the bundle, which was securely corded in thick American cloth, to the trap, and drove home. An hour or so later they were sitting in Hazell's study.

"I think we're entitled to one each before I send them to the Customs," said Hazell, selecting a cigar. "Now, how much do you think he cleared out of this lot?"

Brett looked at the four dozen boxes.

"Well, sir, if he got them, as you say, at Antburg, I can pretty well guess the price he paid. He ought to have saved quite twenty-five pounds in duty—very likely more. Altogether, the run was worth at least fifty pounds. But how did you find it out, sir?"

Hazell told him of his journey to Gantes and of the Customs examination in London.

"I own I was baffled for the moment," he said, "but, of course, I knew that he wouldn't have taken that journey to bring back an empty bag. Inquiry confirmed my suspicions that the guard was in it, possessing a duplicate key to the black bag, and I saw where the solution was. Undoubtedly the cigars were in the country, the only question was their whereabouts.

"The problem was very simple. I had only to keep a watch on Crane. He didn't notice the cyclist who followed him when he took a trap from here the next day, nor did he see that same cyclist lying behind a bush on Pinkney's Common with a field-glass watching him get a parcel from the level-crossing box. The rest you know. I guessed pretty accurately where the guard dropped them, and here they are."

"There's one thing I don't understand, sir," replied Brett, "and that is, why the guard didn't put the cigars in the brown bag and throw that out—or, in fact, why he took two bags at all."

"Oh, but that was where his greatest artfulness came in—the subtlety of the whole thing. The black bag was weighed at Gantes, and its weight registered. It was necessary to have a corresponding weight to it when it arrived in London. That's why he carried those heavy books and used the other bag for them.

"Then he and the guard knew perfectly well that detectives are pretty sharp in these matters, and if it had been noticed that he started back with two bags and only one arrived, especially as he was doing this more than once, suspicion would have been aroused. That's why the other bag was not thrown out. The whole thing was beautifully planned. Now we'll pack up—stop, though—I want three or four more of those cigars. That's right."

He packed up the cigars, and directed them to H.M. Customs.

"There," he said, "we'll send it anonymously. I expect, after his little visit to Pinkney's Common crossing, Master Crane will take a holiday. I must really thank you, Brett, for having given me an interesting little problem. I don't think we need take any further action. The three of them will have quite fright enough to stop them. Good night!"

Hazell was right. Peter Crane suddenly disappeared from view, and the tobacco window was devoted to confectionery again. Harry Brett's prospects so increased with the return of custom that he made a formal proposal for the partnership, which was duly accepted, and the deed signed in the vestry of the parish church. Some weeks after the incident Thorpe Hazell was on the platform of the London terminus of the Mid-Southern and Eastern Railway, watching the incoming of the Continental express. As soon as the bustle was over, he strolled up to the rear guard, who was standing by his van.

"Have a cigar, guard!" he said, offering his case.

"Thank you, sir."

"Take three or four. They're more yours than mine."

"What, sir?"

"I believe you dropped them out of your van—some weeks ago— just by Pinkney's Common crossing. Good-night!"

He turned his head when he reached the end of the platform. There was Guard Crane, standing like a statue, gazing at him with a paler face than was caused by the electric light.

The Tragedy on the London and Mid-Northern

Thorpe Hazell opened his paper lazily as he breakfasted on boiled rice and wholemeal bread in his little West-end flat one very cold winter's morning in January. His interest in passing events was not very much excited until in turning a page he found himself confronted with the headlines:

Shocking Accident on the Railway
Sad Fatality

Folding the paper and shifting his seat so that the electric light fell better upon it, for it was rather dark, and his breakfast was an early one, he read as follows

"A terrible occurrence took place on the London and Mid-Northern Railway last evening. As the express from London, due at Manningford at about a quarter past eight, was entering the station, those on the platform noticed a man leaning out of one of the windows, apparently in the act of opening the door of his compartment, and more than one porter shouted a warning to him to wait until the train stopped.

"When, however, the carriage had come to a standstill, he remained motionless, and those who were near noticed to their horror, that the well-known white panels adopted by this company were stained with an ominous colour, while blood was trickling from the man's head.

21

"Assistance was rendered at once, but it was soon seen that the unfortunate passenger was quite beyond the reach of recovery, although it was the opinion of a doctor who happened to be on the platform that life could only have been extinct for a few minutes.

"The victim of this terrible tragedy was, as has been described, leaning out of the window, his arms and head hanging over the door, which had to be unlocked before he could be taken out. There was a bad wound in the back of his head and neck, as though he had received a violent blow, and a piece of one of his ears had been torn off.

"He had been travelling alone in a first-class compartment, and held the return half of a ticket to Manningford. All Manningford tickets are collected at Bridgeworth, about ten miles up the line, the last stopping station before Manningford, and inquiries have shown that the inspector on duty there had duly taken his ticket, so that he must have met with his death during the last ten miles of the journey.

"The guard of the train states that, on his own request, he locked the compartment at the London terminus just before the train started, and declares that the unfortunate passenger was quite alone during the whole of the journey. His identity has not yet been proved, but, apparently, he is a foreigner. He is tall and dark, with a military-looking moustache, is about fifty years of age, and has a slight scar on his right cheek.

"He had no luggage, and the few papers found upon him were, we hear, written in French, but give no clue to his identification. These papers are in the hands of the police, and the body has been removed to one of the company's offices pending the inquest.

"As to the cause of death, the authorities are inclined to the belief that it was an accident caused by his own carelessness, but nothing definite is yet known. Between Bridgeworth and Manningford there are several bridges over the line, and it is conjectured that his head must have come into collision with the brickwork of one of these structures while looking out of the window.

"It will be remembered that a similar fatality took place near Liverpool some years ago, resulting in the death of a prominent citizen.

"On some of the Continental lines the windows are wisely barred, and in view of the liability to such unfortunate accidents, the railway companies would do well to adopt some means for the prevention of passengers leaning out of windows.

"The inquest will probably be held to-morrow."

Hazell laid down the paper, and sipped his lemonade thoughtfully. It was one of his fads always to take lemonade with his breakfast. Then he read the article through again, and pondered yet more.

"Struck his head against a bridge, eh?" he said to himself. "That's very curious. Wound on back of head and ear torn oft. Umph, I'd like to know a little more about this. Let's have a look at Bradshaw—ah! I can catch that easily. It is not very far down to Manningford, and I know something of Rolfe, the divisional superintendent. It's worth the journey—and there's plenty of time for ten minutes' dumb-bell exercise first."

Half an hour later he was in an express running down to Manningford. As soon as he had passed Bridgeworth he opened the window and kept a careful look out.

"Let's see," he said, "ah, of course, it would be the left side of the train—here's the first bridge "and he put his head out and looked back— "plenty of space there. Well, we shall see presently."

Altogether he counted four bridges between Bridgeworth and Manningford. Arrived at the latter station, he made his way to the office of the divisional superintendent and sent in his card. Five minutes later he was talking with Rolfe.

"Ah," said the latter, "I expect I can easily guess what brings you down here, Mr. Hazell. But I assure you it's not worth the trouble of a journey. The thing's as plain as daylight."

"Oh, you think so, do you?" replied Hazell.

"Why, we've found out everything. There's no doubt that the poor fellow put his head out of the window, and that the bridge caught it as he ran through."

"Which bridge?"

"The second one from here."

"Indeed. And what makes you so certain about it?"

"Why, we've found all the necessary traces."

"And what were they?"

"Several bloodstains on the ballast of the permanent way and sleepers. Just where one would have expected them to be; that is to say, about ten to twenty yards this side of the bridge. The train was running about fifty miles an hour, and the blood wouldn't drop at the actual striking-place."

"Was there any trace on the bridge itself?"

"Not a bit. But that's not at all necessary. Just the corner would have struck him, you see."

"How about the missing piece of his ear?"

"That's been found, too. I tell you there is no mystery about it. It's not in your line at all, Mr. Hazell."

"Ah, well—have you found the reason why he put his head so far out of the window? For he must have stretched it out pretty well to strike it against the bridge."

"Oh, really, Mr. Hazell, that's a mere detail. There are hundreds of reasons why silly persons put their heads out of a train window. You see it done every day."

"I daresay, but I'd like to know this reason. By the way, have you found out who the man is yet?"

"Well, no. But there's been a police detective down, and I fancy he has an inkling of something. The rumour is that the poor chap was a Russian—used to travelling on the Siberian line, where there are few bridges, I should think."

"Can I see him?"

"If you like. It's rather a gruesome sight. Come along."

He took Hazell to an office and unlocked the door.

"I'd rather not go in, if you don't mind," he said. "I've seen enough already, and I'm squeamish about these things."

Hazell nodded, and went up to the table where the dead man lay, covered with a sheet. He removed the sheet from his head, and looked carefully at the wound. Then he seemed satisfied, and rejoined his friend.

"Now," he said, "I want to have a look at the bridge itself. May I walk up the line?"

"Certainly, if you want the trouble. Stop a moment, though— there's a goods train just starting—you can have a lift in the brake, and I'll tell 'em to slow down for you to get off. But you'll have to walk back."

"All right. When's the inquest?"

"To-morrow."

When Hazell got off the goods brake he found a young man standing by the side of the line making a sketch of the bridge.

"Good-morning," said the latter. "Represent a paper?"

"No."

"Oh! I'm on the *Midland Courier*. We shall have a block in to-morrow. Terrible thing. Seen the bloodstains?"

He was very young at his work, and Hazell, with a slight smile at his impulsiveness, replied in the negative.

"Come along then, and I'll show them to you. They're quite plain. Got a bit frozen, and it hasn't thawed to-day."

He took Hazell some twenty or thirty yards beyond the bridge, and pointed out, on the frosty track, a few dark stains on the ballast and ends of the sleepers.

"Must have been killed instantly," he went on, garrulously. "I draw a bit, you see, so I'm making a sketch of the affair—just at the moment when he struck his head against the bridge."

"When he struck his head against the bridge," echoed Hazell, thoughtfully. "Well, don't let me interrupt you. Look out, young man, though, or there'll be a second accident!"

They had gone back to the up side of the bridge, and the young reporter was standing on the line. Hazell had heard a signal fall, and knew a train was coming. The other thanked him for his warning.

"Just what I wanted," he said. "I shall get an impression of the thing now."

Hazell carefully watched the train as it ran beneath the bridge. Then he shook his head, and muttered to himself:

"Just what I thought. He'd have to lean out a tremendous distance. And yet he must have been killed here. It's very strange."

Here he looked at his watch, ate a plasmon biscuit, and solemnly proceeded to go through an "exercise," for which purpose he took off his coat. Having finished his little performance he set to work to examine the edge of the brickwork. This proved unsatisfactory. Then his gaze fell on the metals as he stood, just at the entrance to the bridge, wrapped in thought.

Suddenly he appeared to catch sight of something on the line. The next moment he was down on his hands and knees beside the track. Close to the end of one of the sleepers, outside the left hand rail, he had noticed a hole. That was all. Nothing very curious, perhaps, but he knew very well that holes are never bored in such places.

This one had evidently been done with an auger, for a few shreds of wood were beside the sleeper. It was large enough for him to insert his little finger, and he felt that there was a thread inside. Something had been screwed into that hole.

"Found some more blood?" shouted the sanguinary-minded youth.

Hazell shook his head as he stood up and looked overhead. The sleeper with the hole in it was immediately below the edge of the bridge. He looked long and intently at the bridge, marking with his eyes an imaginary line straight up the brickwork from the hole in the sleeper.

Apparently unsatisfied, he found his way to the top of the bridge, and carefully examined the parapet. An exclamation of triumph escaped him. About a foot above the roadway an exceedingly strong staple had been driven into the brickwork, the fragments of dislodged mortar lying on the ground. He measured a straight line up from the staple to the top of the parapet, looked over, and found the line would drop exactly perpendicular to the hole in the sleeper. A careful examination of the staple revealed a tiny shred of tow attached to it.

He waited patiently till another train was signalled, and then, watching from the top of the parapet, he convinced himself that the imaginary perpendicular line down to the sleeper would just clear the sides of the carriages, as they ran by, by a few inches.

"Good!" he said. "I was certain it wasn't an accident."

He stood on the bridge, thinking, and taking in the surrounding country. A farmhouse and a few scattered cottages stood a little way back from the line and about a couple hundred yards from the bridge. One or two other houses were in the distance. Then he looked at the roadway, which was hard with the frost.

Suddenly he whistled softly to himself. There were tracks of a bicycle coming up the bridge. The machine had evidently been leaned against the parapet. And the rider had returned by the same road by which he had come. There was his second track frozen into the road, and not a sign of it on the other side of the bridge.

Few bicycles of any wear lack some distinguishing mark in the tyres, and Hazell was soon satisfied, after a little examination, that the ones in question were Clipper Reflex, and that a small bit had been chipped out of the back tyre, making its mark plainly in the road.

"How are you getting on?" he shouted to the reporter presently.

"Just finished."

"Where does this road lead to?"

"It's only a bye road, and not much used. But you can get back to Manningford by taking the first turning to the right. If you go straight on it leads to Sandfield."

"Thanks. Nice frosty morning for a walk. I say, do you happen to know when the frost set in in this part of the country?"

"Yes. It wasn't freezing at eight last night, when I went round to my office for some late work, but it was quite hard at ten or so when I came back."

"Thanks. Good morning."

"Good morning!"

"Well," said Hazell to himself, as he walked quickly away, "he was a clumsy beggar to ride a soft road. The whole thing's as plain as daylight, except just one point. How did he know the fellow would put his head out of the window just in the right place?

There's a mystery in this, and I'd like to solve it before I say anything to the police. At present we'll try the only clue there seems
to be."

The bicycle track did not branch off to Manningford, and Hazell
traced it for over eight miles along the road to Sandfield. He broke
the journey at a farmhouse, where he begged for a glass of milk
and a dry crust of bread. When he had partaken of this he astonished the woman who had given it to him by lying down flat on his
back and rubbing his chest violently; after which he gave her half-
a-crown, and explained that "chest massage" was one of the best
aids to digestion. As he drew near Sandfield it became difficult to
follow the track, on account of the increased traffic, but the frost
was his best friend, and he persistently recovered the traces.

At length they led him down a street on the outskirts of the
town, and stopped abruptly opposite a terrace of small houses. He
waited a moment or two in hesitation, not being quite sure which
house might prove the right one, and also wondering whether it
were not his duty to go straight to the police and tell them his con-
jectures. But at that moment, a woman, who had been observing
him through one of the windows, came to the door and accosted
him.

"This is the house you're looking for, I think, sir?"

He turned towards her in surprise.

"The young man's very ill, sir, and I thought I'd better send for
you, me not knowin' anything about him, and feeling if so be as
anything was to happen to him it wouldn't be right not to have no
one to give a certificate, he bein' without friends, leastwise he do
get letters, but when I asked him to send for someone as knows
him he wouldn't hear of it, which I says I'd post a letter or even
write it for him. But he's obstinate, though I told him I'd send for
you, which they said you was out, sir, and would call when you
came home."

The woman paused to take breath, and Hazell fell in with the
situation.

"A lodger of yours, I suppose?"

"Which he's only been with me a short time, and pays his rent reg'lar, sir, though he is, seemingly, a furriner, which I never could a-bear, sir, though he do speak the King's English quite as good as you nor me."

Hazell smiled at her idea of grammar, and asked casually as he went into the house:

"What's the matter with him?"

"It ain't for me to say, sir; but I lost a boy of my own with conjecture of the lungs and browntitis, and I know what the symptoms is, which he wouldn't take no care of hisself."

"Ah, been riding his bicycle in these cold east winds, eh?" went on Hazell as his eyes fell on a machine in the hall.

"Only last night, sir, did he go out, which I told him was a-runnin' against Providence with his cough so bad as the neighbours could hear it over the street."

"Well, I'll go up and see him."

"Do so, sir—the first room on the left."

A sound of coughing struck upon his ears as he opened the door. On the bed lay a young man with fair hair, slight moustache, and hectic cheeks. He turned to Hazell and said feebly, and with a foreign accent:

"Ah, you are the doctor, I suppose. Mrs. Bull insisted on sending for you, but I'm afraid you can't do me very much good."

Hazell locked the door very quietly on the inside, and came up to the head of the bed.

"I'm not the doctor," he began, "though your landlady mistook me for him."

The glow faded from the sick man's cheeks as he raised his head from the pillow. "Who—who are you?" he asked.

"I can hardly explain. I'm scarcely a detective, being only a private individual."

"What do you mean about being a detective?" gasped the other.

"I mean that somewhere in this room—unless you threw them away on the road—you have an auger, a hammer, a large staple with a screw, and a length of very strong rope."

"Good God!" exclaimed the sick man, "how did you find that out?"

"By your own clumsiness. It was a clever thing to stretch that rope from the bridge to the sleeper, but it was foolish to ride your bicycle there in the mud with a frost about to set in."

A violent fit of coughing seized the man for a minute or two. Hazell poured him out a drink of water, and looked at him critically.

"You are very ill," he said.

"I know I am. I don't expect to get over it. What are you going to do? Have me hanged if I live long enough?" he asked bitterly.

Hazell was silent.

"Perhaps you don't know who the man was who was found dead at Manningford last night?"

Hazell shook his head.

"Let me tell you before you do anything. You say you're not a detective, but I suppose you'll tell the police. I don't care. Murder, was it? No, no, no. It was a just judgment and punishment. If ever a man deserved his fate he did. Have you ever heard of Paul Gourchoff?"

"No."

"That was his name. One of the cruellest and most bloodthirsty of all the Russian Police Agents, a man whose life was stained with the foulest crimes. Shall I tell you about him?"

Hazell nodded.

"I will—and then I'll leave the issue in your hands, and you can do as you please. I am a Pole—yes, you can understand something of what I am by the mere word. It is enough for a Pole to be loyal to his country and to labour for the cause of freedom, and then he becomes—if he is fortunate enough to escape Siberia, or prison, or death—an outcast, like myself.

"My father had a little estate; he was one of the old nobility— we are of the Radziwill family, and he plotted, secretly, as every patriot has to plot. This man, Gourchoff, was one of us, trusted with all our plans, but in the pay of the accursed Tsar all the time.

"He waited his opportunity, and then—well, I will spare you the details. My father died on the way to Siberia, a brother and sister are there, somewhere, lost to name even—mere numbers, being slowly done to death. One sister was killed before my eyes— a brutal cossack cut her down with his sword. I was the only one of the family that escaped, and that by a miracle.

"This was five years ago, and since that time I have devoted my life to the cause here in England. There are many of us. Some come over, secretly, from Poland, to keep in touch with those who work in our country. We can do much here, but it is difficult.

"Two months ago a tremendous blow was struck at our organisation. Paul Gourchoff came to England. He is like a sleuth hound, and we knew that if he once tracked our meetings it would mean death or exile to many of our friends in Poland.

"Can you wonder that we determined to take strong measures? Can you wonder that *I* sought my opportunity for revenge? But he was wily. He knew the danger, and it was impossible at first to do anything, although every day he was discovering more and more and running us down. Then I devised the plan which you seem to have fathomed. And it was successful. Gourchoff is dead. Bah!"

Another fit of coughing succeeded. Then Hazell asked:

"But how did you make him put his head out of that window just at the right spot?"

"I am coming to that. I came down here and took rooms, and he was allowed to find out that I was in the neighbourhood. That was the first step. His great plan was to discover the secret rendezvous where we met our compatriots who came over.

"That remains a secret still!

"But it was not in London, and he knew it. So then we went to work carefully. We had discovered that one of us, a man we had never really trusted, was in his pay. Through this man we arranged that he should receive information, which we apparently allowed to leak out. At first the disclosure was made to him that we met in a house somewhere near the London and Mid-Northern Railway in this locality. This, of course, was false.

"Then we let it be known that our friends came to this rendez-vous in various ways, and that signals were arranged to show them if it were safe. He fell into the trap beautifully. So we led him to believe that a meeting was to be held last night, and that two of our number were going from London. Between Bridgeworth and Manningford they were to give a signal by holding a lantern out of the window for a moment. This signal was to be answered by a green light in the window of a certain house near the side of the line if all was well, by a red light if there was danger. These lights were to be flashed, and not stationary.

"Now we knew his object was simply to discover the house, with a view to a raid on some subsequent occasion—oh! you little know of the secret raids that are made by Russian police in England—so that he would journey down alone.

"Our two friends were to get in the back of the train, and of course he was to be allowed to see them get in. That insured that he should go towards the front, and crane his head out of the win-dow between Bridgeworth and Manningford. We let it be thought that the flash should take place from a window at the *side* of the house, so that he would be looking back.

"Heaven knows how I managed that ride last night—it has put the finishing stroke to a long illness. I had taken the most careful measurements beforehand, and knew exactly where to drive the staple in the brickwork, and where to bore the hole in the sleeper. It didn't take me long to fix the rope very tightly—I had it loose till just before the train was due.

"As I stood on the top of the bridge I could see him with his head reached out dimly in the darkness, while one of our friends at the back was holding out a small lantern. I knew, by the sound, that the rope had caught him, and I saw the other man draw in his head quickly. I unscrewed the staple from the sleeper, but I couldn't draw the other from the brickwork.

"There—that is the whole story. To my certain knowledge, Paul Gourchoff has caused the death or exile of over two hundred men and women, whose sole crime was patriotism and love of freedom. Did he deserve to die?"

And Hazell, who had listened to the recital attentively, nodded his head slowly.

"I think he did," he said.

Presently he added:

"Can I do anything for you?"

"No," replied Radziwill. "I don't think anyone can do that. In your kindness you might leave me alone—that is all. I shall cheat the gallows. There is enough money in my clothes here to bury me. I have nothing to live for. Oh, do what you like!"

And he turned over and hid his face in the pillow. Hazell went downstairs. Mrs. Bull was talking to a gentleman at the door.

"Which it's very strange, sir, you bein' the doctor as was sent for, and yet another doctor's with him now, and—"

"I'll put that right," replied Hazell. "Your patient is waiting to see you, sir."

"Oh, I see. Are you a friend of his?"

"Ye-es," replied Hazell. "I'd like to know what you think of him, so I'll wait till you come down."

And what the doctor thought of him was this:

"He may last two or three days, but he won't see the week out."

So Thorpe Hazell kept silence. He asked the doctor to direct him to a vegetarian restaurant, where he lunched on a rice pudding and a dish of prunes. Then he took the local train from Sandfield to Manningford, and saw Rolfe once more before returning to town.

"Well," said the superintendent, "are you satisfied with your investigation?"

"Quite," returned Hazell.

"Only an ordinary case, eh?"

"Only an ordinary case. I beg your pardon, Mr. Rolfe, but how much do you weigh?"

"Fourteen stone, I believe," replied the official, with a puzzled air.

"And you are about five feet six, I should imagine," went on Hazell, looking at him critically. "You really ought to reduce some of it. Try living on lentils for a fortnight; and a very excellent exercise is this—I do it before most meals—take three deep breaths through the nostrils, filling the lungs and letting the air escape through the mouth slowly. At the same time rise on the toes, reach the hands above the head, and bring them slowly down to the sides. Repeat fifteen times. It's a capital thing for digestion. Good-bye!"

Two days later came the result of the inquest. Verdict, "Accidental death, with a recommendation from the jury that the railway officials should carefully examine the width of all their bridges, and take steps, if necessary, to avoid the occurrence of such a painful tragedy."

The Affair of the Corridor Express

Thorpe Hazell stood in his study in his London flat. On the opposite wall he had pinned a bit of paper, about an inch square, at the height of his eye, and was now going through the most extraordinary contortions.

With his eyes fixed on the paper he was craning his neck as far as it would reach and twisting his head about in all directions. This necessitated a fearful rolling of the eyes in order to keep them on the paper, and was supposed to be a means of strengthening the muscles of the eye for angular sight.

Presently there came a tap at the door.

"Come in!" cried Hazell, still whirling his head round.

"A gentleman wishes to see you at once, sir!" said the servant, handing him a card.

Hazell paused in his exercises, took it from the tray, and read: "Mr. F. W. Wingrave, M.A., B.Sc."

"Oh, show him in," said Hazell, rather impatiently, for he hated to be interrupted when he was doing his "eye gymnastics."

There entered a young man of about five-and-twenty, with a look of keen anxiety on his face. "You are Mr. Thorpe Hazell?" he asked.

"I am."

"You will have seen my name on my card—I am one of the masters at Shillington School—I had heard your name, and they told me at the station that it might be well to consult you—I hope you don't mind—I know you're not an ordinary detective, but—"

"Sit down, Mr. Wingrave," said Hazell, interrupting his nervous flow of language. "You look quite ill and tired."

"I have just been through a very trying experience," replied Wingrave, sinking into a seat. "A boy I was in charge of has just mysteriously disappeared, and I want you to find him for me, and I want to ask your opinion. They say you know all about railways, but—"

"Now, look here, my dear sir, you just have some hot toast and water before you say another word. I conclude you want to consult me on some railway matter. I'll do what I can, but I won't hear you till you've had some refreshment. Perhaps you prefer whiskey—though I don't advise it."

Wingrave, however, chose the whiskey, and Hazell poured him out some, adding soda-water.

"Thank you," he said. "I hope you'll be able to give me advice. I am afraid the poor boy must be killed; the whole thing is a mystery, and I—"

"Stop a bit, Mr. Wingrave. I must ask you to tell me the story from the very beginning. That's the best way."

"Quite right. The worry of it has made me incoherent, I fear. But I'll try and do what you propose. First of all, do you know the name of Carr-Mathers?"

"Yes, I think so. Very rich is he not?"

"A millionaire. He has only one child, a boy of about ten, whose mother died at his birth. He is a small boy for his age, and idolised by his father. About three months ago this young Horace Carr-Mathers was sent to our school—Cragsbury House, just outside Shillington. It is not a very large school, but exceedingly select, and the headmaster, Dr. Spring, is well known in high-class circles. I may tell you that we have the Sons of some of the leading nobility preparing for the public schools. You will readily understand that in such an establishment as ours the most scrupulous care is exercised over the boys, not only as regards their moral and intellectual training, but also to guard against any outside influences."

"Kidnapping, for example," interposed Hazell.

"Exactly. There have been such cases known, and Dr. Spring has a very high reputation to maintain. The slightest rumour against the school would go ill with him—and with all of us masters.

"Well, this morning the headmaster received a telegram about Horace Carr-Mathers, requesting that he should be sent up to town."

"Do you know the exact wording?" asked Hazell.

"I have it with me," replied Wingrave, drawing it from his pocket.

Hazell took it from him, and read as follows:

"*Please grant Horace leave of absence for two days. Send him to London by 5.45 express from Shillington, in first-class carriage, giving guard instructions to look after him. We will meet train in town.—Carr-Mathers.*"

"Um," grunted Hazell, as he handed it back. "Well, he can afford long telegrams."

"Oh, he's always wiring about something or other," replied Wingrave; "he seldom writes a letter. Well, when the doctor received this he called me into his study.

"'I suppose I must let the boy go,' he said, 'but I'm not at all inclined to allow him to travel by himself. If anything should happen to him his father would hold us responsible as well as the railway company. So you had better take him up to town, Mr. Wingrave.'

"'Yes, sir.'

"'You need do no more than deliver him to his father. If Mr. Carr-Mathers is not at the terminus to meet him, take him with you in a cab to his house in Portland Place. You'll probably be able to catch the last train home, but, if not, you can get a bed at an hotel.'

"'Very good, sir.'

"So, shortly after half-past five, I found myself standing on the platform at Shillington, waiting for the London express."

"Now, stop a moment," interrupted Hazell, sipping a glass of filtered water which he had poured out for himself. "I want to get a clear notion of this journey of yours from the beginning, for, I presume, you will shortly be telling me that something strange happened during it. Was there anything to be noticed before the train started?"

"Nothing at the time. But I remembered afterwards that two men seemed to be watching me rather closely when I took the tickets, and I heard one of them say 'Confound,' beneath his breath. But my suspicions were not aroused at the moment."

"I see. If there is anything in this it was probably because he was disconcerted when he saw you were going to travel with the boy. Did these two men get into the train?"

"I'm coming to that. The train was in sharp to time, and we took our seats in a first-class compartment."

"Please describe the exact position."

"Our carriage was the third from the front. It was a corridor train, with access from carriage to carriage all the way through. Horace and myself were in a compartment alone. I had bought him some illustrated papers for the journey, and for some time he sat quietly enough, looking through them. After a bit he grew fidgety, as you know boys will."

"Wait a minute. I want to know if the corridor of your carriage was on the left or on the right—supposing you to be seated facing the engine?"

"On the left."

"Very well, go on."

"The door leading into the corridor stood open. It was still daylight, but dusk was setting in fast—I should say it was about half-past six, or a little more. Horace had been looking out of the window on the right side of the train when I drew his attention to Rutherham Castle, which we were passing. It stands, as you know, on the left side of the line. In order to get a better view of it he went out into the corridor and stood there. I retained my seat on the right side of the compartment, glancing at him from time to time. He seemed interested in the corridor itself, looking about him, and once or twice shutting and opening the door of our compartment. I can see now that I ought to have kept a sharper eye on him, but I never dreamed that any accident could happen. I was reading a paper myself, and became rather interested in a paragraph. It may have been seven or eight minutes before I looked up. When I did so, Horace had disappeared.

"I didn't think anything of it at first, but only concluded that he had taken a walk along the corridor."

"You don't know which way he went?" inquired Hazell.

"No. I couldn't say. I waited a minute or two, and then rose and looked out into the corridor. There was no one there. Still my suspicions were not aroused. It was possible that he had gone to the lavatory. So I sat down again, and waited. Then I began to get a little anxious, and determined to have a look for him. I walked to either end of the corridor, and searched the lavatories, but they were both empty. Then I looked in all the other compartments of the carriage, and asked their occupants if they had seen him go by, but none of them had noticed him."

"Do you remember how these compartments were occupied?"

"Yes. In the first, which was reserved for ladies, there were five ladies. The next was a smoker with three gentlemen in it. Ours came next. Then, going towards the front of the train, were the two men I had noticed at Shillington; the last compartment had a gentleman and lady and their three children."

"Ah! how about those two men—what were they doing?"

"One of them was reading a book, and the other appeared to be asleep."

"Tell me. Was the door leading to the corridor from their compartment shut?"

"Yes, it was."

"Go on."

"Well, I was in a most terrible fright, and I went back to my compartment and pulled the electric communicator. In a few seconds the front guard came along the corridor and asked me what I wanted. I told him I had lost my charge. He suggested that the boy had walked through to another carriage, and I asked him if he would mind my making a thorough search of the train with him. To this he readily agreed. We went back to the first carriage and began to do so. We examined every compartment from end to end of the train; we looked under every seat, in spite of the protestations of some of the passengers; we searched all the lavatories—every corner of the train—and we found absolutely no trace of Horace Carr-Mathers. No one had seen the boy anywhere."

"Had the train stopped?"

"Not for a second. It was going at full speed all the time. It only slowed down after we had finished the search—but it never quite stopped."

"Ah! We'll come to that presently. I want to ask you some questions first. Was it still daylight?"

"Dusk, but quite light enough to see plainly—besides which, the train lamps were lit."

"Exactly. Those two men, now, in the next compartment to yours—tell me precisely what happened when you visited them the second time with the guard."

"They asked a lot of questions—like many of the other passengers—and seemed very surprised."

"You looked underneath their seats?"

"Certainly."

"On the luggage-racks? A small boy like that could be rolled up in a rug and put on the rack."

"We examined every rack on the train."

Thorpe Hazell lit a cigarette and smoked furiously, motioning to his companion to keep quiet. He was thinking out the situation. Suddenly he said:

"How about the window in those two men's compartment?"

"It was shut—I particularly noticed it."

"You are *quite sure* you searched the whole of the train?"

"Absolutely certain; so was the guard."

"Ah!" remarked Hazell, "even guards are mistaken sometimes. It—er—was only the inside of the train you searched, eh?"

"Of course."

"Very well," replied Hazell, "now, before we go any further, I want to ask you this. Would it have been to anyone's interest to have murdered the boy?"

"I don't think so—from what I know. I don't see how it could be."

"Very well. We will take it as a pure case of kidnapping, and presume that he is alive and well. This ought to console you to begin with."

"Do you think you can help me?"

"I don't know yet. But go on and tell me all that happened."

"Well, after we had searched the train I was at my wits' end—and so was the guard. We both agreed, however, that nothing more could be done till we reached London. Somehow, my strongest suspicions concerning those two men were aroused, and I travelled in their compartment for the rest of the journey."

"Oh! Did anything happen?"

"Nothing. They both wished me good-night, hoped I'd find the boy, got out, and drove off in a hansom."

"And then?"

"I looked about for Mr. Carr-Mathers, but he was nowhere to be seen. Then I saw an inspector, and put the case before him. He promised to make inquiries and to have the line searched on the part where I missed Horace. I took a hansom to Portland Place, only to discover that Mr. Carr-Mathers is on the Continent and not expected home for a week. Then I came on to you—the inspector had advised me to do so. And that's the whole story. It's a terrible thing for me, Mr. Hazell. What do you think of it?"

"Well," replied Hazell, "of course it's very clear that there is a distinct plot. Someone sent that telegram, knowing Mr. Carr-Mathers' proclivities. The object was to kidnap the boy. It sounds absurd to talk of brigands and ransoms in this country, but the thing is done over and over again for all that. It is obvious that the boy was expected to travel alone, and that the train was the place chosen for the kidnapping. Hence the elaborate directions. I think you were quite right in suspecting those two men, and it might have been better if you had followed them up without coming to me."

"But they went off alone!"

"Exactly. It's my belief they had originally intended doing so after disposing of Horace, and that they carried out their original intentions."

"But what became of the boy ?—how did they—"

"Stop a bit. I'm not at all clear in my own mind. But you mentioned that while you were concluding your search with the guard the train slackened speed?"

"Yes. It almost came to a stop—and then went very slowly for a minute or so. I asked the guard why, but I didn't understand his reply."

"What was it?"

"He said it was a P.W. operation."

Hazell laughed.

"P.W. stands for permanent way," he explained, "I know exactly what you mean now. There is a big job going on near Longmoor—they are raising the level of the line, and the up-trains are running on temporary rails. So they have to proceed very slowly. Now it was after this that you went back to the two men whom you suspected?"

"Yes."

"Very well. Now let me think the thing over. Have some more whiskey? You might also like to glance at the contents of my bookcase. If you know anything of first editions and bindings they will interest you."

Wingrave, it is to be feared, paid but small heed to the books, but watched Hazell anxiously as the latter smoked cigarette after cigarette, his brows knit in deep thought. After a bit he said slowly:

"You will understand that I am going to work upon the theory that the boy has been kidnapped and that the original intention has been carried out, in spite of the accident of your presence in the train. How the boy was disposed of meanwhile is what baffles me; but that is a detail—though it will be interesting to know how it was done. Now, I don't want to raise any false hopes, because I may very likely be wrong, but we are going to take action upon a very feasible assumption, and if I am at all correct, I hope to put you definitely on the track. Mind, I don't promise to do so, and, at best, I don't promise to do *more* than put you on a track. Let me see—it's just after nine. We have plenty of time. We'll drive first to Scotland Yard, for it will be as well to have a detective with us."

He filled a flask with milk, put some plasmon biscuits and a banana into a sandwich case, and then ordered his servant to hail a cab.

An hour later, Hazell, Wingrave, and a man from Scotland Yard were closeted together in one of the private offices of the Mid-Eastern Railway with one of the chief officials of the line. The latter was listening attentively to Hazell.

"But I can't understand the boy not being anywhere in the train, Mr. Hazell," he said.

"I can—partly," replied Hazell, "but first let me see if my theory is correct."

"By all means. There's a down-train in a few minutes. I'll go with you, for the matter is very interesting. Come along, gentlemen."

He walked forward to the engine and gave a few instructions to the driver, and then they took their seats in the train. After a run of half an hour or so they passed a station.

"That's Longmoor," said the official, "now we shall soon be on the spot. It's about a mile down that the line is being raised."

Hazell put his head out of the window. Presently an ominous red light showed itself. The train came almost to a stop, and then proceeded slowly, the man who had shown the red light changing it to green. They could see him as they passed, standing close to a little temporary hut. It was his duty to warn all approaching drivers, and for this purpose he was stationed some three hundred yards in front of the bit of line that was being operated upon. Very soon they were passing this bit. Naphtha lamps shed a weird light over a busy scene, for the work was being continued night and day. A score or so of sturdy navvies were shovelling and picking along the track.

Once more into the darkness. On the other side of the scene of operations, at the same distance, was another little hut, with a

guardian for the up-train. Instead of increasing the speed in passing this hut, which would have been usual, the driver brought the
train almost to a standstill. As he did so the four men got out of
the carriage, jumping from the footboard to the ground. On went
the train, leaving them on the left side of the down track, just
opposite the little hut. They could see the man standing outside,
his back partly turned to them. There was a fire in a brazier close
by that dimly outlined his figure.

He started suddenly, as they crossed the line towards him.

"What are you doing here?" he cried. "You've no business here—
you're trespassing."

He was a big, strong-looking man, and he backed a little towards his hut as he spoke.

"I am Mr. Mills, the assistant-superintendent of the line," replied the official, coming forward.

"Beg pardon, sir; but how was I to know that?" growled the man.

"Quite right. It's your duty to warn off strangers. How long have
you been stationed here?"

"I came on at five o'clock; I'm regular night-watchman, sir."

"Ah! Pretty comfortable, eh?"

"Yes, thank you, sir," replied the man, wondering why the question was asked, but thinking, not unnaturally, that the assistant-
superintendent had come down with a party of engineers to in-
spect things.

"Got the hut to yourself?"

"Yes, sir."

Without another word, Mr. Mills walked to the door of the hut.
The man, his face suddenly growing pale, moved, and stood with
his back to it.

"It's—it's private, sir!" he growled.

Hazell laughed.

"All right, my man," he said. "I was right, I think—hullo!—look
out! Don't let him go!"

For the man had made a quick rush forward. But the Scotland
Yard officer and Hazell were on him in a moment, and a few seconds later the handcuffs clicked on his wrists. Then they flung the

door open, and there, lying in the corner, gagged and bound, was Horace Carr-Mathers.

An exclamation of joy broke forth from Wingrave, as he opened his knife to cut the cords. But Hazell stopped him.

"Just half a moment," he said: "I want to see how they've tied him up."

A peculiar method had been adopted in doing this. His wrists were fastened behind his back, a stout cord was round his body just under the armpits, and another cord above the knees. These were connected by a slack bit of rope.

"All right!" went on Hazell; "let's get the poor lad out of his troubles—there, that's better. How do you feel, my boy?"

"Awfully stiff!" said Horace, "but I'm not hurt. I say, sir," he continued to Wingrave, "how did you know I was here? I *am* glad you've come."

"The question is how did you *get* here?" replied Wingrave. "Mr. Hazell, here, seemed to know where you were, but it's a puzzle to me at present."

"If you'd come half an hour later you wouldn't have found him," growled the man who was handcuffed. "I ain't so much to blame as them as employed me."

"Oh, is that how the land lies?" exclaimed Hazell. "I see. You shall tell us presently, my boy, how it happened. Meanwhile, Mr. Mills, I think we can prepare a little trap—eh?"

In five minutes all was arranged. A couple of the navvies were brought up from the line, one stationed outside to guard against trains, and with certain other instructions, the other being inside the hut with the rest of them. A third navvy was also dispatched for the police.

"How are they coming?" asked Hazell of the handcuffed man.

"They were going to take a train down from London to Rockhampstead on the East-Northern, and drive over. It's about ten miles off."

"Good! they ought soon to be here," replied Hazell, as he munched some biscuits and washed them down with a draught of milk, after which he astonished them all by solemnly going through one of his "digestive exercises."

A little later they heard the sound of wheels on a road beside the line. Then the man on watch said, in gruff tones:

"The boy's inside!"

But they found more than the boy inside, and an hour later all three conspirators were safely lodged in Longmoor gaol.

"Oh, it was awfully nasty, I can tell you," said Horace Carr-Mathers, as he explained matters afterwards. "I went into the corridor, you know, and was looking about at things, when all of a sudden I felt my coat-collar grasped behind, and a hand was laid over my mouth. I tried to kick and shout, but it was no go. They got me into the compartment, stuffed a handkerchief into my mouth, and tied it in. It was just beastly. Then they bound me hand and foot, and opened the window on the right-hand side— opposite the corridor. I was in a funk, for I thought they were going to throw me out, but one of them told me to keep my pecker up, as they weren't going to hurt me. Then they let me down out of the window by that slack rope, and made it fast to the handle of the door outside. It was pretty bad. There was I, hanging from the door-handle in a sort of doubled-up position, my back resting on the footboard of the carriage, and the train rushing along like mad. I felt sick and awful, and I had to shut my eyes. I seemed to hang there for ages."

"I told you you only examined the *inside* of the train," said Thorpe Hazell to Wingrave. "I had my suspicions that he was somewhere on the outside all the time, but I was puzzled to know where. It was a clever trick."

"Well," went on the boy, "I heard the window open above me after a bit. I looked up and saw one of the men taking the rope off the handle. The train was just beginning to slow down. Then he hung out of the window, dangling me with one hand. It was horrible. I was hanging below the footboard now. Then the train came almost to a stop, and someone caught me round the waist. I lost my senses for a minute or two, and then I found myself lying in the hut."

"Well, Mr. Hazell," said the assistant-superintendent, "you were perfectly right, and we all owe you a debt of gratitude."

"Oh!" said Hazell, "it was only a guess at the best. I presumed it was simply kidnapping, and the problem to be solved was how and where the boy was got off the train without injury. It was obvious that he had been disposed of before the train reached London. There was only one other inference. The man on duty was evidently the confederate, for, if not, his presence would have stopped the whole plan of action. I'm very glad to have been of any use. There are interesting points about the case, and it has been a pleasure to me to undertake it."

A little while afterwards Mr. Carr-Mathers himself called on Hazell to thank him.

"I should like," he said, "to express my deep gratitude substantially; but I understand you are not an ordinary detective. But is there any way in which I can serve you, Mr. Hazell?"

"Yes—two ways."

"Please name them."

"I should be sorry for Mr. Wingrave to get into trouble through this affair—or Dr. Spring either."

"I understand you, Mr. Hazell. They were both to blame, in a way. But I will see that Dr. Spring's reputation does not suffer, and that Wingrave comes out of it harmlessly."

"Thank you very much."

"You said there was a second way in which I could serve you."

"So there is. At Dunn's sale last month you were the purchaser of two first editions of 'The New Bath Guide.' If you cared to dispose of one, I—"

"Say no more, Mr. Hazell. I shall be glad to give you one for your collection."

Hazell stiffened.

"You misunderstand me!" he exclaimed icily. "I was about to add that if you cared to dispose of a copy I would write you out a cheque."

"Oh, certainly," replied Mr. Carr-Mathers with a smile, "I shall be extremely pleased."

Whereupon the transaction was concluded.

Sir Gilbert Murrell's Picture

The affair of the goods truck on the Didcot and Newbury branch of the Great Western Railway was of singular interest, and found a prominent place in Thorpe Hazell's notebook. It was owing partly to chance, and partly to Hazell's sagacity, that the main incidents in the story were discovered, but he always declared that the chief interest to his mind was the unique method by which a very daring plan was carried out.

He was staying with a friend at Newbury at the time, and had taken his camera down with him, for he was a bit of an amateur photographer as well as book-lover, though his photos generally consisted of trains and engines. He had just come in from a morning's ramble with his camera slung over his shoulder, and was preparing to partake of two plasmon biscuits, when his friend met him in the hail.

"I say, Hazell," he began, "you're just the fellow they want here."

"What's up?" asked Hazell, taking off his camera and commencing some "exercises."

"I've just been down to the station. I know the station-master very well, and he tells me an awfully queer thing happened on the line last night."

"Where?"

"On the Didcot branch. It's a single line, you know, running through the Berkshire Downs to Didcot."

Hazell smiled, and went on whirling his arms round his head.

"Kind of you to give me the information," he said, "but I happen to know the line. But what's occurred?"

"Well, it appears a goods train left Didcot last night bound through to Winchester, and that one of the waggons never arrived here at Newbury."

"Not very much in that," replied Hazell, still at his "exercises," "unless the waggon in question was behind the brake and the couplings snapped, in which case the next train along might have run into it."

"Oh, no. The waggon was in the middle of the train."

"Probably left in a siding by mistake," replied Hazell.

"But the station-master says that all the stations along the line have been wired to, and that it isn't at any of them."

"Very likely it never left Didcot."

"He declares there is no doubt about that."

"Well, you begin to interest me," replied Hazell, stopping his whirligigs and beginning to eat his plasmon. "There may be something in it, though very often a waggon is mislaid. But I'll go down to the station."

"I'll go with you, Hazell, and introduce you to the station-master. He has heard of your reputation."

Ten minutes later they were in the station-master's office, Hazell having re-slung his camera.

"Very glad to meet you," said that functionary, "for this affair promises to be mysterious. *I* can't make it out at all."

"Do you know what the truck contained?"

"That's just where the bother comes in, sir. It was valuable property. There's a loan exhibition of pictures at Winchester next week, and this waggon was bringing down some of them from Leamington. They belong to Sir Gilbert Murrell—three of them, I believe—large pictures, and each in a separate packing-case."

"H'm—this sounds very funny. Are you sure the truck was on the train?"

"Simpson, the brakesman, is here now, and I'll send for him. Then you can hear the story in his own words."

So the goods guard appeared on the scene. Hazell looked at him narrowly, but there was nothing suspicious in his honest face.

"I know the waggon was on the train when we left Didcot," he said in answer to inquiries, "and I noticed it at Upton, the next station, where we took a couple off. It was the fifth or sixth in front of my brake. I'm quite certain of that. We stopped at Compton to take up a cattle truck, but I didn't get out there. Then we ran right through to Newbury, without stopping at the other stations, and then I discovered that the waggon was not on the train. I thought very likely it might have been left at Upton or Compton by mistake, but I was wrong, for they say it isn't there. That's all I know about it, sir. A rum go, ain't it?"

"Extraordinary!" exclaimed Hazell. "You must have made a mistake."

"No, sir, I'm sure I haven't."

"Did the driver of the train notice anything?"

"No, sir."

"Well, but the thing's impossible," said Hazell. "A loaded waggon couldn't have been spirited away. What time was it when you left Didcot?"

"About eight o'clock, sir."

"Ah—quite dark. You noticed nothing along the line?"

"Nothing, sir."

"You were in your brake all the time, I suppose?"

"Yes, sir—while we were running."

At this moment there came a knock at the station-master's door and a porter entered.

"There's a passenger train just in from the Didcot branch," said the man, "and the driver reports that he saw a truck loaded with packing-cases in Churn siding."

"Well, I'm blowed!" exclaimed the brakesman. "Why, we ran through Churn without a stop—trains never do stop there except in camp time."

"Where is Churn?" asked Hazell, for once at a loss.

"It's merely a platform and a siding close to the camping ground between Upton and Compton," replied the station-master, "for the convenience of troops only, and very rarely used except in the summer, when soldiers are encamped there."*

"I should very much like to see the place, and as soon as possible," said Hazell.

"So you shall," replied the station-master. "A train will soon start on the branch. Inspector Hill shall go with you, and instruction shall be given to the driver to stop there, while a return train can pick you both up."

In less than an hour Hazell and Inspector Hill alighted at Churn. It is a lonely enough place, situated in a vast flat basin of the Downs, scarcely relieved by a single tree, and far from all human habitation with the exception of a lonely shepherd's cottage some half a mile away.

The "station" itself is only a single platform, with a shelter and a solitary siding, terminating in what is known in railway language as a "dead end"—that is, in this case, wooden buffers to stop any trucks. This siding runs off from the single line of rail at points from the Didcot direction of the line.

And in this siding was the lost truck, right against the "dead end," filled with three packing-cases, and labeled "Leamington to Winchester, via Newbury." There could be no doubt about it at all. But how it had got there from the middle of a train running through without a stop was a mystery even to the acute mind of Thorpe Hazell.

"Well," said the inspector when they had gazed long enough at the truck; "we'd better have a look at the points. Come along."

There is not even a signal-box at this primitive station. The points are actuated by two levers in a ground frame, standing close by the side of the line, one lever unlocking and the other shifting the same points.

* The incident here recorded occurred before June, 1905, in which month Churn was dignified with a place in Bradshaw as a "station" at which trains stop by signal.— V. L. W.

"How about these points?" said Hazell as they drew near. "You only use them so occasionally, that I suppose they are kept out of action?"

"Certainly," replied the inspector, "a block of wood is bolted down between the end of the point rail and the main rail, fixed as a wedge—ah! there it is, you see, quite untouched; and the levers themselves are locked—here's the keyhole in the ground frame. This is the strangest thing I've ever come across, Mr. Hazell."

Thorpe Hazell stood looking at the points and levers sorely puzzled. They must have been worked to get that truck in the siding, he knew well. But how?

Suddenly his face lit up. Oil evidently had been used to loosen the nut of the bolt that fixed the wedge of wood. Then his eyes fell on the handle of one of the two levers, and a slight exclamation of joy escaped him.

"Look," said the inspector at that moment, "it's impossible to pull them off," and he stretched out his hand towards a lever. To his astonishment Hazell seized him by the collar and dragged him back before he could touch it.

"I beg your pardon," he exclaimed, "hope I've not hurt you, but I want to photograph those levers first, if you don't mind."

The inspector watched him rather sullenly as he fixed his camera on a folding tripod stand he had with him, only a few inches from the handle of one of the levers, and took two very careful photographs of it.

"Can't see the use of that, sir," growled the inspector. But Hazell vouchsafed no reply.

"Let him find it out for himself," he thought.

Then he said aloud:

"I fancy they must have had that block out, inspector—and it's evident the points must have been set to get the truck where it is. How it was done is a problem, but if the doer of it was anything of a regular criminal, I think we might find *him*."

"How?" asked the puzzled inspector.

"Ah," was the response, "I'd rather not say at present. Now, I should very much like to know whether those pictures are intact?"

"We shall soon find that out," replied the inspector, "for we'll take the truck back with us." And he commenced undoing the bolt with a spanner, after which he unlocked the levers.

"H'm—they work pretty freely," he remarked as he pulled one.

"Quite so," said Hazell, "they've been oiled recently."

There was an hour or so before the return train would pass, and Hazell occupied it by walking to the shepherd's cottage.

"I am hungry," he explained to the woman there, "and hunger is Nature's dictate for food. Can you oblige me with a couple of onions and a broomstick?"

And she talks to-day of the strange man who "kept a swingin' o' that there broomstick round 'is 'ead and then eat them onions as solemn as a judge."

The first thing Hazell did on returning to Newbury was to develop his photographs. The plates were dry enough by the evening for him to print one or two photos on gaslight-paper and to enclose the clearest of them with a letter to a Scotland Yard official whom he knew, stating that he would call for an answer, as he intended returning to town in a couple of days. The following evening he received a note from the station-master, which read—

Dear Sir,

I promised to let you know if the pictures in the cases on that truck were in any way tampered with. I have just received a report from Winchester by which I understand that they have been unpacked and carefully examined by the Committee of the Loan Exhibition. The Committee are perfectly satisfied that they have not been damaged or interfered with in any way, and that they have been received just as they left the owner's hands.

We are still at a loss to account for the running of the waggon on to Churn siding or for the object in doing so. An official has been down from Paddington, and, at his request, we are not making the affair

public—the goods having arrived in safety. I am sure
you will observe confidence in this matter.

"More mysterious than ever," said Hazell to himself. "I can't
understand it at all."

The next day he called at Scotland Yard and saw the official.

"I've had no difficulty with your little matter, you'll be glad to
hear," he said. "We looked up our records and very soon spotted
your man."

"Who is he?"

"His real name is Edgar Jeffreys, but we know him under
several aliases. He's served four sentences for burglary and robbery—the latter, a daring theft from a train, so he's in your line,
Mr. Hazell. What's he been up to, and how did you get that print?"

"Well," replied Hazell, "I don't quite know yet what he's been
doing. But I should like to be able to find him if anything turns up.
Never mind how I got the print—the affair is quite a private one at
present, and nothing may come of it."

The official wrote an address on a bit of paper and handed it to
Hazell.

"He's living there just now, under the name of Allen. We keep
such men in sight, and I'll let you know if he moves."

When Hazell opened his paper the following morning he gave
a cry of joy. And no wonder, for this is what he saw:

MYSTERY OF A PICTURE.

SIR GILBERT MURRELL AND THE WINCHESTER LOAN EXHIBITION.

AN EXTRAORDINARY CHARGE.

The Committee of the Loan Exhibition of Pictures to be opened
next week at Winchester are in a state of very natural excitement
brought about by a strange charge that has been made against them
by Sir Gilbert Murrell.

Sir Gilbert, who lives at Leamington, is the owner of several
very valuable pictures, among them being the celebrated "Holy

Family," by Velasquez. This picture, with two others, was dispatched by him from Leamington to be exhibited at Winchester, and yesterday he journeyed to that city in order to make himself satisfied with the hanging arrangements, as he had particularly stipulated that "The Holy Family" was to be placed in a prominent position.

The picture in question was standing on the floor of the gallery, leaning against a pillar, when Sir Gilbert arrived with some representatives of the Committee.

Nothing occurred till he happened to walk behind the canvas, when he astounded those present by saying that the picture was not his at all, declaring that a copy had been substituted, and stating that he was absolutely certain on account of certain private marks of his at the back of the canvas which were quite indecipherable, and which were now missing. He admitted that the painting itself in every way resembled his picture, and that it was the cleverest forgery he had ever seen; but a very painful scene took place, the hanging committee stating that the picture had been received by them from the railway company just as it stood.

At present the whole affair is a mystery, but Sir Gilbert insisted most emphatically to our correspondent, who was able to see him, that the picture was certainly not his, and said that as the original is extremely valuable he intends holding the Committee responsible for the substitution which, he declares, has taken place.

It was evident to Hazell that the papers had not, as yet, got hold of the mysterious incident at Churn. As a matter of fact, the railway company had kept that affair strictly to themselves, and the loan committee knew nothing of what had happened on the line.

But Hazell saw that inquiries would be made, and determined to probe the mystery without delay. He saw at once that if there was any truth in Sir Gilbert's story the substitution had taken place in that lonely siding at Churn. He was staying at his London flat, and five minutes after he had read the paragraph had called a hansom and was being hurried off to a friend of his who was well known in art circles as a critic and art historian.

"I can tell you exactly what you want to know," said he, "for I've only just been looking it up, so as to have an article in the evening papers on it. There was a famous copy of the picture of Velasquez, said to have been painted by a pupil of his, and for some years there was quite a controversy among the respective owners as to which was the genuine one—just as there is to-day about a Madonna belonging to a gentleman at St. Moritz, but which a Vienna gallery also claims to possess.

"However, in the case of 'The Holy Family,' the dispute was ultimately settled once and for all years ago, and undoubtedly Sir Gilbert Murrell held the genuine picture. What became of the copy no one knows. For twenty years all trace of it has been lost. There— that's all I can tell you. I shall pad it out a bit in my article, and I must get to work on it at once. Good-bye!"

"One moment—where was the copy last seen?"

"Oh! the old Earl of Ringmere had it last, but when he knew it to be a forgery he is said to have sold it for a mere song, all interest in it being lost, you see."

"Let me see, he's a very old man, isn't he?"

"Yes—nearly eighty—a perfect enthusiast on pictures still, though."

"Only *said* to have sold it," muttered Hazell to himself, as he left the house; "that's very vague— and there's no knowing what these enthusiasts will do when they're really bent on a thing. Sometimes they lose all sense of honesty. I've known fellows actually rob a friend's collection of stamps or butterflies. What if there's something in it? By George, what an awful scandal there would be! It seems to me that if such a scandal were prevented I'd be thanked all round. Anyhow, I'll have a shot at it on spec. And I must find out how that truck was run off the line."

When once Hazell was on the track of a railway mystery he never let a moment slip by. In an hour's time, he was at the address given him at Scotland Yard. On his way there he took a card from his case, a blank one, and wrote on it, "From the Earl of Ringmere." This he put into an envelope.

"It's a bold stroke," he said to himself, "but, if there's anything in it, it's worth trying."

So he asked for Allen. The woman who opened the door looked at him suspiciously, and said she didn't think Mr. Allen was in.

"Give him this envelope," replied Hazell. In a couple of minutes she returned, and asked him to follow her.

A short, wiry-looking man, with sharp, evil-looking eyes, stood in the room waiting for him and looking at him suspiciously.

"Well," he snapped, "what is it—what do you want?"

"I come on behalf of the Earl of Ringmere. You will know that when I mention Churn," replied Hazell, playing his trump card boldly.

"Well," went on the man, "what about that?"

Hazell wheeled round, locked the door suddenly, put the key in his pocket, and then faced his man. The latter darted forward, but Hazell had a revolver pointing at him in a twinkling.

"You—detective!"

"No, I'm not—I told you I came on behalf of the Earl—that looks like hunting up matters for his sake, doesn't it?"

"What does the old fool mean?" asked Jeffreys.

"Oh! I see you know all about it. Now listen to me quietly, and you may come to a little reason. You changed that picture at Churn the other night."

"You seem to know a lot about it," sneered the other, but less defiantly.

"Well, I do—but not quite all. You were foolish to leave your traces on that lever, eh?"

"How did I do that?" exclaimed the man, giving himself away.

"You'd been dabbling about with oil, you see, and you left your thumb-print on the handle. I photographed it, and they recognised it at Scotland Yard. Quite simple."

Jeffreys swore beneath his breath.

"I wish you'd tell me what you mean," he said.

"Certainly. I expect you've been well paid for this little job."

"If I have, I'm not going to take any risks. I told the old man so. He's worse than I am—he put me up to getting the picture. Let him take his chance when it comes out—I suppose he wants to keep his name out of it, that's why you're here."

"You're not quite right. Now just listen to me. You're a villain, and you deserve to suffer; but I'm acting in a purely private capacity, and I fancy if I can get the original picture back to its owner that it will be better for all parties to hush this affair up. Has the old Earl got it?"

"No, not yet," admitted the other, "he was too artful. But he knows where it is, and so do I."

"Ah—now you're talking sense! Look here! You make a clean breast of it, and I'll take it down on paper. You shall swear to the truth of your statement before a commissioner for oaths—he need not see the actual confession. I shall hold this in case it is necessary; but if you help me to get the picture back to Sir Gilbert, I don't think it will be."

After a little more conversation, Jeffreys explained. Before he did so, however, Hazell had taken a bottle of milk and a hunch of wholemeal bread from his pocket, and calmly proceeded to perform "exercises" and then to eat his "lunch," while Jeffreys told the following story:

"It was the old Earl who did it. How he got hold of me doesn't matter—perhaps I got hold of him—maybe I put him up to it—but that's not the question. He'd kept that forged picture of his in a lumber room for years, but he always had his eye on the genuine one. He paid a long price for the forgery, and he got to think that he ought to have the original. But there, he's mad on pictures.

"Well, as I say, he kept the forgery out of sight and let folks think he'd sold it, but all the time he was in hopes of getting it changed somehow for the original.

"Then I came along and undertook the job for him. There were three of us in it, for it was a ticklish business. We found out by what train the picture was to travel—that was easy enough. I got hold of a key to unlock that ground frame, and the screwing off of the bolt was a mere nothing. I oiled the points well, so that the thing should work as I wanted it to.

"One pal was with me—in the siding, ready to clap on the side brake when the truck was running in. I was to work the points, and my other pal, who had the most awkward job of all, was on the goods train—under a tarpaulin in a truck. He had two lengths of very stout rope with a hook at each end of them.

"When the train left Upton, he started his job. Goods trains travel very slowly, and there was plenty of time. Counting from the back brake van, the truck we wanted to run off was No. 5. First he hooked No. 4 truck to No. 6—fixing the hook at the side of the end of both trucks, and having the slack in his hand, coiled up.

"Then when the train ran down a bit of a decline he uncoupled No. 5 from No. 4—standing on No. 5 to do it. That was easy enough, for he'd taken a coupling staff with him; then he paid out the slack till it was tight. Next he hooked his second rope from No. 5 to No. 6, uncoupled No. 5 from No. 6, and paid out the slack of the second rope.

"Now you can see what happened. The last few trucks of the train were being drawn by a long rope reaching from No. 4 to No. 6, and leaving a space in between. In the middle of this space No. 5 ran, drawn by a short rope from No. 6. My pal stood on No. 6, with a sharp knife in his hand.

"The rest was easy. I held the lever, close by the side of the line—coming forward to it as soon as the engine passed. The instant the space appeared after No. 6 I pulled it over, and No. 5 took the siding points, while my pal cut the rope at the same moment.

"Directly the truck had run by and off I reversed the lever so that the rest of the train following took the main line. There is a decline before Compton, and the last four trucks came running down to the main body of the train, while my pal hauled in the slack and finally coupled No. 4 to No. 6 when they came together. He jumped from the train as it ran very slowly into Compton. That's how it was done."

Hazell's eyes sparkled.

"It's the cleverest thing I've heard of on the line," he said.

"Think so? Well, it wanted some handling. The next thing was to unscrew the packing-case, take the picture out of the frame, and put the forgery we'd brought with us in its place. That took us some

time, but there was no fear of interruption in that lonely part. Then
I took the picture off, rolling it up first, and hid it. The old Earl
insisted on this. I was to tell him where it was, and he was going to
wait for a few weeks and then get it himself."

"Where did you hide it?"

"You're sure you're going to hush this up?"

"You'd have been in charge long ago if I were not."

"Well, there's a path from Churn to East Ilsley across the downs,
and on the right-hand of that path is an old sheep well—quite dry.
It's down there. You can easily find the string if you look for it—
fixed near the top."

Hazell took down the man's confession, which was duly at-
tested. His conscience told him that perhaps he ought to have taken
stronger measures.

"I told you I was merely a private individual," said Hazell to
Sir Gilbert Murrell. "I have acted in a purely private capacity in
bringing you your picture."

Sir Gilbert looked from the canvas to the calm face of Hazell.

"Who are you, sir?" he asked.

"Well, I rather aspire to be a book-collector; you may have read
my little monogram on 'Jacobean Bindings?'"

"No," said Sir Gilbert, "I have not had that pleasure. But I must
inquire further into this. How did you get this picture? Where was
it—who—"

"Sir Gilbert," broke in Hazell, "I could tell you the whole truth,
of course. I am not in any way to blame myself. By chance, as much
as anything else, I discovered how your picture had been stolen,
and where it was."

"But I want to know all about it. I shall prosecute—I—"

"I think not. Now, do you remember where the forged picture
was seen last?"

"Yes; the Earl of Ringmere had it—he sold it."

"Did he?"

"Eh?"

"What if he kept it all this time?" said Hazell, with a peculiar look.

There was a long silence.

"Good heavens!" exclaimed Sir Gilbert at length. "You don't mean *that*. Why, he has one foot in the grave—a very old man—I was dining with him only a fortnight ago."

"Ah! Well, I think you are content now, Sir Gilbert?"

"It is terrible—terrible! I have the picture back, but I wouldn't have the scandal known for worlds."

"It never need be," replied Hazell. "You will make it all right with the Winchester people?"

"Yes—yes—even if I have to admit I was mistaken, and let the forgery stay through the exhibition."

"I think that would be the best way," replied Hazell, who never regretted his action.

"Of course, Jeffreys ought to have been punished," he said to himself; "but it was a clever idea—a clever idea!"

"May I offer you some lunch?" asked Sir Gilbert.

"Thank you; but I am a vegetarian, and—"

"I think my cook could arrange something—let me ring."

"It is very good of you, but I ordered a dish of lentils and a salad at the station restaurant. But if you will allow me just to go through my physical training *ante* luncheon exercises here, it would save me the trouble of a more or less public display at the station."

"Certainly," replied the rather bewildered Baronet; whereupon Hazell threw off his coat and commenced whirling his arms like a windmill.

"Digestion should be considered *before* a meal," he explained.

How the Bank was Saved

Thorpe Hazell always looked upon the affair of the Birmingham Bank from a distinctly humorous point of view, declaring that it was really not worth calling a railway mystery or adventure, and that it scarcely called forth any astuteness on his part. And yet there were facts in the case that are, perhaps, worth recording.

The banking firm of Crosbie, Penfold, & Co. was an old-established one in Birmingham, numbering many of the leading manufacturers among its customers. At the time of this story the firm suddenly became aware that they had an enemy, and that this enemy was no other than an exceedingly powerful multi-millionaire of Germanic Jewish origin, named Peter Kinch. His reputation was none of the best in the financial world, and it was rumoured that he would stop at nothing to attain an object.

He had a personal quarrel with the senior partner of the bank—old Mr. Crosbie. Kinch's son had met the latter's daughter abroad, and proposed to her before the girl was old enough to know her own mind. Her father was furious when he heard about it, for the young man bore about the same reputation as his father; and although there were hundreds who looked upon him as a "good catch," old Crosbie came of a Puritan family, and retained its instincts strongly.

Samuel Kinch, who was only unbusinesslike when matters concerned his son, whom he foolishly idolised, went to see Mr. Crosbie on the matter, and, it is said, offered to settle half-a-million on his daughter if the old gentleman would consent to the marriage. This only made him more angry than ever, and he retorted that the girl was not to be sold.

A couple of years had passed since then, and Phyllis Crosbie had forgotten her girlish love, and was engaged to Charlie Penfold, the son of the junior partner—the "Co.," in reality of the firm. But Samuel Kinch had *not* forgotten. Deep down in that keen, financial brain of his was a strong instinct of revenge for injuries, and he had taken the affair as a personal slight.

However, outwardly he seemed to have made it up. He was occasionally in Birmingham on business and in contact with Mr. Crosbie, and he never referred to the subject. Then, one day, he deposited the sum of two hundred thousand pounds with the bank.

"I have so much business in Birmingham," he explained, "that it will be a matter of great convenience if you will hold this money."

Old Crosbie didn't half like it, and proposed keeping it intact in their strong room; but the other partners prevailed upon him to invest it in securities. For some months nothing was heard about it. Then some strange rumours suddenly got about with regard to the bank. People began to ask for their cash, and quite a little "run" was taking place. Suddenly Peter Kinch announced that he wanted his two hundred thousand pounds immediately.

The partners were met in consultation in their private room at the bank, which was not yet opened to the public.

"Yes," said Mr. Crosbie, "he wants every penny of it to-morrow. We must face it."

"Under ordinary circumstances we could have paid easily," said Mr. Penfold senior, "but it's very awkward just now. I can't understand matters."

"I can," said old Mr. Crosbie; "I believe we're the victims of a plot, and that Kinch is working it."

"But his object?" asked Charles Penfold.

"Partly private, perhaps—but there's something else at the bottom of it, and he could well afford to sacrifice his money here altogether if he gained his ends."

"What is it?" asked Charles and his lather simultaneously.

"Railway contracts," replied Mr. Crosbie. "It's a question of cutting German estimates by Hill & Co. and a couple of other firms here. If we were to stop payment there would be a serious lack of ready money, because those three firms do most of their business with us. If they can't be sure of ready money now, they daren't undertake the contracts at the price they could otherwise have done. And in steps the German firm, and the firm in question, gentlemen, is really Samuel Kinch. It's a smart bit of business."

He rose from his seat and took a glance out of the window.

"Look here," he said to the others.

It was ten minutes to ten, the hour when the bank opened, and already five or six people were waiting outside, one of them with a cheque fluttering in his hand, tapping the pavement impatiently with his stick. It was obvious that trouble was ahead.

"H'm," exclaimed Mr. Penfold. "I suppose we can hold out to-day."

"Yes, for to-day," replied the senior partner grimly. "We have a fair supply of cash, and I don't think there's any danger. But we must have some more before we open to-morrow. We had better ask Simpson to bring us the securities at once. Also we will telegraph to the Imperial and City, asking them to get the money ready for us. Then, perhaps you, Mr. Charles, and Simpson could go up by the 11.12 train and bring it down this evening?"

The Imperial and City Bank acted as London agents for Crosbie, Penfold, & Co., and it would be their office to raise the necessary funds on the firm's securities. A busy hour was passed in going over these documents and signing transfers. Meanwhile, a steady stream of customers kept coming into the bank, and the cashiers were hard at work paying out money.

Simpson, one of the senior cashiers, who had been selected to accompany Charles Penfold to London, was a particularly smart and level-headed fellow.

"I should like to tell you of a rumour I heard last night, sir," he said to Mr. Crosbie, when the securities had been looked over and packed in a strong leather bag.

"Yes—what is it?"

"Well, sir, we have a powerful enemy, and not over scrupulous . . . am I right, sir?"

"Quite right. What of that?"

"It would be to his interest to prevent us from getting this money in time, sir, and he might not be particular as to what means he took to do it. One of the juniors was asked a lot of questions about us last night by a suspicious-looking stranger he met—er—well, in a bar. He didn't let out anything, but he told me about it, and just now he saw this same man hanging about the bank."

"Thank you," said Mr. Penfold. "Of course, Charles," he went on, "you will take every precaution. You had better telegraph to Scotland Yard, and ask for a detective to travel back with you this evening."

"I'll do better than that, father. I'll wire to my friend Thorpe Hazell. What he doesn't know about railways isn't worth knowing, and I'll ask him to meet me at the Imperial and City. He'll probably come back with us, and I'd really rather have him than an ordinary detective. If there's going to be any attempt at robbery on the line, his advice will be the best to act upon, I'm sure."

Thus it came to pass that Thorpe Hazell found himself in consultation with Charles Penfold a little after three o'clock that day in a private room at the Imperial and City Bank, which, as everyone knows, is situated in Throgmorton Street.

"I'm sure we are being carefully watched," said Penfold. "You noticed it, didn't you, Simpson?"

"Distinctly, sir. Not only on the train, but I'm certain a taxi followed us here."

"Well," replied Hazell, "the thing is very obvious. You say you have reason to believe that an attempt is going to be made to rob you of this large sum of money. By the way, what does it consist of and how do you propose to carry it?"

"Mostly of Bank of England notes, but a certain amount of gold. We shall pack it in this bag. If we all three travel with it, it ought to be safe."

"Well, I'm not so sure of that," said Hazell; "from what you tell me, we evidently have a very wily enemy to deal with, and my experience of railway mysteries tells me there is not always safety in numbers. What train did you think of taking?"

"The 4.55 from Paddington. But if you advised it we might travel by another route."

"Quite so. But the enemy might have thought of that, too, and taken steps accordingly. We must be prepared for all emergencies. Now, suppose you tell me exactly why you think this attempt is likely to be made. Is there any ulterior motive besides robbery?"

Penfold explained that there was, telling Hazell the question of the German contracts. The latter's face brightened during the recital.

"Tell me," he said, "suppose your hypothesis is correct and the robbery took place, what would happen?"

"Well, Kinch would know at once, I expect, and would wire to Germany without delay, anticipating the fact that we should have to stop payment tomorrow. He has everything ready, we know."

"Ah, and suppose he wired and put the machinery in motion, and after all you *could* pay to-morrow, what about that?"

"He wouldn't be such a fool. Why, it would cost him a million. Sure to. Perhaps more. When a man like Kinch once makes a slip it's pretty bad for his reputation."

Hazell got up from his chair and slapped Penfold on the shoulder.

"Excellent, my dear chap," he exclaimed; "I thought at first you were only bringing me an ordinary case of prevention of robbery in a train. But this is really likely to be interesting. Quite a little comedy, in fact. That is, if you will place yourself in my hands entirely?"

"Very well," replied Penfold, "but I don't quite see your meaning."

"Ah, you're rather tired and run down, you see. This affair is making you over anxious. Let me recommend a few hours at the seaside. Bournemouth, now, is a capital place. And, by the way, Mr. Simpson," he went on, addressing the cashier, "it's close on half-past three. Not too soon in the afternoon for a cup of tea. There's an A. B. C. fifty yards from the bank. Go and get some tea, my dear sir, and come back in a quarter of an hour's time; and would you mind bringing me a pint of milk in a bottle and a packet of plasmon chocolate? I shall have to dine *en route.*"

Penfold stared at him in amazement, but Hazell insisted. As soon as he was out of the room Hazell exclaimed:

"Quick now—see the directors here and get the cash; it ought to be ready now. Have it as much in notes as possible. We must pack that bag before Simpson returns. I'm afraid I'm going to impose on him a little. Ah, and I shall want another bag—mine will do. I brought it with me in case I was out for the night; and we'll ask the people here to lend us some weights, or anything heavy will do."

He emptied the things out of his bag, two of the directors came in with the money a few minutes afterwards, and then Penfold began to see daylight. Meanwhile Hazell was rapidly turning over the leaves of a Bradshaw and jotting down notes on a bit of paper, which he presently handed to Penfold.

"Follow these directions carefully. It's best for you to keep out of the way. Now then, here comes Simpson. Not a word, gentlemen, please!"

"Well, Mr. Simpson," he went on, as the cashier came in, "Mr. Penfold agrees with me that you had better take the money down with me. He's not feeling very well, and he's going for a little holiday. You will have to explain matters to his partners. You and I will start directly, but I'm going to see Mr. Penfold off first. Come along, old fellow, you'll catch the 4.10 to Bournemouth easily."

He took him outside the bank, holding his bag in his hand, hailed a hansom, and, as Penfold got in, said to him in a loud tone of voice:

"Don't you worry, old chap. I'll see this thing through. It's much better for you to keep out of it, because Simpson and I can manage it. I hope you'll find your sister better when you get to Bournemouth; it may not be so bad as the telegram makes out."

He noticed, to his intense delight, that a man who was lounging past dropped his stick on the pavement close by, and stopped to pick it up.

"Good-bye, Penfold—oh, I was nearly forgetting your bag; here you are. Now then, my man," he added, addressing the chauffeur, "Waterloo Station, sharp!"

He had the satisfaction of seeing the man who had dropped the stick hail another hansom, which followed in the wake of Penfold's.

"Ah," he said, "they'll see he takes a ticket for Bournemouth, and they won't suspect anything. Now for a little adventure!"

A quarter of an hour later he was seated in a taxi-cab with Simpson, *en route* for Paddington. The leather bag, heavy with the weight of its contents, lay on the floor in front of them. Once or twice Hazell put his head out of the window and looked behind, laughing softly to himself when he drew it back.

"Now, Mr. Simpson," he said to his companion, presently, "you and I are about to run the gauntlet. Perhaps you may think my conduct a little strange, later, but I must beg of you not to question it."

"Very well," replied Simpson, who had hardly taken his eyes off the precious bag in front of him, "I have every confidence in you, Mr. Hazell."

"That's right. Now, suppose—mind, I only say *suppose*—you and I are attacked on the train to-night, you would defend that bag of money, eh?"

Simpson turned to him in surprise.

"Of course—" he began, but a smile on the other's face stopped him.

"It is a considerable sum, I know," he said, "but not so valuable as a human life—*if* you were threatened, Mr. Simpson, eh?"

Again the smile crept over his face, and puzzled the cashier for a moment.

"*I* should prefer to save my life, I think," went on Hazell. "Let us look at the matter seriously. You are attacked, we'll say, and the odds are too great. The villains get away with the money. Perhaps you are able to stop the train. But the money has disappeared. You would go to Mr. Crosbie when you reached Birmingham, and tell him of this terrible misfortune. You would tell the Police. This fellow, Kinch, if he's at the bottom of it, would, put his little plan in action at once. Dear me! A most 'regrettable incident,' as politicians call it. You would throw the whole blame on me. And then—and then—let us suppose that after all the money was at the bank the next morning. What a surprise! Villainy defeated—virtue triumphant. No! Don't ask me any questions. Here we are at Paddington."

A broad grin broke out on Simpson's face as he got out.

"Be careful of the precious bag," said Hazell. "That's right."

The short winter's day was drawing to a close, and darkness had begun to set in. Hazell looked, suspiciously, all round him, and kept close to Simpson, helping him to carry the heavy bag. They took first-class tickets for Birmingham, and tipped the guard to secure them a compartment. On Hazell giving Simpson directions, the latter got in with the bag, and Hazell stood outside on the platform as if on guard.

Presently an old clergyman came along with shuffling step. He was about to get into the same compartment, when Hazell stopped him, telling him it was engaged. He bowed politely, and got into the next one. The carriage was well up the platform and in front of the train, and the majority of the passengers were getting in behind, as is often the case at terminal stations.

A few minutes before the train started a couple of men—strong-looking fellows—came marching up the platform and got into the compartment immediately in front of Simpson. They were dressed rather like farmers, and one of them carried a heavy stick

The positions of the travellers in this particular carriage were now as follows:

1st compartment—the two men.
2nd compartment—Simpson.
3rd compartment—the old clergyman.

Hazell still stood outside the door on the platform. The hand of the great clock was almost on the moment of departure when he suddenly exclaimed:

"I've forgotten to get a paper. There's just time."

He ran back to the bookstall. At the same moment the old clergyman put his head out of the window and watched him. He bought his paper and started back.

At that exact moment the guard waved his green lamp, the whistle sounded, and the train began very slowly to move.

"Look sharp, sir!"

Then Hazell did a very clumsy thing. He caught his toe in the platform and fell, sprawling.

The next moment he was on his feet, but it was too late to catch his compartment. He made a rush for the next carriage; his keen eyes detected an empty compartment; he opened the door and swung himself into the moving train. Simpson, who had his head out of the window, saw what had happened. At first he felt strangely disconcerted, and then, once more, he broke into a smile.

The first stop was at Oxford. Hazell lit a cigar and threw himself back in his seat, laughing softly to himself.

"They are really a very clumsy lot," he soliloquised, "my reputation is quite at stake in allowing it. Never mind, though."

From time to time he looked out of the window towards the front of the train, but it was not until they had travelled a considerable distance beyond Reading that the comedy he was expecting began to be played.

Then he saw, in the darkness, the door of the compartment in front of Simpson's open, and a figure on the footboard. Darting to the other side and looking out of that window he could just discern someone on that side of the carriage also.

Simpson was sitting in his compartment, wondering what was going to happen. Suddenly there was an awful crashing of glass, and the window on the left-hand side was splintered to bits by a violent blow from a stick from outside. Involuntarily Simpson first started back, and then sprang at the window.

The ruse succeeded admirably, for at the same moment the opposite door was opened and a man sprang in. Before Simpson knew what had happened, he felt himself seized by the collar from behind and dragged back. Then the door with the splintered window opened, and the second villain threw himself upon him. Resistance was out of the question. In three minutes Simpson lay on the seat, his hands and feet tied, and a handkerchief bound over his mouth.

"There," said one of the men, "that little job's done. It's lucky for you my friend, that that clumsy detective isn't in with you, or we might have had to use *this*," and he showed a revolver. "But we shan't hurt you. We're just going to search you to see if you have any notes on you, in case they're not all in the bag."

They set to work, coolly enough, but found nothing.

"Well," went on the man, "now we'll clear out. Sorry to have troubled you," he added, to the cashier, "but you should have taken more care of your property. By George, it's precious heavy!"

"Ready?" asked the other.

"Yes—where are we?"

"Between Cholsey and Didcot."

"Right!"

He gave a sharp tug at the chain of the communication-cord with which every Great Western express is provided inside the carriages. A moment or two later there was a shrieking of the engine whistle and a grinding of the brakes.

As the train slowed down the two men, taking the heavy bag with them, prepared to get out. The one who held the bag was actually on the footboard before the train stopped, and Hazell, who was watching from his window, distinctly saw what happened.

The train came to a standstill on an embankment, and the two robbers jumped and ran for all they were worth, but not before more than one of the passengers had caught a glimpse of them. The guard came running along the train, together with Hazell.

The latter made for Simpson's compartment, and was taken a little aback when he found him lying prostrate, but a couple of seconds sufficed to show he was unhurt. He tore the gag off, and the two of them raised a hue-and-cry that was heard all along the train.

"What is it?" asked the guard.

"Robbery!" shouted Simpson, as they cut his bonds, "thousands of pounds, man."

"Money for a Birmingham bank," explained Hazell. "I was in charge of it with the cashier here, only I nearly got left behind at

Paddington and travelled in another compartment. Quick! They mustn't escape!"

"What was the money in?" asked the guard, who thought the men a couple of fools to travel with it as they had done.

"A leather bag—they must have taken it off— there were two of them."

"I saw them running down the embankment," exclaimed a passenger who had joined them, "but I'll swear they were carrying nothing. They vaulted over the fence at the bottom, and each of them used both his hands."

Hazell was standing beside the train and a frown swept over his face. He glanced up quickly at the elderly clergyman, who was looking out of the window.

"Did you see them, sir?" he asked.

"Yes—yes."

"Could you make out if they carried a bag?"

"Oh, yes—I'm sure they did."

"And I'll swear they didn't," said the dogged passenger.

"We'll search the train—sharp, please," said the guard, and he mounted into the old clergyman's compartment at once. But there was nothing there. Nor could anything be discovered in or near the train.

"Now," said the guard, "I'm very sorry gentlemen, but I can't delay the train longer. You should have carried the money in my van. All I can do is to stop at Didcot to let you get out and send a telegram or see the police. That's your affair. It's evident they've made off. Take your seats, please!"

One or two passengers who had started on a chase on the spur of the moment came panting back. Hazell nudged Simpson, and they climbed up into the compartment occupied by the clergyman.

"This is not your carriage," he said mildly, as the train started.

"Oh—so I see," said Hazell. "Never mind. This is a terrible thing—terrible!" and he went on to discuss the robbery.

"You had better wire from Didcot to Mr. Crosbie," he said to Simpson, "see the police there, and then come on to Birmingham by a later train."

"What shall you do?"

"Oh, I think I'll go on. Of course you'll also wire back to London to have the notes stopped. That's all we can do, I think."

An almost imperceptible smile passed over the face of the old clergyman.

"Was it all in notes, may I ask?"

"Oh, no. There was a considerable sum in gold," replied Hazell, who, even for an amateur detective, was strangely communicative.

At Oxford the old clergyman got out for a moment. Hazell saw him hand a paper to an official, and the latter made for the telegraph office. When he came back to the carriage he got into another compartment. Hazell followed him, a sweet smile on his face. The old clergyman grew very grumpy and uneasy.

But Hazell stuck to him like a leech—not only to Birmingham, but all the way to Chester. The old gentleman became more and more uneasy as the train went on. He even told Hazell that he wished to be alone. But Hazell only smiled, and offered excuses. Then he introduced the subject of physical culture, explaining the desirability of lentil and plasmon diet, and giving practical explanation of "nerve training" by holding a piece of paper in front of his face at arm's length and keeping the edge in line with the hat-rack opposite. When they got to Chester he stood about on the platform till the empty train was backed off into a siding.

Then the old gentleman, who had been hovering about the train also, lost his temper, and swore under his breath.

Old Mr. Crosbie and Mr. Penfold, senior, sat in their private room in the bank, with Simpson standing before them. The latter was having a very bad time of it indeed. Questions and rebukes were being hurled at his devoted head by the two partners.

"I cannot understand it at all, can you, Penfold?"

"No," said the latter, "and I'm bound to say I think you have acted in a very strange manner, Simpson. You may go to your place—but there is a detective in the bank, and he has orders to see that you don't leave."

All the papers were full of the robbery that morning. A little crowd had gathered outside the bank waiting for the doors to open. Several Birmingham firms were in consternation. The partners, who had been up all night, looked at each other blankly.

"Can we open?" asked Mr. Crosbie in a hoarse whisper.

The other shook his head.

"We daren't," he groaned.

A few minutes passed in silence. The clock in the office marked seven minutes to the hour. A cab dashed up outside.

The next moment Charles Penfold, fresh and smiling, stood before the partners, opening a bag, and turning out his pockets before their astounded gaze. There was no time for explanation.

Five minutes later the doors of the bank opened, and the foremost of the crowd outside entered, wondering what was about to happen. By common consent they gave way to a coarse-looking man who was forcing his way to the paying-out counter, a smile of triumph on his evil features. For they recognised him as the Nemesis of the bank, Samuel Kinch himself, who had come to take his revenge in person.

He slammed down a cheque upon the counter. The cashier turned it over carelessly to see the indorsement. He did not even ask him to step into the partners' room. He had his instructions.

"You will take it in notes, I suppose, sir?" he asked coolly.

"Yes, if you've got enough," replied Kinch insolently.

"Oh, that's all right, sir."

There was a dead silence, broken only by the rustle and crackling of roll after roll of Bank of England notes as the cashier counted them out and Kinch checked them, with a snarling expression on his face.

Then arose a hum and a buzz. Kinch had been paid. For half-an-hour the paying cashiers were fairly busy, but the tide was beginning to turn, and in an hour's time the receiving cashiers were doing all the work.

The credit of Crosbie, Penfold & Co. was saved, and the tenders for the railway contracts could be delivered without fear of lack of cash for preliminary expenses and raw material.

"One in the eye for old Kinch!" was the verdict of the day.

"Oh, the thing was childish!" said Hazell that evening at the snug little dinner to which old Mr. Crosbie had invited him, but at which he only ate his "plasmon," and partook of seven raw apples— the other partner, Charles Penfold, and Simpson were also present— "I saw that if there was a sham robbery this cunning Samuel Kinch would heap vengeance on himself. So I sent Mr. Charles Penfold here down to Bournemouth, his pockets stuffed with notes, and my own bag stuffed with gold, and slung on the roof of a hansom to avoid suspicion. It would be difficult for them to connect Bournemouth with Birmingham, but we managed to do so by a devious route.

"Then I filled the leather bag with weights and things. Simpson, *of course*, thought we had the money, ha! ha! ha! Oh, *don't* say you didn't, Simpson—don't spoil it. It was a clumsy method of attack, but it answered."

"But what became of that bag?"

"That's just the greatest joke of the whole thing. I was looking out of the window, Simpson, as the beggars got off, and I saw them hand the bag to that sweet old clergyman. The train had hardly stopped before he was out of it. He climbed to the roof of the carriage by the steps at the end, put the bag on the top, and was in at the other side of his compartment in a jiffy. I travelled all the way to Chester to prevent him from laying his hands on that bag, and he was furious. It may be going about the country in that fashion still, for all we know."

"But why prevent him when it was of no value?" asked Mr. Crosbie.

"That was just it. If he had once discovered it was only a sham robbery he would have given the alarm to Kinch—and that would have spoilt all."

"Well, Mr. Hazell. I'm sure the Bank is deeply indebted to you."

"Not at all. It has been a very ludicrous little adventure, and I've thoroughly enjoyed it."

Here he suddenly jumped from his seat, threw himself on his back on the floor, stretching his arms over his head as far as they could reach.

"Good gracious," exclaimed old Mr. Crosbie, "what's the matter? Are you ill?"

"I should be," replied Hazell gravely, "very probably, if I did not take fifty deep breaths in a recumbent position. It is the secret of digesting fruit!"

The Affair of the German Dispatch-Box

Thorpe Hazell often said afterwards that the most daring case which he ever undertook was that of the German Dispatch-Box. It was an affair of international importance at the time, and, for obvious reasons, remained shrouded in mystery. Now, however, when it may be relegated to the region of obsolete diplomatic crises, there is no reason why it should not, to a certain extent, be made public.

Hazell was only half through his breakfast one morning at his house in Netherton, when a telegram arrived for him with this message:

> Am coming by next train. Wish to consult you on important question.
>
> Mostyn Cotterell.

"Cotterell, Cotterell," said Hazell to himself. "Oh, yes, I remember—he was on the same staircase with myself at St. Philip's. A reading man in those days. I haven't seen him for years. Surely he's something in the Government now. Let me see."

He got his Whitaker and consulted its pages. Presently he found what he wanted.

"Under-Secretary for Foreign Affairs—Mostyn Cotterell."

As soon as he had finished his breakfast, including his pint of lemonade, he produced a "Book of Exercises," and carefully went through the following directions:

"Stand in correct position, commence to inhale, and at the same time commence to tense the muscles of the arms, and raise them to an extended front horizontal position; leave the hands to drop limp from the wrists. While doing this change the weight of the body from the full foot on to the toes; in this position hold the breath and make rigid and extended the muscles of the arms, sides, neck, abdomen, and legs. Repeat this fifteen times."

Half-an-hour or so later Mostyn Cotterell was ushered into his room. He was a tall, thin man, with a black moustache that made his naturally pale face look almost white. There was a haggard look about him, and certain dark lines under his eyes showed pretty plainly that he was suffering from want of sleep.

"It's a good many years since we met, Hazell," he began, "and you have gained quite a reputation since the old college days."

"Ah, I see you have read my monograph on 'Nerve Culture and Rational Food,'" replied Hazell.

"Never heard of it," said Cotterell. "No, I mean your reputation as a railway expert, my dear fellow."

"Oh, railways!" exclaimed Hazell in a disappointed tone of voice. "They're just a hobby of mine, that's all. Is that why you've come?"

"Exactly. I called at your flat in town, but was told you were here. I want to consult you on a delicate matter, Hazell; one in which your knowledge of railways may prove of great value. Of course, it is understood that what I am going to say is quite private."

"Certainly."

"Well, let me put a case. Suppose a man was travelling, say, from London to the Continent by the ordinary boat train; and suppose that it was desirable to prevent that man from getting to his destination, would it—well—would it be possible to prevent him doing so?"

Hazell smiled.

"Your enigma is a difficult one to answer," he said. "It would all depend upon the means you cared to employ. I daresay it could be done, but you would probably have to resort to force."

"That would hardly be politic. I want you to suggest some plan by which he could be got into a wrong train, or got out of the right one, so that, let us say, something he was carrying would be lost, or, at least, delayed in transit."

"You are not very clear, Cotterell. First you speak of the man being frustrated, and then of something he is carrying. What do you mean? Which is of the greater importance—the man or his property?"

"His property."

"That puts a different aspect on it. I take it this is some intrigue of your profession. Why not place confidence in me, and tell me the whole thing? I never like to work on supposition. Once some fellows tried to draw me on a supposed case of wrecking a train. I could have told them half-a-dozen theories of my own invention, but I held my tongue, and lucky it was that I did so, for I found out afterwards they belonged to an American train robber gang. I don't accuse you of any nefarious purposes, but if you want my advice, tell me the exact circumstances. Only, I warn you beforehand, Cotterell, that I won't give you any tips that would either compromise me or be of danger to any railway company."

"Very well," replied the Under-Secretary, "I will tell you the leading facts without betraying any State secrets, except to mention that there is a great stake involved. To cut matters short, a very important document has been stolen from our office. We pretty well know the culprit, only we have no proof. But we are certain of one thing and that is that this document is at present in the hands of the German Ambassador. You will understand that the ways of diplomacy are very subtle and that it is a case which makes action very difficult. If we were to demand the surrender of this paper we should be met, I have no doubt, with a bland denial that it is in the Ambassador's possession.

"Of course we have our secret agents, and they have told us that Colonel Von Kriegen, one of the messengers of the German Embassy, has been ordered to start at mid-day with dispatches to Berlin. It is more than likely—in fact it is a dead certainty—that this particular document will be included in his dispatches. Now, if it once gets into the possession of the German Chancellery, there will be a bad international trouble which might even land us in a Continental war. If you can devise any means of obstructing or preventing the transit of this dispatch you would be rendering the country a real service."

Hazell thought for a moment.

"Do you think this Colonel Von Kriegen knows of the document he is carrying?" he asked presently.

"I shouldn't think so, its contents are of far too much importance to trust even to a regular messenger. No, he will probably be told to exercise the greatest care, and his journey will be watched and himself guarded by the German secret police."

"How is he likely to carry the document?"

"In his dispatch-box, together with other papers."

"And he will probably travel with secret police. My dear fellow, you have given me a hard nut to crack. Let me think a bit."

He lit a cigarette and smoked hard for a few minutes. Presently he asked Cotterell if the dispatch-box had a handle to it.

"Yes—of course," replied the Under-Secretary; "a leather handle."

"I wish I knew exactly what it was like."

"I can easily tell you. All the dispatch-boxes of the German Embassy are of the same pattern. It is our business to know the smallest details. It would be about a foot long, eight inches broad, and about five inches deep, with a handle on the top—a dark green box."

Hazell's face lit up with sudden interest.

"You haven't one exactly like it?" he asked.

"Yes, we have. At my office."

"Will the key be with the Colonel?"

"Of course not. The Ambassador here will lock it, and it will not be opened till it is in the hands of the Chancellor in Berlin."

Hazell jumped to his feet and began to stride up and down the room.

"Cotterell!" he exclaimed, "there's just one plan that occurs to me. It's a very desperate one, and even if it succeeds it will land me in prison."

"In England?" asked the other.

"Rather. I'm not going to play any tricks on the Continent, I can tell you. Now, suppose I'm able to carry out this plan and am imprisoned—say at Dovehaven—what would happen?"

He stopped abruptly in his walk and looked at Cotterell. A grin broke over the latter's face, and he said, quietly:

"Oh—you'd escape, Hazell."

"Very good. I shall want help. *You'd* better not come. Have you got a knowing fellow whom you can trust? He must be a sharp chap, mind."

"Yes, I have. One of our private men, named Bartlett."

"Good. There are just two hours before the Continental train starts, and a quarter of an hour before you get a train back to town. You wire Bartlett from Netherton to meet you, and I'll write out instructions for you to give him. He'll have an hour in which to carry them out."

He wrote rapidly for five minutes upon a sheet of paper, and then handed it over to the Under- Secretary.

"Mind you," he said, "the chances are terribly against us, and I can only promise to do my best. I shall follow you to town by another train that will give me just time to catch the boat express. What is this Von Kriegen like?"

Cotterell described him.

"Good—now you must be off!"

Three-quarters of an hour later Hazell came out of his house, somewhat changed in appearance. He had put on the same dark wig which he wore in the affair of Crane's cigars, and was dressed in a black serge suit and straw hat. A clerical collar completed the deception of a clergyman in semi-mufti.

A stiffly-upright, military-looking man, with the ends of his fair moustache strongly waxed, dressed in a frock coat suit and tall hat, and carrying a dispatch-box, walked down the platform beside the boat train, the guard, who knew him well by sight—as he knew many who travelled on that line with their precious dispatches—giving him a salute as he passed.

Two men walked closely, but unobtrusively behind the Colonel; two men whose eyes and ears were on the alert, and who scrutinised everyone carefully as they passed along. Of their presence the Special Messenger took not the slightest notice, though he was well aware of their companionship. He selected a first-class compartment, and got in. The two men followed him into the carriage, but without saying a word. One of them posted himself by the window, and kept a steady look out on to the platform.

The train was just about to start, and the guard had just put his whistle to his mouth, when a man came running down the platform, a small bag in one hand, a bundle of papers and an umbrella in the other. It was only a clergyman, and the man at the window gave a smile as he saw him.

With a rush, the clergyman made for the compartment, seizing the handle of the door and opening it. Frantically he threw his bag, umbrella, and papers into the carriage. The train had just begun to move.

The man near the window had retreated at the onslaught. He was just about to resent the intrusion with the words that the compartment was engaged, when a porter, running up behind the clergyman, pushed him in and slammed the door.

"I thought I'd lost it!" exclaimed the intruder, taking off his hat and wiping the perspiration from his forehead, for it was a very hot day, and he had been hurrying. "It was a close shave! Oh, thank you, thank you!" he added, as one of the men rather ungraciously picked up his bag and papers from the floor, at the same time eyeing him closely.

But Hazell, in his disguise, was perfectly proof against any suspicion. He sat down and opened the *Guardian* with an easy air, just looking round at each of his three companions in such a naturally inquisitive manner as to thoroughly disarm them from the outset. The Colonel had lighted a cigar and said, half apologetically, as he took it from his lips:

"I hope you don't mind smoking?"

"Oh, not at all. I do it myself occasionally," returned the clergyman with an amiable smile.

The train was now fairly under way, and Hazell was beginning, as he read his paper, to take mental stock of his surroundings and the positions in which the other three were seated.

He, himself, was facing the engine on the left-hand side of the compartment, close to the window. Immediately opposite to him sat Colonel von Kriegen, watchful and alert, although he seemed to smoke so complacently. Beside the Colonel, on the seat on his left, was the precious dispatch-box; and the Colonel's hand, as it dangled negligently over the arm-rest, touched it ever and anon. On the next seat, guarding the dispatch-box on that side, sat one of the secret police agents, while the other had placed himself next to Hazell and, consequently, opposite the box, which was thus thoroughly guarded at all points.

It was this dispatch-box that Hazell was studying as he apparently read his paper, noting its exact position and distance from him. As he had told Morton Cotterell, the chances of carrying out his plan were very much against him, and he felt that this was more than ever the case now. He had really hoped to secure a seat beside the box. But this was out of the question.

After a bit he put down his paper, leant forward, and looked out of the window, watching the country as they sped through it. Once, just as they were passing through a station, he stood up and leant his head out of the window for a minute. The three men exchanged glances now that his back was turned, but the Colonel only smiled and shook his head slightly.

Then Hazell sat down once more, yawned, gathered up his paper, and made another apparent attempt to read it. After a bit, he drew a cigarette case from his pocket, took out a cigarette, and placed it in his mouth. Then he leant forward, in a very natural attitude, and began feeling in his waistcoat pocket for a match.

The German Colonel watched him, carelessly flicking the ash from his cigar as he did so. Then, as it was apparent that the clergyman could find no matches, his politeness came to the front.

"You want a light, sir," he said in very good English, "can I offer you one?"

"Oh, thanks!" replied Hazell, shifting to the edge of his seat, and leaning still more forward, "perhaps I may take one from your cigar?"

Every action that followed had been most carefully thought out beforehand. As he leant over towards the German he turned his back slightly on the man who sat beside him. He held the cigarette with the first and second fingers of his right hand and with the end of it in his mouth. He kept his eyes fixed on the Colonel's. Meanwhile his left hand went out through the open window, dropped over the sill, remained there a moment, then came back, and crossed over the front of his body stealthily with the palm downwards.

It was all over in a second, before either of the three had time to grasp what was happening. He had his face close up to the Colonel's, and had taken a puff at the cigarette, when suddenly his left hand swooped down on the handle of the dispatch-box, his right hand flew forward into the Colonel's face, instantly coming round with a quick sweep to his left hand, and, before the Colonel could recover or either of the others take action, he had tossed the dispatch-box out of the window.

They were on him at once. He sprang up, back to the window, and made a little struggle, but the Colonel and one of the others had him on the seat in no time. Meanwhile the third man had pulled the electric safety signal, and had dashed to the window. Thrusting his head out, he looked back along the level bit of line on which they were running.

"I can see it!" he cried triumphantly, as his eye caught a dark object beside the track. The whole affair had taken place so suddenly that the train began to pull up within fifteen or twenty seconds of the throwing out of the dispatch case. There was a shrill whistle, a grinding of brakes, and the train came to a standstill.

The guard was out of his van in an instant, running along beside the train.

"What is it?" he asked, as he came up to the carriage.

The police agent, who still kept his eyes fixed back on the track, beckoned him to come up. Heads were out of windows, and this matter was a private one. So the guard climbed on to the footboard.

"A dispatch-box has been thrown out of the carriage," whispered the police agent; "we have the man here. But we must get the case. It's only a little way back. We pulled the signal at once—in fact, I could see it lying beside the track before we stopped."

"Very good, sir," replied the guard quietly, commencing to wave an arm towards the rear of the train. The signal was seen on the engine, and the train began to reverse. Very soon a small, dark object could be seen alongside the rails. As they drew close, the guard held out his hand motionless, the train stopped, and he jumped off.

"Is this it?" he asked, as he handed in the dispatch-box.

"Yes!" exclaimed the Colonel, "it's all right. Thank you, guard. Here's something for your trouble. We'll hand over the fellow to the police at Dovehaven. It was a clumsy trick."

Colonel Von Kriegen lit another cigar as the train went on, and looked at Hazell, who sat between the two police agents. There was a half smile on the Colonel's lips as he said:

"I'm afraid you did not quite succeed, sir! It was a sharp thing to do, but it didn't go quite far enough. You might have been sure that in broad daylight, and with the means of stopping the train, that it was impossible. Who put you on to this?"

"I accept the entire responsibility myself," replied Hazell—"failure and all. I have only one favour to ask you. Will you allow me to eat my lunch?"

"Oh, certainly," replied the Colonel grimly— "especially as you won't have a chance of doing so when we arrive at Dovehaven. I should like you to travel all the way with us, but the exigencies of international law prevent that."

Hazell bowed, and the next moment was placidly consuming Plasmon biscuits and drinking sterilised milk, expatiating at intervals on "natural food."

"Try a diet of macaroni and Dutch cheese," were his last words to the Colonel. "They both help to build up the grey brain material. Useful in your position!"

When the train arrived at Dovehaven, Hazell was given into the charge of the police there, and marched off to the station. Here the superintendent looked at him curiously. Hazell met his gaze, but nothing was said. It was strange, however, that he was not locked up in an ordinary cell, but in a small room.

It was also strange that the bar of the window was very loose, and that no one was about when he dropped out of it that night. The German police, when they heard about it, smiled. Diplomatic affairs are peculiar, and they knew that this particular "criminal" would never be caught.

Meanwhile, the Colonel journeyed on to Berlin, with the full assurance in his mind that the papers in his dispatch-box were intact. He duly handed the latter over in person to the Chancellor, who, as the result of a cypher telegram, was eagerly expecting it.

Somehow, his key did not fit the lock of the dispatch-box. After trying it for a few moments, he exclaimed:

"Colonel, how is this? This is not one of our boxes, surely?"

The Colonel's face turned pale, and he hesitated to reply. Snatching up a knife, the Chancellor forced open the box, a cry of dismay issuing from his lips as he drew out the contents—the current number of *Punch*, in which he figured in a cartoon, and a copy of the *Standard*, containing an article, carefully marked, on the foreign policy of the Government. Insult to injury, if you like.

German oaths never look well in print, and, anyhow, it is needless to record the ensuing conversation between the Chancellor and Colonel Von Kriegen. At about the time it was taking place the German Ambassador in London received by post the original dispatch-box and its contents, minus the incriminating document, which now reposed safely in the custody of the Foreign Office, thanks to the ingenuity of Thorpe Hazell.

"How was it done?" said Hazell afterwards, when telling the story to a companion. "Oh, it was a pure trick, and I hardly expected to be able to bring it off. Fortunately, Bartlett was a 'cute chap, and followed out all my instructions to the letter. Those instructions were very simple. I told him to wear an Inverness cloak, to provide himself with the duplicate dispatch-box, a few yards of very strong fishing twine, a fair-sized snap-hook, and a

light walking-stick with a forked bit of wire stuck in the end of it.
The only difficulty about his job was the presence of other travellers in his compartment, but, as it happened, there were only two
maiden ladies, who thought him mad on fresh air.

"Of course, I told him how to use his various articles, and also
that on no account was he to communicate with me either by word
or look, but that he was to get into the compartment next to that in
which the Colonel was travelling, and to be ready to command
either window by reserving a seat with a bag on one side and seat-
ing himself on the other.

"The cloak served for a double purpose—to hide the dispatch-
box and to conceal his movements from the occupants of his
carriage when the time for action came. Fortunately, both his
companions sat with their backs to the engine, so that he was
easily able to command either window.

"I was to let him know which side of the train was the sphere of
action by putting out my head as we ran through Eastwood. He
would then look out of both windows and get to work accordingly.

"What he did was this. He had the snap-hook tied tightly to the
end of the fishing-line. By leaning out of the window and slinging
this hook on the fork of his walking-stick he was able to reach it
along the side of the carriage—holding his stick at the other end—
and slip the hook over the handle outside my door, where it hung
by its cord.

"He then dropped the stick and held the cord loosely in his right
hand, the slack end ready to run out. This, you will observe, kept
the hook hanging on my handle. With his left hand he drew the
dispatch-box from under his cloak and held it outside the carriage,
ready to drop it instantly.

"Of course he was standing all the time, with his head and
shoulders out of the window.

"When I leant forward to light my cigarette at the Colonel's
cigar, I slipped my left hand out of the window, easily found the
hook hanging there, grasped it, and kept it open with one finger.
Bartlett, who was watching, got ready. You can easily guess the
rest. I swung my left hand suddenly over to the dispatch-box,

Bartlett allowing the line to run through his hand, snapped the hook over the handle before they could see what I was about, and pitched it out of the window as lightly as possible.

"The same instant Bartlett dropped the duplicate box from the train, grasped the line tightly as the real dispatch-box flew out, and hauled it in, hand over hand. He very soon had the dispatch-box safely stowed under his cloak, and, on reaching Dovehaven, took the next train back to town, to the no small satisfaction of his chief.

"Unluckily, I quite forgot to ask Cotterell to mention in the wire I knew he would be sending to the police at Dovehaven to have a dish of lentils ready for me in my brief imprisonment. It was very awkward. But they made me an exceedingly well-cooked tapioca pudding."

"But," said the Bishop of Frattenbury, "while—er—agreeing with you on the question of consuming alcohol, I cannot follow what you say with regard to animal food. Many animals were—er—in point of fact designed by a beneficent Creator for the sustenance of human life."

"You've no small opinion of yourself, my lord," rejoined Thorpe Hazell, "if you really believe that the pig was created in order that you might have ham for breakfast."

The Bishop of Frattenbury reddened. He was not accustomed to be spoken to like this by a mere layman, and he would have resented it even in a church dignitary.

"I scarcely commend your flippant way of putting things, sir," he rejoined severely, "even for the sake of argument. I was alluding to the general scheme of creation, and the—er—fitness of things."

"But it amounts to this: You are in favour of killing pigs, and I am not," went on Hazell calmly, drawing a cigarette from his case; "and the question is: Are you a better Christian for killing your pigs, or am I, who have a certain amount of respect for the life of a hog, which you haven't?"

The Bishop frowned angrily.

"What you say is quite beside the mark," he answered; "I am not in the habit of taking the life of *any* animal."

"No; but you encourage butchery in others, which is degrading. But to go back to the subject we were discussing. Have you ever had any practical experience in the analysis of foodstuffs?"

"Of course not," said the Bishop; "I'm not a chemist."

"More's the pity, because, being a Bishop, it might be good for you to know something of the laws of health—capital subject for a charge to your clergy! Now, there are four excellent foods, each of them excelling the nutritive powers of animal flesh—oatmeal, macaroni, lentils, and Dutch cheese."

And he ticked them off one by one on his fingers.

"Really, sir!" exclaimed the Bishop, who was now in a very bad temper indeed, "I must ask you to excuse me from taking a further part in this conversation."

And, opening the book he had been reading, with a vicious gesture, he composed himself in the corner of the first-class compartment in which both were travelling. Thorpe Hazell smoked his cigarette quite calmly, a smile on his lips. He had not intended to say anything rude, but the Bishop's dogmatic manner had rather put his back up.

Presently he removed his coat, stood upright in the carriage, and commenced throwing his arms to and fro violently.

The Bishop of Frattenbury laid down his book and gazed at him in astonishment.

"A digestive exercise, my lord," explained Hazell, pausing for a moment. "It is now a quarter to seven, and I hope to dine at eight. You draw in a very deep breath—so!—then you move the arms ten times—so!—then you exhale the breath—slowly. It is also a safeguard against unnecessary flesh development. You should have practised it years ago!" And he lit a fresh cigarette.

There was a crash and a rattle and a heavy bumping. The Bishop was suddenly shot forward into Hazell's arms. The lamp went out, and total darkness followed. Then the carriage reeled like a drunken man, the panes of glass splintered, there was a dull shock, and Hazell, who had managed to get his hand outside the door and open it, fell out of the compartment on to the soft turf beside the line. He heard the Bishop follow him. A moment or two afterwards there was a heavy splash, and then a muffled cry somewhere below.

Thorpe Hazell blew the fragments of his cigarette out of his mouth, sat up, rubbed an injured elbow, and looked around him. There was an awful hissing of escaping steam from the engine. The driver was on the ground, a lamp in hand; another lamp was dancing about as the guard appeared on the scene.

"What's up?" cried Hazell, as he went towards the engine.

"She's off the line, sir," replied the man.

"Anyone hurt?" yelled the guard.

"I think not," replied the driver, "we weren't running fast. Jim!"

"Hullo!"

"All right?"

"Aye, mate, I jumped the other side," exclaimed the fireman.

"How about the passengers?" asked Hazell of the guard.

"There were only four in the train, sir," replied the guard— "two thirds—ah, here they are—yourself, and the Bishop."

"Ah, the Bishop, of course," said Hazell. "I think he got out just after me," he added, with a slight chuckle. "I hope he's not hurt."

At that moment a faint cry for help came from the foot of the embankment. Hazell and the guard hurried down, and there, by the light of the lamp, they beheld a sorry sight. At the bottom of the bank was a ditch, bordered by a barbed wire fence. The unfortunate prelate had fallen into the very muddiest part of the ditch, and in trying to emerge therefrom had caught his clothes on the barbed wire. He was a mass of mud from head to foot, his apron hung in ribbons, one of his coat tails was torn clean off, and one of his sleeves ripped up from elbow to wrist. Blood was trickling down his face from a slight cut on the cheek.

"Are you hurt, my lord?" asked Hazell.

"No," replied the Bishop grimly, "I don't think so—except a few bruises. But I'm exceedingly uncomfortable."

There was a look on the Bishop's muddy and bloodstained face as the lantern flashed upon him that suddenly appealed to Hazell.

He gave him his arm and helped him up the embankment. Then they found out what had happened to the little branch train in which they had been travelling. The crank axle of the tiny tank engine had broken, the leading wheels had left the rails, and one of the three carriages composing the train had jumped the metals with the shock. No one was hurt, and the Bishop's plight was really the worst of the lot.

The line upon which the catastrophe had taken place was the little branch one from Heston to Cathfield, a distance of some seven miles, and a single track. Only four or five trains are timed to run per day upon this little bit of line, and even then it scarcely pays the company to run them, so small is the traffic. This train, from Heston to Cathfield, was the last one of the day. It was a winter's evening, exceedingly dark, and a hurried consultation took place between guard and passengers as to what was the best thing to be done.

"We're about three miles from Heston," said the former, "and it's impossible, as you see, to go on. The nearest breakdown train is at Blayford, and it's not likely that it will be despatched till the morning. There's not a house anywhere near here, and the best thing we can do is to walk back along the line to Heston Junction. There's a very fair inn there where you gentlemen can get beds for the night."

Then the Bishop of Frattenbury—dirty, grimy, blood-bespattered—stood forth in his torn, fluttering garments, and spoke.

"I *won't* go back to Heston," he exclaimed. "I am due to speak at an important meeting at Redminster to-night, and I insist upon your making some arrangements for getting me there. I *must* be there!"

Hazell looked at him with admiration. The true British spirit had come out in his lordship—the spirit of pig-headedness that refuses to be daunted by obstacles because it has a grievance against someone.

"I'm very sorry," said the guard, "but I don't see how you're to get to Redminster to-night."

"I tell you I must be there," said the Bishop, the marks of episcopacy manifesting themselves despite the mud. "You ought to have guarded against this breakdown, but, since it has occurred, it is your plain duty to devise some plan by which passengers shall reach their destination. I am the principal speaker at this meeting to-night, and in my whole career I have never failed to keep an engagement. I intended catching the 7.30 from Cathfield to Redminster, arriving at the latter place at 7.50, in time for me to reach the hall at 8. It is your duty to assist me to do this."

It was splendid to hear him speak. Even the driver, who was standing by, felt that somehow he had committed a perfectly heinous offence, and, although he was a Baptist by choice, it began to dawn upon him that a Bishop's anathemas might perchance affect Nonconformists in certain cases.

"If it weren't for the broken axle," he said apologetically, "we might get her on the rails with the screw-jack and try running her on."

"Do so," commanded the Bishop, "and, if necessary, proceed without the axle."

"It is absolutely impossible to go on," broke in Thorpe Hazell, "but, if you are determined to speak at this meeting, I might perhaps make a suggestion."

"The officials ought to get me out of the difficulty," replied the Bishop loftily, "but what do you propose?"

"It is now close on seven," said Hazell, "and the distance to Cathfield is nearly four miles along the line. It is out of the question trying to catch the 7.30, but there is a later train which would get you into Redminster by 8.45, and if we started walking at once we might catch it. Perhaps you would allow me to accompany you, as I wish to go on to Redminster myself."

The Bishop thought for a moment.

"Ahem! I suppose it is the only course to take, and I am much obliged to you. But I shall write to the general manager," he went on, turning to the guard.

"Yes, my lord," said that individual meekly.

"We ought to lose no time," said Hazell, "but—er—if we catch that train—your lordship—well, is hardly in a suitable costume to speak at a meeting."

"Dear me!" exclaimed the Bishop, "I never thought of that. How exceedingly unfortunate. I have no change in my bag, either—only my—er—night—attire. But I could possibly borrow a coat from one of the clergy."

"Meanwhile," said Hazell, "if you will allow me, I have a spare jacket I could lend you—just for the walk—that is, if you can get into it."

"You're welcome to my coat," broke in the guard, with the idea of a peace-offering in his mind. "I've another in my van—and I'm about your size."

Finally, the Bishop of Frattenbury took off his coat and tattered apron, and accepted the guard's offer. But he stuck to his own hat, which he had left in the carriage. Then Thorpe Hazell borrowed a lantern from the guard and set off along the track with the Bishop, whilst the others prepared to walk back to Heston.

"I'm afraid you will find it rather a stiff walk," said Hazell. "Might I offer you some refreshments? I seldom travel without them."

"Thank you," replied the Bishop, "but I am a teetotaler."

"The refreshments to which I allude are chocolate and milk," rejoined Hazell.

The Bishop accepted a bit of chocolate, and they stumbled along the centre of the single track in silence for a while. It was rough work, but the Bishop well understood that the catching of the later train at Cathfield meant a quick progress, and that even then it was a mere chance. Yet the prelate was a man of grit, despite his pompous demeanour, and he was determined that the Redminster meeting should not lose his speech on the Education Question if he could help it.

They had gone about a quarter of a mile along the track, Hazell leading the way, and considerately directing the light of the lantern on to the ground so that his companion might best see where to tread, when the former suddenly uttered an exclamation of joy.

The flash of his lantern had fallen upon an object lying beside the line. He stopped short.

"What is it?" asked the Bishop.

"If you're agreeable, I think we might make our progress a bit easier," said Hazell.

"How?"

"Here's a trolley. If we can get it on the line, we could ride on it."

"But how about the motive power? I hardly see—"

"*We* shall have to be the power," broke in Hazell; "and we've not only a stiff wind behind us, but, if I am not very much mistaken, most of the line from here to Cathfield is on a down gradient. Kindly give me a hand!" The Bishop, in some surprise, did as he was asked.

Under Hazell's directions his lordship assisted him to put the two pairs of wheels on the rails and the heavy frame on to them. There was a shunter's "coupling staff" among the tackle, and Hazell placed this, together with the lamp, on the trolley.

"Evidently the platelayers have bagged it to push with," he said. "Well, we may find it handy? Now, then, can you kneel on one knee on that side? That's right. I'll take this. Press your other foot on the ground and give a shove—so! Off we go. Can you manage it?"

"It's work to which I'm scarcely accustomed," said the panting prelate grimly, "but I'll do my best."

"Good!" replied Hazell, in admiration. "We're picking up speed fast now. Steady—long strokes, please!"

The trolley began to run along rapidly. Presently the light of the lamp fell with a passing flash on a short post beside the line, with two arms, one level, and the other at a downward angle.

"A falling gradient!" cried Hazell. "Climb right on. That's it!"

He gave the Bishop a hand while the latter struggled on to the trolley, falling flat as he did so. He clutched his hat with one hand and the edge of the trolley with the other. Hazell knelt, holding the Bishop's coat just at the small of the back to steady him. The trolley felt the momentum every instant, and was soon running on the down grade quite furiously.

"I—hope—there's—no—danger!" jerked the Bishop as he bumped. "If—we—met a—train—I—"

"All right!" broke in Hazell cheerfully. "It's a single line, and our driver had the staff. No other train can run."

The exact meaning was dim to his companion, who gathered, nevertheless, that his fears in this direction were groundless.

"But—suppose the—line's—not—clear—or the—things they—call—points—are not—set—right!"

Hazell laughed.

"Don't worry. There are no points between Heston Junction and Cathfield—not even a station. It's quite safe."

"But—how—can we—stop?" went on the Bishop, as the trolley bounded forward.

"This gradient won't last long, and we can always stop by putting our feet on the rails and pressing—a human brake!"

"I—hope it—won't—end in—a—human breakage!" exclaimed the Bishop, with a grim and noble attempt at humour which went straight to Hazell's heart.

"Good old chap!" he muttered. Presently the speed began to slacken, and the Bishop slowly rose to his knees from his recumbent position. Simultaneously both men broke out into a hearty laugh.

"Enjoying the ride?" asked Hazell.

"I was thinking that some of the younger clergy might enjoy seeing me taking it," remarked the Bishop.

"A coincidence—so was I!"

"Shall we catch that other train?"

Hazell managed to look at his watch.

"Easily! We must push again a bit. I'll use the staff."

He stood upright to do so. The Bishop kicked out manfully once more. As Hazell had said, the wind was behind them, helping them tremendously. They struck another gradient—a long one this time. Hazell looked again at his watch.

"It's rather different from walking," he said. "We shall be in loads of time for the 8.45. That will get us to Redminster a little after nine."

"No chance of catching the 7.30, I suppose?" asked the Bishop.

"No. It's not very far off that time now—and we've the best part of two miles to go. Besides which, the last half mile or more is a steep up gradient, and we shall have to walk it."

They set to pushing again. The line was almost level now. Presently the Bishop exclaimed: "What's that light?"

Far away, on their right, a sudden flash of radiance had sprung up in the darkness of the black wintry night.

"Opening the coal-box to fire a locomotive," replied Hazell. "And what's more, I'm pretty sure it's the train you wanted to catch running along towards Cathfield. Hullo!" as he caught sight of another gradient post, "there's a steep drop here—one in fifty, if I recollect rightly. Jump on and hold tight! There'll be a curve presently."

The trolly had already begun to gather speed. Even Hazell, who was on the right of the Bishop, had to hold on. Once more the light of the main line train flashed upwards, like a searchlight, and this time Hazell gave vent to an excited "Hullo!"

In order to explain the thought that had suddenly struck him, it will be necessary to give a brief description of the railway at this particular spot. As has been said, the little single line from Heston Junction to Cathfield was about seven miles in length. From about two miles beyond the scene of the breakdown it bore round gradually to the left, until at length it met the main line at a point a little over a mile from Cathfield.

But this point was not a junction. That is to say, the single line, instead of crossing on to the main by facing points controlled by a signal-box in the angle, ran parallel on the left of the main track all the way to Cathfield, where it had its own little "bay" terminus.

This arrangement, involving a little more capital expenditure at first, had its advantages in that the necessity for a "junction-box" and the maintenance of its signalman was obviated, thus making it cheaper in the long run. Similar instances may occur to the reader, as, for example, the running of the Midhurst single line from Fishbourne to Chichester alongside the up main South Coast track; or the bit of the Abingdon branch that runs parallel with the main down Great Western for some little distance into Radley. The arrangement, also, has another advantage in leaving both main and branch lines absolutely clear at all times.

Now the trolley, rushing downwards at fairly high speed, was just approaching the point from which it would continue running close along the main up track. And on this main up track, further away from the point, the express, that would ultimately stop at Cathfield, came thundering along. They were, naturally, in front of her, and Hazell knew by her head-lights, which just appeared in view—a green light above a white—that she was the train in question.

"Hullo!" he shouted, as a sudden idea took possession of him.

"What's—the—matter?" cried the Bishop, who was on the jerk again.

Hazell's reply was unintelligible to his lordship.

"The tail-lights of the branch train are a red *and* a white, but the main-line trains carry a red light only!"

"What—on—earth—"

"Hold *on!*"

They came swinging round the curve with a clatter, and then the light of the lamp glanced on the shining up rail parallel with them and some five feet from the right edge of the trolley.

Hazell looked back. The head-lights of the express were out of sight now, there being a bit of a curve on the main line. Kneeling upright, as well as the shaking trolley would let him, Hazell took up the guard's lamp and turned the red shade on. Then he hooked its handle to the hook on the end of the coupling staff.

"Hold on to the edge with your left hand, my lord! Right! Now take my left hand with your other. Don't let go, for goodness' sake. Good! Here she comes. Just in time!"

Holding the coupling staff with his right hand, he reached it out, till the lantern was just over the middle of the parallel up track, the red light pointing back towards the approaching train.

"What—are—you—doing?"

"Trying to get you in time for your meeting!" replied Hazell. "Hold on. We're nearly on the level now."

As the driver of the express came round the slight curve, he saw the red tail-light, apparently of an up main line train, for it was on his track, moving on in front of him. Instantly he shut off steam and whistled furiously.

And then, as Hazell glanced back, he saw the sparks flying under the train, and he knew that the Westinghouse brake was doing its work.

"I can manage by myself now," he cried, for the trolley was slackening speed. "Stop her, my lord!"

Very gingerly the Bishop applied the brake—to wit, his episcopal boot—and slowly they came to a standstill. So did the train—not fifty yards behind.

The front guard jumped from his van and came running forward, expecting to see a train—or, at least, a detached truck in the way. When he caught sight of the trolley and the two men on the other rail, his indignation expressed itself in pretty strong language as he inquired what they meant by it. Hazell briefly explained the breakdown and how they had journeyed on.

"But, why the — did you stop my train, even if your story's true?"

"Because," said Hazell imperturbably, "my friend the Bishop here did not wish to lose his connection."

"Bishop be—" began the guard, as he turned his lantern on the prelate.

"Hush!" checked Hazell, "his lordship is unaccustomed to such language."

"A pretty Bishop!" sneered the guard, as he looked at the extraordinary figure. "But you'll have to pay for this!"

"Oh, no," replied Hazell sweetly. "We've both got first-class tickets. But we're wasting precious time. Clear this trolley off—we're coming with you."

"And I will see that you are properly recompensed," said the Bishop loftily, recovering something of his episcopal dignity.

They went on in the guard's van. At Cathfield Hazell explained matters to the stationmaster, who was getting anxious about the non-arrival of the branch train.

"You'll have to settle with the authorities for stopping the train," he said, as Hazell gave him his card.

"Oh, I think that will be easy enough—I've done one or two little amateur jobs for the G.M." replied the railway expert; "he knows me very well."

The run on to Redminster was in a first-class carriage.

"Let me thank you exceedingly for all your trouble," said the Bishop, who was still attired in the guard's coat. "How can I repay you for it?"

"Easily," replied Hazell. "May I refer to our former conversation—just after we left Heston?"

"Certainly."

"You appeared to be sceptical as to the food values of oatmeal, macaroni, Dutch cheese, and lentils. It would be such a pleasure to me, my lord, if you would lose that scepticism, after personal experience."

"I don't quite understand."

"If, in return for any small service I have rendered, you would try these foods exclusively, with the exception of milk as a beverage, for, say a fortnight, I'm sure you would be convinced."

His lordship pressed his lips and frowned, but the frown soon developed into a grim smile.

"Very well," he said, "I *will*."

"And you will let me know?"

"I will let you know."

"Thank you, my lord. Ah, here we are at Redminster. But you cannot speak in that costume?"

"I shall drive straight to the Deanery first, and borrow some clothes from the Dean. I am staying the night there."

At a quarter past eight the Bishop of Frattenbury, rigidly clad—a little *too* rigidly, perhaps, for the Dean was the sparer man of the two—was addressing a crowded meeting at the Redminster Town Hall as only his lordship, who was famed for platform eloquence, could.

And here followed the postscript, after the lapse of a couple of weeks.

The Palace,
Frattenbury.

My Dear Sir,

I have faithfully kept my promise to you, and
strictly adhered to the abominable diet you pre-
scribed for a fortnight—which ends to-night. I am
much looking forward to resuming my ham for
breakfast tomorrow, and rejoice that Providence
provided the necessary animal for its production. I
am still more than grateful to you for your kind and
shrewd services on the eventful evening when I first
made your acquaintance, and should you ever be in
Frattenbury, hope that you will remember that the
Apostle has enjoined bishops to be "given to hospi-
tality." You shall, on that occasion, have your four
abominable (the word suits admirably) foods *ad lib.*,
but you will find me carnivorous.

Believe me,
Yours very truly,
G. Frattenbury.

The Adventure of the Pilot Engine

When a special train is to be run on our railways, papers of directions are printed and issued to station-masters and others. These contain minute details concerning the timing of the run, and the keeping of the line clear, how this train is to be shunted into a refuge siding at one station, and that train has to be kept clear at another point.

In the case of any important or Royal personage travelling, these instructions are marked "private," and are jealously guarded.

Some three years ago, at a juncture when European politics were considered by diplomatists to be in a very delicate state, an announcement might have been seen in several Continental papers to this effect: "Count von Neglein, being slightly indisposed owing to his arduous duties, has retired for a few days, under the direction of his physician, to his country house at B—. He hopes to be able to resume work in a week's time."

At the same time, a messenger from Downing Street called upon the general manager of the London and East Midland Railway and gave him an order with strict injunctions that the matter was to be kept private.

A special train was required the following Tuesday to run from London to Singlehurst. Every precaution was to be taken for the safety of this train, as a most important person was going to travel by it. The general manager immediately summoned the superintendent of the line, and before the morning was out a proof of the "special working instructions" had been laid on his desk, damp from the company's printers.

That same morning three men were closeted together in a house in the West End of London. Two of them were of a distinctly foreign appearance, the third might have belonged to any nationality. He was a man of medium height, clean-shaven, with close-cut hair, ordinary features, and mild-looking grey eyes. The only thing of any note about his face was a certain set and resolute compression of his lips.

The language in which the trio were speaking was French, and the subject under discussion was that of Count von Neglein's little indisposition.

"The news is of the gravest character," said the elder of the two foreign-looking men. "There can be no doubt about it that if Count von Neglein has an interview with the English Prime Minister in the presence of the King during the ensuing week our plans will be frustrated completely."

"You are sure that your information is correct?" asked the other man.

"Positively. Besides, Dubourg here can corroborate it," and he turned to the third man.

"Quite correct," said Dubourg. "The Continental journey will be made to Ostend, and thence to London by private boat. These little steam yachts are handy."

"There is no possibility of, er—persuading the Count to relinquish his journey on the Continent or by sea?" said the first speaker, with a curious interrogatory lift of his eyebrows.

"None," replied Dubourg. "The arrangements are excellent—for them."

"Well, you ought to know something about that," said the second man.

Dubourg bowed slightly.

"It is my business," he said.

"The King," went on the first speaker, who was evidently the one in authority— "the King is staying with the Duke of Worcester, and will be there all next week. Singlehurst, I believe, is the nearest station. The Prime Minister and the French Ambassador are invited there to dine on Monday. That means staying the night."

"And that yacht will arrive early on Tuesday morning," put in Dubourg.

"Exactly. Well—er—my instructions are to prevent an interview between von Neglein and the Prime Minister at all costs. Now, Dubourg, what have you to say?"

Dubourg thought for a minute, his lips tightly compressed.

"We must find out," he said presently, "how he is going to travel from London to Singlehurst. If it is an ordinary train, as you know, I have done something in this line before. But if it is a special—well!"

"Well?"

"It may be a question of stopping at nothing."

"Then stop at nothing," said the chief coldly. If he is removed altogether, so much the better for our interests."

"I will make inquiries and see you this evening," said Dubourg rising.

"Do so. Good-morning. A most excellent person this Dubourg," he went on to his companion, "he has been an engineer and an actor, and he knows ten European languages fluently. If the thing's to be done at all, he's the man to do it—especially if it is a question of railways. That's his chief line."

The same evening Dubourg called again at the West End house. A dinner party was in progress, and the elder of the two foreigners sat at the head of the table, an order across his breast, and was addressed with much deference by his guests. As soon as the servant handed him Dubourg's card, he begged to be excused for a few moments, and left the table.

"Well?" he said to Dubourg, when they were seated in his private room.

Dubourg laid a printed paper on the table.

"It was difficult to get," he said, "but fortunately the printers were open to a fee."

The paper, which was marked "Strictly Private," was headed:

"Instructions for working special train from London to Singlehurst."

Then followed a long list of details. The train itself was to leave the London terminus at 8.30 a.m., preceded by a pilot engine at 8.20.

"They are taking extra precautions with that pilot engine," remarked Dubourg, with a light laugh.

The other looked at him narrowly.

"Why do you smile?"

"Because I think it would have been as well for Count von Neglein's restoration to health if they had not determined to run a pilot."

"It is going to be a serious affair?"

"Very serious. And dangerous—that is, if my plan is successful."

"And your plan?"

"No," replied Dubourg, "I won't give you the details, lest I should fail. But the key to it lies here."

And he put his finger on a paragraph of the "Instructions."

The other read:

"Inspector Inglis will travel on the engine of the express, which will be worked by Driver Forbes and Fireman Scott. The pilot engine will be worked by Driver Fraser and Fireman Norris."

"Four of the best enginemen on the line," remarked Dubourg. "I happened to see Driver Fraser and Fireman Norris bring a train in to-day—excellent men!"

"I don't see your point, but I know I can trust you. Koravitch, who was with us this morning, will give you any funds or assistance."

"I shall want the latter. To-morrow I am going to make certain inquiries about Fireman Norris. I've taken quite a fancy to the look of him. On Monday I shall take a journey down the line, merely to refresh my memory of a few details. I shall be back that evening. If my little plan succeeds, I don't think there will be any interview. Good-night!"

Late on Monday evening, Dubourg sat in his lodgings poring over a rough map of a section of the London and East Midland line that he had made as the result of his trip that day, and referring closely to the "Special Working Instructions" that lay beside it on the table.

The first fifty miles of the London and East Midland consist of a quadruple track, the two main lines on the left for up and down fast trains, and the others "relief lines" for slow trains. There are places where a train can cross from the main line to the relief, or *vice versa*, the points being, of course, controlled by signal-boxes; and there are also places where, for shunting purposes, trains can cross from the down line to the up, or *vice versa*, but in this case they must first stop and then reverse.

Thirty-five miles down the line is Rushwood Station. Two and a-half miles further is Alton Siding Box, which commands crossing points on the relief line only, the main line metals being clear. Five miles on is Holt Box, where points are so arranged that trains may cross in all the ways I have mentioned. Half-a-mile further is the long Roxton Tunnel, with a signal-box at the entrance.

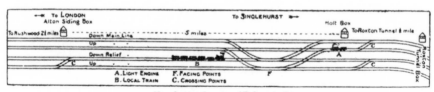

Map showing the scene of Dubourg's plot.

When a train has passed the Roxton Box the man on duty signals "line clear" to Holt, and the signalman at Holt is free to admit a train on his section from Alton Siding Box.

In the case of very special trains, such as those carrying Royalty, and when a pilot engine is used, all traffic on the adjacent line must come to a standstill between the passage of the "pilot" and the "special" following it; while, with regard to trains running in the same direction on relief lines, a stop must be made for extra precaution wherever there is a crossing-over place, when the "special" is timed to run by on the main line just at that moment.

The two special notices which Dubourg was studying so intensely were these

"Directions to the signalman on duty at Holt Box. Light engine No. 321, running on the up line to Rushwood, must stop opposite box, and the 9.5 local down passenger train from Rushwood must be stopped outside facing points on relief line during passing of pilot and special." A "light engine," by the way, is an engine running by itself.

The man called Koravitch came in presently and glanced at the map.

"Well, Dubourg," he said, "is everything ready?"

"So far as it can be," replied the other. "There are several weak spots in the plan, but I must trust to luck. And here is the weakest, I think."

He laid his finger on the rough map at the point marking the Roxton Tunnel Box.

"As for myself," he went on, "it is a risky thing. After our little business of to-morrow morning you must start off with the motor. I want you to be waiting a little after nine on the main road just outside the village of Roxton, on the London side. Are all the other things ready?"

"Yes."

"The carriage?"

"Yes. Our men are warned."

"Good! Then we'll have some rest. Six o'clock to-morrow, mind. It'll be quite dark then."

About half-a-mile from the terminus of the London and East Midland Railway are a couple of streets of small houses belonging to the company, and entirely occupied by railwaymen. You may see them going in and out of their houses at all hours of the day or night. Drivers and firemen starting to "work" trains to the Midlands, goods brakesmen returning after a weary run up, smart guards, dingy engine-cleaners, the rank and file of the great railway army.

It was pitch dark on the morning of the eventful Tuesday, when a closed carriage drove up to one of these little houses, and a man, with his cap drawn down over his face, sprang out and rapped violently at the door. The people were well accustomed to these sudden calls, especially in foggy weather. A minute later and a window opened, and a head appeared at it.

"Who's there?"

"Mr. Walters," growled the man below. "I want Norris at once."

"I'm Norris, sir."

"Sharp, then. You're firing the pilot for the special?"

"Yes, sir; but she don't start till 8.20."

"There's an alteration. Quick! Put on your clothes and hurry up!"

The window was shut down, and in a very few minutes Norris came out of the house, clad in his working clothes and ready for the "run," his little bag with provisions and the familiar blue tea-can in his hand.

"There's not a moment to lose," said the supposed Mr. "Walters," holding the door of the cab open. "Jump in—Fraser has gone on."

Norris got into the cab, and Dubourg, for it was he, followed. The driver whipped up his horse, and before the unfortunate fire-man had realised what was happening, he found himself in the grasp of two powerful men, who snicked a pair of handcuffs on his wrists, and then proceeded to gag him.

"Now, if you keep still," said Dubourg, "we won't hurt you; but, if you make any resistance or refuse to do what we tell you, I can't answer for the consequences."

They drove along at a furious pace, and presently drew up at a house in Camden Town, the door of which opened immediately. Dubourg and Koravitch took the fireman by the arms and hurried him into the house, the door was closed by a third man, and the cab drove off.

The room into which they carried Norris was brilliantly lighted, and a looking-glass stood on the table. Dubourg lost no time.

"We're going to trouble you for your clothes, my friend," he said quietly, "and then you shall enjoy a rest."

In ten minutes the fireman had his outer clothes stripped from him and Dubourg had put them on. Then he opened a small tin case, took out a wig, some false hair, spirit gum, and other make-up materials, and set to work on his own face, carefully studying first Norris and then the reflection in the looking-glass. In a very short time he was transformed into the exact likeness of the fireman. By this time Koravitch had gone, but not before he had assisted the other man in binding Norris securely.

"Now," said Dubourg to Norris, as he put a small life-preserver in his own pocket and carefully examined a revolver, "you'll suffer no inconvenience beyond remaining here for a few hours. A letter will be posted to your wife stating where you are, and she'll receive it this afternoon. I'm sorry to leave you gagged, but there are neighbours who might hear you."

With that he walked out of the house with his fellow-conspirators.

Dubourg went his way to the engine-sheds of the London and East Midland Railway to all appearances an ordinary fireman, returning nods of greeting which were given him by men he met.

He had served in the secret service of a powerful European nation for ten years now, and his chief work had been in connection with railways, steamers, and other methods of travelling. Railways and their working were his speciality, and to a man who had driven locomotives scores of Limes, the details of a fireman's work were nothing. He knew exactly what was required, and gave in his name at the check office with as much unconcern as if he had been Norris himself, glancing at the notice board with quite a practised eye.

Fraser had arrived before him, and, lamp and oil-can in hand, was in the pit beneath the great engine, carefully inspecting every portion of the works. He gave a nod to his mate presently, as he joined him on the foot-plate; it was dark inside the engine-shed, and he did not notice anything strange.

Afterwards Dubourg took care to keep his face turned away from him as far as possible, besides which, it was a gloomy winter's morning, and men on the footplate have too much to do to look narrowly into each other's faces. Their eyes are fixed on other things, and driver and firemen on duty are not talkers. A dozen words in a hundred miles' run is often as much as they exchange.

Presently they "whistled up" to be run off the shed road, backed down to the "special," and stood at the end of the platform ready to start. Dubourg forgot nothing. He saw that the tail-light was properly fixed on the back of the tender—there were tunnels on the route—he placed the special head discs, denoting the character of the engine, in front of the smoke-box, and when a loco. inspector strolled up to the engine, he gave a twist to the hand-brake in the most approved manner.

Punctually to the minute they moved out. Dubourg stood slightly behind the driver, carefully noting the pressure-gauge, the needle of which soon began to move up as the blast operated. Directly the steam began to "blow off" at the valve he was ready for coaling. In a few seconds, as the needle began to go up once more, he commenced to put the feed on by setting the injector to work, screwing down the water-regulating wheel with such easy method and adjustment, that the driver's suspicions were never once aroused.

So the "pilot" ran on.

A dozen words had not been exchanged between the two men, so perfect was the working of both. Exactly at scheduled time they passed Rushwood, and the pseudo-fireman began to keep a sharp look out on his own account. At Holt Box he noted, with much satisfaction, that the local train stood on the "down relief," and the light engine on the "up main," according to instructions.

The half mile on to Roxton commenced with a sharp curve after leaving Holt, and through a deep cutting. One more coaling operation, and Dubourg had his hand in his pocket, grasping the life- preserver.

The instant the train had entered the tunnel he acted. With his left hand he dashed off Fraser's cap, standing behind him, and at the same moment, struck him on the top of the head with his weapon. The driver, stunned with the blow, fell on the footplate like a log. Dubourg sprang to the regulator, shut off steam, and then put on the brake, the engine coming to a standstill in the tunnel.

Now came the ticklish part of his dastardly plan, and well he knew it. The signalman he had just passed at the mouth of the tunnel was like a sentry, to be overcome by foul means, before he could attain his object. But Dubourg was a man absolutely devoid of either fear or feeling.

Reversing his engine, he slowly backed out of the tunnel, stopping before the box, to the intense surprise of its occupant. The latter came rushing out on to the platform outside his door, first glancing to see that his signals were set against the "special."

"What's up?" he cried.

"This!" shouted. Dubourg.

There was a sharp crack as his hand flew up with something glittering in it. The signalman staggered to his door, but fell on the threshold. Dubourg, calm as ever, lifted the insensible form of the driver and dropped him beside the track. Then he threw open the regulator and jumped off himself.

The engine began to move backwards.

Very coolly Dubourg mounted the steps of the signal box. He stooped to look at the man.

"H'm! Don't think I've killed him," he muttered.

Then he went into the box, deliberately selected an instrument, and gave the signal "Line clear" back to Holt Box.

And all the time that pilot engine was running back on the very metals over which the special was approaching. The signal that would have been given by the man on duty would have warned his colleague at Holt in time for him to clear off the light engine which stood there to the "up relief," and cross the runaway engine over to the "up main." The next moment Dubourg was running across country to catch his motor and escape.

The signalman at Holt Box stood in front of his instruments, expecting every moment the sharp ring on his bell warning him from Alton Siding that the special was passing that point and entering upon the section between them. He never dreamt of any danger, having received the signal from Roxton Box that the line ahead was perfectly clear beyond that point.

Suddenly he heard a roar and a rattle round the curve and, as he glanced in that direction, his horrified gaze met the runaway pilot engine. Never was signalman placed in such an awful dilemma. The immediate danger crowded all else from his mind as he grasped a lever.

There flashed before him this:

If he set the crossing-points the pilot would crash into the light engine on the "up main." If he set the other points it would come into collision with the passenger train standing on the "down relief." There were but a few seconds in which to choose either course, and in his hesitation he lost them. The engine ran by both sets of points. At that moment there came the signal from Alton Siding Box:

"Train entering section."

Dubourg had made his calculations with diabolical cunning. For even if the special had not passed Alton Box, and it had been possible to stop her there, unless she could have pulled up and backed into Rushwood in time, which was hardly likely, the smash would still have taken place, there being no crossing points at Alton over which the runaway engine could be switched.

The case stood thus: The special, with Count von Neglein aboard her, and the pilot engine were rushing towards each other on a five-mile stretch of line with absolutely no possibility of changing metals, the former travelling at fifty and the latter at forty miles an hour. Surely it seemed that Dubourg's diabolical plot could never be frustrated by human means.

But it was, through a page-boy in the first instance, and through Thorpe Hazell in the actual working.

It came about in this way. Hazell had had in his employment a sharp boy named Sam Thorne. Making a change, however, in his domestic establishment which led to the employment of an older servant instead, this page-boy had left him and had taken a situation in a large boarding-house in Bloomsbury, the very house, as it happened, where Dubourg had his apartments.

On the Monday night when Dubourg was discussing affairs with Koravitch, Sam Thorne came into the room with some hot water and glasses. He overheard Dubourg make a remark in which he caught the words "Halt Signal Box," and his quick eye caught sight of the map of the railway which was lying on the table and the words "Special Working Instructions" on the paper beside it. Neither of the men dreamt that the boy had noticed anything.

Now while he had been in service with Hazell, Sam Thorne had gained a great admiration for his master as a railway expert, especially as, on one occasion, he had been made use of in finding out some little detail. He knew well how much Hazell loved getting hold of any mystery of the line.

The idea that something was up struck him forcibly, the fact that Dubourg had asked to be called at five o'clock exciting his suspicions. He was a boy of strong imagination and of action, so he determined to put Hazell on the track. For this purpose he begged paper and envelope of the cook, and scrawled the following effusion:

> Dear Sir,
> Two furrin men staying here are up to something to-morrow—I think about railways. Is there a place called Holt Signal Box on the London and East Midland? And they were looking at speshul working instruckshuns. I saw them, and I thought Ide let you no. Yours truely,
> Sam Thorne.

It was nearly ten o'clock. Sam asked leave to post his letter, and as soon as he was outside the house he started off for Hazell's flat, taking a 'bus on the way. Here he found that Hazell was out of town, but had left his address with the porter. He was staying in the country at Holmfield.

"Better post it if it's particular. He'll get it to-morrow morning," said the man.

"It's very particular," replied the boy. "Give us a stamp, gov'nor."

He posted the letter, and received an awful wigging when he got back at half-past eleven. But he felt, somehow, that he had done his duty—even if the letter arrived too late.

As a matter of fact, Hazell got it at breakfast the next morning. He read it with a smile at first. Then he suddenly remembered that an official had told him the previous Saturday that a very important special was to be run that morning on the L. and E.M. He did not know, of course, who was to travel in it, but the mention of "two furrin men" aroused his suspicions.

Holmfield was a village in the heart of the country, devoid of railway or telegraph. But there was one point about the place—it was within fifteen miles of Roxton, and not much further, therefore, from Holt Box.

"Weston," exclaimed Hazell to his host, pulling out his watch at the same time, "you will have to excuse me, but this letter has disturbed me greatly. Will you lend me your bicycle and a local map? I want to be off in ten minutes."

The other, rather surprised, acquiesced, and in ten minutes Hazell was pedalling for all he was worth on the Roxton Road, keen on discovery, but little dreaming what was before him.

After riding some fifteen miles he deviated from the main road by a turning that his map showed him would lead him along the line close by Holt Box. He reached the top of a little hill commanding a view of the railway, and as he did so he saw the pilot engine run through. He could also discern the stationary train and light engine, and these facts told him at once that the engine running through must be the pilot of a special. He wondered, as he rode on, whether anything really was likely to happen, or whether he had only had a false alarm. Presently he arrived opposite Holt Box—which was on the further side of the line—got off his bicycle, and climbed the railing. He was now exactly opposite the light engine.

At that moment he saw what the terrified signalman had grasped—the reversed pilot engine running back. He even heard the two strokes of the bell that announced to his practised ear the entering of the special on the same section, and he knew in an instant the awful danger. An idea swept upon him like an inspiration. Dashing over the metals he made for the light engine, climbed the foot-plate, and cried to the astonished driver:

"Open the regulator—quick—brakes off, fireman. We can save her!"

He had seized the regulator himself as he spoke, and the engine had already begun to move, the fireman mechanically taking off the brake, the driver standing dumb-stricken.

"*Overtake her!*" yelled Hazell, pointing towards the retreating pilot.

Then the driver grasped his meaning.

"It's an awful risk," he cried, as he took the regulator, "steady, mate"—to the fireman— "don't coal her, man, yet—for Heaven's sake. We shall want all our steam."

"How long have we got?" asked Hazell.

"Two minutes at the outside," replied the man; "will you do it, sir—or shall I?"

"I will."

"It's dangerous—fearful."

"I know. Go on!"

The driver carefully "notched up" with his reversing wheel, and got her out of "full throw" as the speed increased. The pilot had a fair start, and nearly six hundred yards separated them now. He and Hazell looked grimly ahead. The distance between the engines gradually grew less. The driver glanced at his watch.

"Half a minute gone!"

Then he muttered:

"She's not running more than forty; she's in full gear, thank God!"

Which means that the pilot's cylinders were fully open to steam, and that, at the speed at which she was running, the strokes of the piston were somewhat retarded.

Another thirty seconds passed in anxious silence. At length there were only fifty yards between the engines.

"Look out, sir!" cried the driver.

"What are you going to do, sir?" asked the fireman, speaking for the first time.

"Jump!" said Hazell.

"You *can't*, sir!"

"I'll try, anyway," replied Hazell, going to the side. Twenty seconds more and the two engines were running side by side.

"Keep her so, driver! Steady!"

At length the footplates were opposite, some three feet of space separating them. Hazell grasped the handrails and calculated the distance. Then he gave a forward spring, and landed fair on the pilot's step, clutching at her handrail.

"Thank God!" he cried as he flew at the regulator, closed it, and turned on the brake. Then he glanced over his shoulder.

Not a quarter of a mile behind the special suddenly came round a slight curve. There was a furious whistling, then the white steam was shut off, and a minute later the train had stopped, barely a hundred yards from the engine that had so nearly destroyed her.

The affair was hushed up. The loco. inspector and Driver Hicks, of the light engine, went forward with the pilot, while the light engine was run on to Rushwood by her fireman. Hazell accompanied him, and took train to Roxton to recover his bicycle—walking out to Holt Box afterwards.

Von Neglein only knew that "a block had occurred on the line," and his views of English railways were rather lowered in consequence.

The signalman at Roxton and the driver of the pilot both recovered, an important treaty was duly signed, and a "diplomatic triumph" ensued.

Dubourg was never discovered, in fact, the police received an intimation that it was useless to pursue their "clues," and the railway officials in high places were also advised to hold their tongues. So they did. As to Hazell, he was warmly thanked by the superintendent of the line, and Driver Hicks was substantially rewarded for the part he had played in what might have been an awful tragedy.

THE STOLEN NECKLACE

Thorpe Hazell was dining at his club. They were accustomed to his eccentricities there, and hardly a member had looked up from his newspaper when he had divested himself of his coat, and gravely gone through his "digestive exercises" in a convenient corner before proceeding to the dining-room. Here preparation had been made, for he had told the head-waiter he was coming. A table was reserved, and on it stood a carafe of milk, a little loaf of brown bread, and a dish of his favourite biscuits. A bowl—he never would use a soup-plate—of lentil soup was soon put before him, and he commenced his meal.

"Hullo, Hazell," said a voice presently, as the speaker clapped him on the shoulders, "don't you overfeed yourself, old chap!"

"Oh, it's you, is it, Masters?" exclaimed Hazell, as he looked up. "I thought you were out of town."

"So I was till half-an-hour ago. I've just come up by the West-Northern, and I'm frantically hungry. Thought I'd come round for a meal at once before going to my chambers."

Hazell motioned him to take a seat at his table. The waiter came up and presented the menu. Hazell listened while his friend ordered dinner. Then he said:

"Oxtail soup is very heating. Whiting is a fish that ought to be cooked within two hours of catching. Curry is deadly for the liver. How you can digest Welsh rarebit is more than I can imagine, and alcohol in any form has been proved by the leading doctors to be a poison."

Frank Masters laughed heartily.

"Your life must be a misery to you, Hazell!"

"Not at all. I never suffer from indigestion."

"Neither do I."

"Not now, perhaps, but your old age will be a misery to you."

"How do you know yours won't, too? You haven't put *that* to the test with your system yet!"

Hazell shook his head sadly as the other fell to on his soup. There were few converts to be made at the club.

"Did you have a good run up to town?" asked Hazell presently.

"Capital."

"Where did you come from?"

"Redminster."

"Ah, you took the express arriving in town at 7.28?"

"Yes, Mr. Bradshaw!"

"Mr. Bradshaw" was Thorpe Hazell's nickname at the club, and he rather rejoiced in it than otherwise. No man ever, attempted the fag of looking at a railway guide when Hazell was near at hand.

"Was it in to time?"

"To the minute."

"Generally is. Did you notice whether a compound drew it?"

"What?"

"A compound locomotive."

"My dear fellow, I haven't the slightest idea what you mean. As long as I get to my journey's end I don't worry about the engine. Jolly good train, that express. No stop at all except at Wisden Junction, and I can't see the necessity for that."

"They take tickets there," replied Hazell.

"I know. But why the johnny can't collect 'em on the train instead of only just looking at 'em is one of those railway mysteries that you know more about than I do."

"They could collect them on the train, of course," replied Hazell, "or even at Redminster. But there's another reason why the train stops at Wisden—in case there are any passengers for South London."

"Then why do they disturb you on the train, and make you hunt in all your pockets just to see your ticket?"

"They don't," said Hazell, in blunt contradiction, as he helped himself liberally to boiled rice—for his second course had just arrived.

"But I tell you they do," replied his friend.

"Oh, well," said Hazell, "it must be something new. I travelled by that train a fortnight ago, and they didn't do it then. Oh—what an ass I am! Of course, I know what it was. A ticket inspector must have been on the train. The railway companies are not so foolish as you think, Masters, and they often catch fellows in that way."

The conversation took a general turn, and, after a bit, Hazell finished his meal and said good-night to his friend, with another gentle remonstrance against the savoury he was enjoying.

The next morning he had scarcely finished breakfast at his flat when there came a ring, and he heard his servant show someone into his study. The next moment he was looking at a visiting card.

"Miss St. John Mallaby."

When he went into the study he found himself confronted by a remarkably pretty young lady, whose face, however, was wearing a very anxious expression.

"I hope you don't mind my coming here, Mr. Hazell," she began, "but I think you've met my brother."

"Do sit down," he answered, "yes, of course I have."

"He told me about you, and what a clever railway detective you are, and I've come to you. I thought you might advise me."

Hazell smiled.

"I'm afraid I have a reputation that I don't deserve," he said. "I'm scarcely a railway detective, as you put it."

"Oh, but you *will* help me—please!" said the girl earnestly.

"Of course, I'll do anything I can for you, Miss Mallaby. But tell me what it's about?"

"I don't want anyone to know—I mean I want you to promise you won't tell anyone. I'm in great trouble. I've done something awfully wrong, and it's like a judgment on me."

"My dear young lady," replied Hazell gravely, "before you make a confidant of me are you sure that it is wise to do so?"

"Oh, yes—yes—yes. Because you may be able to help me. Please let me tell you."

"Very well, then," said Hazell encouragingly.

"Well, I've lost a diamond necklace!" she blurted out.

Hazell nodded and waited.

"I ought not to have worn it all," she went on, "and that's the terrible part of it. It belongs to my aunt. I'm staying at her house in town. You see it's going to be mine one day—she has promised to give it to me when I come of age, and that's why I borrowed it."

"Suppose," said Hazell kindly, "you begin at the beginning and try to tell me exactly what has happened?"

"Yes, I will, as well as I can. My mother and I came up last week to stay with aunt for the season. It was then that she showed me the necklace. I'd often heard about it, for it's been in the family a long time. Well, last Monday aunt had to go away unexpectedly, owing to her brother being taken ill. She left her keys in charge of mother. On Tuesday I was to go down to Appledon to Sir Roland Hartingford's. His daughter, who is a great friend of mine, came of age that day, and there was a ball at the house. Just before I started, the idea suddenly struck me that I would dearly love to wear the necklace at the dance. I know it was awfully wrong of me, but the temptation was a strong one, and I found myself saying that if aunt had been at home she would have lent me the diamonds. And then I yielded and took them."

"How did you get them?"

"It was very simple. I had to borrow my mother's keys for something, and she gave me her chatelaine. In it were the other keys. Almost before I realised what I had done, I had gone into my aunt's room and unlocked the safe which is fixed there. The necklace was in a small leather case. I took it out, locked up the safe again, and gave my mother back the keys."

"Did you tell her what you had done?"

"No. She does not know even yet."

"Where did you put the necklace?"

"In my dressing-case, which contains my own jewellery and which never leaves me when I travel. Well, I went down to Appledon with my maid and wore the diamonds at the ball. It was on the return journey—yesterday—that I lost them."

"In the train?"

"Yes. That's why I came to you, Mr. Hazell. At least, I think it *must* have been in the train—and yet—I hardly know what to say. It is all so terrible."

"Well, you must try to tell me."

The girl thought for a moment.

"Appledon is on a branch line," she said, "and you join the main line at Redminster."

"Quite so," said Hazell indulgently.

"It must have happened in the main line train, because after we had got in I wanted something from my case and unlocked it. The necklace was there then; I'm positive of that."

"What train was it?"

"The 5.40 express from Redminster. I was travelling with my maid in a first-class compartment. It was a corridor train."

"Was anyone else in the carriage with you?"

The girl hesitated and blushed slightly. Then she said:

"One of the guests at Appledon—Mr. Kestron was coming up to town by the same train, and he travelled with me."

"The Honourable George Kestron?"

"Yes."

"I know him slightly," replied Hazell, remembering that a rumour was abroad to the effect that this same Kestron was rather hard up—had borrowed money, so it was said.

Miss Mallaby noticed a certain tone in Hazell's voice as he replied.

"No—*no!*" she exclaimed, "I can't suspect him."

"Had you, then?" asked Hazell.

"The thought *would* come into my head. It was partly for that reason that I did not go to the police. Oh, Mr. Hazell, I don't know what to think."

"Well, go on with your story, please. Perhaps you will tell me how you were seated in the carriage?"

She explained that she was at first seated in the corner next to the corridor with her back to the engine, and Kestron was opposite. Her maid was on her left by the window, with the dressing-case, covered over by a rug, between them. After a while, Kestron had suggested changing places, as she had said something about travelling with her back to the engine. She was careful to move the dressing-case over to her side. Afterwards Kestron had changed his place again and had sat next to her until Wisden Junction was reached—the dressing-case being between them.

"Have you known Mr. Kestron long?" asked Hazell.

"I had only met him a few times before the ball. We danced a good deal together that night, but I had not known him very long—that was why I asked my maid to stay in the compartment."

"How came he to travel with you?"

"He had asked me the night before what train I was going by."

"I see. Well, when did you miss the necklace?"

She told him it was after the train had left Wisden Junction. She put her hand into the outside pocket of the case, where she kept her purse, and discovered, to her horror, that a long slit had been cut through the inner side. She unlocked the case, and the necklace was missing. Kestron had got out at Wisden, having to take a train from there on business before he went home that night.

"Do you know his address?" asked Hazell.

"Lancaster Crescent—number eight, I think."

Having discovered the loss of the jewels, she was terribly upset, and even asked her maid if she had taken them. The latter was indignant, and wanted to be searched on the spot. They looked everywhere in the compartment. It was still broad daylight, and she was certain that neither of them had left the compartment between Redminster and Wisden.

"Did anyone else come in?"

"No—even the ticket-collector only opened the door, and stood half outside when he asked to see our tickets."

Hazell suddenly remembered that the friend with whom he had been dining on the previous evening had travelled by the same train. He thought for a minute, and then asked her to tell him how the three were seated when the ticket-collector came, and who gave him the tickets.

"Mr. Kestron was next to me—it was after he had changed places the second time. I handed his ticket to the man, who glanced at it and returned it. My maid had both our tickets—she always sees to that—and she showed them to him."

"But as she was near the window, how did she do it?"

"Why," exclaimed the girl rather petulantly, "she naturally moved across to him."

"I see," said Hazell thoughtfully. "The corridor, of course, was on the *left* as you faced the engine. Can you remember whether the ticket-collector came from the front or back of the train, and whereabouts your carriage was in the train?"

"About the middle. The collector came from the front, but he had passed along the corridor just before."

"Only *just* before?"

"Yes."

"Ah! Well, I think you've told me all I want to know. It's a troublesome case. By the way, what happened when you arrived at the terminus?"

"My aunt's brougham was there to meet me, and the footman got my luggage from the van. My maid and I went straight to the brougham. I was foolish, perhaps, but I didn't tell anyone what had happened. I dreaded the police knowing. I felt like a thief myself. And—and—"

"You suspected Mr. Kestron, I suppose?"

Her eyes fell before his gaze, and she nodded slowly.

"I don't wonder," said Hazell.

"But—but—do you think he took it, Mr. Hazell? I don't know what to do about it—and my aunt comes home this evening. I shall have to tell her. If—if—he took it, are you going to try to find out?"

"I shall have to keep you in suspense for a little while, Miss Mallaby," said Thorpe Hazell. "I want you to go straight home and say nothing about this visit. Please give me your address, and I will call as soon as possible—to-day, I expect. I can't promise anything, but there is just a chance of getting on the track."

She thanked him. He put on his hat and saw her to the door, where her taxi was waiting. Then he hailed another and directed the driver to take him quickly to the terminus of the West-Northern Railway.

"Wait," he said as he got out. "I shall want you again directly."

He made his way to the office of the traffic-manager, whom he knew.

"I want some information," he said. "Will you tell me if there was a ticket-collector or inspector on the 5.40 p.m. express from Redminster last evening?"

"Another mystery?" asked the official.

"Yes—but the chances are against a solution, I'm afraid."

The manager rang for a clerk and gave some orders. In ten minutes' time the report was brought in. *No ticket inspector or collector had been on the train.*

"That settles it," cried Hazell. "I'd advise you to look after your old uniforms, Mr. Street. Good- morning."

His next move was to drive to Frank Masters, whom he found busy with a pile of briefs in front of him.

"Sorry to disturb you," said Hazell, "but the matter is of importance. It's about your railway journey last night. That ticket-collecting incident is the clue to a mystery. Can you remember what the fellow was like?"

"Yes. A man with a black beard and moustache, and rather a gruff voice."

"After he'd looked at your ticket did he go back along the corridor?"

"No. He passed first, and asked for tickets Coming back."

"From the front of the train—yes, I know. Now, whereabouts in the carriage were you—which compartment were you in, I mean?"

"The last but two—a first-class."

"Last but two from the engine?"

"Yes."

"H'm. I wish I knew about those two compartments behind you."

"I can tell you."

"Good!" ejaculated Hazell. "How?"

"There was a fellow in my compartment who lit an Egyptian cigarette. I can't stand the smell of 'em, so I went out."

"After the tickets were looked at?"

"Yes—some ten minutes later—just before we got to Wisden. The next compartment was evidently reserved for ladies, so I avoided it; the last was a second class, but I didn't mind that. There was only one man in it."

"Oh, that's grand," cried Hazell, with great glee. "I'll have a drink on the strength of it." And he pulled out his milk flask.

"What was he like?" he went on.

"A clean-shaven fellow, with the exception of slight whiskers. He was reading a paper when I went in."

"That's the man I want," said Hazell. "You see, I happen to know that the doors at the ends of the coaches on this train were locked, the key being with the guard. So it was impossible that anyone could get through to the next coach. If only I could find out where that man is now!"

Masters wheeled round his chair suddenly.

"Will you tell me why you want to know?" he asked.

"I can't, my dear chap."

"Will you assure me, then, that no harm will come of it if I can give you a clue?"

"On the other hand, you will be doing a very great service in the cause of justice."

"Very well, then. I took a taxi straight to the club when I arrived at the terminus. And I happened to notice that my travelling companion took the next on the rank. He had a large Gladstone and a smaller bag with him."

"That settles it. I'm off," exclaimed Hazell.

In half an hour's time he was back at the terminus, in consultation with the cab inspector, who keeps watch at the station gates.

"I want the number and destination of the taxi that followed immediately after the one bound for the Avenue Club last evening—from the 7.35 from Redminster."

He knew, of course, that every cabman has to shout out his destination to the inspector as he passes the little office at the gate. The man consulted his book.

"Number 28,533. Destination, Eight, Lancaster Crescent."

Thorpe Hazell stood as one stunned.

"Kestron's address!" he muttered to himself. "The girl must have been right, after all. It's pretty bad!"

"I think you'll find the taxi on the rank now, sir," went on the inspector.

It was there, and in answer to his inquiries the driver informed Hazell that the address was quite correct, and that his fare had certainly gone in at number eight.

"I'm sorry for her," said Hazell to himself, as he told his own cabman to drive him there; "but at least I can try to bluff him. Still, it's very strange. There's a hitch in my reasoning somewhere. Except, of course, this man must have been his tool. *I* can't make it out."

He rang the bell of number eight, and a servant opened the door.

"Is Mr. Kestron in?"

"No, sir; he went out half an hour ago."

Thorpe Hazell paused, then he said:

"Ah, he has returned from the country, then?"

"Yes, sir. He came back late last night."

"About eight?"

"No, sir; not till after ten."

"Oh," said Hazell nonchalantly, "I thought he returned by the train arriving at about half-past seven and drove straight home."

"No, sir; the valet came back with the luggage then, but Mr. Kestron arrived later."

Instantly the solution flashed across his mind. Producing half-a-sovereign, he said to the girl: "I want to see his valet."

The girl looked at him doubtfully, and hesitated.

"I am a friend of your master," said Hazell quietly.

Then the bribe acted. In a couple of minutes the valet came into the room where Hazell had been shown. Without a word the latter walked to the door and locked it. Then he turned upon the man.

"Do you find ticket-collecting a paying business?" he asked.

The other turned very pale.

"I don't understand," he said.

"I can prove that you were amusing yourself asking for tickets on the express from Redminster last night. I have all the details."

The man was thoroughly taken aback. At first he denied everything, but something in Hazell's quiet manner was too much for him.

"Well," he said sullenly, "and if I was? It was a harmless enough joke. You're from the railway company, I suppose?"

Hazell ignored the question.

"I want that diamond necklace that was handed to you by Miss Mallaby's maid," he said, "sharp!"

The man gave a bound forward.

"It was a clever scheme you both hatched out at Appledon—no!" he cried, "I know exactly what happened. If you attempt any nonsense you're done for, my man." Then he went on to explain that if the necklace were restored quietly nothing more would be said.

"Not for your sake, you know," he added grimly, "but because it's best to hush it up. If you refuse, I'll open the window and tell my cabman to fetch the police. These are my conditions. You give me the necklace, and clear out of here before your master returns. For I fancy *he'll* know about this one of these days."

"Who are you?" blurted out the man.

"My name's Thorpe Hazell—if that's any use to you, and this isn't the first little affair of the railway I've solved."

"I've heard of you," said the valet. "Were you on the train?"

"No. Now then—that necklace, please."

"I'll—I'll go and get it."

"Then I'll come with you."

He looked at Hazell for a moment, then, putting his hand in the inner pocket of his coat he drew out a small case, and handed it over to Hazell with a curse. The latter opened it, and saw the diamonds were intact.

"Thanks," he said. "I've two questions to ask you—out of mere curiosity. Why did you trouble to ask for tickets in every compartment of that carriage?"

"I thought it might allay suspicion if the alarm were given before the end of the journey. The other passengers would—"

"Oh, it is very weak!" interrupted Hazell. "How should you have changed into uniform if there had been anyone else in your compartment?"

"There was the lavatory."

"I see. Good-morning. You may think yourself very lucky, my friend."

In an hour's time the necklace was in the hands of Miss St. John Mallaby, who was profuse in her expressions of relief and gratitude.

"And you are sure that—"

"That Mr. Kestron had nothing to do with it? Absolutely. Now, please ring for your maid."

The latter came in. Hazell held the necklace in his hands.

"Your mistress thinks you had better take yourself off at once," he said. "Mr. Kestron's valet is also out of a situation. Did you use your scissors or a knife to slit open that dressing-case under cover of the rug?"

She stood for half-a-minute gasping for breath. Then she left the room without a word.

"It has been an interesting case, Miss Mallaby," remarked Hazell, "and I am glad to think that the last of my little investigations of railway mysteries has cleared a good man of suspicion and ended happily."

The Ruse That Succeeded

A spick and span little steam yacht was slowly entering the tiny harbour of Porthaven. The tide was ebbing fast and the pier master shouted a few directions, for the channel of available water was not very wide. She flew the French tricolour flag astern, and the pennant of a well-known French yacht club on her foremast. On the bridge, smoking a cigarette, stood a little man, every bit as spick and span as the yacht herself; a typical Frenchman, dressed in a spotless white duck suit, with very sharp, piercing brown eyes which scanned the quayside narrowly.

There was nothing remarkable in the entrance of a French yacht into the little harbour of Porthaven. It was the height of the yachting season, and a dozen other small private craft lay there at anchor, or were moored alongside the quay. The owner of one of them, standing on deck with a pair of glasses, remarked to a lady who stood by his side:

"That's *Hirondelle* coming in. She belongs to a chap named De Natoye—there he is, on the bridge. I met him at Cannes this spring."

"A Frenchman?"

"Yes—and a rich one too. A very jolly chap. I'll have the dinghy out and pay him a call when he comes to anchor. Welcome him to English waters."

For the next few days De Natoye was welcomed not only by this particular owner of a yacht, but also by everyone of note in Porthaven. He was an agreeable little man, bright and vivacious, and his presence added much to the society gathered at the seaside

resort. Once or twice he pleaded excuses for not accepting invita-
tions to lunch or dinner, and on these occasions it might have been
noticed that he took an express to London, and was not arrayed in
yachting garb.

But with Monsieur De Natoye himself and his elegant steam
yacht this story does not deal directly, although he was the leading
cause that led to a curious railway incident. It will be necessary,
therefore, to leave *Hirondelle* at her moorings in Porthaven
harbour, and to transfer the scene to London—hot and out of season at the end of August.

Night had set in when, out of one of the little side streets in
that strange district called Soho, there came into Wardour Street
an unobtrusive little man, who glanced once or twice over his shoulders as if to see whether anyone were following him or not. A look
of satisfaction passed over his face as he made up his mind that,
apparently, he was unobserved. Porthaven yachtsmen, looking at
him closely, would have noticed that he was Monsieur De Natoye,
and would have remembered that he had refused, with most polite
excuses, to attend a dinner that night on board Lord Feverel's yacht
Firefly.

Arrived in Piccadilly Circus he lit a cigarette, unbuttoned the
light dust-coat he was wearing, disclosing an expanse of shirt-front
beneath, and strolled leisurely in the direction of a famous *café*,
where men of all nations congregate. It being out of the season,
there were not many present.

Seated in a corner, a Benedictine on the table in front of him, a
cigar in his mouth, was a tall, military-looking man, with a big
moustache and keen grey eyes. Anyone who knew anything of the
diplomatic world would have recognised him at once as Colonel
Sibthorpe, attached to the Foreign Office, "a deuced good berth,
and nothing to do, what?" as some of his military friends said.

In fact, no one seemed to know quite what the Colonel's exact
mission was. He made pleasant little Continental tours, he lounged
about town, was an agreeable companion, and knew what was
going on in the world. That was all most men could say about him.

Monsieur de Natoye walked up to him. The Colonel nodded affably.

"Hullo!" he exclaimed, "you in town? What brings you to this dull metropolis?"

"Business—a leetle business, Colonel," answered the Frenchman, sitting down beside him.

The Colonel motioned to a waiter.

"A Benedictine?" he asked.

"Certainly. Thank you."

"Bring me another, too."

"Yessir."

When the drinks arrived the Colonel, leaning back in the chair, said nonchalantly in a low tone: "Well? Settled it?"

"Yes," answered De Natoye, sinking his voice to the level of the other.

"When?"

"Wednesday."

"What time?"

"He takes the 7.15 train from London."

"And reaches Porthaven?"

"At 10.42."

"You sail at once?"

"No. The tide will not serve before half-past one in the morning."

The Colonel puffed at his cigar thoughtfully. "Anyone suspect?" he asked presently.

"We think not, but we are not sure."

"Humph."

"You will help us?"

"Only as far as I can—you know my position?"

The Frenchman nodded. Someone sat down at the next table, a foreigner apparently. The Colonel raised his voice.

"You are staying in town to-night?"

"Yes."

"Ah! Glad to have seen you. I must be off. Good-night!"

He finished his liqueur, shook hands with De Natoye, strolled outside on the pavement, and hailed a taxi.

"Kensington High Street."

"Whereabouts, sir?"

"Oh, the station will do."

Arrived there, he got out, dismissed the taxi, and walked some little distance in the Hammersmith direction till he came to a row of ugly-looking houses standing back from the Street. Taking a quick glance on either side first, he went up to the door of one of these houses and rang the bell. The servant came.

"Mr. Brett at home?"

"Yes, sir, but I think he's engaged."

The Colonel took a card from his pocket, a blank one, wrote a few words upon it, and handed it to her.

"Give him that and I think he'll see me."

In less than a minute the servant was showing him into a room at the back of the house. An alert-looking, clean-shaven man of middle height rose from the desk at which he was seated.

"I didn't expect you, sir," he said quietly.

"No," replied the Colonel as he took a seat, "but I've a bit of work on hand that I think requires your services."

Brett closed the door and locked it, his face betraying no surprise. He was accustomed to secret commissions from the Foreign Office; in fact he made his living chiefly by this means. Not that he stood in any official capacity. He knew very well the risks he ran, and that if he walked into trouble he could expect no open help from those whom he served. The secret agent of a Government often has important work to do, and does it well as a trusted servant, but he must never expect to be recognised officially.

The Colonel lit a cigar, took a notebook from his pocket, and consulted it carefully. Presently he said:

"You know a man named Koravitch—a Russian, don't you?"

Brett thought for a moment. Then he replied: "Yes. Goes by the name of Martin sometimes." The Colonel nodded. Brett unlocked a cabinet and took a small, indexed book from it.

"Here he is," he said presently, "Koravitch, Russian subject. A suspect in Russia. Gave information on Roumanian question. Known to the French Secret Service. Useful man."

The Colonel nodded.

"That's the chap," he said, "do you happen to know where he is now?"

Brett again consulted his notebook.

"Yes—in England—unless he's left the country during the last fortnight—which would have been difficult," he added grimly.

"It would have been difficult, as you say," replied the Colonel. "I see you're up-to-date, Brett."

"It's my business, sir. Do you want Koravitch? I can soon lay my hand on him."

"So can I. But we don't want him just now. Let me give you the facts of the case. Koravitch, as you said just now, is a useful man—both to us and the French Government. But the Russians don't want him on the Continent. They know very well he's here—they made it too hot for him in his own country—and the Russian police have been keeping him under observation. But as long as he remains in England they'll leave him alone. Well, as it happens, there's a very good reason why he should go to France just now."

"I see—and you want me to get him over there quietly?"

"No, I don't. That's the affair of the French Secret Service, not ours. And it's been arranged. You know Monsieur De Natoye?"

Brett's eyes sparkled.

"One of the cleverest little fellows they've got."

"Quite so. Well, he's got a yacht lying at Porthaven, ready to take Koravitch off. I owe him a good turn, and although, as I said, the affair is not ours, and we can't take any definite action, still I'm anxious he should get Koravitch away."

"What do you want me to do, sir?"

"The case stands thus. Directly the Russian police suspect the man's leaving England, they'll arrest him. They've got a plausible reason—so plausible that international complications would arise if any department went to the Home Office and stopped interference."

"You mean, sir, that our police would have to help the Russians if called upon?"

"Exactly. They're hardly likely to do that—I don't think they will—but our police must be kept out of it. Now, Koravitch takes the 7.15 train to Porthaven at the terminus of the London Eastern and Porthaven line on Wednesday night. He arrives there at 10.42, but De Natoye's yacht can't get out before one, because of the tide. What the Russian police will do, if they suspect anything, is this. They'll either have Koravitch arrested before he leaves London, or they'll go down to Porthaven and nab him on the boat. He's not out of the wood till the yacht starts. Then De Natoye will see to it."

"What do you want me to do, sir?"

"If you can, shadow the whole thing unostentatiously, and, if there is a danger of the arrest taking place, prevent it. You'll earn a big fee. But, remember, I can give you no support in any way."

"That's understood, sir. Anyhow I'll try my best."

The Colonel shrugged his shoulders.

"Right! You know your game then. Don't come to me about it—at all events, until Thursday, when it will have been played out one way or another. Good night!"

Turning over the papers on the bookstall at the London terminus of the London Eastern and Porthaven Railway stood Brett, apparently a nondescript individual with plenty of time on his hands. But he was by no means idle. The centre of observation was the gateway to number 7 platform close by, from which the 7.15 express to Porthaven started. It was just after seven now, and the train was drawn up in readiness. Brett scrutinised quietly every person who went through the gate. He also kept his eyes from time to time on the door leading from the booking office, and took searching glances round the big open space between the station buildings and the entrances to the various platforms.

At ten minutes past seven a man walked quickly across this space to where Brett was standing; it was one of his subordinates.

"All right," he said, "he's taking his ticket. I followed him all the way in a taxi."

"See anyone?"

"They're artful," replied Brett, "I've had to deal with them before. Go outside and watch everyone who comes to the station. If you see them, come at once. If we can, we must stop them somehow."

The man went back. In a couple of minutes an individual came across to platform number 7, a man with a large head and wearing a soft hat turned down over his forehead. Brett recognised him by his walk.

"Koravitch!" he said to himself. "I expect the poor beggar feels precious nervous."

He watched him take a seat in the train. A sudden thought occurred to him. He glanced at the clock. It was now 7.10.

"Allow me to speak to a friend who is leaving by this train?"

"Certainly, sir," said the polite official, letting him through the gate.

He went up to the carriage. The man within gave a start as Brett's head poked itself into the window.

"All right," said the latter, "I know. The coast is clear, but if they should come at the last moment drop out on the other side and let them board the train. If not, when you get down make your friend take his yacht out the instant the tide serves. That's all."

Without waiting for a reply he hurried back to his post of observation and watched the clock.

Twelve minutes past—thirteen—fourteen—surely it was all right now.

No! Suddenly he saw his fellow detective rushing across. He ran forward to meet him.

"Three of them!" said the man.

"Right. Charge!" exclaimed Brett, in a low voice.

Three men came dashing out of the booking office close on each other's heels. Without a word Brett and his assistant rushed forward with their heads down to meet them. As they did so Brett heard the bell ring at the platform entrance.

They tilted against the first man, fell in a heap, and the other two came tripping over them. There was a little chorus of strange oaths; one of the men picked himself up and made a dash for number 7 platform.

"Too late, sir," said the collector, indicating, with a jerk of his thumb, the outgoing train.

"I don't know whether you ought to apologise to us, or we to you," said Brett, blandly, "the meeting was so mutual!"

The leader of the three men looked at him with a scowl of suspicion. Brett raised his hat politely, and passed on, remarking:

"*I* don't mind apologising. I'm very sorry to have caused you any inconvenience."

"That's all right," said his subordinate, as they passed out of the station.

"Not a bit of it," replied Brett.

"What do you mean?"

"If they've as much common sense as I have—and I certainly give them credit for that—they'll find an easy way out of the difficulty."

"But it's the last train to Porthaven!"

"On this line," said Brett, drily. "Come in here and have a drink. This thing's got to be thought out."

Brett explained as they sat in the corner of a private bar.

"The case is like this," he said. "There's one way, and only one way of getting to Porthaven tonight before the yacht sails, and it's this. You know Melfield, don't you?"

"Yes. About a hundred miles down the line, isn't it?"

"That's right. A local train leaves Melfield at 11.5, arriving at Porthaven just after half-past twelve. If they catch that, Koravitch won't get out of the country."

"But how can they catch it?"

"By taking the 9.5 on the South Midland Railway to Melfield. It arrives there at 10.48. The South Midland and the London Eastern and Porthaven stations at Melfield are just over a mile apart. They'd do it easily if they took a motor."

"I see—but not if the train were late?"

"That train never is late. It nearly always runs to time."

"If it could be delayed on the journey—"

"Exactly," replied Brett. "That's just the problem I'm trying to work out. I want to delay that train and I want to do it without any risk of danger to anyone—that is, of course, if they travel by it—as I think they will. And there isn't much time."

He lit his pipe and smoked thoughtfully for a few minutes. Then a smile came into his face.

"I know something about railways," he said, "and the way they're worked. And I have an idea I can make that train late at Melfield."

"How?"

"With a good strong gimlet!"

"A *gimlet?*"

"I haven't time to explain. You go straight to the South Midland Terminus and keep a look-out. Don't let them see you. At ten minutes to nine you'll see me by the bookstall—I shall be dressed as an old man. Let me know if they are there. That's all. I've just got time to run home and change first."

Before he called a taxi to take him borne, Brett entered a shop close by and purchased a large, strong gimlet, with a sharp screw point, carefully examining it to see that it was good steel.

About a quarter to nine an old man walked slowly into the terminus of the South Midland Railway. Clouds had come over the evening sky, and darkness had set in prematurely. He loitered about by the bookstall till his subordinate came up.

"You were right," said the latter, "they're all three here, and they've taken tickets for Melfield."

"Good! You needn't wait. If you like to come to my house in an hour's time I'll explain things to you."

The South Midland Terminus is constructed on a different principle from that of the London Eastern and Porthaven, in that passengers have free access to all the platforms. Brett made his way to number 4, from which he ascertained the Melfield train started. It was just being slowly backed in, the red tail light gleaming as it came down the line to the buffer stops at the "dead end." Brett knew that the chief difficulty of his task was to escape the notice of the officials. He entered a compartment at the rear end of the train, crossed the floor of the carriage, opened the further door, and, closing it behind him, dropped down on the line beyond, between the train and another that stood on the neighbouring metals.

Then he made his way cautiously to the back of the train and crawled under the last coach, coming out behind it—between it and the "dead end." It was fairly dark here, with the exception of the gleam from the red lamp.

It was this red lamp that Brett wanted—for less than a minute. Making up his mind for a bold attempt he reached for it, removed it from its socket behind the coach, put it on the ground, and, stooping down, removed the lamp itself from its outer case. Then, with a sharp prod from his gimlet, he bored a hole at the bottom of the oil receptacle, giving the tool a quick turn afterwards. The oil came dripping out.

In ten seconds the leaking lamp was replaced on its socket, and Brett was under the coach again. He managed to slip out unobserved, and to gain platform number 5 through the other train. Before he left the station he saw the three Russian police agents enter the Melfield express. Then he went home satisfied, saying to himself:

"Even if they order a special to Porthaven at Melfield they can't get there in time. It would take too long to get one out. I should like to be on that train and see the effect."

The effect was very simple. A red tail light is placed at the rear of a train for several reasons—to protect it should it be at a standstill, and, more especially, to notify to signalmen on duty that the whole of the train has passed, and that the line behind, therefore, is clear.

Slowly, but surely, the oil trickled out of that particular lamp, until none was left. The train had run some fifty or sixty miles of its journey when the light finally drooped and went out. The first man who noticed something was wrong was the signalman in charge of an obscure roadside cabin named "Cherrington Box." He gave a little start as the train whisked by, and then promptly obeyed his printed orders. That is to say, he went to his signalling apparatus, and sent forward to the next box the code signal of his line, seven beats, a pause, and a final beat. In the next signal-box the man on duty heard the eight rings in this particular order, and, to his ears, they carried the very plain message:

"Stop and examine train!"

Which he proceeded to do by keeping the home signal against her.

"What's up?" cried the driver, as he stopped beside the box.

"Cherrington telephones you've got no tail light," shouted the signalman.

Down jumped the guard and ran behind the train. The lamp was there right enough, but out. He tried to light it, and swore at the lampmen fifty miles behind him.

"Forgot to fill it!" he muttered.

In his van was a spare one. But it took several minutes before it was fixed behind the train. Three men were anxious, and one of them shouted out of the window to the front guard, with a foreign accent:

"Why do we stop?"

"All right, sir; we're just off."

"We shall be late at Melfield?"

"Yes, sir, I'm afraid we shall."

"A sovereign if we're in time."

"Hope we shall be, then," said the guard; "but it doesn't rest with me. Right away, George! Try your best, and it's shares."

For he guessed the driver had overheard. But, at Slade Junction box, a cross-country express, well up to time, got the road on to Melfield first, and the London train steamed in thirteen minutes late. For the second time that night three men failed to get to Porthaven, and perhaps they guessed it was not pure accident.

On Friday Brett saw Colonel Sibthorpe.

"Well," said the latter, "he got off all right. I suppose the coast was clear after all?"

"I rather fancy *I* made it clear for him," replied Brett, with a smile.

"How?"

He drew a gimlet from his pocket and showed it to the Colonel.

"With this, sir."

And he proceeded to explain.

The Slip Coach Mystery: A Railway Adventure

If it were possible to write the secret history of a European Ambassador what a revelation would stand before the eyes of the astonished public! We read our newspapers and form our opinions on great international questions from their pages, or from speeches in the House of Commons, while all the time those "behind the scenes" are smiling to themselves at the very small amount of knowledge which the press and public are really permitted to obtain; or else, while the people are flattering themselves over the prospect of a "peaceful political outlook," as contained in the "leaders" of the daily paper, those in whose hands the "outlook" is really placed are trembling with anxiety lest some piece of delicate diplomacy should fall through. Nor is the public aware of the plots and counterplots which take place among a class of men chosen especially for their diplomatic faculties, and often pitted against one another in a warfare that demands more brains than the most skilful military leader in Europe.

The incident I am about to narrate forms a small part of the secret annals of the diplomatic service, though at the same time soother equally secret element entered into the plot.

It will be remembered that in 189- there were rumours going the rounds of the press concerning friction between some of the great Powers of Europe, nor were there wanting those who prophesied "wars and rumours of wars." The centre of the agitation was that great field of international trouble and dispute vaguely known unto us as "The East." Some fresh troubles had arisen in the "Eastern Question," owing to the unexpected attitude of one of the smaller Powers, which appeared to be setting her more powerful neighbours at defiance, and encouraging them to quarrel among themselves. The Prime Minister was harassed on every side. Questions were asked in the House, but cleverly evaded, and the foreign policy of this country seemed for a few weeks to he wrapped up in sphinx-like mystery, until suddenly the crisis was at an end, the stocks rose merrily, and the public once more breathed freely. But it is little known that a far different result might have been the case; and therefore the incident about to be chronicled will be of all the more interest. One stipulation must be made, and that for obvious reasons. The names of those who took part in the adventure must not be disclosed, for it was from one of these that the facts of the case will be set down. There is no fear of his discovery, and I have permission to publish his story, which runs as follows.

It was during a prolonged stay in the East of Europe that I first became aware of the existence of a secret society which has its members spread through many countries, and which I will refer to under its Anglicised name of "The Watching Brotherhood." Why and how I became a member myself matters little in the incident I am about to narrate. Perhaps I was young and foolish, and fired with false ideas of "Liberty." Perhaps it was because, being a cosmopolitan, I had few patriotic instincts, and was the more ready to devote myself to the cause which "The Watchers" professed to have in hand. On my return to England I found a little handful of the "brothers" in London. Perhaps it will be better understood when I say that most of these were of Russian extraction, and probably exercise more influence even in this country than might be supposed. Among the few who constituted our branch of the society the most important was a man whom we will call Koravitch, a fine muscular fellow of English descent by his mother—a man who would stick at nothing, and the narration of whose exploits would form a volume in itself. Koravitch was our chairman, and one evening, when we met at his summons in a quiet house not a hundred miles from Tottenham Court-road, he came into the room with a more serious expression than I had ever seen him wear.

"Comrades," he said, an soon its he had taken his seat, "we have serious business before as to-night, and before long some of us may be called upon to act."

"What is it?" we asked breathlessly.

"The peace or the war of Europe, perhaps," he answered. "Great things are being weighed in the balance. But listen while I read you this message from B—"

B— was one of the heads of the society, and a word from him meant much. We anxiously listened while Koravitch read the following:—

"To our brothers, greeting! The time has come and the great opportunity has arisen. The Powers of Europe are looking one another in the face in anger and in terror. Irresolution characterises three Governments, and peace is threatened with destruction. Let there be war! Let the nations fight, for then shall follow the rising for Freedom."

The explanation was this: If Europe could be involved in an Eastern war it was determined to light the torch of a great revolution in Russia and other countries in sympathy with such a movement. How far such a rising would be successful it is difficult to judge, but "desperate men use desperate means to attain their ends."

"Now," went on Koravitch, "there is something more. I have a most important matter to put before you. Two of the Powers are bringing pressure to bear on the British Cabinet to induce England to act with them independently of Russia. If they are successful the chances for war will be increased tenfold. So grave has this political outlook been considered at St. Petersburg—for, somehow or other, the affair has leaked out—that it has been determined to send an Extraordinary Embassy from the Tsar's Government, armed with a treaty of a private nature, by the signing of which England will agree to act with Russia, in agreement with certain proposals the latter Power intends to make—the end of which will be peace. So important does the Tsar consider the question that this embassy is being kept a dead secret, and even the Russian Ambassador in this country is unaware of it."

"Is this true?" asked one of the "brothers."

"Did you ever know me to lie?" asked Koravitch, sternly. "Of course it is true. Our society has its agents everywhere—and evens the Tsar's palace is not free from them."

"And who is the Ambassador chosen?"

"Sklavotski," said the chairman.

"What! Sklavotski?" we echoed.

"Ay—none other. A pretty good handful to cope with, eh?"

For the name carried terror with it. Sklavotski had been one of the cleverest secret police agents in Russia. Then he was appointed to diplomatic service of a dangerous character, and it was commonly reported that no one had ever got the better of him.

"Yes," continued our chairman, "it is none other. And now comes the point that concerns us. It is ordered that every possible delay be placed in the way of his journey here. Right across the Continent our agents are at work, and no pains have been spared. Even a railway accident has been planned on one of the lines on which he has to travel. But one thing has been strictly ordered, and that is that his life is not to be attempted. The question stands thus: His interview with the British Prime Minister must be prevented until the representatives of the other two Powers have prevailed upon him to take the other course. Also, if possible, the private treaty which he carries must be obtained. Now you may be sure that he will take every precaution, for no man knows the risk he is running better than himself."

"And how does this affect us?" asked a "brother."

"Well, you see, in the event of his slipping through the hands of our friends on the Continent we must try to got the better of him on this side of the water."

"Which way will he come?" I asked.

"It is not quite certain, but in all probability via Kingboro', coming on to town by the 'Catton and Slowbridge' line. If he doesn't meet with any accident abroad, he ought to be on our shores on

Friday evening. Now, listen, and I'll tell you what our plans had
better be. First of all, which of you knows Sklavotski by sight?"

"I do," I replied. "I shouldn't seen forget him, with that scar
over his eyebrow and his big white moustache and imperial."

"Very well. Then you and the 'Lynx' (a sobriquet for another
"brother") and myself will go down to Kingboro' on Monday, and
I'll arrange to have a cipher telegram sent to me there detailing
movements abroad. I'll leave you, G—, in charge here, and wire
you instructions if he doesn't come by that route. But remember,
all of you, be faithful to your oath, and do your duty."

It in not worth while to mention the details of the meeting which
followed. Suffice it to say that on Monday night we three above
mentioned found ourselves meeting by appointment in a road outside the East Coast seaport of Kingboro'.

"Hold yourselves to readiness to act to-morrow," said our
leader. "My advice states that the Ambassador's all right so for—
he's a clever one, he is—and he may get over here after all. Now
the boat is timed to arrive at seven to-morrow evening. It's dark at
six, so we'll meet in the road at the back of the station."

"Have you got any plan?"

He shook his head.

"I simply can't think of anything. But if he comes we'll have to
nab him somehow. Perhaps we'll do it in town. Anyway, we'd better separate now. So, goodnight."

At six o'clock the next evening we met as arranged.

Koravitch had important news for us.

"I've had cipher telegrams to-day," he said, "which make the
affair more pressing than ever. Sklavotski is on his way. There's to
be an attempt to tamper with the boat's engines, though they don't
think it will come off. But on Ambassador Extraordinary from one
of the opposition Powers is making for England, and will be in
London early to-morrow morning, arriving at Dover by the first
boat. At all risks he must have some hours' start of Sklavotski, or
else the whole thing falls through."

"That means that Sklavotski must be prevented from getting to
London tonight," I said.

"Aye, not only presented. He must be kidnapped, and kept till midday to-morrow."

"How is it to be done?"

"We must get him on the train, somehow."

"Are ordinary passengers allowed to travel by it?"

"Yes—you go and take first-class singles to London. And we'll keep an eye on each other, and on him."

The boat was late in arriving that night. We heard that some of the machinery had got out of gear during the passage, but after a short delay had easily been set right again. Anxiously we three watched the passengers as they disembarked from the boat. There was the usual medley—groups of laughing foreigners, two or three phlegmatic Dutchmen, pale-faced ladies, oven to the inevitable clergyman, an old man who was evidently nervous of the landing platform, and who slipped at the end of it. I stepped forward and helped him to his feet, receiving his thanks in a voice choked with a cough. Presently we three spies instinctively glanced at one another as an individual appeared on the landing platform, a man wearing a heavy fur-lined coat, conspicuous for his large white moustache and imperial. His soft hat was drawn down over his forehead, but not no closely as to prevent a scar over his eye from showing. It was Sklavotski! He appeared to have no luggage except a handbag, and when this had been examined by the Customs officers we followed him to the platform.

The train was drawn up—rather a long one—and behind the rear brake-van was an extra coach containing a luggage, two first, and two second compartments. The bulk of the passengers made for the centre of the train, but Sklavotski, casting a searching glance around him, walked straight to the last carriage and got into the first-class compartment nearest the back of the carriage, tipping the guard to lock him in.

It was at this moment Koravitch suddenly exclaimed:

"Oh, the fool—he's played right into our hands! Now, quick, you two, get in that carriage."

"What—with him?"

"No, you can't do that. Get into the other first-class compartment—the one at the front end of the carriage, and get the guard
to reserve it. I'll be with you in a minute."

We got in, and, curious to know what our leader was about, I
leaned out of the window to watch him. First he carefully observed
the space between the last carriage and the one in front of it. Then
he walked to the end of the train and gave a glance behind. His
next move was to run down the platform, and, looking round to
see if he were unobserved, he darted into a room, the door of which
opened on to the platform. In a moment he had emerged, apparently holding something beneath his great coat. Then he joined us
in the carriage, and the guard locked us in.

"No stop before London, guard, is there?"

"No, sir."

In five minutes we were off, and Koravitch produced from
under his coat a railway lamp.

"What on earth are you going to do with that?" we asked.

"Well, it isn't worth while to make big accident out of this trip,
and I want the train itself to go on," he replied.

"What do you mean?"

"You'll see presently—there's a big job before us. Now, do you
think you two can tackle Sklavotski?"

"How?"

"Well, you'll have to go along the footboard, and get in with
him. Then, somehow or other, you must persuade him to drink this
little refresher" (and he took out of his pocket a small bottle); "you
needn't be afraid, it will only make him sleep comfortably."

"But what are you going to do?"

Koravitch first proceeded to light the lantern, and to turn on
the red glass. Then he answered:

"Well, I've got a very dangerous job. I'm going to uncouple this
carriage, and let the rest of the train go on. I shall put this lamp
behind the coach in front of us, for if the train ran on without the
tail light, she'd be pulled up pretty soon by a signalman, and I want
to leave the light on behind our carriage, so that the next trains on
the 'up' line will pull up at the red light ahead of her, and so there

won't be a smash. As to the uncoupling, it's a difficult job, of course, but I know how to go about it. It's lucky he did not travel by the opposition route, as those trains are fitted with the auto-vacuum brake, and I should not have been able to work it. But the 'Catton and Slowbridge' use the 'Westinghouse,' and I can turn off the cocks, and manage all right. I know how that works. Then there's the electric communication to unfasten. Then there are the safety chains on each side of the coupling—they'll be easy enough—and lastly, the actual coupling itself. There'll be just footing enough, or I'll manage to hold on somehow while I unscrew the coupling, manipulate the brake, and then when the coupling gets slack I'll slip it off the hook as we go down a gradient. The train will go on, and we shall slowly pull up. I know just the spot where it had better be worked, so that we shall pull up in a quiet place. But there isn't any more time for talking now."

"One moment," I said. "What do you propose doing if you manage to stop the coach?"

"Oh, we'll get Sklavotski out of it."

"And then?"

He shrugged his shoulders.

"Then we'll think of further developments. Sufficient to the moment is the danger thereof—quite sufficient. Now, then, off you go. Stop, here's a railway key in case his door's locked. Take care not to let those people in the other compartments see you. Good luck, and I'll be with you presently. Steady, now. One out of each door, so as to take him on each side!"

So saying, he put the lamp under his coat, so as not to be seen by anyone as he walked along the footboard, while "the Lynx" and I stepped out, one on either side of the carriage, I taking the key, as it was on my side that the guard had locked the door. Very stealthily I crept along the footboard, carefully avoiding being seen by the occupants of the second-class compartment I had to pass. At length I arrived opposite the door of the compartment in which Sklavotski was travelling, and ventured to look in at a corner of the window. He was lying down on the seat, with his bag for a pillow, apparently fast asleep. At this moment I caught sight of my

companion's face at the opposite window, and saw that he was
ready for the attack. Quickly and noiselessly I inserted my key and
unlocked the carriage door. To open it and spring in was the work
of another instant, and simultaneously my companion entered by
his door. Sklavotski sprang up and uttered a curse in Russian; but
in less time than it takes to tell the story we were on him, and,
holding him down firmly to the seat, notwithstanding his violent
struggles we managed to force his mouth open by holding his nostrils, and to pour the contents of the little bottle down his throat.
A shudder or two ran through him, his struggles grew less and less,
and very soon he was resting quietly, to all intents and purposes
fast asleep.

Then we turned our thoughts to Koravitch. He had not yet appeared, and we were still rushing along at 50 miles an hour. I
looked out of the window, craning my neck to see as far as possible, and then to my joy observed that the train in front of our
carriage was leaving us, and that a red light was gleaming brightly
behind as she sped into the darkness. At the same moment a dark
figure appeared creeping along the footboard, and Koravitch
entered our carriage.

"Bravo," he said, "capital! You fellows have managed it splendidly."

"And you?"

"It was a terribly tough job, but I meant to do it. The screw
coupling was the difficulty. I've got my left wrist sprained holding
on—lucky I've gone in for gymnastics, for I couldn't have managed
it else. But there's no time to talk now—we're slowing down. There's
a bit of an up gradient here that will soon pull us up."

"What's the next move, then?"

"To get this fellow out of it. Ah, the handbag." He ran hurriedly
through its controls. "No, it's not in that. I'll pitch it out, then.
Now—we're slowing up. Open the door on this side. Good! We're
on an embankment. As seen as we stop, I'll get out, and you drop
him and follow. We must chance those people in the 'seconds' seeing us, but it's precious dark, and I don't think they will. As soon
as the carriage pulls up it will begin to roll back down the incline,

and from what I know of the line will go half a mile before stepping. We're stopping—I'll jump," and he sprang out into the six-foot way. We had got the sleeping ambassador ready on the floor, and in half a minute we were all out of the carriage, just before it stopped.

"Lie down," said Koravitch.

We did on. The carriage, surely enough, began at this moment to roll back. A window was opened and a head thrust out. The speed increased as the coach passed us, and we heard a voice say in German:

"Ach Himmel! we've broken loose!"

That was all, and we waited for no more. Then we carried the ambassador down the embankment, and found ourselves in a field.

"What shall we do now?" I asked.

"Well, the first thing is to get as far away from the line as possible," answered Koravitch, "and we must take him with us—better carry him by turns. He's not extra heavy; who'll take first?"

"I will," I said. So Sklavotski was hoisted on to my shoulders, and we started off. Presently we struck a narrow country lane, which led us away from the railway. We had gone nearly three miles down this lane, carefully avoiding a little row of houses in it, when Koravitch, who was carrying the ambassador, suddenly stopped, and exclaimed:

"Look here, we can't go on like this. We must hide the fellow somewhere. He'll come to presently."

"But what are we to do?" asked "the Lynx." "Where can we hide him?"

"Shall we get him to some wood?" I said.

"But it's precious cold, and we ought to stick to him for some hours yet; in fact, he ought not to be allowed to get free till well on in the morning. Now let's think. Hullo! I've got a plan. What's that building in front of us?"

"Looks like a church," I said.

"Exactly so; it is a church—I know the country now. It's Little Prebbleton Church, and there isn't a house to speak of within a quarter of a mile of it. It's the last place anyone would dream of entering this time of night, for it's nearly nine o'clock; so let's make for it. We shall be safe inside, and I've got a little dark lantern with me that will help us look over things a bit."

So saying, he led the way to the church, and we were soon picking our way over the churchyard, among the tombs, which stood out in ghastly dimness. Koravitch made for one of the windows, and after some little trouble, managed to force it open. He got in first, and then we lifted Sklavotski through the window and followed ourselves. It was a grim, uncanny feeling that possessed us as we stood in the church. After fumbling about for a few moments we found our way to the vestry, a snug little carpeted nook divided from one of the side aisles by a heavy curtain. Then Koravitch lit his lantern, carefully turning it away from the one window which the vestry possessed.

"Are you going to stay here all night?" I asked.

"Well, perhaps it might be as well," he answered, "unless we tie him up, and leave him here. To-morrow's Saturday, and I should think someone would find him then—they're pretty well sure to come in and get the place ready for Sunday. If not, he won't die if he isn't found till Sunday morning, for we could give him a feed before we go. But the first thing to do is to search him, and to see if we can find anything of importance."

So saying, Koravitch went carefully through the ambassador's pockets. He found some money of various nations, and at length brought out a pocket-book.

"Here it is," he exclaimed, and we gathered round him eagerly as he opened it. But disappointment awaited us; beyond a few receipted hotel bills and unimportant papers, the pocket-book was empty.

"Where can it be?" said Koravitch.

"In London with Monsieur Sklavotski!" said a voice, which made us start and look round. The ambassador had risen upon his feet, and was smiling at us.

"What?" we exclaimed. "How—"

"Pardon, gentlemen," said the other, "I have awakened before you were quite ready for me. No, you needn't attempt to attack me, for I am not going to run away. There is no need. You were asking, I think, for the whereabouts of a certain little paper you thought I had in my possession. I replied that it is now probably in London, and in the safe keeping of Monsieur Sklavotski, whose person it has not left since he started from St. Petersburg. I see I astonish you. Gentlemen, you have been labouring under a slight misapprehension, and I will now make things clear to you. Allow me to introduce myself as Monsieur Klaboulf, a servant of the Ambassador."

And so saying he tore off his moustache and imperial, wiped the scar from his forehead with a handkerchief, and bowed to us with a smile. We were too much astonished to utter a word, and he went on:

"You see, gentlemen, it was only to be expected that Monsieur Sklavotski would find his journey dangerous and inconvenient, and so he hit upon a simple little plan. He shaved himself, and managed to paint out the scar, so that no one could possibly recognise him. And then he paid me to take the danger and inconvenience upon myself. Ah, it has been a very troublesome journey, I assure you. I only just escaped six inches of cold steel besides other disagreeable adventures. And when I came on shore to-night I was tired out. But I had my work still. I knew someone was watching me, so, in order to draw attention from Monsieur Sklavotski himself, who was travelling with me. I went ostentatiously to the last carriage."

"And where was the Ambassador?" hissed Koravitch.

"Don't worry, my friend. Didn't you see an old clergyman get off the boat? Ah, you didn't think to notice him, did you? Never mind. Well, as soon as the train started I fell asleep, and was only awakened by the somewhat violent intrusion. Then they kindly sent me to sleep again, and the first thing I remember was being lifted in at the window just now—and that's my story."

Koravitch bit his lip with anger.

"Then it's all up?" he said.

"Exactly so, gentlemen. Monsieur Sklavotski intended going straight to the Foreign Office, where he was expected, on reaching town. Your scheme was a bold and clever one, though how I got here I don't know. And now that you have failed what do you intend to do with me? I presume you bear me no ill-will; and, as we've both played our little part, there's an end of it."

"Curse you," said Koravitch.

"Oh, of course, if you like. Well, gentlemen, I'm in your hands. What are you going to do with me?"

"You take it pretty coolly," said Koravitch.

"Why, yes; I've been accustomed to dangerous predicaments."

"I like your courage."

The man bowed.

"Are you willing to solemnly swear that you will take no steps against us till the morning?"

"My friends, we had better let the matter end here. I don't want to take any steps against you. Why should I?—the game's ours. If you let me go now, I promise to find my way to the nearest inn, and to say nothing whatever about you. Are you satisfied?"

Well, the end of it was that we agreed to let him go, for we didn't want murder on our hands, and we were rather struck with his coolness. So once more we found ourselves outside the churchyard gate.

"Good night, gentlemen," he said. "You will take more care the next time you try to trick Monsieur Sklavotski. I assure you he's not an easy man to be caught napping—but there, you know it."

He walked off in one direction, and we in another. In a couple of hours we found ourselves in the neighbourhood of C—, and arranged to get a lodging for the night.

We heard afterwards that a signalman saw the escaped carriage running back past his box and gave the alarm. The passengers remaining in the detached coach were "intelligent foreigners," so they were politely told that "they had got into a 'slip coach' that did not work to London. Before starting they should have enquired of the guard, who would have put them in the front part of the train for London." Much excitement was caused when it was found that some of the passengers were missing, but the real state of the case was never known. The result is now a matter of history, though few knew at the time how nearly the settlement of peace came to be frustrated.

A Perilous Ride

It is astonishing how at times the wisest and most careful men are befooled into performing acts of considerable trouble to themselves only to serve a purpose useless to them. Everyone knows the story of Sir Isaac Newton, who, being much annoyed by a cat and her kitten continually crying to come into or go out of his study, made *two* entrances by sawing out pieces from the bottom of the door—a large opening for the cat, and a small one for the kitten! So, in the story about to be related of Koravitch, that astute individual, as will be seen, was once prevailed upon to undertake what proved to be a very dangerous adventure, and certainly by no means to his advantage. But I had better let the chronicler of his exploits relate the details, as follows:

It was on the occasion narrated in a former memoir of my remarkable friend Koravitch—the time when I ran across him in America—that he told me, together with several other personal adventures—some of which have already been narrated—the following extraordinary story. I had been saying to him:

"Well, you certainly seem fated to take part in adventures of the railway. Have you anything else you can tell me in connection with the line?"

He thought for a moment, and then replied:

"Yes; I could tell you several little stories that would interest you. You see, before I turned my hand to political intriguing I had a few years of railway life, mostly in India, where I did a bit of engineering work, besides a few months in Australia. I must tell

153

you some day of an exciting time I had at a little station in the latter country, when some bush-rangers captured the station as a preliminary to boarding the train, and bound the only two occupants—the station-clerk and myself—hand and foot; and another little story of a ride I once had on a locomotive in India, when I was doing driver's duty owing to shortness of hands, and the native fireman 'ran amuck' on the footplate."

"I should think that's about the worst ride you ever had—worse even than the night when we tried to capture Sklavotski, eh?" I asked.

Koravitch removed the cigar he was smoking from between his lips and gazed at it, pondering for a minute or two. Then he said, slowly:

"The worst ride I ever had? Well, not exactly. There was one that beat it, though I'm not very fond of talking about it, because I made such a fool of myself on one occasion. It was a nasty experience, though, and I wouldn't go through it again in a hurry, I can tell you."

"Where was it—India?"

"No, England, on a 'racing' train—the Scotch express."

"How did it—"

"There, don't ask me any more questions about it. I suppose you want to hear the whole yarn, so you may as well have it. You remember the great 'race to the North' of a few years ago, don't you?"

"Rather! I took a great deal of interest in it at the time."

"Humph! Well, there's a little incident connected with that race that may re-awaken your interest when you hear of it, for I don't expect it's known to you. And, moreover, it will serve to explain why one of the racing trains went wrong on one occasion."

"Which—the Great 'North Eastern' or the—"

"Didn't I tell you not to ask too many questions? Now let me begin at the beginning. At the time of the 'race' I was living in the neighbourhood of Tottenham Court Road—the old place, you know—and, if you will mind back to that particular year, you will remember that our 'Secret Society' was more than usually busy.

Several important political intrigues were in operation, and some of our most cherished interests were at stake. More than one of the 'heads' of the Society had come over to England, and in one way or another our work was well cut out.

"It was one morning towards the end of August that I received by post—what was not very unusual for me—a mysterious missive, which began with the secret name by which I was known in the Society, and read thus:

"'Use every effort to prevent Scotch Express 8 p.m. from Newston to-morrow (Thursday) arriving at Aberdeen before Great East Northern train. Most important. See papers.'

"This letter was signed by a very influential member of the Society, and I had no doubt that some important interest was at stake. The day on which I received the letter was Thursday, so, if I was to carry out the order, there was certainly no time to be lost. A last night's paper was lying on my table, and, heeding the warning at the end of the letter, I took it up and scanned it. My attention was arrested by the following paragraphs, which seemed to bear on the case in point:

"'The Queen is still staying at Balmoral. She drove out yesterday accompanied by the Princess Beatrice.

"'It is rumoured that the Prime Minister will pay a special visit to Her Majesty, travelling by the Scotch Express to-morrow evening. This visit is said to be occasioned by fresh complications which have arisen in the Bulgarian Question.'

"Not being satisfied, however, with this, I sent out for a morning paper, and found still more to interest me. There was a paragraph something to this effect:

"'Count von Scheuzinger, Envoy Extraordinary from the Austrian Government, is expected to arrive in London late this afternoon. His Excellency will seek the earliest opportunity for an interview with the Queen, and will in all probability proceed to Aberdeen immediately after a brief visit to the Foreign Office.'

"I began to see daylight. Evidently it was wished that this individual should be able to steal a march on the Premier, and the latter had selected the 'West Northern Route' for his journey northward.

I turned to Bradshaw, and hunted up the trains from Aberdeen to Ballater. The 'Queen's Special' left the former at 3.50 a.m. That was too early for either express to catch. The next train from Aberdeen was at 7.10, and at the time of the 'race' either express would catch it easily. So the only alternative at which I could arrive was that the foreign ambassador, if he reached Aberdeen before the Prime Minister, would *drive* to Balmoral. At all events, one thing was clear, and that was that I was ordered to delay the West Northern express. Again I turned to the paper, and read the following:

"THE RACE TO THE NORTH.

"'Yesterday morning the West Northern express was again to the front in the railway race, arriving at Aberdeen at 5.15 a.m., while its rival from Queen's Cross reached that station at 5.31. Last night both trains started at 8 o'clock, the drivers keenly alive to the work required of them, but, of course, we go to press too early to know the result of their respective journeys. To-night, however, it is anticipated that the race will be more exciting that ever, for the West Northern officials state that they will not only run the express in two portions, but that the first half will only consist of four coaches, and they are pretty well determined that it will not only beat their rival, but also prove a record run. Those who favour the Great East Northern Route will also be interested to hear that every possible pains are being taken in order that to-night's run shall also be a record.'

"Here was a pretty problem for me to work out! I was accustomed to all sorts of intrigues and risks, but to undertake the delaying of a special racing train seemed rather a large order. I sallied forth, trying to hatch some scheme, and wended my way first to Queen's Cross. Here it was my luck, on pretending to be a representative of the Press, to get a brief interview with the man who had been told off to drive the train on its first stage that night.

"'Shall we beat 'em, sir?' he remarked. 'Can't say, I'm sure. It's a ticklish point. They've had the pull of us yet, for, you see, although they've 540 miles to our 523, they've got an advantage in being able to pick up water as they go along, and so their tenderweight's a good deal less than ours. They've got a bit better track, I believe, too, though it's a stiff pull up the Snap bank between Breston and Carline. Of course, we shall do our best, but I wouldn't like to promise you the G.E.N.'ll win.'

"This was discouraging, and I sought the rival terminus. There I managed to learn that every effort was being made to run a record that night, and that it would be very surprising if the G.E.N. got the better of them. I tried to get into the engine sheds in the hope of having a chance to tamper with the locomotive that was going to do the first stage of the journey, or at least to get at the driver. But it was all of no use. The officials seemed particularly reticent, and I could get no information whatever. Tired and cross, I returned to my rooms to rest as best I could and think out the situation. All sorts of ideas presented themselves to my mind: going down the line, capturing some lonely signal-box, and keeping the signals against the express; setting a red light on the line to stop the train, as I did once on the Nord Belge Railway; but nothing seemed feasible, and at length I determined to travel myself on the express, in the hope that some unforeseen opportunity would turn up and help me to delay the train. With this purpose in my mind I started from my lodgings some little time after seven o'clock in the evening. It was darker than usual for the time of year, for the sky had become overcast with heavy clouds, and a severe thunderstorm was threatening to break.

"I was wending my way through some of the back streets in the neighbourhood of N.W. London, where itinerant vendors of fruit and vegetables are apt to expose their wares for sale on barrows, when one of these gentlemen, who was packing up his scales, let a weight slip just as I passed, with the result that it struck my foot in falling.

"'Beg pardon, guv'nor!' he remarked, in answer to my some-what angry ejaculation. ''Ope it ain't 'urt ye, but 'tain't only a two-pounder, and it might have been worse.'

"'Bad enough as it is,' I replied, 'for it caught me a nasty knock.'

"'Better than 'avin' a twenty pun' wyte on yer foot, same as one of my brothers did once—that's enough to lime a bloomin' great elephant.'

"I was about to pass on when a sudden idea struck me, and I turned to the man.

"'What's the biggest weight you have in stock?'

"'Only four pun'. There ain't no use for anything above that on my barrer.'

"'Where can I buy a twenty-pound weight?'

"'Eh! Are yer goin' in fur sellin' coals, guv'nor? Well, on the second turnin' to the right there's an ironmonger's shop, where they sell such things; and let me—'

"I was off to the shop before he had finished, and somewhat astonished the proprietor by purchasing a twenty-pound weight, with a bar-handle let into it, and taking it away with me. It was an awkward thing to carry, of course. I had it done up in brown paper, and grasped the handle through this as well as I could. What did I want it for? Wait a minute and you'll see.

"When I reached the portico of the station the storm had begun to break, and, in spite of the fact that it was still only a quarter to eight, darkness had set in. I was very glad of this, as it favoured my plot—in fact, it was necessary that it should be quite dark. As I strolled on to the platform the engine was just backing in with full steam up—one of the well-known compounds of the 'West North-ern' type. Of course there were a number of people looking on, and at first it seemed as though I should not succeed in my plan, which was to travel unobserved on the front of the engine that pulled the 'Scotch Express.'

"Four minutes to eight, and still the opportunity had not come. Then a brilliant idea seized me. One compartment of the train was still unoccupied, except by the light luggage of three passengers, who were standing on the platform, one of whom I recognised as the Prime Minister. To dart into the 'sleeper,' open the opposite door, and get out on the other side was the work of a few seconds, and to my joy I found myself in the six-foot way *between two trains*—the 'Express' and an 'empty' drawn up alongside, so that my movements were quite concealed from observation. Along in between the trains I crept, lugging my big weight with me, past the tender of the engine, past the cab—the driver and fireman being too much engaged on the other side to notice me—past the two sets of driving-wheels peculiar to this type of engine, until I stood close to its front. How I wished at that moment that the West Northern Railway built their engines on the 'bogie' system, for, of course, that would have given me a much larger space in front of the smoke-box. But I screwed up my courage, placed the weight on the narrow platform in front of the engine, and prepared to spring on myself as soon as she started.

"Nor had I very long to wait, for, punctually to the moment, the driver opened the regulator, and off she steamed on her journey north, with Screwe as her first stopping-place, *unless I managed that it should be otherwise.* At the same moment I grasped the frame and drew myself up on to the narrow platform in front, taking care to crouch down as much as possible, so as to avoid being seen by anyone on the platform. As we cleared the roof of the terminus the rain pelted down in torrents, and before we reached the first tunnel I was wet to the skin. The darkness had become intense, for which I was only too thankful, as it prevented me from being seen. By the time we ran through Williamsden Junction the speed was very great, and it was as much as I could do to hold on by the vacuum brake-pipe in front as I lay with my knees drawn up on my narrow and jolting resting-place.

"Out into the country and the black night we raced, running against time and our rival of the Great East Northern, with the blast thundering up the chimney close behind me, and the good engine quivering with the strain. No joke even to be on the footplate behind a comfortable cab on such a night; but to be riding where I was might strike a feeling of uneasiness into the heart of many a man bolder than myself.

"Once I was in great peril of being discovered. I happened to raise myself from my crouching position for a moment, holding on to the hand-rail in front of the chimney, when, as I looked back, I saw the fireman coming to the front with his oil-can. In horror I crouched round to the opposite side, stooping as far as possible in case the driver should see me through the weather glass. Fortunately the fireman went back the way he had come, or I must, of course, have been caught.

"But the worst was to come, for I had stationed myself there for a purpose, and, as our head-light shone upon the narrow trough of water between the rails at Thorney, I laid hold of my weight and prepared to act. But, no, we were not to pick up water here; the scoop was not let down, I knew, because I heard no splash. So on we went, until I was chilled to the bone with the rain and rush through the storm, until at length we reached the top of the long gradient that rises more or less all the way between London and Wing, and were dashing down at fearful speed through Sheddington and Laytown.

"When we were through Bletchton I prepared to act once more, and presently I had grasped the weight by its handle and was holding it over the buffer-plate exactly in the centre, as far down as I could possibly reach—right over the middle of the track. It seemed ages, and I thought I could never hold on; but presently I caught a glimpse of something shining ahead, and we were over the watertrough at Castledean.

"Splash! The driver had let down the scoop, and there was not an instant to lose. Reaching as far down as possible, I dropped the twenty-pound weight into the water-trough between the rails. A moment afterwards and there was a crash—faint enough beneath the roar of the locomotive, but sufficient to distinguish in it the ripping sound of tearing iron. Immediately the splashing ceased, and I knew the weight had done its work. It had fallen into the trough, and, naturally, the scoop struck it as it came along and was completely destroyed, the effect being that it was impossible to pick up any more water *en route*, and that the driver would be compelled to stop and replenish his tank before he reached Screwe.

"And stop he had to. I very soon knew by the sound of the engine and her blast that he had notched her up as much as he dared, and was afraid to open his damper much. The speed slackened slightly, and it was evident that it would be a ticklish job for him to get as far as Mugby without his lead plug blowing off. But, as I afterwards heard, he understood his engine thoroughly, and he did it. I was too much occupied in getting off unobserved as we drew up at Mugby to notice things, but I just heard him shout to someone on the platform:

"'Look alive there with that water! It's a fine night's work this! What's up? Why, someone must have fouled the road and put a big block of iron or something in the water-troughs. We'll not win the race to-night, that's certain!'

"Nor did they. What the West Northern's record would have been without that stop it's impossible to say, for as it was they ran into Aberdeen at 4.51 the next morning. But the Great East Northern was there already, a good eleven minutes in front of them at Linaber Junction, and for once the West Northern had to take a 'back seat,' for of course it was on their portion of the track that the mishap occurred.

"And what was the result, do you ask? Did Count Scheuzinger reach Balmoral before the Prime Minister, and why was it that the Secret Society wanted him to do so? No, the Austrian Ambassador, as it happened, had travelled down with the Prime Minister by the West Northern Route, and I had been made a fool of. How? Why, the next evening, after arriving back in town utterly done up with my exertions, you may imagine my feelings when a letter came by the last post for me, which read somewhat as follows:

"'My dear sir,—I really cannot refrain from writing both to thank you for a service you have, as I suppose, rendered me, and also to congratulate you on what must have been an exceedingly daring exploit. But let me explain myself.

"'I may as well state that for some time past I have been acquainted with the methods of your Secret Society, and, in fact, in order to further certain

ends of my own have succeeded in more than once
penetrating into some of your meetings. It was at one
of these that I first became aware of your daring and
ability in a certain adventure of the railway undertaken by yourself, and based upon your technical
knowledge and skill; and I well remembered how it
was said at the time that when any difficult enterprise connected with the line had to be undertaken,
you were the man, *par excellence*, to evolve the
scheme and to carry it out. It was this that led me to
select you to aid me in a little matter that concerned
myself. The fact is, there has been a good deal of
betting lately on the 'Race to the North,' and, of
course, the odds have been the last few days very
much against the East Coast Route. Being myself one
of that class of people known as 'prodigal sons,' and
not yet having eschewed the husks of fortune for the
ways of piety, it occurred to me that there was something in taking heavy odds as above if I could claim
your assistance in delaying the West Coast train. I
accordingly wrote to you, taking the liberty to sign
myself as one of those whom I knew you would obey,
suggesting that you should stop the express from
Newston, while certain paragraphs in the papers to
which I mysteriously alluded probably lent colour
to my request

"'At all events, when I saw you at Newston platform last night (for naturally I was there) I felt sure
that my little plot had succeeded—especially when I
observed that you had chosen a somewhat novel
method of travelling northwards, for I just caught
sight of you in front of the engine as the train started.
What was your exact method of procedure I do not
know, but as there was a breakdown I naturally sur-
mise that you had something to do with it. Your journey must have been, to say the least of it, somewhat

unpleasant, but you will have the satisfaction of knowing that you have earned the gratitude and substantially increased the wealth of

"'Yours very truly,

"'East Coast Route.

"'P.S.—I am sorry I cannot sign my real name but the reason must be obvious to you.'

"And so," added Koravitch, "you see I had been fearfully and wonderfully sold. I never discovered who the individual was that I had unwittingly served; but, at all events, that was the most terrible ride I ever had on a locomotive, and I don't think I'd care to undertake such an experience again."

NOTE.—It is worth recording that in the race to the North of 1895 the times of arrival at Aberdeen on the last three days were as follows:—

	West Coast.	East Coast.
August 20th	4.58	5.11
August 21st	4.51	4.40
August 22nd	4.32	6.23

Also I have it on reliable information that on the night of the 21st an L. and N.W. engine broke down in some way between Bletchley and Crewe and considerably delayed the train. I mention the coincidence as a remarkable one. Perhaps "Koravitch" has explained another railway incident!

THE MYSTERY OF THE BOAT EXPRESS

It was a gusty, stormy morning in January, with the wind blowing a cold rain from the north-west. There were very few passengers by the Great Southern Boat train to Porthampton that morning, for it was not the day one would choose, if one could help it, for a cross-Channel journey, especially as the telegram from the coast on the station notice-board proclaimed that the Channel was "rough and stormy."

It wanted but three minutes to the starting of the train. A passenger came running from the booking office, a man of about forty years of age, with fair beard and moustache, carrying a small Gladstone bag, a soft hat pulled well down over his eyes, and the collar of his great coat turned up.

"What class, sir?" asked the guard as he drew near.

"Second—please," replied the man.

The guard noticed that he spoke with a slight foreign accent, and opened the door of an empty compartment. The passenger glanced hurriedly along the train, and then got in.

"Will you please lock the door? I do not wish to be disturbed."

The guard took the proffered half-crown, drew a key from his pocket, and turned the lock. The man pulled up the window.

One or two more belated passengers came hurrying to the train—one just as it was about to start. The latter looked hastily into each carriage as he moved along the train.

"Now then, sir—in here, please!" And the guard opened the door of a compartment, blew his whistle, and the train started.

At Porthampton the guard remembered the locked door, and ran down the platform to release the passenger. He opened the door, and gave a start of surprise.

The occupant of the compartment was huddled up in a heap upon the floor on the further side, his head, with its back to the guard, leaning against the edge of the seat. And staining the cushion of the seat, and the man's shoulder, were splashes of blood.

The guard gave a cry of alarm; a few station officials and passengers pressed forward. One of the latter, an elderly gentleman, exclaimed:

"Then it was a shot I heard!"

"I'll trouble you for your name and address, then, please sir," said a quiet voice. "I am one of the company's detectives."

The other produced his card.

"I am the manager of the City and Southern Bank," he said.

"All right, sir—now let's have a look at the poor chap, and you shall tell us your story later. Someone fetch a doctor."

He went into the compartment, and gently raised the head of the unfortunate man.

"He's dead, I'm afraid—looks as if he shot himself."

"There's a revolver on the seat," exclaimed the guard.

The detective took it up, glanced at it sharply, and put it into his pocket.

"Was he travelling alone?"

"Yes," replied the guard.

"Anyone in the next compartments?"

"This is at the end of the coach. No one was in the next. I'm certain of that."

A doctor came bustling up. They lifted the body on to the seat, and the medical man made an examination.

"A bullet through the brain," he said. "Life must have been extinct for nearly an hour."

"You say you heard a shot, sir?" asked the detective of the bank manager.

"Yes—some time ago. I thought it was a fog signal. I little imagined it meant suicide. Do you want me? I am on my way to Paris, but I shall be back to-morrow."

"You could attend the inquest here if we held it to-morrow evening?"

"Certainly."

The whistle of the steamer sounded, and the little group of passengers hurried away. The detective looked at the doctor, raising his eyebrows.

"Queer, I think, sir?" he asked.

The doctor nodded.

"Half-a-minute," said the other.

He darted out of the carriage.

"Jenkins," he said to a subordinate on the platform, "it's lucky you're here. I want you to board the boat and cross on her. Bring back an account of all the passengers, if you can—there's not a score of them."

"Very good, sir."

The detective went back to the carriage.

"I understand a revolver was found," said the doctor. "Where?"

The other showed the exact spot on the seat where the weapon had been lying. Then he took it from his pocket and showed it to the doctor. The latter examined it.

"As you say—it's queer," he said. "D'you see what he's got in his right hand?"

The detective looked.

"A handkerchief!" he exclaimed. "Will you see about getting the body to the waiting-room, sir? It may as well lie there. I'll examine the clothes afterwards. I've some work to do here first."

He was a long time in the compartment, and before he left he summoned the guard once more. That night the evening papers had a paragraph stating that an unknown man had apparently committed suicide by shooting himself in the Porthampton boat express. The detective smiled when he read it. His smile changed into a frown, however, when Jenkins returned by the night boat and handed in his report.

"Nothing suspicious about any of them," he said.

"Then he must have slipped off on this side—out of the station," replied his chief enigmatically, "I've bungled it a little."

At the inquest the guard was the first to give evidence. He mentioned that the deceased had spoken to him with a German accent.

"How do you know that?" asked the coroner.

"You can't be guard of the boat train for five years running, sir, without picking up hints. I can generally spot a Frenchman or a German."

He concluded by giving a brief account of his discovery of the body. The coroner asked a few questions, adding:

"No one else could have got in with him?"

"Impossible, sir. The further door was locked already, and, as I said, he asked for the other to be locked."

"He seemed to want to be alone?" asked a juryman.

"Yes."

The juryman nodded sagaciously.

"Suicide—premeditated," he murmured.

Mr. Clinton, the bank manager, was allowed to give evidence next, as he was anxious to catch the last train back to town.

"I was travelling in the compartment next but two to the deceased's," he said, "and was half dozing over a book when I heard a slight report. The wind was very high and both windows were shut."

"A report of a pistol?"

"I didn't think so at the time. There were three other passengers with me, and we all imagined it was probably a detonator on the line, such as is used in fogs or in warning the driver that a gang of men are at work. I am interested in railway matters, and I jumped up at once and looked out of both windows. There was nothing to be seen, and the train did not slacken speed, so we all thought no more about it till I was told at Porthampton what had happened."

"When did you hear the shot?"

"About half an hour after leaving London."

Next came the doctor. He stated, concisely, that death had been caused by a bullet which had entered the deceased's head at the right temple, passed through the skull, and carried away a piece of the bone on the further side. He agreed that the time which had elapsed might reasonably coincide with the shot that Mr. Clinton had heard, and described how he found the body lying on the floor close to the further door.

"As a man might naturally have fallen after he had shot himself?" asked the juryman who had spoken before.

"I don't think so," replied the doctor shortly.

A sensation ran round the court.

"Why not?" asked the coroner.

"There are circumstances in the case which are baffling. The wound was just in the position likely for a man who had shot himself with a pistol, holding it in his right hand with the muzzle against his temple. Death must have been instantaneous. But the strange thing is that the deceased was clutching a handkerchief with his right hand, and that there were no powder marks round the wound. The shot must have been fired at a further distance."

"But," said the coroner, "I understand that a revolver was found in the compartment?"

"It was found before I was on the spot," replied the doctor, "and the next witness will tell you more about it. It is not my professional business," he went on, "to hazard speculation; but I do say emphatically that, in my opinion, it is certainly not a case of suicide."

The detective corroborated what the doctor had said.

"Tell us about the revolver, please," said the coroner.

"It was lying on the seat—away from the deceased. It was loaded in every chamber, and had not been discharged recently. The barrel was quite clean inside.

"I examined the compartment carefully," he went on, "and although, as the doctor has told you, the bullet went through the skull, carrying away a piece of the bone, I could find neither bone nor bullet—nor any mark of either—in the carriage."

"Was the window open?" asked a juryman.

"Yes—at the end where the body had fallen. The other was shut. I know what your question implies; but, if the man had been shot by someone outside the open window, the bullet mark would have been found at the opposite end of the compartment. If, on the other hand, the bullet, after penetrating the skull, had gone out of the open window, the shot must have been fired inside, which appears impossible, especially as both doors were found locked; and the murderer could not have opened the other window from outside and then fired through it."

"What is your opinion, then?" asked the Coroner.

"Murder," he replied, "but *how* I cannot say."

"You have taken steps?"

"As far as is possible."

He stated further that there was no clue to identify the dead man. "He carried no papers, his bag only contained clothing, and his linen was not marked."

"Nothing else?"

The witness hesitated.

"There was something which *might* be a possible clue, sir; but I will ask you not to make me mention it—at present."

An adjournment was made for a fortnight at the request of the police. But at the adjournment the detective said bluntly that he had no more evidence, and the inspector of police who was in charge of the case was equally reticent.

Finally, the jury returned the rather strange verdict of "Found shot—apparently by some person unknown," and the newspapers curtly referred to the case as "another unsolved railway mystery."

So much for the story. I had the sequel from the very man who unravelled the mystery, now retired from business on a comfortable pension. He was telling me some of his exploits one day, when I happened to mention the Porthampton Murder.

"That was a curious affair," I said. "You never solved it, did you?"

He filled and lit his pipe thoughtfully.

"I can't say I didn't do that," he replied; "but"—and he laughed—"I wasn't allowed to get the credit of it. The official police stopped me. Look here," he went on, "it happened five years ago, and is forgotten; I don't mind telling you the tale, if you like."

"I'd better begin at the start," he continued. "I was pretty convinced from the first that the murderer—if there were one—had been on the train, and probably given us the slip at Porthampton Station. But I had very little to go upon. As a sort of forlorn hope, however, it dawned upon me that something might be discovered if I found the exact spot on the line where the bank manager—Mr. Clinton—had heard the shot. He had said it was about half an hour after leaving London. I ran up to town the morning after the inquest, and called on him.

"'Can't you recollect exactly *where* it was on the line?' I asked.

"He thought for a minute.

"'Let me see—yes, I can. We ran through Hazleton Station a minute or so afterwards.'

"'Hazleton;' I exclaimed. 'A big village, I think? Now, Mr. Clinton, when you looked out, you're sure you saw no one—on the footboard, for example?'

"'Positive. I couldn't have helped seeing anyone if he had been there. I glanced both up and down the track on both sides.'

"I took the next train to Hazleton, determined to patrol the line for a mile or so up from the station. It was just a remote possibility that I might find something—perhaps, even, a pistol!

"It was a fruitless search, however. So, giving it up, I made up my mind to seek a place of refreshment. A road ran parallel with the up side of the line, quite close. I climbed over the palings for easier walking, and got into the road. There were a few small houses, almost new, of the suburban villa type, for Hazleton was getting a name as a picturesque neighbourhood, being only half-an-hour's run from town.

"As I walked along, thinking that the train must have been passing close by the spot when the mysterious tragedy happened, my glance fell on the gatepost of one of the villas. On it was the name of the house, 'The Maples.'

"I gave a start, and I'll tell you why. You may remember that at the inquest I stated there was a small, possible clue, which I wished to keep to myself. In the pocket of the murdered man I had found a current number of a newspaper, on the outside cover of which was scrawled in pencil those very words— 'The Maples.'

"At once I made up my mind. I found my way to the only news-paper shop in the village, and made some inquiries. At what hour could I have a morning paper delivered? I was told the newspaper train arrived pretty early, and that the boy started on his rounds at seven. I chatted away, leading the conversation up to 'The Maples.' Yes, they sent papers to that house.

"'Who lives there?' I asked casually.

"'Foreigners, I think, sir. They haven't been long at Hazleton. I've quite forgotten their name for the moment.'

"I was evidently on a track. Sometimes boldness is the best action for discovering things, so I determined to call at 'The Maples.' The point was this: The paper found on the man had evi-dently been left at this house the very morning he was murdered. The obvious deduction was that the poor wretch himself had been in the house.

"The door was opened by a fair-haired young woman, with a pale, anxious face. I saw, at a glance, she had been crying.

"'What is it, please, you want?' she asked nervously, with a strong foreign accent.

"I came to the point at once.

"'Information about a fellow-countryman of yours who left this house early on Tuesday morning and was found dead in the Porthampton boat express,' I said.

"She clasped her hands together, and gave a little cry.

"'*Ach!*' she exclaimed, 'are you of the *English* police?'

"'Not exactly,' I replied, 'I am in the service of the railway com-pany.'

"She hesitated. I thought she was about to faint. Then, pulling herself together with an effort, she said:

"'Will you come in? You need not fear—there is no one else in the house.'

"She led me into a sitting-room, sat down, wringing her hands, and said, in a low voice:

"'He was my brother!'

"'Your brother? But if you knew—why have you not identified him?'

"She shook her head.

"'I was afraid—they might kill me, too—*Himmel*—but you do not know how I am suffering.'

"'Then you know he was murdered?' I asked in surprise.

"She nodded.

"'I saw it,' she gasped, 'it has haunted me ever since—it was terrible—and I could do nothing. Poor André!'

"'Come,' I said, 'you must tell me everything. I want to be your friend.'

"'But—but,' she faltered, 'it is the police whom I fear—and the others. You do not know.'

"'My dear young lady,' I said, 'I assure you you have nothing to fear from the police. They are only too anxious to find the murderer. And, if you know, you can help them.'

"She shook her head again.

"'You do not understand,' she said. There was a long pause. Then she spoke again, more calmly:

"'I will tell you,' she said. 'Since you have discovered so much. I was afraid of this. My name is Cambon. André and I are natives of Alsace, of French extraction, but of German nationality. And, you see, we were both in the Secret Service of the German Government. I cannot tell you how it all happened, but Herr Otto Schuster had us in his hands—he is a bad man. It began by accident; a little sketch that I made of one of your English forts, and André mentioned it. Schuster paid us for it; we were poor, and ever since he has held us in his hand.'

"'There is a retired officer of your artillery living here in Hazleton, Major Dent. He had invented a new gun, and your War Office was going to make experiments with it. Schuster told us we must come down here and try and get the drawings, so he took this house for us. We got to know the Major—I taught his little girl German, and—well I got hold of the plans and made a rough copy.'

"'And sold it to Schuster?'

"'No. That is why it all happened. It was Pierre Duprez who interfered. You do not know him? Oh, he is one of the cleverest spies of the French Government, and he found out what we were doing. He came here and saw my brother, just as we were about to send the plans to Schuster. He appealed to André's French parentage—he entreated—reviled him for being a false Alsatian—for many of us still hate the Germans, though we obey them. And André gave way. He gave the plans to Pierre Duprez, and Duprez was to pay him twenty thousand francs—to his order at a bank in Paris. We meant to retire then—to get away from the power of Otto Schuster. That was last Monday, and Duprez took the plans back with him to London.

"'It was early on Tuesday morning that the warning came, by the first post. Pierre Duprez sent it. He said that Schuster had found out, and advised my brother to go to Paris at once. There was scarcely time to arrange anything, for André saw that he must take the next train to town to catch the boat express. I packed up a few things in his bag, and he put in his revolver. He was very nervous and afraid of Schuster, and said he should keep the weapon ready during the whole journey. I was to follow him in a few days' time. Then we arranged a signal, so that I should know he had caught the express. He was to wave his handkerchief from the window as the train passed this house.

"'Can you guess now? Schuster must have tracked him to the train, but was too late to get in with him. I stood just outside the front door, waiting. Then the train came in sight, and I saw André leaning out of the window, waving his handkerchief. I waved mine in return. Schuster must have seen me doing so, and that evidently gave him the idea that André was leaning out of the carriage, and that an unexpected chance of killing him had offered itself.

"'For, suddenly, just as the train was opposite the house, I saw a man's head and arm come out of a window two compartments behind my brother. Something shone in his hand; he leant forward, took aim at André, there was a flash, and I saw my brother fall back into the carriage, while Schuster, for it was near enough to recognise him, immediately retired into his.'

"Now I understood why no traces of bone or bullet were found. The latter went through Cambon's head while it was outside the carriage.

"Well, by strong arguments, I prevailed upon his sister to go to town with me at once. Now she had told her story a new idea seemed to have got possession of her. The phase of fright was passing. Vengeance was taking its place.

"'Yes, I will go with you,' she said, 'I don't care what your police do with me—if they find Otto Schuster.'

"But I had my doubts and said nothing. It was as I had expected. The Chief Inspector at Scotland Yard took down the information without comment, thought for a few minutes, and then said:

"'I will ask you to stay here a short time, I am going to the Foreign Office. This is a very peculiar matter, and I cannot handle it without advice.'

"In an hour's time he was hack. A grim smile was on his face. He turned to Fräulein Cambon.

"'It may be some satisfaction to you to know that any charge against you for purloining valuable secrets has fallen through. Major Dent is not so artless as you supposed. His drawings were under lock and key at the War Office.'

"'But—!' she began, in astonishment.

"'What you copied were old designs, of no value,' he interrupted drily, 'as M. Duprez will doubtless discover before long.'

"She sprang from her seat.

"'So!' she cried, 'André has been murdered for nothing! But you will find this Schuster—ah, you English police are so clever! You will hang him, yes—'

"The Chief waved his hand.

"'Madam,' he said, 'my instructions are simply to see that you leave the country at once. With the rest we have nothing to do. When one enters the Secret Service of a Government one takes all risks, and you and your brother ought to have known this. You will understand,' he went on, turning to me, 'that nothing is to be done by us, and that you are to proceed no further.'

"'You will not find Schuster. You will not avenge my poor brother?' she shrieked.

"He shook his head.

"'Then,' she said, in a low voice, 'I will avenge André myself. I will never rest until—'

"The Chief cut her short. He evidently had little sympathy with spies.

"'You may do what you please, madam, but I warn you that it must not be in this country.'

"Whether she carried out her threat or not I often wonder. At all events Otto Schuster, the German Secret Service agent, was found stabbed in the back in one of the narrow streets of Genoa not a year afterwards, and I have sometimes thought it may have been the sequel to the Porthampton boat express mystery."

How the Express was Saved

The strike on the Mid-Northern Railway was not very prominent in the public eye. The daily papers, full of a murder sensation, had devoted only small paragraphs to it—paragraphs which had been relentlessly slaughtered with blue pencil before they left the sub-editors' room. Passengers on the railway noticed nothing at all. Trains still ran fairly up to the scheduled time, guards and porters took tips as usual. Nothing seemed amiss to the casual eye.

The reason was that only one section of the great army of workers of the Mid-Northern Railway had laid down their arms, or rather their tools, and these particular tools were shovels and pickaxes, and crowbars and spanners. It was a platelayers' strike—based on a shilling a week extra and an obdurate board of directors.

In this particular instance the officials considered the strike was unjustified, a breach of certain contracts made in a recent conciliation, and they had taken the strong line of not only refusing to discuss the men's demands, but also of giving it out that certain of the ringleaders need not trouble to return to work at all. The strike was by no means general; a certain proportion of employees remained on duty, and no trouble had been encountered in obtaining the services of a few hundreds of "out of works."

A dozen men were gathered together in the stuffy little bar of the "Red Lion" at Hillingdon. At all times you would have expected the railway element to predominate in that particular bar, for

Hillingdon was a big junction on the Mid-Northern and the "Red Lion" stood in the very centre of a district, nine-tenths of the inhabitants of which were employed in the Company's service.

The subject of discussion was, naturally, the platelayers' strike.

"Well, there ain't much wrong with the road," remarked the fireman of a goods engine. "Everything up to time. You wouldn't know anything was up at all."

"It's those blacklegs that are upsetting things," replied a thick-set man with a scowling face who lounged in a corner. "If it wasn't for them takin' on our job you wouldn't ha' had such an easy run down."

The fireman laughed. He was young and cheeky.

"They'll want someone to take on *your* job for good and all, Yates," he said, "from what I hear."

Joe Yates darted an angry look at him and replied with an oath. He was one of the men whom the Company had refused to take back, he and another named Ford being the ringleaders of discontent at Hillingdon.

"Steady on, Tom," growled one of the men to the fireman, "your tongue's too loose, my lad."

"Got many chaps at work up the line?" asked another platelayer.

The fireman nodded.

"Yes—a lot. You haven't even stopped 'em putting down the new rails 't'other side o' Cranbury. There's a good forty of 'em there—hard at it."

"Ought to be shot," muttered Joe Yates, "what business have they to take the bread out o' the mouths o' us, eh?"

The fireman drained his glass, and replaced it on the counter.

"Might as well ask what business have you chaps to take the bread out o' the mouths o' your wives and children," he answered as he went to the door.

With another oath Joe Yates sprang forward. A few hands were stretched out to stop him, but he had almost gained the door when a newcomer entered and barred the way—a tall, sinewy man in corduroys.

"Chuck it, Joe," he exclaimed. "If it's that young fool of a Stimson you're after he ain't worth wastin' muscle on. Come and have a drink with me."

It was Harry Ford himself. By mutual consent the others dropped the subject of the strike while the two men drank sullenly and in silence. Presently Ford said to the other:

"Coming out?"

"Don't mind if I do."

"Come on then. Good-night, all."

It was raining steadily, and very dark. The two men walked slowly along the street, and then Ford led the way to a waste, unfrequented bit of ground.

"Look here," he remarked suddenly, "it's not much of a look-out for you and me, is it Joe?"

"That it ain't—curse 'em!" replied the other.

"Curse 'em by all means, but *that* won't do 'em no harm. Ain't you game for something more?"

"What d'ye mean, Harry?"

"I heard a bit o' news just now. The G.M.s* coming down to Hillingdon to-night—by the express that gets here at 11.53."

"Well, what o' that?"

Ford's voice sank to a low whisper.

"Well, supposing that train was to run off the metals just afore it got to Buckley Bridge."

"Eh?"

"I say, supposing a length o' rail was taken out just t'other side o' the bridge—chance for the whole train and the G.M. in it to pitch into the river, eh?"

"What are you driving at, Harry?" asked Joe Yates, sinking his voice to a whisper.

"A spanner and a hammer 'ud soon do it," replied the other, "and the night's made for it."

"But—if we were seen?"

* General Manager.

"Look here, Joe. How far off is Buckley Bridge?"

"Matter o' four miles up the line."

"Then if we were seen here in Hillingdon at a quarter to eleven no one 'ud even suspect us o' the job, eh?"

"But how would we get there in time?"

"The 10.55 goods to Wharnton. Leaves No. 5 siding. We could easily get into a truck. And she has to slow down at Buckley signal box to get the staff for the Wharnton branch. We could drop off there and be right on the job. Are you game for it?"

"Done!"

"Right. You show yourself in the 'Red Lion' later on; I'll go to some other pub. Meet me alongside the goods just before 10.55. She'll be marshalled ready for starting. And bring a spanner. I'll get hold of a crow-bar."

Buckley Bridge, or "Bridge No. 74," as it was technically called, was an iron bridge, of some fifty yards in length, spanning the river, some four miles away from Hillingdon on the up line. It was used for the service of trains only, and was guarded by a light iron railing on either side.

A little way on the Hillingdon side of the bridge stood a signal box. This box guarded the junction where the single branch line to Wharnton struck off from the main line. The customary signals were placed to protect this junction, of which two only need be described in the present narrative. These were the "distant" and the "home" signals which warned approaching trains on the down main line, and they were both on the side of the bridge farthest away from the signal box.

The "distant" signal was half-a-mile up the line, the "home" signal about a hundred yards before the bridge. There was, therefore, ample protection for the down trains, as if the junction or the block beyond it on the Hillingdon side were not clear the train would be brought to a stop well before it reached the bridge.

Beyond the bridge, where the main line ran on to the signal box, it curved slightly to the right, so that the man on duty could not actually see the down home signal. But, by means of that

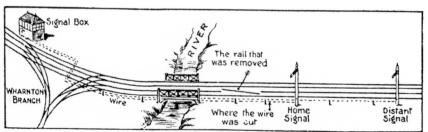

Map showing clearly the position of the signals, the box, and the bridge where the accident was planned to take place. Only signals necessary for the story are shown.

wonderful little instrument, the electric repeater, he could tell its position exactly, the miniature semaphore arm in the little glass case in front of him imitating every movement of the signal itself as he pulled or replaced the lever.

In the signal box were two men, the signalman on duty and a young linesman. It was the duty of the latter to patrol a certain length of the road with a view to inspecting and repairing electric and signalling apparatus. Some trifling defect had been found that evening in the interlocking gear beneath the Buckley box, and Charles Palmer had been working at it overtime. He had now come up from the network of bars and wires below the box, and was smoking his pipe in the cabin.

He was packing up his tools as he smoked. One or two, such as his folding rule and a small pair of wire cutters, he put in his pocket from force of habit. The rest he arranged in his bag.

A ring came at the bell.

"The Wharnton Goods," said the signalman, as he returned the answer and pulled the levers that "took off" the up main home and distant signals.

"You'll be wanting the staff for her," said Palmer.

"That's right."

He went up to the curious-looking electric machine that held the staves for the Wharnton Branch, signalled forward to the block ahead on the single line, obtained, by means of electric release, a long brass staff from the machine, and then threw open his window and peered down the line. Two flickering lights, a green above a white, showed that the goods train was approaching. The engine came to a standstill just beside the box, and the signalman ran down the steps and handed the staff to the driver.

"A rough night, Bill."

"No mistake," replied the driver, as he opened the throttle valve. "Good-night, mate!"

Out of a low truck midway along the goods train Yates and Ford dropped stealthily to the ground on the side farther from the signal box, climbed the fence bordering the line, and, stooping down, hurried along parallel with the track through fields until they came to the bank of the river. Here they turned aside, reclimbed the fence, and passed over the iron bridge.

"Got your spanner, Joe?" asked Ford, in a low voice.

"All right."

"There's not too much time—we shall have to look sharp."

"Can't start till the local's gone by."

"Ah, I forgot that. Hullo—there's the signal for her."

"Crash!" went the arm of the down home signal which stood about a hundred yards beyond them. The two men hid themselves as the local train came by, and then sprang on to the track.

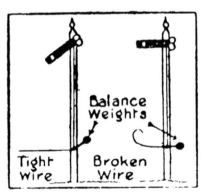

Diagram showing the mechanism of the balance weights and signals.

"Here you are," said Ford, "we'll soon have it out. I only helped to put it in three weeks ago," he added, with a grim chuckle. "You take that end, I'll tackle this."

Rails are secured to each other at the ends by flat pieces of metal known as "fish plates," to which they are fixed by bolts. The object of the two men was to remove one of the rails immediately in front of the bridge, rightly calculating that if the engine ran off at that point the train would probably be wrecked in the river.

It was work to which they were well accustomed, and accustomed to do it smartly as well. As a rule old rails are replaced by new ones without in any way interfering with the running of the trains, and over and over again the passenger little dreams as he runs along securely that a new rail was inserted only a few minutes before.

With their stout, curved spanners, they loosened and unscrewed the nuts which fastened the bolts holding the two fish plates to the rails. In a very short time the fish plates themselves were off and lying alongside the line. Then came the knocking out of the wooden "keys" which held the rail in the "chairs" fixed down to the sleepers. They looked round once or twice, for they could not loosen the keys without a slight noise of hammering, but the wind was rising, drowning all sounds. Then the rail lay loose.

Next came the supreme effort. Long rails weighing 106 lb. to the yard take some moving. Both men were strong, but it wanted all their strength put forth before the rail was lifted out of the chairs and fell with a muffled clang at the side of the line.

Then the unexpected happened. Charles Palmer had started for his home, and his home was in a village the further side of the river from the signal box. There was a road bridge two miles away; there was the convenient railway bridge close at hand. And he, naturally, chose the nearer route. The sky was clearing a little, a waning moon had risen and was showing a pale light through the rain-clouds. Half-way over the bridge he fancied he saw something moving; just as he was over there came the clang of the metal, and when Yates and Ford looked up he was there—right upon them—with his fists clenched.

"You scoundrels!" he cried, as he rushed forward.

Ford, however, was perfectly cool. His brawny arm went out straight from the shoulder, and his fist caught Palmer right on the chin. The young man went down like a log.

"Curse him!" cried Ford beneath his breath, "look sharp, Yates. There's no time to lose. Got any cord or anything?"

"Here's a bit o' stout twine."

"Tie his legs together—ah, would you!" he exclaimed as Palmer made an attempt to cry out. "I'll stuff something in his mouth and tie it in with a handkerchief—we must fix his arms, too. I know—good, he's got leather laces in his boots—that's better than cord."

In five minutes Charles Palmer lay beside the line gagged, his feet tied together and his hands cruelly fastened behind him with his own bootlaces, while Ford and Yates had gained the further side of the river and were hurrying back to Hillingdon along unfrequented by-roads.

They paused once for breath.

"He'll be smashed up," whispered Yates, thinking of Palmer.

"Let him be!" replied the other savagely, "if he isn't we'll have to make tracks—for I believe he recognised us."

Charles Palmer lay for a few minutes half dazed. Then he began to realise not only his own terrible position, but the fact of the gaping void between the line of rail. Nothing could save the express from being wrecked. It was, he knew almost due now.

"Twang—crash!" the sounds came simultaneously. The down home signal was pulled off. He glanced at the place where the post should be. Yes—the extinguishing disc had passed over the white "back light," so that green showed on the other side.

"Twang!" That was for the distant signal. The train was on the block now, and the line was signalled "clear."

And then a desperate thought, arising from a pain in his thigh, came into his mind. If only he could do it! Writhing and twisting he wriggled himself slowly away from the metals to the side of the line. His face touched something cold. Good! It was what he was seeking for—the wire that communicated with the home signal.

A great effort, and he lay with his back to the wire. Could he do it? With extreme difficulty and with the laces cutting into his flesh he managed to get a couple of fingers into his hip pocket, felt for the cutters, drew them slowly out, held them in his hand, and groped for the wire behind him.

The weighted safety lever at the base of the home signal, re-lieved of the tension of the wire, fell, resetting the semaphore arm at "danger," and showing the red light.

A whistle, the grinding of brakes, a shower of sparks along the wheels, and the great express came to a standstill.

What was up? In the signal box the man knew something had given way. The tell-tale repeater stood at "line blocked." The engine whistle clamoured for a clear road. The road was clear. Seizing a lantern he came down from the signal box and ran along the line, past the curve, till he could see the back light.

He waved the lantern for the train to advance slowly, running forward over the bridge as he did so.

Then, with a shout, he turned on the red glass of his lantern and waved it frantically. He had seen the gap in the metals—and the man beside the line. The train was saved!

And to-day Charles Palmer holds a prominent position in the electrical and engineering department of the Mid-Northern.

A Case of Signalling

The 2.15 goods train moved slowly out of No. 14 siding at the big terminal station of Sterrington on the Great Southern Railway, and commenced its ponderous journey on the main up line. To railway men the train was ironically known as the "afternoon flier," a name given to it in scorn and derision. All the way along the line it stopped at every station to pick up empties, and was shunted into every refuge siding in between stations to make way for its betters.

Finally, it accomplished the seventy or eighty odd miles of its journey in something under seven hours, more or less. It was rumoured that at more than one point the brakesman had his regular nap while the driver and fireman comfortably read stray newspapers in their cab.

Along the route they were subjected to mild chaff from porters on platforms or signalmen who hauled them up. "Broken the record to-day, Jim?" "Been racing a funeral?" "What sort o' weather did you leave at Sterrington last week?" These, and similar observations, broke upon the ear of old Jim Harvey, but without the slightest impression.

On the return journey at night he made up for it. He backed his engine on to a "fast mineral" train that came pounding down at twenty or thirty miles an hour, with only three stops to take off loaded trucks until she was held up in Fairdale refuge siding three miles out of Sterrington for fifteen or twenty minutes, to allow of the passing of the night passenger down express.

Jim Harvey stood on the footplate of his dingy, but powerful goods engine, "notching her up" slightly as she took the road and gained in speed, his eyes fixed on the signals in the distance. His grey head turned occasionally to observe the manner in which George Ledbury, his young fireman, put on coal—a task calling for the exercise of more skill than the outsider is aware of.

George Ledbury was a new mate, having only recently been promoted from the footplate of an insignificant "local goods" to work on the main line. He had great visions of the day when he should drive a crack express train like the one that came snorting past them on the down road.

"That'll do," said the driver with a grunt of approbation; "she won't want any more before she gets to the Belton rise."

The fireman put down his short shovel, gave the footplate a brush round, wiped his hands on a bit of waste, and took his place on the other side of the cab. He was a good-looking young man, in spite of the fact that at this particular moment he had a big smudge on one of his cheeks. He gave one the idea of being quick and alert, and there was a twinkle in his blue eyes that spoke of happiness.

They were passing through the suburbs of the large town of Sterrington now, and the streets of small houses had given place to broad avenues with large villas of a superior class. This suburb of Fairdale was noted for its quiet and beauty. Many of the wealthy manufacturers and business men had their houses there, together with a sprinkling of the "retired."

The country began to open out, and fields appeared. About three hundred yards from the line were some half-a-dozen good-sized detached houses standing in their own grounds with their backs to the railway—almost the last houses of the suburb. The fireman's gaze shifted from the signals ahead to one of these houses; he drew a clean-white handkerchief from his pocket, and, turning his back to the driver, suddenly began waving it to and fro with peculiar motion.

Jim Harvey, glancing over his shoulder across the cab, suddenly caught sight of these mysterious movements. He was about to speak, when, looking beyond over the field, he saw something else which brought a grin over his weather-beaten face.

Standing at an open window at the back of one of the aforesaid houses a female figure in a white apron could just be discerned, and there came the answering waving of a handkerchief.

"Is she a pretty girl, George?"

George Ledbury turned round, stuffed the handkerchief into his pocket, and the smudge on his face showed upon a crimson background.

"Ask me to the wedding when it comes off, won't you, mate?"

George laughed uneasily.

"All right," he said, "there's nothing to be ashamed of."

"Not a bit, my lad," replied the old driver cheerily. "I've been through it myself and I wish you luck. Got a place over there?"

And he jerked his thumb in the direction of the house.

"Yes. She's a parlourmaid to a fussy old retired major and his wife."

"You were waving your handkerchief in a funny way—and so was she," went on the driver.

"Morse code," replied the fireman.

"What do you mean?"

"Before I was in the sheds, I was in a signal-box for a year and learnt the code. I've been teaching it to Maggie."

"Oho!" exclaimed Jim Harvey, "signalling, eh? What was it you said?"

The young man blushed crimson again and looked uncomfortable.

"*Best love*," he blurted out.

The other laughed heartily.

"And what did she say?"

"Oh—something—something about a kiss—only she didn't spell it quite right. She hasn't quite got hold of the code yet."

"Well I'm blowed!" said the driver. "Hullo—bit o' stick against us. Brakes, George!"

A "bit o' stick" in the shape of a semaphore arm at right angles to the post faced them. The driver shut off steam, the fireman screwed down the hand brake.

George Ledbury had each second Sunday off. Maggie Bond's alternate Sunday afternoon out, strangely enough, coincided with it. Therefore it came to pass that the following Sunday they might have been seen in the country outside Fairdale walking arm in arm. Only, instead of his dirty dungaree overalls, George wore a well-fitting dark blue serge suit, had a face that was clean enough for the occasional kiss he got in return for a dozen given, and looked, in every way, an exceedingly spruce young man. The conversation need not be recorded, being of the "As it was and ever shall be, world without end" description.

"What's the time, George?" Maggie asked presently.

"Five forty-seven," he replied, in true railway parlance, after glancing at his watch.

"That's ten minutes to six," she exclaimed, with a woman's usual comprehension of exact figures, "and if I'm not back by six there'll be an awful row. The master is just about irritable if you're not back exactly in time."

"Bother the master," replied George, "we'd best be getting back, then."

It struck six before they reached the house. Outside the gate he demanded a farewell kiss, got it, and gave three in exchange, the entire performance being observed, unknown to the actors therein, by Major Blake, who was strolling round his garden.

Off went George Ledbury, walking with head erect and heart aglow down Sinclair Avenue—the name of the quiet little street—and in through the gate went Maggie, to be confronted by the stern little Major.

"Margaret, you're ten minutes late."

"Very sorry, sir."

"Who was that young man you were kissing?"

Maggie blushed violently.

"He's—he's a friend, sir."

"Margaret, I'm ashamed of you."

She drew herself up a little.

"We're engaged to be married, sir," she said a trifle defiantly.

"Oh, are you! Why, you're not out of your teens. Understand me, Margaret, that I won't have any followers about my house. I object to it. Who is he?"

"A fireman on the railway, sir."

"Oh! One of those fellows who are always going on strike; a lazy lot. You'd better have nothing more to do with him. Anyhow, don't let me catch him about my house. Go indoors at once. Your mistress wants you."

He spoke as one addressing a private in a regiment, and started for a walk, very satisfied with himself. He did not notice two well-dressed men who were strolling along Sinclair Avenue, although they, apparently, eyed him with interest. He might have seen one of them the next day talking casually to his gardener at the dinner hour, and eliciting certain information about himself.

He returned from his walk and found his wife in the drawing-room. She was a weak little woman. But then she had been married five-and-twenty years to Major Blake.

"I've had to give Margaret a lecture, my dear," he began. "The girl has a sweetheart."

"Oh, I know," she replied, "Margaret has just given me a month's notice."

Major Blake's periodical "lectures" to the domestics meant a constant source of worry to Mrs. Blake and an increase of fees to the local registry office for servants.

"Impudent hussy!" exclaimed the Major, "we're well rid of her."

His wife sighed.

"I'm sorry she's going, dear. She's been a very good servant—and they are not easy to get."

"Pooh!" rejoined the Major. "I won't have men coming about my house. I'd rather be without servants altogether. I don't want to be robbed."

Later on that evening he smoked his cigar and sipped his whis-key and water in a little room he called his "study," but which was not blessed with many books. In one corner was a large iron safe. The Major was a collector, and a collector with expensive tastes. That safe contained a variety of precious stones, chiefly uncut.

He opened it, glancing with a collector's pride at the contents, which were arranged in various trays. It was his silver wedding day soon, and he was going to give his wife a necklace made from uncut Indian sapphires. He picked out about a dozen of the pale blue stones.

"These will do very well," he said to himself, "I can take them up to town with me when we go on Tuesday. By the way, I must go and talk over trains with Kate."

It was on the following Tuesday afternoon that Major Blake and his wife went to London. He had a parting shot at Maggie Bond as he was going out of the house.

"Now, Margaret," he said, "remember what I told you. I won't have that young fellow about my premises while I'm away."

The little servant tossed her head. She was not over particular in her reply.

"Very well, sir. I'll leave myself now if you don't think—"

"Nonsense, Margaret," broke in Mrs. Blake. "We shall be back Thursday morning. See that the fire is lighted in your master's study."

So it came to pass that Maggie was left alone with the cook. The latter was slightly deaf and fond of reading penny novelettes, so Maggie was left much to her own resources. She waved her hand-kerchief as usual to George Ledbury as his train passed on the Wednesday afternoon.

At ten o'clock that evening she accompanied the cook, who was a trifle nervous, round the house to lock up. Then both servants went to bed, the cook sleeping in an attic in front of the house and Maggie occupying a similar room at the back.

It was about one a.m., and unusually dark, when two men came stealthily down Sinclair Avenue, each of them carrying a large black bag. Arrived at Major Blake's house they entered the gate, crossed the lawn on tip-toe, and proceeded to a window at the side of the building.

Then, with the help of a glazier's diamond and a circular bit of leather soaked in water, they quickly and skilfully removed half a pane of glass. The rest was easy, and in five minutes' time they were bending over the safe in the Major's study on the second floor, examining it with a small electric lantern.

"A good two hours' work," whispered one of them.

"Let's get at it, then. Out with the tools."

It may be that they made a slight noise in opening their bags and arranging their tools. At any rate, Maggie awoke with a start and listened attentively. She was by no means a nervous girl, and, somehow, the fear or even the thought of burglars never entered her head. What was really agitating her mind was the problem as to whether she had shut the window in her master's study. She remembered opening it in the morning, but she could not recollect whether she had closed it with the other windows in the afternoon. A slight wind was rising. She got out of bed, opened the door, and listened.

A gentle "swishing" sound came from below, just such a sound as the wind blowing about the curtain in a room might make. She determined to be certain. Throwing on a skirt and jacket, after having lighted a candle, she went downstairs quietly, so as not to awaken the cook, and threw open the door of the study.

Two men were on their knees in front of the safe. Before she could recover from her surprise or utter a cry they were upon her, and she felt a strong hand pressed over her mouth.

"All right, my dear," whispered one of them, "don't be frightened. We won't hurt you. But we'll have to keep you quiet. Joe—your handkerchief—that's right—sorry to deprive you of your voice, miss."

"Is it safe?" whispered the other.

"Safe as nails. There's only the cook in the house beside her, and she's deaf. We won't run for this. But we must tie her up."

The gardener had been pumped effectively.

In one of their bags was a bit of rope. The girl struggled, but they tied her feet together.

"Let's take her into the bedroom—next door, Joe."

This was Major and Mrs. Blake's room. They laid Maggie on the bed, drew one of her arms through the brasswork at the head of the bedstead, and tied her wrists together.

"Sorry if it's a bit uncomfortable, my dear," said the first man, "but it can't be helped. Cook'll find you all right in the morning—here, you mustn't catch cold—"

He threw the eiderdown over her, and the two men left the room, locking the door on the outside cautiously.

"Come along, Joe, we've got to get this safe open—and it's worth it."

Maggie lay on the bed, bound and gagged. But the tight cords round her wrists and ankles did not hurt her half so much as the thought that she was to blame. For she felt sure the burglars had entered through the window which she believed, wrongly, she had left open.

It made her nearly mad to think of her employers being robbed while she was helpless to do anything. She did not quite know what was in the safe, except that certain valuables were kept there. What could she do? If only cook would wake! But, if she did, she would probably lock herself in her bedroom from fear, and the thieves would get off. *If* she could give the alarm!

She turned and twisted in a vain endeavour to free herself, but, as she did so, one of her hands came in contact with something against the wall by the head of the bed. It was the button of the electric light. She twisted it, and the room was illuminated instantly by a lamp hanging from the centre of the ceiling. Just then the clock on the mantelpiece struck two. An idea suddenly occurred to her. She turned off the light and thought it out—trying to remember certain things. The window was at the back of the house, and, fortunately, she had not troubled to draw down the blind.

For a quarter of an hour she lay waiting—waiting —listening to every tick of the clock. She heard a train go by. That was the up "fish special." It could not be long now. No! There came a series of sonorous puffs, suddenly ceasing, and then, "bang—bang—bang" as the brakes of the down goods engine were put on and the buffers of the heavily-laden trucks behind came crashing together.

A whistle—then more puffs—and she knew that the train was being shunted back into the refuge siding just opposite the house, where it would remain till the up express passed. And George

Ledbury was on the footplate of that stationary engine. If only he would look that way! With this prayer on her gagged lips, she felt again for the little electric button.

Driver Harvey filled his pipe, struck a match and lighted it. He was looking forward to the end of his run and the comfortable bed awaiting him. He folded his arms and leant against the side of the cab meditatively.

Suddenly he exclaimed:

"Hullo! Does that girl of yours try to talk to you in the middle of the night?"

George Ledbury was down by the side of the engine with a lamp and an oilcan.

"What's up?" he asked.

The driver pointed to the dark outline of the houses in the near distance.

"Look there," he said, "that's your girl's place, ain't it? What's she up to? Blowing you kisses when she ought to be in bed and asleep? I'm ashamed of her!"

And he gave a quiet chuckle.

But George's gaze was fixed on a certain window. Flashes of light were coming from it in irregular succession, some of them momentary, others prolonged. He recognised the Morse code in a second.

"What's she saying?" asked the driver, with another chuckle.

The fireman sprang on the footplate.

"Two words—over and over again—this is the third time."

"What are they, mate?"

"'*Help—Whistle!*'" exclaimed the other, reaching for a little handle at the top of the fire-box.

"What are you up to?" cried the driver.

But George gave no heed to him. A series of shrill screams rose in the night. He was signalling back with the whistle—just two words.

"*What's up?*"

Then he waited, his eyes fixed on the distant window. Back came the flashes of light.

"Well?" asked the driver.

"*Thieves—in—the—house—help*," exclaimed George Ledbury, as he made out each word. At this moment the express came thundering by.

"I must go," cried George.

The driver put a heavy hand on his shoulder.

"No, my lad," he said, quietly, "you mustn't leave your duty. Besides, I've a better notion than that. Whistle back '*Help coming soon*,' will you? Ah, the signal's off. Go on whistling, mate."

He opened the regulator and the train moved slowly forward, the whistle screeching out its message. Opposite the signal-box he pulled up. The man on duty had his head out of the window.

"What's the matter?" he shouted. "What's all this row about help coming?"

For, of course, he understood the code.

"All right," sang out the driver, "there's burglars in one o' those houses yonder. Tell him which, George."

"Major Blake's house— 'Alma,' Sinclair Avenue."

"You telephone on to Sterrington and ask 'em to send the police out—sharp!" cried the driver. The signalman tumbled to it at once, asking no further questions.

"Right, mate!" he exclaimed, rushing to the telephone. In three minutes' time the message was transmitted from Sterrington main box to the superintendent's office. In another three minutes they received it at the police station. In five minutes more a sergeant and three constables were pounding along on their bicycles through the silent streets. The open window was a fairly easy thing to find, and as the burglars looked up from their work for the second time that night they stared at the flash of a bull's-eye lantern and felt the snap of handcuffs before they realised what had happened.

"Just in time," said the sergeant, pointing to the safe, the door of which was open.

"Curse you!" muttered one of the men.

"The game's up, Joe," said the other philosophically. "There's a young woman in the next room, sergeant; she'll feel a bit more comfortable if you go in and untie her."

They were removing the gag from Maggie's mouth when the sergeant remarked:

"Smart bit o' work. I wonder who gave the alarm."

"I did!" exclaimed Maggie triumphantly.

"You?"

And then she explained.

When Major and Mrs. Blake returned at a reasonable hour that same morning, they found a policeman on the premises. He announced bluntly that the house had been broken into. The Major began to fume.

"It's that girl and her followers!" he cried, "I knew what would happen."

"Excuse me, sir, but it's owing to your servant and her sweetheart that you haven't lost your stones."

And he told him the story. The Major turned to Maggie, who had come into the hail.

"Well done!" he cried, "I was a bit hasty. Where does that young man live?"

"Please, sir, he's in the kitchen, sir. He came to see how I was."

"Bring him up!" shouted the Major.

Whereupon it fell out that Maggie revoked her month's notice, and that a nice little sum shortly stood to her credit in the Post Office Savings Bank. And as George Ledbury is now fireman of a passenger express, part of that sum will shortly be withdrawn for the purpose of partly furnishing a little house in the railwaymen's quarter of Sterrington.

Winning the Race

Monsieur De Courcelles, the French Ambassador, sat in the luxurious little study of the French Embassy in London, pale of face, hollow eyed, and with brows knitted in dire perplexity. Those who knew Monsieur de Courcelles in Society, where he was famous for his courteous manners and his subtly humorous *bons môts*, would scarcely have recognised him in the person of this worried and haggard-looking man.

Though, possibly, just the very few men who knew what was going on at some of the embassies at that particular time might have guessed the cause to a certain extent. Diplomatic negotiations of extreme delicacy were being conducted between three of the great European powers, a sort of triangular duel in which each minister for foreign affairs had the interests of his own particular country to think of, together with possible difficulties with the other two.

That morning Monsieur de Courcelles had ventured to smile a little, rub his hands together, and murmur:

"*Bon! Ca marche bien!*"

Things seemed going smoothly then. And now, at five o'clock in the afternoon, a cypher message had been brought in, which upset all his hopes. He had translated it from the code book himself, and it lay before him, pencilled on a bit of paper, together with a time table. Presently he rang the bell.

A well-dressed young man entered the room. A glance at his chief told him something was wrong. The ambassador shrugged his shoulders, spread out his hands, and exclaimed:

196

"De Natier left Paris an hour ago. He will be in London to-night—and he carries the Treaty with him."

"But that is good, is it not?"

"Yes. If I can get that Treaty into the hands of the British Minister before a messenger arrives from Berlin. Otherwise"—he threw out his hands again— "well, you know clause number three will be struck out, though it is to the advantage of both of us."

"Well, there should be no difficulty, monsieur. Our information this morning from our Secret Service in Berlin told us there would be a delay, and that no messenger would leave Germany till to-morrow."

The ambassador pushed the paper across the table.

"I have just received this," he said. "Read it."

The Vicomte de St. Croix took the paper and read out loud:

"Von Kriegen left Berlin by Nord Express this morning, crossing Bayende Challover."

He whistled thoughtfully, arching his eyebrows as he did so.

"Which means?"

"This. De Natier crosses from Belleporte to Fairholt. The boat starts at 7.10 this evening and the train leaves Fairholt at 9.5, arriving in London at 10.45. Von Kriegen takes the Bayende Crossing. His boat leaves about a quarter to four with a passage of about three and a half hours to Challover. The train leaves Challover at 8.20, arriving in London at 10.20, just twenty-five minutes before De Natier does. The result is obvious."

"You mean that Von Kriegen gets his despatches through the German Ambassador to the Foreign Minister *first?*"

"Exactly. Which is fatal to us."

The Vicomte de St. Croix, secretary to His Excellency, thought for a moment or two.

"It's the same line, of course," he said, half to himself, "both trains run on the East Southern, only the one from Challover has the start—running through Fairholt twenty-five minutes before De Natier's train starts. As you say," he added, turning to the time table, "it is obvious!"

"What's to be done?" asked the ambassador irritably, tapping the table with his pen. "Can *anything* be done to prevent Von Kriegen getting here first, St. Croix?"

The young man pursed up his lips.

"A motor's out of the question," he said, "so is a special train. De Natier *can't* arrive at Fairholt before the other train has started."

"Can you suggest anything?"

St. Croix shook his head.

"There's only one thing," he said. "If anyone can help us it's Charlier. He's a wonderful man—especially with his knowledge of railways."

The ambassador looked at his watch.

"Half-past five," he said. "When can you get Charlier here?"

"I'll telephone to him at once. If he's at home he'll motor down in less than fifteen minutes."

"Yes—telephone immediately. I'd promise him ten thousand francs if he could in any way delay Von Kriegen, without causing complications."

A quarter of an hour later Charlier came and was shown into the private room of St. Croix. He was a short, dark man, with clean shaven face. A Frenchman by nationality on his father's side, Charlier's mother was English, and he himself a mixture. He spoke both languages fluently and without accent, and had long been employed in the French Secret Service as an extremely useful and capable man.

To him St. Croix gave an account of the situation. Charlier took notes carefully. Then he asked to be supplied with an East Southern time table.

"Can you suggest anything?" asked St. Croix.

Charlier thought for a minute.

"It is a very difficult problem, *monsieur*," he said. "I can't promise anything. If you will allow me, I would like to think it over alone."

"Certainly—but the time?"

Charlier glanced at the clock on the mantelpiece.

"I know," he said, "there is not a moment to lose. But, unless I have a plan we can do nothing. Stop a minute. Can you send to the East Southern terminus and ask for the conditions of both crossings to-day, and the direction of the wind."

"I'll do so at once," replied St. Croix, leaving the room.

Charlier lit a pipe, spread out a map of the East Southern railway on the table, and then commenced to study it intently, referring every now and then to the time table.

"It's really a little more than twenty-five minutes' start," he muttered to himself, "the second train is scheduled a bit faster than the first. I remember that. Now here's the problem, and a knotty one it is, too. How to make number two train arrive before number one. *Can* it be done? Let's see."

Again he squared himself, and pored over the map.

"Could number one train be got out of the way and number two pass it? Sounds impossible!"

Suddenly his eyes brightened and his finger went down on a particular place in the map.

"It *is* possible—if the time is short enough. Twenty-five minutes' interval is too long. Yes—but how? The job is, how to tackle the interlocking apparatus."

At this moment St. Croix entered with a message:

"Strong south-westerly wind, channel passages up to time, crossing from Bayende to Challover probably average."

"Good!" exclaimed Charlier, "Von Kriegen's got the wind against him. If he's only ten minutes late, that's something. Don't speak—and don't go, *monsieur*. I have an idea."

St. Croix watched him. He was making rapid drawings on a bit of foolscap paper. They looked liked a jumble of lines and curves. Sometimes he scribbled a few words against a point in his drawings.

"Lucky I know the place," he said beneath his breath.

Suddenly he sat up.

"It *can* be done, *monsieur*," he said.

"What?"

"It is possible that De Natier should arrive before Von Kriegen, but it's a big risk."

"We—we should not countenance an accident," began St. Croix.

"*Monsieur*," interrupted the other, "my plan entails no accident—not a soul would be hurt in any way. The risk would be to the men who undertook the job, and there must be three of us. If we were discovered, it would mean heavy imprisonment."

"We would give you ten thousand francs. Can you find the other men?"

"Only one—Duquesne. And I must give him at least a thousand."

"You shall have it, Charlier. And I will offer my own services."

"I've told you the risk, *monsieur*."

"I'll take it. What is your plan?"

Charlier looked at his watch. It was a quarter to seven.

"There's no time to explain. You have a powerful motor?"

"A sixty-horse Daimhard."

"Good. Duquesne can drive it. You know where I live—my flat is close to Westminster Bridge. Can you be there in half-an-hour?"

"Yes—I'll drive myself."

"Before you start, send someone to the East Southern people. Ask them to have a special at Fairholt on arrival of the boat. You can wire down to De Natier to take it?"

"Yes—but even then he'll start *after* Von Kriegen."

"I know. But he'll get off ten minutes before the ordinary boat train, and that ten minutes is everything. Of course, you'll have him met here?"

"The ambassador will do that."

"Certainly. It's not my affair. I'm going to get him here if I can. In half-an-hour then, *monsieur*. That will give us ample time."

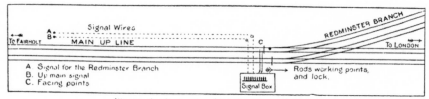

Diagram showing position of the signal-box and signals.

An hour and a half later a powerful motor was running at high speed along the main road from London to Fairholt, out in the open country. Duquesne was driving, and St. Croix and Charlier occupied the rear seat, the latter explaining the details of as wild a scheme as ever entered his subtle brain.

"I cannot quite understand what you mean by the word interlocking," said St. Croix.

"Apart from technicalities it's really a very simple thing," replied the other. "The idea is this: You want to prevent a signalman from pulling a wrong lever accidentally, and you arrange a series of intricate locks beneath his box so that he is under the control of his own signal apparatus. Let us say that A is the lever which sets the point to run a train off the main line to a branch, and B is the lever which pulls off the semaphore signal. Well, you can't pull B before you've pulled A. The pulling of A unlocks the bar which keeps B rigid."

"Oh, I see."

"So what we're going to do—oh, here we are. I'll soon show you."

They had arrived at a very lonely part of the country where the road ran through a common. A red light here and there betokened the vicinity of a railway, while some four or five hundred yards across the common was a little blaze of light from a signal box.

Charlier spoke to the driver and the car stopped. All lights were extinguished, and they proceeded to run the car a hundred yards or so over the common.

"No one will suspect it's here," said Charlier. "Yes, turn her round. We shall have to run off in a hurry by and by. Here are pistols. They're not loaded, by the way—only for show. And masks —we'll put 'em on. Right! Bring the tools and the wire, Duquesne."

Then they crept quietly along towards the signal cabin, passing behind it, and crossing the line at a point about fifty yards beyond where two tall signal posts showed dimly side by side against the sky, their two small white back lights shining in the direction whence the men had come, and their red lights glaring towards the down track.

At the suggestion of Charlier the three men lay down in some long grass beside the track.

"There's plenty of time," whispered Charlier, "and I'll explain the situation. There's only one man in that box, and he is stationed there to control the Redminster branch line which leaves the main track opposite his cabin. It's unnecessary to enter into the complicated details of signalling, but I must just say that he can't pull the levers to signal a train on to the branch line, until he has first pulled the lever that sets the points which transfer the train off the main line to the branch.

"Now these are the 'home signals,' close by us. Two of them. The inner one is for the main up track and the outer for the branch line. So, when the inner one shows a green light the driver knows the main up line is clear, and when the outer one shows 'green' he knows that his train will go on to the Redminster branch. We've only to wait till the up express from Frimwell has gone by. The next train will be the Challover up boat express."

Presently, on the still night air, they heard the bell in the signal box ring.

"The up train," whispered Charlier.

The wire close beside them creaked as it stretched, and the semaphore on the inner post went down with a crash, the red light changing to green. Another wire followed—the back light of the "distant" signal ceased to shine like a star in the darkness.

"Directly she's run by we must set to work," said Charlier. "Duquesne, get the tools ready."

The headlights of the train showed up. Then she passed them with a roar. The signal arm flew up to danger.

"Quick," said Charlier. "Be ready to lend a hand, as I tell you."

Then Charlier did a very curious thing. With his cutters he severed the wires leading from the signal-box to the two signals close by. He took the broken end of the one attached to the main up signal and told Duquesne to make a loop at the end of it. Then he did the same with the end of the other wire leading from the cabin. With a bit of the wire he had brought he joined these loops together, the two other men keeping them at a tension. Then he gave Duquesne his final instructions.

"Directly the train has passed, run along the line about a couple of hundred yards on the Redminster branch. Light the red lamp we've brought and stand it in the six-foot way pointing in the Redminster direction.

"Then hurry back here, and when you see a green light waved from the signal-box, raise this weighted lever at the foot of the up main signal. That will depress the arm. Keep it raised till the next up train runs by, and then rush for the motor, light the lamps, and start the engine. Now, Monsieur de St. Croix! Got your pistol? We'll give our friend the signalman a fright."

Bill Watson, an oldish man, was making an entry in his log book, when suddenly he heard the door of the cabin open behind him. Turning, his astonished gaze fell upon two masked men, holding revolvers pointed straight at him.

"Don't move!" cried the shorter of the two men, "we won't hurt you, but you've got to do what we tell you."

"What do you want?" asked Watson, with a quick side glance at his telegraph instruments.

"What we *don't* want is for you to give an alarm. Understand, we won't have any nonsense."

"What's your game? Train wrecking or robbery?"

"Neither. We shan't do any damage to anybody or anything. In the first place, remember that I know all the code signals of the East Southern. Keep him covered," he added, turning to St. Croix.

Charlier stepped forward to the row of signal levers, and studied the plan of the junction exposed on a board in front.

In order to make quite sure, he asked a few sharp questions of the signalman, who answered him surlily.

"All right," he exclaimed presently, "now I know just what to do. Hullo! What train's that?"

"The Challover boat express."

"Good. Accept it—no tricks now!"

Almost trembling with fear the man gave the "line clear" signal to the previous block, and was about to pull the levers when Charlier pushed him aside.

"I'm going to send that train *on to the branch*."

"You can't," said the man doggedly.

"Can't I?"

He pulled over two levers. The points opposite changed as they moved. Then he pulled a lever marked "number 6." The signalman grinned a little.

"I don't know what you're up to, but you'll only stop her," he said. "The driver will see you've taken off the branch signal, and he won't run on."

Charlier laughed.

"Look at the back lights," he said.

The man looked and exclaimed:

"Well, I'm blowed! You've taken off the up main with the branch lever."

"Exactly! Merely a matter of cutting and joining the wires. You must see to that afterwards. Now, what train runs after this?"

"A special—had a wire about her only half an hour ago," admitted the signalman.

"That's all right. All I want is to get that special in first. Ah, here comes the boat train!"

The head lights—green over white—drew near. She was travelling at sixty miles an hour. On she came. All right! The line was clear. And then, just as she reached the box, she swerved off and went dashing down the branch.

"Signal back 'line clear'!" thundered Charlier, reversing the three levers and pulling over number 1. "She'll go a mile before she pulls up. Good!"

For he saw Duquesne dash past. Three minutes later a warning red light shone on the branch track towards the train that had passed. The driver might back her flow, but he would never dare to pass that light without explanation. St. Croix, his revolver always pointed at the signalman, waited in tense expectation.

The minutes passed slowly. A series of sharp whistles sounded down the branch. The driver had discovered the mistake.

Five—seven—ten minutes. Then the tail light of the express appeared. She was backing. Another whistle. The red light was seen.

Charlier snatched up the cabin lamp, turned on the red shade, and waved it from the door.

"I hope the guard won't run back!" he muttered. Twelve—fifteen minutes—and then a ring on the bell.

"The special?" exclaimed St. Croix.

"Yes!" cried Charlier. "Take her, man—and send on the line clear—hurry up!"

"You can't get her by," said the man. "You can't pull off the home signal."

Charlier, without a word, turned on the green shade and held out the lamp. The next instant the back light on the up main disappeared. Duquesne had carefully obeyed instructions, and, standing at the foot of the post, had set the signal for the approaching train. Again the bewildered signalman exclaimed; "Well, I'm blowed!"

"Here she comes!"

Yes—the violet and green headlights of a special, pacing furiously. The men in charge of the express would understand now why there was a delay in backing on to the main line. At length she reached the signal post and came dashing past the box.

"Off with you!" cried Charlier to St. Croix. "Sharp. Good-night, my man—you're all right. There's no harm done!"

The signalman rushed to the door after them as they ran down the steps.

"Help!" he yelled at the top of his voice. The guard of the express, who had run back, came stumbling over the metals, almost touching St. Croix as the latter vaulted the boundary fence.

"Whiz!"

Duquesne had reached the motor, started the engine, and was in his seat, steering-wheel in hand. The two men jumped in; off went the car—bumping over the grass on the common.

"Which way?" asked Duquesne, as they reached the road.

"London, of course," said Charlier. "Oh, I see what you mean. Better make a bit of a *détour*. We've done our work, and there's no hurry."

At the terminus of the Fast Southern Railway Monsieur de Courcelles himself waited on the platform. Somewhere about ten o'clock he ventured to ask an inspector if the Challover boat express would soon be in.

"No, sir," replied the inspector. "The train's delayed. Something queer seems to have happened down the line, but we don't exactly know what."

"How long will it be?"

"I can't tell you, sir. There's a special from Fairholt due almost directly. Seems to have overtaken the express and passed it somehow."

Then the ambassador knew the situation was saved. In ten minutes' time he was whirling along towards the Foreign Office, the precious document in his breast pocket.

And, when he left, the document duly signed, he found the German Ambassador's motor had just dashed up.

"You are paying a *late* visit, Baron!" he exclaimed, as he raised his hat courteously. To which the other replied, under his breath, with a throaty German swear word of several syllables.

A week later the French Ambassador met the British Foreign Minister at a society crush.

"Oh, by the way," said the latter, "a strange thing seems to have happened on one of our railways the night I saw you last. They were talking about it at the Home Office. I gave them a hint, Monsieur de Courcelles, that perhaps it might be as well if Scotland Yard did not press their investigations."

"That was thoughtful of you, my Lord," replied the ambassador, the vestige of a twinkle in his eye.

[Note for the benefit of railway experts:—

In order to simplify the story I have made no reference to the "distant signals." They would, however, have been worked as follows: For the boat express the "up distant" could not have been taken off, but, of course, the driver would have run by it. For the special, Duquesne would have taken it off, first pulling the lever actuating the "home main," but, in this case, only pulling a broken wire. The interlocking details will readily occur to the expert.]

Three third-class coaches were being slowly shunted into the "bay" at the busy station of Maplehurst. There was nothing out of the ordinary in the appearance of these particular coaches, beyond the fact that some of their quarter-lights bore the label, in red lettering, "Reserved," to which was added in a hasty scrawl, "3.10 p.m. down."

A man, lounging on the platform, eyed them with interest, and then casually inquired of a porter who was going to travel in them, speaking with a slight North country accent.

"Soldiers, I think," was the reply. "There was fresh trouble at Northbury last night, and they're going down to stop the row—at least, that's what I've heard."

The other man thanked him quietly for the information, and glanced at his watch. It was about one o'clock. Then he strolled towards a time-table, which he consulted carefully, and with apparent interest in the 3.10 p.m. down train.

He satisfied himself that this train, an express, arrived at Northbury at 4.32, and then he made his way out of the station to the post-office, from which he dispatched a telegram addressed to Northbury.

A smile of satisfaction appeared on his rather sickly and saturnine face as he emerged into the street.

"Well," he said to himself, "at any rate, I've given them due warning of what's going to happen, and I hope they'll take advantage of it. Sending hired butchers—that's what I call it."

That morning the newspapers were full of the strike riots at Northbury. A dispute had occurred, a few weeks previously, between some iron-foundry owners and the workers, and all attempts at settlement had proved futile. Then the trouble had broken out, and mobs of nondescript hooligans had allied themselves to the more discontented of the strikers, and violent measures had been the result. Property was wrecked indiscriminately, machinery damaged, and many of the local police seriously injured.

The authorities—actuated perhaps by humane but, as the sequel had proved, not too wise motives—had been reluctant to call in the aid of the military, and the reinforcements of police from the surrounding district had proved quite inadequate to cope with the tumult. Men's passions had been aroused to a very dangerous degree, and the whole neighbourhood was seething.

What had roused the anger of the strikers especially was the fact that one or two foundries were being partially worked by "blacklegs," and that a few mineral trains laden with pig iron were leaving Northbury daily.

There was already much violent talk of reprisals against the railway company, and the station and sidings at Northbury were carefully guarded by police.

In travelling down to Northbury, one came upon the iron district quite suddenly. A little over an hour's run by express train from Maplehurst was the sleepy old country town of Raebon, situated in the midst of a quiet agricultural district, and showing little sign of life.

Beyond Raebon the railway ran through a lonesome, desolate bit of country, with tracts of heath and woodland and a few scattered houses. There was no station until one reached Tarlington, some eight miles distant from Raebon, and this was only a little wayside place with scant accommodation for any shunting purposes.

Then the train, after running another mile or so, entered a deep cutting through a range of hills, and passed beyond into an entirely different country. Fields and trees and moors seemed to have vanished as if by magic, their places being taken by rows of sidings, the tall chimneys of the foundries, and colonies of little houses, between all of which the train ran till it reached the large and important station of Northbury, three and a half miles beyond Tarlington.

At this same station of Tarlington no one could have guessed, on that particular afternoon, that just over those low hills to the north, half the men of the countryside had gone mad. There was an air of serene repose about the little wayside station. Harding, the station-master and booking-clerk combined, was seated in his office making out returns; Jameson, the solitary porter, was whistling merrily as he trimmed lamps in the porter's room.

At the up end of the platform stood the signal-box, and the stern warning on the outside to the effect that no unauthorised person was allowed therein was being disregarded in the most barefaced manner in the person of Johnny Harding, the station-master's small boy, aged ten, who was enjoying his Saturday holiday in the company of Crake, the signalman, and more especially those moments of it when Crake allowed him to return a call or to pull over such of the levers as yielded to his boyish strength.

Truth to tell, Johnny knew as much about the working of the Tarlington box as Crake did himself. The boy was a railway enthusiast, and could tell you the name or number of every engine on the system, and had the code signals by heart, to say nothing of the scheduled, time of every train, stopping and express, that ran through the station, with an accuracy of memory equal to the "working time-table" itself.

The bell suddenly rang out, the "be-ready" signal. Crake returned it. Then he went to the telephone.

"What is it?" asked the boy.

"An up mineral train just leaving Northbury," replied the signalman as he hung up the receiver.

"Minerals" were running anyhow that week. Crake accepted it, and a little disc marked "train on line" appeared in the instrument in front of him. The "mineral" had started from Northbury.

The boy took up the pen on the booking-desk, and glanced at the clock. All movements of trains have to be entered carefully.

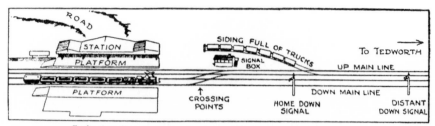

Explanatory diagram, showing the station at Tarlington and the adjacent track.

"3.36," he said, as he wrote it down; "how about the 3.58 slow passenger train from Northbury?"

"She's to pass the mineral train here," replied Crake.

Which meant that the mineral train was to be shunted off the up main line at Tarlington to allow of the passage of the slow passenger train, and was then to follow the latter.

The boy took a glance out of the window. There was a "refuge siding," leading back from the up main line, and this siding was full of empty trucks. The accommodation at Northbury was becoming limited, and these trucks were an "overflow."

"There won't be room," he said presently.

"Doesn't matter," replied Crake, as he pulled off the home signal, "the down main's clear for the next-half hour or more. She can go into that for the time being."

Heavy wreaths of steam came puffing up through the cutting. The mineral train came lumbering along. The driver shut off steam and crawled through the station, bringing his engine to a standstill opposite the box.

Crake slid the window open and looked out. The train was a heavy one.

"You'll have to go on the down main," he said.

"Right!" answered the driver, exactly understanding the situation.

"How are things going yonder?" asked the signalman, jerking his thumb in the direction of Northbury.

"Bad, mate—bad as can be. They've lost their heads. We shouldn't ha' got out half an hour later—there ain't enough police to stop 'em. There's a talk o' the soldiers coming down."

"Pretty nigh time something was done," replied Crake, who had little sympathy with the strikers.

"You're right, mate. Well, I'm glad I shall be out of it to-night."

He started the engine and the train moved slowly on, coming to a halt when it had gone a few hundred yards. Then Crake pulled the necessary levers and signalled with his arm through the box. The train came back, crossing over to the down line, and remained stationary alongside the platform. Thus the up line was made clear for the coming passenger train.

In a few minutes the train from Northbury was signalled, the station-master and the porter appeared on the up platform, together with three or four passengers, and the train came in.

It was just at this moment that Johnny, looking out of the signal-box, caught sight of a dense black mass coming along the road down the hill; as the train moved out of the station the sound of singing arose.

"Look there!" exclaimed the boy, "what's up?"

Crake threw back the starting signal lever and glanced out of the box. A crowd of men was rushing down the hill towards the station, singing and shouting.

"Hullo!" he cried, "they must be some of the Northbury lot—what are they doing here?"

Remembering his duty, however, he turned towards his instruments again. It has been said that the next station on the up line was Raebon, but the next "block" was a little signal-box halfway between the two stations known as "Tedworth level-crossing."

There were no sidings or cross-over points at this box; it merely guarded the level-crossing of the country road which gave it its name. Crake waited till the bell warned him that the passenger train had passed this box; he returned this signal, and the disc in the "up" instrument changed from "train on line" to "line clear." He could now send the mineral train forward.

He had already pulled over the levers once more for this purpose when the crowd of men and hooligans burst into the station. Before they knew what had happened, the unfortunate station-master and porter found themselves seized by rough hands and forced into the porter's room, and the key was tamed upon them.

Crake stood, hand on the lever he had just turned over, thunderstruck. The boy's quicker wits grasped the situation—or, at least, part of it.

"Quick—the telephone!" he cried.

Crake turned to the instrument when half-a-dozen men rushed up the steps and invaded the cabin. Johnny, half from fear, slid behind the desk and crouched down on the floor.

"No you don't!" exclaimed a tall, stalwart man, evidently the leader, as he struck down Crake's hand from the bell push. "We're not going to do you any harm, mate, if you keep quiet and do as you're told—if not, you'll bring it on yourselves. Tie him up, lads!"

In two minutes Crake was bound down to the solitary chair the box contained. The boy breathed hard behind the desk. He was not discovered.

"Now," said the leader, "which of you chaps said you knew how to work these things?" and he pointed to the instruments and levers.

"I did, Sinclair," said a short man, stepping forward, "I was on the line myself once."

"Right. Then see to it that no messages get through—and that the down express comes along—d'ye understand, Macpherson?"

"Aye! I can get her through—if that's what you want, mate."

"It's not quite what I want," exclaimed the other, "I haven't made up my mind yet—the first thing to do is to clear out this pig iron. I'll be back directly."

Outside, the mob had already attacked the hated mineral train. The driver, seeing the points rightly set, had attempted to start, but was quickly dragged off the footplate together with the fireman. Sinclair stood on the little platform outside the box, surveying the scene. They were letting down the sides of the trucks, and the heavy pigs of iron came crashing out upon the platform on one side and the six-foot way on the other.

An ugly expression came over the face of the strike leader. Three days' rioting had turned him from a usually phlegmatic north countryman into a brute, and there was a gleam of murder in his grey eyes. Within his breast pocket was a certain telegram which he had received from Maplehurst a few hours previously.

They were going to send soldiers down, were they? Soldiers who might possibly fire upon him and his comrades. Let them see to it, then. If anything happened they would bring it upon their own heads, curse them!

Suddenly he turned and came back into the signal-box.

"What time does the down express pass Raebon?" he asked Crake abruptly.

"4.17," replied the signalman sullenly.

Sinclair looked at the clock. It was very nearly that time now.

"And what time does she run through here?"

Sinclair went out again and shouted to the madmen below. They stopped in their work of destruction.

"Let's hear Sinclair!" cried a voice.

"Ah, hear me, lads!" shouted the ringleader. "There's a train coming down—it's nearly due now—with three carriages full of soldiers. D'ye know what *that* means?"

Wild yells of execration answered him.

"Once they're let loose on ye," he went on, "there'll be murder done. But I've a plan for stopping them. Leave yon train in the way, and they'll have to stop here. There are a couple of hundred of us. We can storm the carriages before they know where they are and break up their rifles. Who's game?"

Wild voices answered him and hoarse cheers rose from the maddened crowd.

"We'll do it, mate!"

"Right. *What are you doing with the engine?*"

He had suddenly seen some of the men uncoupling the engine of the mineral train, while one had sprung on the footplate. It was just at this precise moment that the bell rang out in the cabin and Macpherson received the signal from Tedworth level-crossing box that the express had left Raebon.

In obedience to the orders of Sinclair he began to pull the levers which actuated the signals for the express. But they would not move because they had been locked by Crake when the latter pulled the two levers to shunt the mineral train from the down to the up line. Macpherson saw this and replaced these two levers. He could now set the signals for the express.

"Good heavens, man," exclaimed Crake, observing what was going on— "there's a train standing there—on the down road."

"I know there is," said Macpherson, pulling off the home and distant signals. "That's our game. When the driver sees it he'll stop the express—don't you worry, mate."

"What are you doing with the engine?" cried Sinclair once more.

"Going to send her up the line," answered the man on the footplate, "she shan't have a chance of drawing a mineral train this journey."

"Stop, you fool!" thundered Sinclair.

But the man had already opened the throttle valve and jumped off the footplate. The great engine began to move forward.

"Good heavens!" screamed Macpherson, seeing what was happening, "the crossing points are not set! She'll run into the express!"

The old habit had come back to him. He was no longer the mad ironworker on strike, but the signalman on duty.

But it was too late now for him to transfer the engine to the other line. The heavy locomotive gathering speed, took the down metals, and rushed forward to meet the express *on the same line of rails*. Sinclair saw what had happened in a moment. He also grasped the fact of the awful catastrophe that must take place when the two engines met. And a thrill of diabolical joy welled through him. Let it happen, then! No human power could prevent it now.

"Clear out, Macpherson!" he cried. Then, addressing the mob, who stood paralysed on trucks and platforms, he shouted:

"Out of the station, lads! Back home, every one of you!"

There was a scramble out of the trucks and across metals and platforms. A panic seemed to have seized the men as they realised the horrible thing that was going to happen. They poured out of the station faster than they had entered it, leaving Harding the station-master, the porter, driver, and fireman under lock and key, and the signalman fast bound.

The only other railway official, the brakesman of the mineral train, had long since jumped from his van and hurried back along the line towards Northbury to summon assistance.

One person, and one person only was left free at the station, and that was Johnny Harding. He came out from behind the desk, ghastly pale, but with all his wits about him. And he flew to the telephone.

"It's too late," said Crake, "nothing can save the express now. Look at the clock!"

The clock marked 4.20. The express was approaching from Raebon at full speed—and the engine of the goods train, a tiny speck in the distance now, was rushing forward to meet it.

Nevertheless, in sheer desperation, the boy pushed the little knob to ring up Tedworth level-crossing box—where the express was due at 4.22.

Old Joe Salter sat in his little box at Tedworth level-crossing, stirring the fire in his stove with his wooden leg. Years before, he had lost a leg in the company's service, and was relegated to his present post, which was a light one. He had to open and shut the gates of his crossing, and act as the midway "block" between Raebon and Tarlington. His signal cabin, with its five levers, two each for up and down home and distant signals, and one for locking his gates, was on the ground level.

He had received the signal that the express had left Raebon, and duly accepted it and passed it on to Tarlington. His gates were open to the line, and his down signals pulled off. All was right. Over one of the gates hung a youth, with a team of horses behind him, drawing a felled tree trunk on a low waggon, waiting till the train had passed. It would do so in another two minutes, for it was just 4.20 o'clock, and the train was well up to time.

Suddenly there came a ring at the bell. Somebody wanted to speak to him from Tarlington. He rose, went to the telephone, and gave the answering ring. Then he raised the instrument to his ear. Johnny Harding's voice came through.

"Stop the express—quick—stop the express."

It was unusual, but the old man never stayed to question it. "Clang—clang" back went the two levers, and two signal arms rose to "danger," one, the distant, half-a-mile up the line, and the other about three hundred yards from his box, in the same direction. The express might pass the "distant," but not the "home."

He returned to the telephone.

"What's the matter, then?" he asked.

His face blanched as the appalling news came through.

"The strikers—they've sent on a goods engine—on the down metals—by itself—no one on footplate—it'll wreck the express—can you do anything?"

The old man dropped the receiver, dazed for a moment. Then he shouted back:

"When did it start?"

"Four or five minutes ago—can you do anything?"

Joe Salter gazed round wildly. Then the inspiration came.

"Yes!" he shouted, and threw back the locking lever.

The next moment he was stumping over the lines to the gates. The whistle of the express sounded, shrieking for its right of way. He glanced in the other direction. A puff of white rose above the distant trees. Hauling the gates open, he cried to the astonished youth:

"Bring your lot across—quick! There's no time for question—hurry up, lad!"

Wondering dimly why a train should be stopped to make way for his load, the yokel gee'd up his horses and led them forward slowly. The great tree trunk was across the down metals.

"Stop—unlatch the chain your side—look alive, sonny—I'll see to this one."

The chain traces were quickly loosed.

"Now!" thundered the old man, "off with those horses—for your life, lad! Lash them up!"

Just then the goods engine rounded a curve and came thundering along. The youth, his dull brain roused at last, needed no further warning. He struck out with his whip at the horses, and ran after them as they plunged at a gallop along the road, followed by old Joe Salter stumping along as fast as his wooden leg would allow him.

As the crash came, he turned. It was an appalling sight. The great engine ran full tilt into the waggon and tree trunk, seemed to push both out of its way, literally staggered on, tearing up metals and throwing ballast in clouds, shook, tottered, thundered, and hissed. Finally it rolled over on its side, a mass of metal, steam, and flying wheels, dragging itself many yards along the side of the line, breathing its dying breath in the form of a white cloud of vapour intermixed with glowing embers.

The express was saved—by not much more than a hundred yards!

Half-an-hour later the breakdown train, with its wonderful hydraulic crane and lifts, came down from Northbury, and a gang of men set to work instantly to clear the road of the masses of *débris*, and to lay rails for the passage of the express over the ruined gap. Long before then soldiers and passengers had clustered round the plucky old man to whom they owed their lives, and not one of them grudged his coin when the hat went round.

The soldiers reached Northbury several hours late, but their services were not required that night. A fear—a horror had run through the hearts of the more violent of the strikers. Besides which, they wanted leaders, and Sinclair and Macpherson were nowhere to be found, then or at any other time.

A week later two persons "trod the carpet" in the General Manager's office, an old wooden-legged man and a small boy. And the "G. M.," when he had finished his complimentary speech, which was accompanied by something else of a substantial nature, remarked:

"Well, Salter, I think it's time you were placed in honourable retirement—you've well earned it. As for you, Johnny, I hope you *won't* retire. We must make a railway man of you, my boy, later on. And I hope you'll never have to sacrifice an engine to save an express again. But it was worth it, and the company is proud of the services of both of you!"

The Convict's Revenge

"Ugh!" said my companion to me, with a shiver and a little clutch at my arm. "That's a thing I hate!"

We were standing by a level-crossing as he spoke. We had almost started to cross the rails, when a rumble and a whistle and the bright glare of the head-lights heralded the close approach of a train. So we stood back for a moment or two to let the iron steed and his load pass. The lights from the carriages flashed out upon us, then there was a swirl of wind as darkness came on once more, and the red tail-light vanished round the curve beyond.

"Why," I remarked with a laugh, as we went on again, "surely an old soldier and ex-prison warder like yourself isn't afraid of a passing train?"

"Ah, sir, every man has his weakness, and I'm not ashamed to confess that I've got mine. And, perhaps, if you'd had an experience that happened to me some ten years ago, you'd flinch a bit when an express train rattled past you."

"Oh, there's a foundation for it, is there?"

"There is, sir, and if you care to step inside my little place and rest for half an hour, I'll tell you the yarn, such as it is."

I expressed myself only too delighted to pick up the proffered information. I must explain before I go further that until the evening in question my companion had been unknown to me. I had been staying for a few days at the little cathedral city of Dullminster, and had been on a day's fishing excursion in the neighbourhood with no companion save my pipe. It was while pensively watching my float in the quiet little stream that a fine-looking old fellow appeared, bent on the same sport as myself, and took up his position close by. As bites were few and far between, we entered into conversation, and when dusk set in, by mutual consent, we packed our traps and set off together over the pleasant fields that lay between us and Dullminster. He told me something of his past history as we trudged along, from which I gathered that he had begun life in the Army, and afterwards he had been a warder in the well-known convict prison of Dartport, from which post he had retired into private life some few years since, and had come to eke out a restful existence on savings and pension in Dullminster, the place of his birth.

A few hundred yards beyond the level crossing we stopped at the door of a little house in one of the streets in the outskirts of the town.

"Come in, sir," said the old fellow. "I'm all by myself—yes, an old bachelor, sir. And if you'll condescend to have a cup of tea, while I spin you the yarn, you're welcome to it."

It was a chilly autumn evening, and the bright fire and singing kettle in the little sitting-room looked very inviting, so I gladly accepted mine host's invitation.

"And now, sir," said he, when we were comfortably settled, "I'll tell you why I don't like to be near an express train at night.

"Of course, as you can imagine, we used to have some queer customers at Dartport. Her Majesty's private hotels take all kinds of folk, and we are not particular as to character. One of the worst gaol-birds that I ever remember was a certain convict whom I will call by his old number—36. He was in for a long sentence—in fact, as far as I know, he's doing time yet; though if there'd been a little more evidence forthcoming at his trial, his term of imprisonment would have been a short one, ending in the prison-yard on the scaffold; but as it was, though his list of crimes was a pretty black one, murder couldn't quite be proved, though there were few that doubted he hadn't stuck at that.

"From the moment I set eyes on him at Dartport I knew there'd be trouble with No. 36. It wasn't only the size and strength of the

man, but a certain nasty look about his eyes that told me this. Nor
was I mistaken, for he proved to be one of the most unmanageable
brutes we ever had. He soon took a particularly strong dislike to
me, for, as ill-luck would have it, I was the first to have to report
him for misconduct, and it was through me that he had his first
taste of the cat. When I went into his cell that night, he broke the
strict rule of silence, and hissed out:—

"'You devil of a turnkey, I'll kill you before I've finished with
you.'

"It was a threat I had heard more than once before, and it didn't
affect me very much at the time, though I had good reason to remember it afterwards.

"Two years passed, and No. 36 showed no signs of improving.
He had a marvellous physique, and the prison diet seemed in no
way to diminish his strength. He had to be most carefully watched
in the quarries, and in fact always, for he had a nasty knack of being dangerous in more ways than one. At length, towards the end
of the summer of the year of which I am speaking, he suddenly
turned over a new leaf, and became quiet and tractable. I felt less
sure of him than ever, nevertheless, for I had seen something of
this phase of character before, and I knew it generally meant
mischief. Nor was I mistaken, for one afternoon, when a fog had
come on rather unexpectedly, the sharp crack of a rifle betokened
the escape of No. 36. Taking advantage of the mist, he had suddenly struck the nearest warder to the ground, hurled a big bit of
stone with deadly aim at one sentry, completely bowling him over,
taking the chance of a bullet from another—and was off!

"A search party was, of course, organized at once, but somehow or other he managed to show a clean pair of heels and escape
over the moors. As darkness set in, a poor old man was found dazed
and half naked, about a couple miles from the prison, and, after
being revived, he told how No. 36 had met him and insisted upon
having all his upper garments, so that the runaway had an extra
good chance of getting clear.

"It was between nine and ten o'clock at night that I, in company with several other members of a search party, halted for a

little consultation just by the embankment of the railway, the main 'West Southern,' line to London, that runs through the desolate bit of country some five or six miles north of Dartport Prison.

"'I wonder whether it's any use having a look at Westmoor Station,' said our chief.

"Westmoor Station was about two miles up the line from where we were standing.

"'Aye,' I replied, 'it's just possible that he might be lying around there, looking out for a train; though it's my belief that he's making northward—at any rate, it's more likely.'

"'Well, Davis,' said the chief, after a moment or two's thought, 'suppose you go to Westwood. It may be worth trying. I think we ought to go on to Hartwell, or that direction. What do you say?'

"'I'm willing to do as you suggest,' I answered. 'It's just as well to see the station-master, I think.'

"'All right. You slip away, then, Davis. You'd better keep along the line—it's the nearest way.'

"So I started off along the line. It was a very dark night, though the fog had lifted, and it was some moments before I got used to the track. After a bit, however, I made pretty fair progress, walking between the down pair rails on the right-hand side, so that I could see the head-lights of any train coming towards me. I hadn't gone far before I did a very foolish thing. I slung my rifle over my shoulders, so as to leave my hands free.

"I had gone about half a mile or more up the line when a great longing for a pipe came over me. I hadn't had a pipe all day, and as you're a smoker, sir, you know pretty well how I was feeling. As I walked along I took out my pouch, filled my pipe, and then felt in my pocket for a match. After nearly turning it inside out I found one solitary wax vesta. Now, there was a bit of a wind blowing over the moor, and fearful lest I should waste my precious match, I refrained from striking it until I could get behind some shelter. The desired object presently appeared, looming through the darkness, in the shape of a little platelayer's hut on the same side of the line as I was walking, the door facing towards the rails. Getting into the shelter of the doorway, I struck the match, and was just about

to light my pipe, when, as I leaned against the door, to my astonishment it opened inwards with my weight, almost precipitating
me to the ground, and before I could recover myself the light of
the vesta revealed to me the hideous face of No. 36, who was
hiding within.

"With a snarl he was upon me, and had clutched me by the
throat with his strong, bony hands. It was all done so suddenly
that I had scarcely time to think of what was happening, and had
hardly realized the situation, when I found myself sprawling on
my back with the ugly brute on the top of me. Of course, I made a
mighty effort to defend myself, but I was quite powerless in his
strong grip.

"'Ah,' he growled, with a curse, as he held me pinned to the
ground, 'it's you, is it? Well, I've got a few old accounts to settle
with you, and I don't think there could be a better opportunity.'

"'You brute!' I ejaculated, trying to twist myself out of his grasp.

"'Ah—would you? Not so fast, Warder Davis. The tables are
turned now, and you're the prisoner.'

"At this moment something flashing bright in the dim star-light
fell out of my pocket and clanged on the gravel ballast of the railway track.

"'Good,' said No. 36, making a snatch at it; 'these bracelets were
meant for me, I suppose. Perhaps they'd prove as good a fit on
your wrists. At any rate, we'll try. And as we haven't a cell handy
to fix you in, we'll fasten you down to something secure—do you
hear?'

"And putting forth all his strength, in spite of my desperate
struggles, he half dragged, half rolled me on to the down track close
beside us. Then, kneeling on my chest, he forced my right hand
beneath the outer rail between the sleepers, and my left arm over
the rail, then there was a sharp click, as with a savage chuckle he
snapped the handcuffs over both my wrists, and I realized my terrible position. *I was handcuffed down to the rail!*

"He jumped up in triumph, felt in my pocket, drew out the key
of the handcuffs, and hurled it away.

"'How now, you white-livered skunk?' he snarled. 'I could kill you outright with a knock on the head if I chose. But *I'm* not going to commit murder, oh, no! I'll leave that to the down express. Do you understand? If it runs at the same time as it used to, it ought to come by here about eleven o'clock, and I guess there'll be a little obstruction in its way to-night. Ah! I've got to fix you a bit tighter, my friend, just to make sure, you know.'

"And he went into the hut, reappearing in a few moments with a piece of rope, which he had, I suppose, previously noticed there.

"'You'd feel a little bit more comfortable if I tie your feet down too, eh?' he sneered; and, to my horror, he put a loop of rope round my right leg, drew it underneath the inner rail, and then made the end fast to my left ankle, above the rail. I was thus fixed right across the track, and escape from a hideous death seemed impossible. But the villain had not finished yet.

"'There's just a chance that you might call out,' he said, 'so I'll tie your mouth up. You can say your prayers just as well with it shut as open, and the sooner you say them the better, for you never needed to more.'

"He stuffed part of my handkerchief into my mouth and tied it round with another bit of rope. Then he proceeded to rifle my pockets.

"'Got any loose cash about you? That's right. I'll take care of it, for it won't do *you* any good now, I reckon, and you'll have the dying satisfaction of having helped me to get off to London. And now, you skunk of a warder, good-night! I told you I'd be the death of you one day, but, by Heaven, I never hoped for such a paying-off of old scores as this. Remember, you'll see the head-lights of the engine coming towards you—you'll hear the roar of the train that's going to squash you. It's a good revenge, isn't it? I'd stay here and see the end of it if I could, only I've no time to spare, so now good-night, Warder Davis, curse you!'

"And with a brutal kick at my defenceless body he started off in the direction of Westmoor. I could see his bulky form for a moment or two in the dim light, and could hear for several minutes the tread of his feet crunching the gravel on the permanent

way. I had no doubt in my mind that he had been making for
Westmoor previously, and had used the old platelayer's hut as a
hiding-place until it was about time to take a chance of getting on
one of the up trains.

"My situation was a truly awful one. He was quite right about
the down express: it was timed to run through Westmoor just about
eleven o'clock. It was past ten now, so that there was not an hour
between me and a hideous death. I lay still for some minutes and
tried to compose my mind to think a little. Was there anything I
could do? Yes! With an effort I might manage to remove the gag. I
pushed my head as far as it would go over the metals, and to my
joy was able to undo the knots with my chained hands and to get
the handkerchief out of my mouth. This was a relief, certainly, but
only a very small one, for it soon dawned upon me that if I yelled
my loudest there would be no one within hearing on the lonely
moor through which the track ran. To get my hands free was
impossible, but there might be a chance for my feet. I began to
kick them about, and discovered that the wretch had simply passed
the rope between my ankles *once* round the rail, so that by alter-
nately kicking and pulling with each foot I could draw it backward
and forward against the rail. With the energy of despair I began to
work with all my might to fray the rope against the rail, and so set
my feet free.

"I must have kicked away for over half an hour—kicked and
pulled till I was stiff and in agony, and still the rope held, but I
could *feel* it rubbing away and getting thinner, and I tried to work
it so that the friction took place where the rail rested in the 'chair'
on the sleeper, so as to have a sharp corner to cut. Fiercely I
struggled to get free, but the rope was a strong one, and it seemed
as if it would hold for ever.

"A whistle! Hardly discernible in the distance, but still I knew
what it meant. The down express was running through Westmoor
Station. A fresh struggle—and *still* the rope held. Then came an
ominous rumble in the distance, and there, half a mile away up
the straight bit of track, I could see the glimmer of the engine's
head-light. A desperate pull! I hung on to the outer rails with both

hands, and pulled with arms and legs like a man on the rack of old—every muscle of the body was strained with the fearful tension. Snap! The rope broke and my feet were free.

"There was not a moment to lose; the train was little over a quarter of a mile away, and in twenty seconds it would be on me. But a desperate man can do a lot in that time. With a quick movement I rolled over to the outside of the track, so that my *left* arm came under the rail. Then I threw myself at full length parallel to the track, feet towards the approaching train, and as far from the rail as possible. At the same moment I drew down my hands on either side of the rail so that the short chain between the steel wristlets was on the top of the rail, the centre being on the inner top edge of the rail where the wheels would strike.

"With a roar the train was on me. I expected to have one of my hands cut off, and there came a sharp thrill of pain to both wrists as the leading wheel of the engine struck the chain, while the thought flashed across me that I might not be far enough from the rail to escape being struck in my body.

"The passing of that awful train seemed to be an hour. Wheel after wheel ran close to my face with a hideous clatter—until the momentary red glare of the taillight and a big rush of air told me that the danger had passed. For about five minutes I lay perfectly still, and not till then did I discover that my hands were falling further apart.

"Scarcely daring to hope, I drew them slowly towards me. Yes! I was free! The heavy train had snapped the swivel-link that joined the handcuffs, and with the exception of a severe bruising in my wrists, I was perfectly uninjured.

"Well, to make a long story short, sir, I toddled to my feet with the most profound feeling of gratitude to Providence that I had ever experienced. And then, weak and nerve-shattered as I was, there came upon me the intense desire to recapture the brute who had condemned me to such an awful death. My rifle was still with me, and uninjured; so, as well as I could, I set forth in the direction of Westmoor, starting in fright after I had gone a short distance at the noise of a heavy goods train, that rumbled past me on the up track.

"When I got to the station, the platform and offices were closed, but this same goods train was being shunted in the yard, preparatory to making a fresh start on its journey towards London. Two or three trucks, covered with tarpaulins, were detached, and I fancied I caught a glimpse of a dark figure crouching beside one of them.

"I stopped and watched, smiling to myself as I saw No. 36 climb into the truck, and disappear beneath the tarpaulin. Then I went quietly to the brakesman and explained matters. He, the driver of the engine, a couple of shunters, and myself surrounded the truck, and in a few minutes No. 36 found himself brought to bay, with the man whom he had thought dead presenting his rifle within a foot of him. He saw the game was over and gave in, and that's the end of the yarn.

"Yes, of course, he was pretty severely punished, but that didn't compensate me for my terrible experience; and now perhaps you don't wonder why I should give a bit of a shudder when an express train passes me in the dark!"

In the Rockhurst Tunnel: The Ganger's Story

"Well, sir," said the railway ganger, as he slowly lit the short clay pipe so dear to an English labourer's mouth, "I'll tell you the tale, as you seem bent on hearing it. It was hushed up at the time, d'ye see? but I suppose there ain't any particular harm in letting it become public after all these years.

"I was just an ordinary platelayer on the Mid-Northern Railway when it happened. It was in the Rockhurst Tunnel, and the Royal special was—, but there! I'd better start at the beginning and make a few explanations, or you won't get the hang of the thing."

So we sat down together by the side of the line. He had only just come off duty and had asked me for a light just as I strolled over the level crossing. A railwayman of any grade is always worth talking to, and one thing had led to another until the man had dropped a hint that he had a story to tell. That settled it, and here is the ganger's tale.

"When the King or some other person of the Royal Family takes a little run over the line, it ain't a question of just buying a ticket at one end and giving it up at the other, like you or me does. There's all sorts of things to be arranged by the Company beforehand, and when the Royal special's run, a lot of trouble that most people don't dream of is taken, so that nothing shall fall foul of it. Orders are given all along the line for shunting other trains into sidings to let it pass, and on a busy bit of the road this ain't no joke for the traffic super. to arrange.

"A pilot engine is run 'light'—that's by itself—a quarter of an hour ahead of the train, and nothing's allowed on the metals between the two. Every station-master gets his special instructions, not only for use at the stations themselves, but orders for the protection of every inch of the line.

"At every bridge under or over which the train is to run, at every level crossing, at all 'facing points' and junctions, in every tunnel, a man is stationed long before the Royal train is timed to pass. It is his duty to see that the line is clear, that no suspicious persons are loitering about, and generally to act as sentinel over the Royal safety. Most of these men detailed for special duty are drawn from the permanent wav gang. Many a time I've held the green flag when Queen Victoria (God bless her memory!) was a-rushing by, and though she didn't see me I felt as proud as though I'd been a sentry guarding her at Windsor Castle.

"The gang I was working in at the time I'm telling you of knew there was going to be a Royal journey on the London and Mid-Northern, and one morning just as we were going to begin work our ganger told us that the special was to run that afternoon, and that he'd got his orders from the stationmaster in our district for placing the men.

"All that morning we spent in overhauling the five miles of down metals that belonged to our gang. Keys were driven in more firmly between the chairs and rails, fish-plate bolts were tested and the spanner clapped on to all loose nuts to tighten them, and everything was done to make the permanent way as safe as possible.

"'Jackson, Holloway and Stone,' said our ganger, 'you're told off for the Rockhurst Tunnel. You take the south end, Jackson; you the north, Stone; and,' turning to me, 'you'll be in the middle, Holloway.'

"'All right,' I answered.

"'Don't forget your lamp, Holloway,' he went on, 'and be sure you've got enough oil in it. You'd better be in your place before two. The pilot's timed to run through at 2.55.'

"Now, of course, you've heard of the Rockhurst Tunnel. It's just over a mile long, and runs under as wild a bit of moorland as you'd find in a day's march. There's a signal box in the cutting at each end, so the tunnel is a 'block' in itself. It's not quite straight through; there's a slight curve just at the centre, but by standing on the outer side of this curve you can see the spot of daylight—for it's only a spot—at each end. I knew every inch of the tunnel. Many a long day I'd spent in it, working by the light of naphtha lamps, and it was only natural that I should stand a chance of being placed on guard in it.

"I remember well how I chuckled over what seemed to me an easy afternoon's job—just a spell of rest. Folks know little of the work of the P.W. men. The passenger, as he rushes by and glances at a group of chaps leaning on their shovels and picks, doesn't realise that the very rail he's running over has very likely only been keyed into its place five minutes before. He growls at the slowness of his journey when 'reduced speed' is ordered for a P.W. job, little thinking that tons of heavy ballast must be shovelled in and levelled by the despised platelayer before it will be safe to run at sixty miles an hour again. And there's dangers in the life, too, not only from the running of the trains, and fools pitching empty bottles out of windows, and fogs and such like, but lots of other things that you never dream of, sir.

"I had my foot jammed in a facing point once, when it was being closed; lucky for me, the signalman heard me shout in time, or I'd only have troubled the shoemaker for one boot for the rest of my life. This scar on my cheek was cut by a bit of a detonator that flew off the rail when the engine struck it, and it might have cost me an eye. And my teeth—but there, that reminds me, I'm getting clean away from my yarn.

"Well, about a quarter to two, carrying an ordinary railway lamp with a green and red shade to it, and a few detonators, or fog signals, in my pocket in case of accident, I walked through the tunnel from the south end till I reached the centre. It was pitch dark, of course, except for just a dim spot of light that shone over the rails; for just above was a ventilating shaft opening into the moorland.

"Very soon after I'd got to my place the ganger himself came through, making a last examination By his doing this it was impossible that anyone else could be in the tunnel.

"Now, I must tell you exactly what my duties were. They were very simple. Of course, I had to know that the line was perfectly clear ahead. The green lamp that Stone, at the north end, had, would shew me this. When the pilot engine entered the south end I was to shew a green light towards the driver, and also to wave it in the other direction, so that Stone could see that all was right. Exactly the same precautions were to be observed when the special itself came along. In case of anything wrong happening, I was to shew the red light, of course.

"It must have been nearly half-past two. I was standing a few yards away from under the air shaft when I was startled by hearing a noise. I turned round to see what was up, and I tell you my heart gave a sort of jump when I saw the figure of a man close by, while another one seemed to be dropping from the roof of the tunnel.

"'Hullo, what are you doing here?' I said, pulling myself together as well as I could.

"'Look sharp, Bill, drop! Here's our man—right under our very nose!' cried the fellow I had seen.

"I saw something was up, and turned the red shade on to my lamp, hurrying to the side of the tunnel as I did so.

"'Ah, would you?' shouted the man. I saw him lift up his arm, and the next moment I felt a heavy blow on my head, and staggered forward.

"'Quick, Bill, or they'll see the red light. Down with him!'

"The other man had now come up, and the two, springing at me, bore me down to the ground between the metals. I still held the lamp, but it was wrenched out of my hand and the green shade turned on once more.

"'Got the cord, Bill?' asked the first speaker.

"'Here it is,' said the other. 'You hold him down and I'll make short work of him.'

"In five minutes they had lashed my arms closely to my sides, cutting my wrists almost to the bone, and bound my legs firmly together.

"'What—what are you going to do with me?' I asked.

"'You'll soon see, my friend,' said the man who had spoken first. 'You never expected visitors, eh? But angels drop from the sky sometimes, and we just slung a rope from the airshaft overhead and came down it, see? Pity your people don't take more pains when they have Royal passengers.'

"'There was a man there—' I began.

"'A clumsy youth, yes! He's in the same case as you now. Listen; we won't kill you outright, because you've not done us any damage, but we'll give you a chance of seeing one of the biggest railway accidents known, and of telling your friends about it—if you're lucky enough to escape yourself, which I doubt.'

"'For God's sake, what are you going to do?' I cried. 'Do you know *who* is travelling? Do you know?'

"'Exactly; that's why we're here. You don't suppose we should have taken so much trouble over an ordinary train, do you? But there isn't any time to waste on you. The pilot engine will be through directly. Hurry up with that bag, Bill. Stow it safely and fix the end of the rope to the up side of the tunnel till we want it again. That's right. Now help me lift this fellow into the manhole in the wall and stick by him there while I work the pilot through. Clap your hand over his mouth if he tries to shout. Afterwards he can yell as much as he likes.'

"They put me into the manhole, propping me up against the sides of the wall. I tell you, I was in a 'blue funk.' I'd guessed pretty well the meaning of the thing. They were a couple of Anarchists, and they meant to wreck the Royal train in the middle of the tunnel. And I couldn't prevent it, for they'd planned it too well.

"Presently I heard a roar from the South end of the tunnel. The pilot engine was coming through. The man who had charge over me laid his hand on my mouth, but I could see what the other was doing. He was holding the green light towards the engine, every now and then turning to wave it in the opposite direction, so that my mate at the other end of the tunnel would think that all was right.

"With a rattle and a roar the pilot engine ran past us. Then the man with the lamp drew a hammer from his pocket and drove a nail in the wall of the tunnel as high as he could reach, hanging the lamp on it, green light towards the south.

"'You can't reach *that* to *blow* it out,' he said to me with a nasty, chuckling laugh. 'And now we're going to fix a pretty little fog-signal of a patent pattern on to the rails. It's warranted to stop any train!'

"And in the dim light from the shaft I saw them draw something out of a bag, and carefully fix it on to the metals, using some tools as they did so.

"'There,' said the brute when they had done, 'I think that'll settle matters. Quick, Bill! We've not a moment to lose. The train will be through in five minutes or so. Up you get! Good-bye, my friend,' he shouted to me as the other man started climbing up the rope, 'There's an exciting time before you!'

"And then he disappeared, leaving me alone in the tunnel. It was about as ugly a fix as a chap could be in, and you can fancy I felt pretty queer. But even before they went there came to me just a glimmering of an idea, faint as the spot of daylight under the shaft, but a dying man will clutch at a straw, they say, and I was in the same sort of case. Besides, it wasn't only my own life I was thinking of.

"I told you they'd put me, propped up against the wall, in an upright position. Bound hand and foot as I was, in that position lay my last chance. I might yet save the Royal train.

"If only I could get across to the other side of the tunnel, between which and me lay a double set of metals!

"Why? I'll tell you. The Anarchists didn't know, and perhaps you don't either, that the safety of that tunnel didn't only depend on my shewing a green light. The Rockhurst Tunnel, like several other long ones in England, such as the 'Box' and the 'Severn,' on the Great Western Railway, is fitted with a special apparatus for giving an alarm signal in case of danger or accident.

"This apparatus is a very simple one; a telegraph wire is fixed in the tunnel and connected with a 'tell-tale' bell in the signal boxes at each end in such a way that if the wire is broken the bells start ringing at once and give the alarm. Then each signalman knows that something is up in the tunnel, and can put his signals against all trains and prevent them coming in.

"This wire, which is a thin one, so that you can easily break it, is fixed to the wall of the tunnel on the up side of the line, about five feet from the ground. I remembered this, and I knew if I could only break it in time the signalman in the box at the south end would never let the Royal train pass without an examination of the whole tunnel.

"As I say, I was tied up. Still, a sort of plan came before me, and I determined to have a good try at it. I was upright, and I felt I might be able to move by short jumps. The worst thing I had before me was the getting over the four rails, for, if I fell down, I knew it would be pretty difficult to get up again.

"I gave one or two hopping jumps forward, very carefully, till I felt my shins against the first rail. Then I pulled myself together, jumped as high as I could, and lurched myself forward. It was a narrow squeak. I felt the heels of my boots just touch the inner edge of the rail, but down I came safely on the other side. A few more jumps and another effort brought me into the 'six-foot way.' Half the battle was over. Then I jumped the third rail and only one was left.

"Whether I was nervous, or over confident like, I don't know, but when I tried to jump that last rail my toe caught in the top of it and sent me lunching forward. My shoulder came an awful bang against the wall of the tunnel, but, luckily, my feet had landed on the ground, and I felt myself sort of propped up in a slanting position against the wall. I managed to get myself upright, and then came the nastiest job of the lot.

"I felt against the wall with my face till my nose touched the signal wire. Then I grasped it—*with my teeth.*

"Talk about a dentist, sir! It wasn't in it. I bit hard on the wire, and pulled and strained with all my might to break it I thought I never should have stood the pain long enough, but at last the wire snapped, and, at the same time, out flew three of my teeth, torn out of the gums. I was pretty well done up, I can tell you, and had to lean against the wall.

"It might have been a minute or an hour I waited, for all I knew, but anyhow I heard, after a bit, a long whistle from the south end of the tunnel. Then came silence, and I knew the train had stopped.

"A long time seemed to pass, and then I heard voices and saw three or four white lights coming through the darkness.

"'Here's his green light, all right,' said someone.

"'Here I am,' I shouted. 'Look out how you come forward.'

"'What's the matter, my man?'

"'There's something on the line under the air shaft. Take care how you touch it.'

"'Why, he's tied up, and covered with blood,' cried one of the party, as he flashed his lantern on to me, 'whatever's happened? Are you hurt?'

"'Not much sir. Only a tooth or two gone,' I answered.

"It was the loco. super., who had been travelling on the footplate of the Royal engine. With him was a guard, and a couple of officials who had special charge of the train. A penknife soon set me free, and I told them what had happened.

"Then we went up to the thing that had been fixed to the line, screwed on by a bolt passing underneath the rail, so that I could have done nothing *there* with my teeth.

"'Great heavens!' gasped the loco. super., as he stooped down with his lamp, 'A couple of dynamite cartridges! My man you have saved the Royal train; but for goodness sake keep your mouth shut.'

"Well, the result was that they examined the tunnel from end to end, and then the Royal train was allowed to run slowly through.

"A few days later, I 'trod the carpet' in the general manager's room. He thanked me for what I had done and asked me to keep the whole thing to myself—for the sake of the Company, I expect—and ended by giving me an envelope with a nice little sum in bank notes.

"'Also,' he said, 'you'd better go to a dentist's and get some false teeth put into those gaps. You can send in the bill to the Company.'"

A Warning in Red: The Story of a Railway Mystery
Victor L. Whitechurch and E. Conway

"Yes," said the Colonel, as he lit another cheroot, "many a man when he is in action is simply mad for the time being, and fights like a demon because he sees red."

"Sees red?" I asked, with a start.

"Don't you know what I mean?"

"No."

"Ah, it's a curious psychological problem that I've experienced myself. I was leading a cavalry charge at Joonpore, and suddenly the enemy, the country, everything seemed to fade away into a blood-red mist that blinded me with colour—I could see nothing else. And then the mad desire came upon me to slash and slay. They told me afterwards that I behaved like a fury, and I can believe it, for I've seen many a man in the same condition. It only comes in battle, I believe. That's the only time you can 'see red.'"

"Are you sure?"

"Yes. But what's the matter, Forbes? You look completely startled."

"Oh, it's nothing," I replied, "only a fanciful presentiment I had when I arrived this evening, and you put me in mind of it."

"What! you don't mean to say you saw red," asked the Colonel, with a laugh.

"Not in your sense of the word, Colonel; and you'll only laugh at me if I tell you. It's a mere fancy, that's all."

"Well, drown your fancies in a whisky and soda, and then get a good night's rest after your journey. That's the best thing for you,

Forbes. But if you like to tell me what's upset you I won't laugh at you."

So in the end I told him about the strange effect I had experienced in alighting at the station. I had come down from town to spend a couple of days with Colonel Ward at Manningford. Although I had known him for many years, and had often seen him at his club, it was the first time I had ever been to stay at his country house. He expected me by a late train, but judgment being given in a case in which I was professionally engaged as solicitor rather earlier than I had expected, I was able to get away from town in the afternoon, and reached Manningford station about six o'clock. I had not thought it worth while to wire, as I had determined to take a trap if it was far to walk, and surprise him.

Manningford was a tiny little country station, I was the only passenger who alighted, and one solitary official, who seemed to combine the offices of stationmaster, porter, and ticket-collector, met me on the platform.

"Tickets, please," he said, gruffly.

I gave him my ticket. As I did so, the train in which I had been travelling glided off the platform, and I caught a glimpse of the red tail-light showing in the fading day.

Grasping my Gladstone bag, I was about to depart, when the idea struck me that I would ask the stationmaster about a conveyance. He had retired to his office and was standing at the ticket-issuing window, which was open. He had lit the lamp inside, as the office was rather dark.

"Can I get a cab anywhere?" I asked.

He looked up. He was a red-faced man with red hair, and the strong light showed his colour vividly. In accordance with the rules of the railway company he served, he was wearing a red tie.

"No," he said, rather shortly. Perhaps I was staring a little rudely at his illuminated countenance.

"But," I persisted, "surely there is some conveyance to be had near, isn't there?"

"You can hire a dog-cart at the Star," he said.

"Where is that?"

"Cross the line and go out on the other side of the station. Turn to the right, and it's about five minutes' walk."

And he slammed down the window.

I went on to the platform once more, and slowly crossed the line. I say slowly, because the *red* colour of my surroundings began to grow upon me. The station itself was painted a chocolate colour of a reddish tinge. The tiles bordering the flower beds were of a deep red colour, enclosing for the most part scarlet geraniums. Looking down the line I caught the crimson rays of the setting sun reflected upon the rails, and glancing in the opposite direction noticed that the red light on the up starting signal was burning brightly. It was a strange, indescribable sensation that attacked me, this predominance of blood-red colouring; and I gave a little shiver as I walked to the inn, which was a good quarter of a mile from the station, though apparently the nearest house. A two-mile drive brought me to the Colonel's, and after dinner his mention of "seeing red" recalled what had happened.

"Well," said Colonel Ward, as he bid me good-night, "I won't laugh at you, because I'll admit that we're none of us accountable for peculiar brain sensations at times. Monk, the stationmaster, isn't exactly a beauty to look at, is he? But he's a capital official. You've been overworking yourself lately, Forbes, and you must take things easy. Good-night, old chap. Pleasant dreams. I hope your red sensation is not the preliminary to a nightmare."

The next morning, as we were sitting at breakfast, a servant burst into the room with a very frightened expression, and told the Colonel that a man wanted to see him at once. He was absent for about a quarter of an hour, when he returned in great agitation.

"Great heavens!" he exclaimed, "my poor friend Geoffrey Anstruthers has been murdered—killed on the line when coming down from town last night. Your blood-red impression had something in it, perhaps, Forbes."

"Tell me about it, Colonel."

"I will. It's upset me dreadfully. Poor Anstruthers was my nearest neighbour, living about a mile off in that big white house you noticed between the station and my place. We were the greatest of friends, for although he was a very peculiar man we got on thoroughly. The poor fellow was to have met you at dinner here tonight."

"How did it happen?"

"Well, they tell me his body was discovered by the side of the line near Barton—about midway between London and Manningford. A platelayer found it early this morning. There were marks of a struggle and a couple of knife stabs, and he seems to have been attacked and killed in the train and then thrown out."

"Have you any idea if there was a motive for the crime?" I asked.

"Unfortunately, yes," said the Colonel. "Poor Anstruthers was a man of most eccentric habits, and one of his fads was that he would bank nowhere but at the Bank of England, and that he would pay nobody by cheque. He also settled all his accounts once a quarter only, and the tradesman who asked for an earlier settlement, or the servant or labourer who demanded monthly or weekly wages, was sure to be dismissed by him. Regularly every quarter we went up to London and drew several hundred pounds in gold out of the Bank of England, bringing it back in an ordinary brief bag. I often warned him that he was doing a very foolish thing, but he only laughed at me.

"Yesterday he went up to town for this purpose. His servants thought that as he had not returned last evening by his usual train, which arrives at 10.15 p.m., he was staying the night in town. But evidently some blackguard got hold of his movements. Poor old Anstruthers!"

"Is anything being done yet?" I asked.

"I hardly know," said the Colonel; "I think his nearest relations are abroad. At all events I'm the greatest friend he had, and I'm going to take the matter up. I shall go to Barton by the next train."

"I'll come with you," I said.

"That's very kind of you, Forbes; your assistance will be most valuable, for I know your hobby—railways. It might help us."

We finished our breakfast quickly and drove into the station. On my way I asked the Colonel a few particulars concerning the train by which Anstruthers had travelled the night before. It ran as follows:—

> London (dep.) . . . . . . 8.45 p.m.
> Muggridge (stop) . . . . 9.10 p.m.
> Barton (stop) . . . . 9.37 p.m.
> Manningford (stop) . . . 10.15 p.m.
> Porthaven (arrive) . . . . 10.30 p.m.

So that the only stops between London and Manningford were Muggridge and Barton. The body, so the Colonel had heard, had been found about two miles on the London side of Barton.

The red-faced stationmaster was in his office when we arrived at the station.

"Sad job this, Mr. Monk," said the Colonel.

"Terrible, sir. It regularly upset me when the down train brought the news this morning. Poor Mr. Anstruthers! I knew him well, sir. I'd seen him go up in the morning, and wondered why he didn't come back by the 10.15 as usual. Are you going by the up train?"

"Yes. We're going to Barton to inquire into this awful affair. Two first returns, please."

The stationmaster reached to his rack for the tickets. Now, as often happens in small country stations where the supply of tickets to various stations on the line is limited and becomes exhausted, he did a very common thing. Selecting two blank tickets he dipped the pen into ink and wrote on their respective halves, "Manningford to Barton," "Barton to Manningford," and the fare, 7s. 8d.

Then he passed them through the window and I took them up. He had written the names in *red ink!*

"I hope they'll catch the wretches, sir," said the stationmaster a few minutes afterwards, as he opened our carriage door for us.

Arrived at Barton, we took a trap and drove to the scene of the tragedy. The body, we were told, had been removed to an inn close by the railway, but at my request we went first to the line, as I was anxious to see the exact spot where Mr. Anstruthers had been thrown out of the train. We found a local policeman and two plate-layers at the place, which was in a cutting. One of the latter told us that he was the man who had discovered the body.

"He was lyin' just here, gentlemen," he said, pointing to the six-foot way between the two lines of metals.

"Of course he was dead when you found him?" I asked.

"Yes, sir, but it's my opinion he wasn't altogether dead when they threw him out."

"Why?"

"'Cause he seemed to have moved afterwards. One of his arms was just restin' on the down rail."

"Well?"

"Well, sir, he couldn't ha' fallen like that in the first place, cause the wheels o' the train would ha' cut his arm."

"Stop a minute," I said. "What time did you find him here?"

"'Tween three and four this mornin', sir."

"And he was thrown out about 9.30 the night before?"

"Yes, sir."

"Was that train the last down one?"

"The last passenger train, sir."

"Was there a down goods train after that?"

"Yes, sir, between half-past one and two."

"Ah, then, why didn't *that* train crush his arm?"

The question staggered the platelayer and the policeman too. They evidently hadn't thought of this.

"I s'pose 'e must ha' bin alive when the goods train passed, and moved afterwards," said the platelayer presently, and the police-man entered a note to that effect in his pocket-book.

"What are you driving at?" said the Colonel.

"Never mind yet," I answered. Then, turning to the platelayer again, I said, "He was stabbed, wasn't he?"

"Yes, sir."

"Where?"

"In the chest, sir."

"Any bloodstains?"

"Yes, sir. He was wearin' a white weskit, and it was quite red when I turned him over."

"He was lying on his back, then?"

"Yes, sir."

"Well, where are the blood-marks on the stones here? Have you cleared them up?"

"*There wasn't none*," said the man.

"Strange!" I murmured to myself, as we left the spot.

"You'd make a good detective, Forbes," said the Colonel.

"Not a bit of it," I replied. "It's simply because there is a mystery connected with my hobby—railways. That's what makes me a little extra sharp."

"A *mystery?*" said the Colonel.

"Yes," I replied, "more than you think. But now let's see the poor fellow."

Mr. Anstruthers was lying on a bed at the inn, just as they had found him. The neighbouring police inspector was there, very imposing and important. The Colonel gave his card, and we were allowed to see the body.

It was a gruesome sight, and my friend turned away to ask some questions of the inspector. I looked at the dead man carefully. There were signs of a struggle. His clothes were torn, and one of his hands was tightly clenched. Then I saw what, apparently, the wily country police had passed undiscovered—a shred of paper clasped in his hand. Without exciting the inspector's attention, I wrested the fingers open and drew from them a tiny scrap of torn paper, evidently clutched by a dying hand. It bore the following in writing:— "ord—on." It was such a tiny scrap, such an insignificant thing to go upon, but I slipped it into my pocket-book nevertheless.

"Come," said the Colonel, "I can't stand this any longer. Well, inspector, I hope you'll get the villain."

"Ah, we're on the track," said the officer, sagaciously. "They got out at Barton, that's about it; and we'll have 'em yet."

"Do you want to see anything else, Forbes?" asked the Colonel.

"Yes. I should like to see the doctor who examined the body."

"It's Dr. Moore," said the policeman. "He lives at Barton."

So we called on Dr. Moore on our way to the station. He declared that he had seen poor Anstruthers at six o'clock in the morning, and was positively certain that he must then have been dead *seven or eight hours*. The mystery was thickening.

Passing on to the platform at Barton, we had to show our tickets. As I took mine back I gazed at it in a listless sort of way, when suddenly I gave a start. The last three letters of "Manningford"—where had I seen them? That peculiar elongated "o" and the curiously tailed "d"—Ah! I remembered!

Hastily I drew the scrap of paper from my pocket-book, and compared it with the ticket. The "ord" was in the same handwriting! It was part of the words "Manningford station."

In a moment a clue flashed across my mind, and I searched for a porter.

"Is there any official about the station with whom I can have a word? It's about an urgent matter."

"Yes, sir; Mr. Smart, the district superintendent is here; he came down about that murder. You'll find him in the station-master's office."

"Come with me, Colonel," I cried, turning to the office.

Hastily I introduced myself to Mr. Smart, telling him my errand was connected with the murder.

"Tell me," I asked, "is there any train from Manningford to London after 10.15?"

"Only a goods," he said.

"Exactly. What time does it leave Manningford?"

"About midnight."

"And Barton?"

"It stops here for shunting. Generally starts on about 1.45 a.m."

"Mr. Smart, can you lay your hand on the men who worked that train last night?"

He consulted some return sheets.

"Driver Power and fireman Hussey," he murmured. "They're on the Slinford branch to-day—they don't often run on the main line—and brakesman Sutton. He works a goods back to Porthaven to-day. He'll arrive there in half an hour."

"Does he always work main line trains?"

"For several months past he has."

"He's the man then, Mr. Smart. It's of the utmost importance that you should wire to Porthaven to have him closely watched. I'll explain presently."

The district superintendent hastily scribbled a line on an official telegraph form and rushed out with it. When he returned I said—

"Have you any of the company's detectives at hand?"

"Yes, two," he answered.

"Bring them then, and come along."

"My dear fellow," said the Colonel, who had been patiently silent up to this point, "*what* does it all mean?"

"Yes," said the superintendent, "I'm in a fog."

"I hear the down train coming in," I cried. "We must all return to Manningford—quick, sir—I'll explain everything in the train."

A few minutes, and the Colonel, the superintendent, and his two detectives and myself were in the train bound for Manningford.

"Now, sir?" said Mr. Smart.

"Well," I replied, "we're going to arrest the murderers, or one of them I think, at all events."

"And who's that?"

"Monk, the stationmaster at Manningford," I answered.

"*Monk?* Impossible. Why, the murder occurred forty miles away."

"No," I replied, "it occurred at Manningford station last night shortly after 10.15. Listen. Poor Anstruthers came down from town, got out of the train, and was done to death by the stationmaster, who was *alone on the station*, for the sake of his money. In the struggle the murdered man clutched a letter that Monk had written and was probably carrying in his breast pocket. This scrap of it I found in his hand just now. It is in Monk's handwriting. Look!" and I compared it with the ticket.

"But how about the body being found where it was?" asked the Colonel.

"It was taken there afterwards, probably in Sutton's brake van, and thrown out. This would account for two facts: first, that no blood was found on the permanent way, although Anstruthers had bled; and, secondly, that his arm was lying on the down rail. The down goods had passed before he was thrown from the up goods brake van. That's my theory, gentlemen. Here we are at Manningford, and the least you can do is to arrest the stationmaster on suspicion."

The latter was on the platform when we arrived. I noticed he gave a start as he saw so many of us get out of the train. The superintendent went up to him.

"Mr. Monk," he said, "a very painful duty brings us here. These two gentlemen are members of our police force, and they will have to detain you on suspicion."

"Of what?" gasped Monk, his red face growing paler.

"Of participation in the murder of Mr. Anstruthers last night."

"But he was killed in the train," said the stationmaster.

"That remains to be proved. At all events we are going to detain you, and to search your house."

"I won't submit to it," began the man; but he subsided when a pair of handcuffs were slipped over his wrists. Then we all repaired to his little house, just across the road. Again he proved turbulent, but it was no use. With skeleton keys one of the detectives opened a box in his bedroom.

"Ah!" he exclaimed, as he drew out a brief bag, "this seems rather heavy. No wonder. It's full of money."

"That's Anstruthers' bag," exclaimed the Colonel.

The wretched man saw the game was up, but, wretch that he was, he exclaimed—

"It's not me—it's Sutton—the brakesman of the up goods train. He had as much to do with it as I did. He took the body away; and he's got a lot of the gold."

"All right," said the superintendent, "we're seeing after him. You have to thank this gentleman," pointing to myself, "for unravelling the mystery."

"Curse you!" yelled the stationmaster at me.

Sutton turned against Monk, and between the two of them the whole story came out. Monk's accounts were short, and he owed money all round—the usual story—racing. He had half planned to murder Anstruthers several times, and at last the opportunity presented itself. He was the only passenger to alight that night, and Monk noticed that the guard had not observed him. So he asked him to step into his office for a moment under pretence of something, and then went for him. There was a struggle, but Monk was the stronger man. In this struggle Anstruthers hid grasped the bit of paper, but without the other's knowledge.

Then came the disposal of the body. Sutton was a man of doubtful character, and Monk knew enough about him to ruin him if he disclosed certain cases of goods stealing. So, when the goods train came along, he gave Sutton twenty pounds, and promised him another thirty to take the body in his van and pitch it out so that people would think Anstruthers had been murdered in the train. It was the easiest thing possible on a dark night to halt the train with the brake van opposite Monk's office, and to slip the body in without driver or fireman knowing anything about it.

The sequel was the gallows for Monk, and fifteen years at Dartmoor for Sutton.

"There was something uncanny after all, Forbes," said the Colonel, after dinner on that eventful day, "about your blood-red impression of Manningford station and its master!"

A Jump for Freedom: An Engine-Driver's Story

Steady lot, us drivers? Well, we have to be, there's no choice in the matter. Driving wants a clear head, and a man who can make up his mind what to do in a moment. The majority of people don't half realize the work there is to do, or the responsibilities of the "foot-plate."

I often think, myself, the difference there is between us chaps and the captain of a Channel-boat. I used to think of it more when I was on the "Sou'-Western," running the Continental train to Southampton. Maybe I had a couple of hundred lives in tow; but I'll venture to say very few of them thought of the man who had them and the train in sole charge, for though the fireman's along with you, the driver is responsible for everything, including him. Yet when the passengers stepped aboard the Channel-boat, if they got a glimpse of the captain they'd look at him with a kind of awe.

I don't say all this out of jealousy, but I've often thought if we had a uniform, with gold lace round our caps and collars and an engine worked on our shoulders, folks who were going a long journey would think more of us, and say: "That's our driver," just as you hear them remark "That's our captain."

Still, as I say, I wouldn't change. There's a charm about the "foot-plate" and a pride in your engine that only a driver knows. Why, I've seen men get quite affectionate over a favourite engine, and almost cry when they were changed to another. Adventures? Well, the life's full of adventures, more or less; not very interesting to the general public, perhaps, but exciting enough to us. Stop,

246

though. I can tell you one adventure I had years ago, which will interest you—about the most remarkable thing that ever happened to me, and about as curious an affair as you could find in the history of the line, I reckon. It was when I was on the Sou'-Western, and before I became a regular express driver.

Before you can quite understand it, I must tell you something about the line itself. From Clapham Junction to Hampton Court there are four lines of rails, two of them used for up and down "fast" trains, and the others for up and down "slow." You have the same sort of thing on some of the other lines: the London and North-Western, for instance, has four lines as far as Roade, beyond Bletchley, only they are worked differently to the South-Western.

The London and North-Western run their up and down fast trains on the two left-hand lines of rails from Euston, and the up and down slow on the two right-hand, so that, when two trains are going in the same direction, there is always a line of metals between them. But from Clapham to Hampton Court Junction the outer left-hand rail is used for slow, and the next to it, the inner left-hand, for fast, the outer right and inner right being used for up-slow and fast respectively. The "up-slow" extends all the way to Woking, but this has nothing to do with my story.

Thus, you see, if one train passes another going in the same direction, the trains are close together. Sometimes I have known two trains travel alongside each other at the same rate for two or three minutes, and more than once I have spoken from my engine to the driver of another train, and given or received a bit of 'baccy when we were going at the rate of forty or fifty miles an hour.

The Northern system is generally considered to be the better of the two, but the South-Western still stick to the other plan.

One day, in the winter of 188-, there had been a special cheap excursion from Portsmouth to Waterloo: I forget what the occasion was; but, anyhow, I was detailed on duty to take this train back to Portsmouth.

We were to start at 9.27, and as far as Hampton Court Junction to run on the outer, or slow, line. The last train before us was the nine o'clock, so you see we expected a clear run. We were not to stop anywhere before reaching Portsmouth.

The train was a heavy one, as a good number of people had taken advantage of the excursion, and it seemed that we should hardly get off to time. As a matter of fact, however, we were only two minutes late in starting, and were soon bowling away merrily towards the south.

The boat-express to Southampton leaves Waterloo at 9.35, and runs from there to Basingstoke without a stop, travelling to Hampton Court Junction on the fast line. We had just passed Rayne's Park when I heard the approaching roar of the express coming down behind us. We were travelling a good forty miles an hour at the time, and the other train began to pass ours very slowly. Presently the express engine was alongside ours, and the driver sang out a cheery "What ho! mate," as the two "cabs" came together. Creeping gradually past us, the carriages of the boat-train became visible, and as I glanced at them I could distinguish the passengers plainly. Five coaches had already passed us, when I stood well on the left-hand side of the foot-plate, furthest from the other train, to allow my fireman to perform his office.

At this moment my engine put on a little spurt, and the two trains were running almost exactly at the same pace, the other just slightly gaining. I happened to glance over my shoulder, when, to my astonishment, I saw a man in the other train deliberately opening the door of his compartment, which was just drawing opposite to the "cab" of my engine. Before I could recover from my surprise he had stepped out on the footboard of the carriage, and in another second he sprang upon the foot-plate of my engine, clutching at the rail on the cab, while the door of the carriage he had left, obeying the motion of the train, shut with a slam.

In an agony of terror, my mate and I seized him and dragged him into a position of safety, while the other train spurted forward and passed us. For a moment or two neither of us spoke. I was the first to recover my presence of mind, and the habit of duty mastered my curiosity for the instant.

"Hold on here," I shouted. "Jim fire her up, man; wait till we get through Woking—then we'll see to him. Steady, sir! Keep over in that corner, please, and thank Providence you're not a dead man."

"Mad, I should think," said my fireman, as he set to work again shovelling on the coals, while I riveted my attention to the mass of red and green lights we were ever and anon approaching and passing.

At Hampton Court Junction we were switched on to the "fast" line, following the boat-express by about six minutes, and in half an hour or so we were through Woking, and then I turned to the stranger. He was a young man, clean-shaven, and well-dressed; deadly pale and trembling, clutching hard at the support. The footplate's a bit shaky to a novice.

"Are you mad, sir? Do you know you've had a fearful escape? What, in the name of all that's wonderful, do you mean by it?"

"N-no; I'm not mad. I—I was forced to do it."

"Forced to do it? Why, you were alone in the carriage, as far as I could see."

"Yes, yes, I know that. But I was desperate. I'll explain everything."

"Wait a minute or two; I can't attend now. Tell me when we're through Guildford."

How he started as we entered the Guildford tunnel just beyond the station! I thought he'd fall at first, and my mate had to hold on to him for a minute. When we were clear of the tunnel, I asked him for his explanation.

"I wanted to escape," he said, "and it was the only way."

"Escape? Who from? The police, I suppose? Well, don't you think you've done that, my friend."

"No, no, no! Not from the police. I'm not a criminal. Listen, and I'll tell you. I've got mixed up with a terrible secret society—a set of people composed of the very worst sort of Anarchists—men of several nations. It would be too long a story to tell you how I came to join it, but when once among such people, there is no drawing back. We were pledged with the most awful oaths to secrecy,

and terrible penalties were ordained for those who proved trai-
tors. I would have given anything to set myself free, but it was
impossible.

"Well, one evening last week, we held a meeting to determine
the performance of an awful act. I can't tell you exactly the truth,
but I will go so far as to say it was the assassination of a certain
great personage on the Continent. We drew lots, in order that the
assassin might be chosen. The lot fell upon me. In vain I begged to
be excused, the others were relentless, and the president said to
me:—

"'George Felton, you have sworn obedience, and obey you must.
The lot has fallen upon you, and you must perform the deed. If you
refuse, or if you even hesitate, there is only one penalty, and that
you know. It is death, and it is useless for you to try to escape from
it. This is how you will proceed: Until Thursday you will be carefully watched. The evening of that day you will take the boat-train
via Southampton and Havre for Paris. You will travel by that route
because it is the less frequented. You will go absolutely alone, but
every step you will be watched. The "brethren" will be posted all
along the line of route. At Waterloo two of them will watch you
into the train. At Basingstoke two others will keep their eyes on
you while the train is stopping there. At Southampton you will be
watched on board the boat, and the same thing will happen at Havre
and Rouen, your only stopping-places. At Paris you will be met by
two comrades, who will keep you in view until the final arrangements have been made, when you will be told how to act. So do not
think to escape, as every movement will be watched.'"

The train flew on; my mate and I were interested, as you may
well guess. He paused for a moment to allow of the engine being
coaled once more, then I said:—

"But you might have stopped the train by pulling the communicator, and—"

"I'm coming to that. I had thought of trying to escape thus, but
just as the train moved out of the station a little note was thrown
in at the window by a 'comrade,' who had been watching me. I
opened it and read as follows: 'We never thought the other night

that perhaps you might try to escape by stopping the train *en route* and jumping off. In case such an idea has entered your head, you may as well know that the "brothers" are on the train. You know what that means. You are helpless. Be brave for the sake of the "cause."'"

"Have you got that letter?" said the fireman.

"No; I tore it up. Well, I tell you, I was desperate. I had half made up my mind to jump and risk it, when we gradually began to pass your train. I was alone in my compartment, and could see the well-filled carriages close to me. I sat looking at them mechanically, when the idea suddenly seized me, and I asked myself the question, 'Why shouldn't I change trains?' By this time I was opposite to the guard's van in the front, and there was not a moment to be lost. It was too late to try for that when I opened the door, and my only course was to jump on to your engine. Thank God, I did so safely!"

"Aye, you've had a lucky escape, and you may well thank God. Well, what's to be done now?"

"Where are you bound for?"

"Portsmouth."

"Do you stop anywhere first?"

"No."

"Well, look here. Can't I slip off on the outer side as we come into the station?"

"I don't know so much about that. You've come on the footplate uninvited, and you ought to give an account of it to the authorities. If I let you get off without, I'm liable for a row myself. Besides, how are we to know your story's true?"

"Before God I swear it's true. And no one need ever know I was here. I'll make it well worth your while. Besides," he added, piteously, "it's my only chance. When they know I've escaped they'll search high and low. If this isn't kept quiet they'll know about it before I have the start of them, and that means certain death. I couldn't escape. As it is, I've got money enough to get well out of the country before they know."

Well, it seemed rough enough on the poor chap, but my mate stuck out against letting him go. I argued the matter out with him as well as I could, and he was beginning to come round to my point of view when I suddenly exclaimed:—

"Look out, mate, there's a block at Petersfield."

The distant signal was shining with a red light instead of a green, and we put on the brakes until the train was almost at a standstill.

"For God's sake, let me get off," begged the stranger.

My mate and I looked at one another. The train came to a stop close to the signal.

"Don't refuse me. See here," and he held out five sovereigns and literally pressed them into my hand. I looked at Jim again. He nodded.

"All right, get off and keep quiet till we've gone on. Good luck to you. Here, I don't want your money."

But he was gone in a moment. Then the semaphore arm fell with a crash, the green light shone out, and we started once again; nor did we stop till we had reached Portsmouth. Later on, my mate and I talked the matter over between us, and agreed that we would not mention it to anyone, as it was better for all that it should be kept quiet. Then I offered him half the money.

"No," said he, "I won't take it. If his story's true, it's something like the price of blood. They must have given him the cash for his journey and expenses."

I hadn't seen it in that light.

"Well, mate, I believe you're right. I never thought of that. I sha'n't touch it either, I couldn't bring myself to do it. But what shall we do with it?"

Finally, we agreed to send it anonymously to a railway charity, and the next morning we did so.

Two days after that, I was off duty, when the fireman came round to my house, with a curious expression on his face and a newspaper in his hand. "Read that," he said, quickly, pointing to a paragraph. I read as follows:—

"MYSTERIOUS DISAPPEARANCE OF A CRIMINAL.

"On Thursday evening last, a strange occurrence, the facts of which are unknown, must have taken place somewhere on the main line of the South-Western Railway between Waterloo and Basingstoke. Our readers will remember the case of embezzlement and forgery at the head offices of the 'Amalgamated General European and Colonial Exchange,' a forgery on a large scale, in which the under cashier, Charles Winfield, a clever, and unfortunately well-trusted young man, was deeply implicated. Winfield, by some means, managed to escape arrest, and the police have been assiduously following his track since. On the evening in question, Detective Baxter, of Scotland Yard, recognised Winfield in a first-class compartment of the 9.35 boat-train from Waterloo to Southampton. The train was just moving out of the station, and it was impossible for the detective to get in, but he ran along the platform by the side of the window, clearly identified his man, took the number of the carriage, and noticed which compartment it was, and immediately wired to Basingstoke, the first stopping-place. When, however, the train arrived at this place, the police, who had assembled on the platform, found no trace of the criminal. It was ascertained that the train had not pulled up once; the particular compartment was empty, but a thorough search was made throughout the train, it being thought that he might have changed carriages by the foot-board. It is supposed that Winfield recognised the fact that he had been discovered at the last moment on his way to the Continent, and guessing that he would be arrested at Basingstoke, must have jumped off the train in a moment of desperation. Whether the unhappy man

was killed or escaped remains a mystery, no trace of
him having been discovered."

"What do you think of that?" said my mate.

"Well," I said, "I think he half deserved to escape on account of
his pluck. And—well, he was the finest liar I've ever met!"

The fireman nodded his head slowly, and then said:—

"Well, I had my doubts most of the time. He was too fine a liar
for me!"

Special Working Instructions:
A Station-Master's Story

"I really believe," said the station-master, "that the majority of the travelling public imagine that the sum total of my duties consists in wearing a cap with a gold band round it, and strutting about the platforms starting trains and answering questions, many of which would puzzle the general manager of the line himself.

"Now, look here," he went on, pointing to the heterogeneous mass of documents lying on the table of the office, and taking them up one by one as he enumerated them. "This is the sort of thing—from early morning till dewy eve, and often starry midnight—a complaint from some old lady saying she's left her umbrella either in the waiting-room, or on the book-stall, or in a train she travelled in yesterday (she doesn't say which), and will I tell her where it is and send it on at once. A notice from the district superintendent asking for full details why the 12.53 was delayed here yesterday. Instructions for submitting plans for ventilating the cloak-room. Pamphlet of new fog-signalling arrangements, requiring a complete alteration of posting the men. A claim from a local brewer demanding compensation for beer arriving short (it's marvellous how beer casks are always being staved in—accidentally—on our night goods trains). Instructions for working three 'specials'—excursions—to-morrow morning, and so on. It's never finished, and sometimes I'm sick of it."

"This is rather interesting," I remarked, taking the last paper he had mentioned from his hand and glancing at it. "How wonderfully every detail is arranged, down to the names of the guards and the time of passing every little signal cabin!"

255

"Those working instructions for the 'specials'? Yes, they have to be set down pretty accurately. You see, we have to work them as far as possible without interfering with the ordinary traffic, and that means a lot of detail."

It certainly did. On the printed form was portrayed the running of the trains in question, the number of coaches of which they were to be composed, the class of engines to draw them, the stops for taking in water, the shunting into "refuge sidings" *en route* to allow of the passage of certain express trains—everything was put down most carefully.

"I'm not sure that I ought to allow you to handle that," went on the station-master, with a laugh. "You know, it's private information, 'For the Company's servants only,' as you see."

"Well, I'll give it up at once—though I don't see what harm it could do for me to know a little more than the outside public about these excursion trains."

"No; as you say, there's no particular harm in anyone seeing these papers. But," he added, musingly, "sometimes we receive certain working instructions that might prove very dangerous if outsiders were to get hold of them."

"How so?" I asked.

The station-master took a key from his pocket, unlocked a drawer, and produced a crumpled and torn paper.

"This is a paper of working instructions for a special train," he said, "which nearly caused a most frightful catastrophe, and which got me that nasty scar you may have noticed over my left eye."

I took the paper. It was headed:—

"Specially urgent and private."

"Instructions for working through down special train from London to Porthaven on March 7th, 189-."

I looked at my companion inquiringly.

"I see you want to know all about it," he said; "so as it's a slack half hour, and I can get through my correspondence afterwards, I don't mind telling you."

Then he related the following startling experience:—

"I suppose that some of our chief railway officials could, if they chose, throw many a light upon the political history of Europe. I mean that often visits of the utmost importance take place between the Ambassadors of different countries, aye, and between those who are higher than Ambassadors—visits that are kept jealously secret and guarded, but upon which hang sometimes the great fates of diplomacy—of war and peace. It is here that the railway companies are often requisitioned to provide swift and secure means of transit. Many a special train has traversed the length and breadth of England, for instance, the identity of whose passengers was only known to a few officials who made arrangements for the journey, and who could be absolutely trusted in the matter. Often it has been the work of a master railway mind to run such trains at the precise time needed, a work of great anxiety when perhaps the traffic superintendent knows an international problem is trembling in the balance, and the solution rests upon the speed with which a diplomatic journey is accomplished. Then, although it is true we do not, happily, have to take the immense precautions which are observed when the Czar travels in Russia, still it is often necessary to arrange as strictly for the safe transit of an important personage as for his speed. For, indeed, those who move in the highest circles have enemies always, including the times when they travel.

"When I received the circular of instructions which you now hold in your hand, I guessed, from the caution and secrecy to be observed, that some person of great importance was about to pass over the line. Who this exalted personage was it matters not; except, perhaps, you might probably call to mind that in the year 189- a certain great Sovereign of Eastern Europe was paying a private visit to the Queen—a visit which, so it is said, formed the basis of a subsequent diplomatic treaty.

"I was at the time the station-master of Millbridge, a small station on our main line some forty or fifty miles from the London terminus. It was a lonely spot at best, especially at night, for no passenger trains stopped there after eight o'clock, though there were plenty of through expresses. The station staff was a very small one, as you will readily imagine.

Victor L. Whitechurch

"The circular in question was delivered to me on the evening of March 6th, inclosed with a letter from the superintendent of the line enjoining me to observe the very strictest caution and secrecy in carrying out its instructions. The instructions were, briefly, these. A special train was to leave London at 10.30 p.m. and was to run to Porthaven. Not only were all pains to be taken to see that she ran to time, but certain precautions, very much like those observed when the Queen travels, were to be put in operation. Twenty minutes before the special's 'time' each block was to be clear, and patrols—chosen in each case from the platelayers of the district—were to be placed along the line at stated intervals two hours before the passing of the train, which, by the way, was timed to pass Millbridge at 11.23 p.m.

"I recognised that somebody of the greatest importance was travelling to Porthaven, which is, as you know, a seaport town from which many vessels sail to the Baltic. The next morning I proceeded to carry out instructions. I arranged with the ganger of the district for the placing of the platelayers. I caused the signals, etc., to be carefully inspected; in fact, I did all that was necessary and sent up a report to town by a late afternoon train.

"Of course I intended to be on the watch to see such an important special through, and I detailed my head porter to be on duty with me at 11 p.m. I must also tell you that I had given orders to my signal-man, in accordance with the instructions, that a down goods train which was due at 10.45 should be shunted into a siding till the special had passed.

"About half-past nine that evening I was seated in my office, making up my accounts. I have told you that the station was a lonely one. My own house was the nearest, and that was a couple of hundred yards away. My office, which opened on to the platform, was, of course, very quiet at that hour. In feet, I was the only person on the station, the signal-man on duty in the cabin just off the platform being the nearest man. There were no more stopping trains that night. The booking clerk and porters had gone home, and, as I have said, the head porter was not to come on duty till eleven.

"I was feeling a certain sense of satisfaction over my arrangements for the 'special,' knowing that the men were properly posted and that everything was clear, when, without a word of warning, my door was suddenly thrown open, and two men, with masks on their faces, entered.

"'Good evening,' said one of them, abruptly. 'You're the station-master?'

"'Yes,' said I, in astonishment.

"'Well, we've come on a little matter of business, and if you're quiet we won't hurt you, though we shall have to take strong measures.'

"'What on earth do you want?' I began.

"'First of all we want to see your instructions about a special train that's to run down from London to-night.'

"'You're not going to see anything of the kind,' I cried, attempting to rush through the door and give an alarm.

"But they were too quick for me. In a moment they had tripped me up and sent me sprawling on my back.

"'Give up that paper!'

"'I won't!' I shouted, springing to my feet— 'Help! help!'

"'Quiet, you fool!' said the man who had not yet spoken, aiming a blow at me with a heavy stick. It caught me just over the left eye and fairly stunned me for a few minutes.

"When I came to I found myself gagged, my arms bound behind me, and one of the ruffians finishing binding my feet together. The other was eagerly rummaging my pocketbook.

"'Here it is,' he exclaimed.

"'Good!' said the other, as he tied the last knot. 'Now let us hear all about it.'

"'Here we are,' said his companion, as he consulted the paper. 'Head-lights on engine a white one over a green one—'umph, we must bear that in mind. Leaves London 10.30—passes through here at 11.23—passes "Ash signal-cabin" at 11.28, and Frambourne 11.36.'

"'Ah, well, the bridge is about midway between Ash cabin and Frambourne, eh?'

"'Yes—so she'll pass there about 11.33.'

"'Good. What's the time now?'

"I could see the other man first take out his watch and then look at the clock in my office.

"'Why, I'm over five minutes slow,' he said; 'it's three minutes past ten by this clock. I'll set my watch by it, and then we'll be off.'

"Really his watch was right. For many years I have been in the habit of keeping my office clock five minutes in advance.

"'As for you, Mr. Station-master,' he exclaimed a moment later, as they both turned to depart, 'I fancy you'll have to keep quiet for a while. Good-night, and pleasant dreams!'

"So saying he turned out my lamp, and I heard them locking the door on the outside after they had left me. I tell you I was pretty uncomfortable. Not only was I lying bound hand and foot, unable to speak, and suffering from the cut on my face, but I realized that something dreadful was going to happen to the special train—*what*, I could not guess. Then I remembered how particular the instructions had been, the secrecy, the unusual precautions, and the urgent way in which it had been laid down that the train should not be one minute delayed in any way.

"I began to suffer agonies. What had they meant by the bridge? Were they going to wreck the train? The latter seemed impossible in view of the patrols. There was only one bridge between Ash cabin and Frambourne, and that was over the line where a road crossed it. Close under this bridge a platelayer had been stationed, I knew. It was a mystery.

"And then as regarded myself. When should I get free? The head porter would come on the platform about eleven. He would try the door and find it locked. I should be unable to answer him. He would think I had gone up the line, home—*what* would he think? I struggled in my rage, but it was useless.

"So the time went by. It seemed hours— I heard the goods train come in. 'Tap, tap!' The head porter was knocking at the door.

"'Are you there, sir?'

"No answer. He shook the door.

"'That's a rum go,' I heard him exclaim, as his steps retreated. Then my clock struck eleven.

"I rolled over on the floor with a final effort, and managed to get my feet against the leg of the table. Why had I not thought of it before? I was wearing elastic side boots. Hurrah! I wrenched one off by the heel, then the other—*then*, with a supreme effort, I wedged a coil of rope against the table leg and tugged—tugged till I pulled the skin off my heel, *but* the coil slipped slowly over my foot. That loosened the rope—kick, kick—in a few minutes I had kicked myself free. My hands were still bound, but I could use my feet, and I did. I banged against the door with them with all my might in the hopes of attracting attention from outside. And I did.

"'Are you inside, sir?' It was the head porter's voice.

"'Bang—thud'—was all I could answer.

"'All right, sir, I don't know what's up, but I'll smash the door in, so look out!'

"In half a minute he was at work with a platelayer's crowbar. The door came crashing in. A stream of light from his lantern fell upon me. He took in the situation at a glance, whipped out a knife and cut the cords that bound my arms, and the handkerchief which the blackguards had stuffed in my mouth.

"'For Heaven's sake, *what's the time!*' was my first cry, heedless of his questions.

"He flashed the lantern on the clock. *A quarter past eleven!* Ten minutes past by the right time. In thirteen minutes the special was due! What followed was an inspiration. The head porter thought me mad for a few minutes, and I could not even now fully explain *why* I acted as I did. I only felt that at all costs I must send a counterfeit special on first.

"'Rush to the signal cabin and keep back the special till I come. Don't stand there staring like a fool, Gordon. Quick—don't let him take off the home signal!'

"Then, scrambling across the lines and points, I hurried towards the engine of the goods train that was waiting in the siding.

"'Driver—driver!' I cried.

"'Yes, sir.'

"'Put on fresh head-lights; you've got one white one, get a green lamp lighted. Do you hear? And put the white one over it. Quick, now!'

"'What's the matter, sir?' said the astonished driver.

"'Never mind—only—are you prepared to carry out orders at once?'

"'What are they, sir?'

"'Uncouple your engine, then back into No. 2 siding, take on the three empty passenger coaches there, and run on to Frambourne with them without a moment's delay, at your highest speed.'

"'All right, sir,' said the driver, producing the head-light. 'Uncouple her, Jim,' he added to the fireman.

"I was off like a shot to the signal box to direct the slight shunting operation involved. It was wonderfully quick work. At exactly eighteen minutes past eleven the improvised train steamed out of the siding on to the down line. She was *five minutes before the special*. The signal-man saw something unusual was the matter, and forbore from asking questions, simply sending the 'make ready' signal to Ash cabin, and receiving the usual replies. There was a telephone to Ash, and I seized hold of it and gave some directions.

"'I suspect danger on the line between you and Frambourne,' I said, 'and have sent on a pilot train in front of special. Get ready to receive special directly she has passed, but hold up the special till you hear from Frambourne that all is clear. Tell Frambourne to shunt pilot train immediately on arrival.'

"'All right, sir!' came the reply.

"At the same moment there was an ominous whistling in the distance.

"'She wants the signal taken off,' said the signal-man, referring to the special.

"'She'll have to wait, then.'

"The head-lights appeared, slackening down beyond the home-signal. Then came the message from Ash cabin: 'Line clear.'

"Crash! the lever was pulled, the special came on, gathering speed as she passed. There was a locomotive inspector on the foot-plate of the engine, and I heard him shout: 'You'll have to answer for this!'

"Then came a period of suspense, minute after minute passed—then, at last, the 'line clear' signal from the block ahead. The special had passed Ash cabin. Several more minutes—then a ring up on the telephone. 'Pilot train has reached Frambourne, but there's something up. Line clear, and have sent on special.'

"Another pause, and then a telegraphic message from Frambourne: 'Your action highly commendable. You have saved special. Engine of pilot train returning on up line for goods train. Driver will give information.'

"You may be sure we waited in a tension of excitement until that engine arrived, travelling tender first. It was some time before it did so, and when it came it carried a detective and an extra driver, for it appears old Goodson had been too much overcome to take his engine in hand. He came into the little office, and told me the following extraordinary story:—

"'When you sent me on with them three empty passenger coaches,' he said, 'I was dazed like. I never even stopped to pick up the brakesman. Then I begun to think it out. I knew by the head-lights you wanted me to pretend I was the special, and, thinks I, there's danger ahead, that's it. So I kep' a sharp look-out, not knowin' what might be on the line, though I knew 'twas well guarded. It was fairish dark, too, and I couldn't see far ahead.

"'Well, we passed Ash all right, and was bowlin' along for all the world like a racin' train, when I see as I comes up to it the outline of a couple o' men standin' on the top of a bridge. It was all so sudden like that I can't tell exactly what happened, but Joe, my fireman, sings out, as we passes under the bridge, "Halloa," and I see summat fallin' on top o' the train as I turns round to look. Then there were a couple o' awful explosions, and a splinter o' wood copped me on the head. "Go on," ses Joe, as I put my hand on the regulator, "Go on," 'e ses, "the bloomin' train ain't quite smashed up—she'll run all right." So we ran on to Frambourne, and there we find that two carriages were shivered about frightful. Lor' bless us, sir, if there'd been anyone in 'em they'd ha' been killed for certain. They was a mass o' splinters runnin' on frames, that's what they was. You see what they'd done?'

"'Dropped explosives on the train from the bridge?' I gasped.

"'Aye—they thought we was the special. Ah, that was a sharp bit o' work o' yours, sir.'

"'And the special?'

"'Oh, she come through all right, nearly five minutes late. They won't know what happened till she gets to Porthaven. But you saved her, sir.'

"Yes, it was true, I had saved the train and its Royal—well, er—important occupant. I was ill with brain fever for weeks afterwards, but when I recovered I heard that the wretches had never been caught. They had evidently driven in a dog-cart from my station to the bridge, and, owing to setting their watch to my clock and the changed head-lights on the goods engine, had imagined the 'special' was running to time, and had dropped two dynamite bombs on to the tops of the empty coaches as they passed beneath the bridge. The torn paper of working instructions was found on the bridge, and, as you see, I have it now. The other results of that night were promotion to this junction, and a beautiful diamond scarf-pin that was sent me from—well, er—Russia. Yes, passengers sometimes tip even the station-master!"

Wandering through the old city of Rheims one sultry summer evening, I had lighted upon an insignificant little *café* in the neighbourhood of the station, and had sat me down to have a cool "bock" and a smoke. At the next table to mine sat a group of two or three workmen, seemingly connected with the railway, more especially one of them, whose smoky blouse and not over-clean visage proclaimed him as an engine-driver; in fact, as I looked at him I remembered having noticed him on the foot-plate of the engine that had drawn my train from Mézières to Rheims the previous day.

I think it was the request on my part for a light, or something equally trivial, that first caused me to enter into conversation with my neighbours; but certain it was that before long we had drifted into a subject that is rather a dangerous one to touch upon, even now, with a Frenchman: the subject of the Franco-Prussian War.

"Ah, yes, monsieur," said one of the men, "I well remember the coming of the Prussians into Rheims, though I was but a lad at the time. It was early in the afternoon of September the 5th, a few days after the Battle of Sedan. I was lounging about in the streets when I heard the clatter of horse-hoofs, and sure enough four Prussian soldiers came riding into the city. *Ma foi*, how we hissed them!"

"What did they do?"

"Oh, they bought some food at a confectioner's. One old man tried to stop them by taking hold of a horse bridle. The soldier struck him with a pistol, but he would not let go. Then he shot him through the arm. They galloped off directly afterwards, and a shot was fired at them. In a few hours, though, we had twenty-five thousand soldiers, with the King of Prussia at their head, quartered upon us."

"How long did they stay?"

"Oh, they left immediately. They were marching on to Paris, nothing seemed to stand in their way."

"Except old Pierre Cournet," said the man I had guessed to be an engine-driver, taking his cigar from his lips reflectively.

"Ah, but that is true," remarked the other, adding, as he and a third man who had not spoken rose to go, "Monsieur should ask Jean Martin to tell him the story—he is not on duty for another hour yet."

Left alone with Jean Martin, I begged leave to replenish his glass of ordinary wine with a bottle of Burgundy, offered him a more fragrant cigar than the one he had been smoking, and, in return, drew the following extraordinary narrative from him:—

"No, monsieur, I was not in the army at the time of the war, and it is no story of a soldier that I am going to tell you. True, I served afterwards, as every man must do in France, but then I was only eighteen, and yet, although so young, was already a fireman on this very same line where now I drive a locomotive.

"I had only been fireman for a few months before the war broke out. The driver of the engine to which I was attached at the time of which I am speaking was an old man named Pierre Cournet. We were running trains between Rheims and Mézières, and, therefore, were in close touch with the first great battlefield of the war. I shall never forget that terrible time. Every sort of vehicle we had on the line was used for carrying troops. We took over 20,000 men from Rethel to Mézières, men belonging to Marshal MacMahon's army, and among them were Pierre Cournet's two sons.

"They had just time on reaching Mézières to run to the engine and bid their father farewell, for he happened to be driving the very train by which they travelled, when the bugle-call tore them away from him—tore them away for ever. For only a few days afterwards the sword of a Uhlan and the bullet of a Prussian needle-gun claimed the lives of Pierre Cournet's two sons in the awful fight of Sedan.

"When the news was brought to him he almost went mad. He swore he would turn franc-tireur and be revenged ten-fold for their deaths. Ah, monsieur knows well he was not the only parent in France who made such threats, and carried them out, too! And Pierre Cournet would assuredly have carried his out but for that which happened.

"We were at Rethel when the news came. Our countrymen were flying in every direction, and the railway was falling metre by metre into the hands of the enemy. Mézières still remained in possession of the French, and did not surrender for some weeks, but the railway communication was cut off. We tried to get down there with some stores, but our train fell into the hands of the Prussians at a station about twenty kilometres this side of Mézières.

"Then it was that Pierre Cournet's patience was put to the test. A great, bearded Prussian officer came on the foot-plate and addressed him in broken French.

"'You will take this train back to Rethel, after we have loaded it with cannon and ammunition. You understand?'

"'I will not,' replied Cournet, trembling with fury. 'I will not take your cursed guns one inch towards Paris.'

"'Oh, very well,' replied the officer, calmly drawing out his watch and making a sign to some of his soldiers to come near. 'I will give you two minutes to decide. If you refuse, why then you will be shot instantly—I have no more time to waste on you. I would not even give you this chance, only there are no engineers with me, and I have no one who can drive a locomotive.'

"He stood, watch in hand, and the old engine-driver, pale with fury, stood beside him. I watched Pierre Cournet's face. For the first half minute it was still, with a set purpose; then a gleam of light seemed to flash into his eyes, and his lips parted in a smile. He had changed his mind.

"'Very well,' he said, as the Prussian closed his watch with a snap. 'I will drive the engine for you.'

"'Good!' said the officer. 'But if you think you're going to play any tricks you're mistaken, for see here!'

"He called to two of his men, who came on to the foot-plate, and gave them some instructions in German. Each of them drew a pistol.

"'Now,' he added to Pierre Cournet, in French, 'these soldiers have orders to shoot you and your young friend on the very slightest suspicion of trickery, and as one of them understands French, you'd better be careful what you say. And now, while we load the train, you get your engine to the other end and be ready to start.'

"Pierre Cournet shrugged his shoulders and told me to get down and uncouple the locomotive and to work the points so that he could shunt it to the reverse end of the train. I did so, one of the soldiers accompanying me and keeping guard over me all the time. We had been running from Rethel tender first, so now the engine stood in its right position, smoke-jack in front. I coupled her to the train.

"It was nearly two hours before we were ready to start, and during that time we watched the Prussians get six guns on to as many trucks and fill all the available waggons with ammunition. There were two old third-class carriages at the rear end of the train, and some fifty artillerymen were ordered into these. Finally, the officer who had spoken to us before came up, and dismissed one of our guards, taking his place instead.

"'I shall travel with you,' he said, cocking his pistol, 'and see that all goes right. Besides, I am not sure yet how far we shall go. Now then, start!'

"I had set the points to bring the train on to the up-line. Cournet laid his hand on the regulator, there were a few sonorous puffs, and we were off.

"I knew by my companion's face that he meant to do something desperate before our journey was over. He had given me one sharp, questioning glance that seemed to mean, 'Will you help me?' and I had nodded in reply, though what his plans were I could not guess. Still, I determined that, if need be, I would strike a blow against the hated Prussians.

"We had gone a few kilometres, and were getting up a fair speed, when the mouth of a tunnel loomed ahead. I saw a strange expression flit across Cournet's face, and I think the Prussian officer must have noticed it too, for he said a few words in German to the soldier, and the latter grasped me by the neck just as we entered the tunnel, while at the same moment I felt the cold ring of his pistol-barrel pressing against my forehead. The officer had seized Cournet in the same manner, and if the old driver thought he was going to do anything in the tunnel he was mistaken. When we were through our guards released their hold. We went on. Presently a smile of triumph shone in Pierre Cournet's face, instead of the disappointed look he had worn as we emerged from the tunnel. I felt instinctively that the moment of action was arriving.

"'Get me a spanner, Jean!' said the driver, quietly; 'a bolt is loose.'

"I opened the tool chest and took one out. The officer's suspicions were aroused in a moment, and he levelled his pistol at Cournet as the latter took the spanner. But Cournet only smiled contemptuously, and began tightening a nut, saying to me: 'More coal, Jean.'

"I took up the heavy shovel and put a few loads on the fire, my guard handling his pistol in a menacing manner all the time. Evidently the slightest movement on our part was being watched with scrupulous jealousy. What *was* the driver going to do? I asked myself this question as I looked ahead through the weather-glasses after putting on a third shovelful of coal. We were rushing along a high embankment now, and travelling at a much greater pace than we usually went. In a few seconds we should be rounding a very sharp curve, but Cournet did not seem inclined to slacken speed. He was still engaged in screwing up the nut.

"I was just turning towards the tender again for more coal, when a sudden swerve told me we had left the straight and were rounding the curve. At that very moment Pierre Cournet, his back towards the officer, with a very quick movement of his wrist struck the glass tube of the water-gauge with his spanner and sprang on one side.

"In an instant a cloud of steam and a jet of scalding water poured forth on to the footplate, blinding and burning us; at the same moment two sharp reports rang out, and I heard Pierre Cournet shout, 'Strike him, Jean!'

"I was quick to take it in. Notwithstanding what had happened, I never lost my nerve for a moment; in fact, the breaking of the water-gauge was no new experience to me, though this was the first time it had not happened accidentally. My shovel was already half poised in the air, and I brought it down with all my might on the Prussian soldier's head. Reeling backward he fell off the foot-plate, rolled down the embankment, and I saw him no more.

"Meanwhile Pierre Cournet had not been idle. With a second blow of his weapon he had felled the officer immediately after the latter had fired his pistol, and the big Prussian lay unconscious at our feet. All this was but the work of a few seconds, but I shall remember that terrible little fight in the midst of the scalding steam as long as I live.

"The next moment the fearless old driver had rushed to the broken gauge, and, scalding his hands severely in the attempt, had turned off the steam and water-taps. Once more the foot-plate was clear. But this was by no means all. There was a terrible plan formed in Pierre Cournet's brain that day, and he worked it out to the bitter end.

"We were now beginning to rush down an incline, at the end of which, on the level, was a long tunnel. The old driver turned to me:—

"'Go back,' he cried, 'over the coals, and uncouple the engine. You can do it, can't you?'

"'I'll do it!' I shouted. We were only working with ordinary chain-couplings, and I knew these would be slack as we ran down-hill.

"In ten seconds I was behind the tender, astride one of the buffers, stooping down and separating the loose chain dangling between the tender and the leading truck. Then I clambered back over the coals to the foot-plate. I found Pierre Cournet slackening speed with his hand on the regulator.

"'Tie him up,' he exclaimed, with a glance at the officer. 'He's coming to.'

"There was a piece of rope in the tool chest, and I tied the Prussian's arms securely behind his back, making the end of the rope fast to a ring in the footplate. Hardly had I done so when we entered the tunnel.

"We were running very slowly now. Although uncoupled, the momentum given it by the incline had kept the train close behind our engine, and, of course, its leading buffers were still touching our rear ones, because, by slowing his engine, Pierre Cournet had been checking the speed of the train behind.

"In the middle of the tunnel we stopped dead for a moment.

"'Good,' said Cournet, as he immediately opened the regulator once more; 'it is level here, and the train will stay in the tunnel until—until—but you shall see for yourself, Jean. *Mon Dieu*, grant that I may hold out!'

"Out of the tunnel into the bright daylight we rushed with great speed. Still I had no idea of what Cournet meant to do.

"'Put on the brakes,' he shouted as he shut off the steam. 'Quick and hard, my son!'

"We came to a standstill about three-quarters of a kilometre from the tunnel's mouth. It was a perfectly straight bit of line, and, looking back, I could see the black entrance behind us.

"'Get off, Jean,' said the driver.

"He was reversing the gear of the engine now, and it seemed to me that it cost him a great effort to pull the lever over the sector. Then came another voice, that of the Prussian officer. He had come to.

"'For God's sake, what are you going to do?' he asked.

"'Going to do? Why, send you back to your friends as fast as we can. Adieu, monsieur—a speedy and safe journey to you—and the journey ends *in the tunnel!*'

"So saying, he opened the regulator to the full, and sprang from the foot-plate to my side as the great engine began to move backwards, along the line we had come, towards the tunnel. It was some moments before I grasped the horror of the thing. Then, as I saw the locomotive hastening away from us, gathering fresh speed every moment as it neared the dark opening of the tunnel, I realized the awful nature of Cournet's revenge.

"He grasped me by the arm. I think he had gone mad for the moment.

"'See,' he cried, 'André and Jacquet will be avenged by their father. They are caught like mice in a trap, and all their guns and ammunition will be destroyed. Ah, it has nearly reached the tunnel!'

"Horror-struck, I watched the locomotive until at length it disappeared into the dark aperture, and the white steam rolled in cloudy columns from the tunnel's mouth. The next few seconds seemed like hours, but at last, straining every nerve, we heard a dull, muffled sound from the direction of the tunnel, followed by a deep, growling roar. Then all was quiet.

"I turned to Pierre Cournet. He had released his hold on me and had sunk on the grass by the side of the line. His face was an ashen grey, and for the first time I noticed a streak of red running down his blouse.

"'Why, you are wounded!' I said.

"'Yes,' he gasped. 'He hit me when he fired; I hardly thought I could have lasted it out—but—but—I have not died too soon—goodbye, Jean—escape quickly—Ah!'

"In a second or two it was over, and I was running for my life through the wood by the side of the line—for my life, I say, because I knew the country round was infested with Prussians, and it might have been difficult to give an account of myself had I been captured.

"Afterwards? Oh, they thought it was a strategy of some French engineers, this blowing up of the tunnel.* For blown up it was. Probably the engine crashing into the first truck that was full of

---

* Several railway tunnels on the lines which the French knew would prove useful to the Prussians in their advance on Paris were purposely blown up.

shells caused the explosion. But the whole train was buried, and with it the bodies of the Prussian artillerymen.

"And now I must wish monsieur goodnight, for it is nearly time for me to take my train to Mézières. Without doubt my journey will be less exciting than the one I have recounted."

BETWEEN TWO FIRES:
THE STORY OF A LOST GUN

It was, at the most, an affair of outposts, but Colonel Baxter was anxious to make the thing successful, although the force under his command was scarcely a thousand, all told, including four guns. For some days the Boers had been retreating northward and had crossed the Zandgolo River, entrenching themselves upon the farther side, after having destroyed the railway bridge over the river. The Colonel's little force had followed closely, and was encamped to the south of Vredeburg, slightly over a mile and a half from this same bridge. Although he hardly had hopes of dislodging the enemy before the arrival of reinforcements, he was determined to push forward as far as possible, and at least worry them if he could do no more. For this purpose a reconnaissance with a hastily-prepared armoured train was ordered.

Now, Major Finch did not believe in armoured trains, and he was the more inclined to grumble on this occasion because one of the precious four guns had been "commandeered" to go to the front on a coal-truck protected with bits of boiler-plate. As an artillery officer he mistrusted the whole arrangement, and made no secret of it; but the Colonel only scoffed at his scruples, and so he had to watch Lieutenant Sangate and a dozen men climb into the truck and disappear behind "that rickety tin armour," as he called it.

There was not much time for growling, however, for the worthy Major had to take up a position with the remaining guns on the summit of a kopje that commanded the railway line as far as and beyond the river. It was the duty of these guns to protect the advance of the armoured train.

"It's a fool's game," muttered the Major to himself as he swept the veldt with his field-glasses, till his eyes rested on a ridge of hills some three miles from where he was standing, and about a mile and a half beyond the river. "They've got guns there, to a dead certainty, guns that we can't touch; and as soon as that rotten little, tinkered-up fad of Baxter's gets within range she'll draw their fire. It'll be sheer luck if they get out of it, too. If he wanted to send 'em a target why couldn't he have run out a dummy, and not chanced losing my precious barker? Halloa, they're off!"

For as he glanced at the line just below him there came some spurts of steam from the engine as it slowly moved forward on its dangerous errand. Besides the locomotive there were only two trucks, one in front with the gun, and the other behind, containing a Maxim and a score of Tommies. The Major watched the train as it wound its way round the bases of the low hills until it reached Vredeburg "Station," an apology consisting of a platform, a couple of sheds, a few sidings, and a signal-box, the latter being on the other side of the station.

From this point the line ran perfectly straight and on a dead level with the veldt as far as the river, which was distant about a quarter of a mile from the station. It was the object of the reconnaissance to discover how far the bridge had been damaged, and, by drawing the enemy's fire, to unmask his position.

"Now the game will begin," muttered the Major, as he turned his glasses once more towards the distant kopjes.

He was right. A puff of white smoke came from the summit of one of them, and a few seconds later there was another smaller puff a couple of hundred yards in front of the advancing train. Another and another followed, and shells began to drop thick and fast about the little fort on wheels. Then there came a spurt of fire from the leading truck. The enemy's compliment was being returned.

Slowly the train ran on. Half the distance between Vredeburg Station and the river was traversed when, suddenly, another sound arose distinct from the boom of the guns. It was the rattle of Mausers.

"There they are!" cried the Major, "on the other side of the river. Let 'em have it—a little under 3,000yds!"

The three guns opened fire, and the range was speedily found. Shrapnel began to drop unpleasantly close to the Boer riflemen the other side of the river, who still, however, kept up a withering fire on the approaching train. The latter had now arrived within a hundred yards of the river, when suddenly the Major saw three of the enemy's shells, aimed with splendid precision, fall almost simultaneously apparently right into the train immediately in front of the engine and burst, with clouds of smoke. This was followed by a perfect hail of shells dropping in rapid succession all round and upon the devoted train, supported by a terrific rifle fire from the Boer infantry at a range of little more than 300yds.

"Why don't she come out of it?" muttered Major Finch. "It's madness trying to stick there." For the train had stopped dead, and the one solitary gun was doing its little best. The enemy had not, at all events, succeeded in silencing it.

"Good," went on the Major, as puffs of steam once more rose from the engine's smoke-stack; "she's coming back—what!— Great heavens, they've left my gun behind!"

For as the train steamed quickly back into Vredeburg it was evident that she was coming away without the front truck, which still remained on the line within a hundred yards of the river, the plucky gunners working their solitary gun for all they were worth.

The enemy's shells had burst between the engine and the truck, completely shattering the couplings. Two men lying dead across the track showed that an attempt to recouple the truck had been in vain, and under the fearful fire the engine had been compelled to retreat. She left her other truck on the British side of Vredeburg Station, and twice attempted a dash to the front, supported by Finch's three guns. But it was no use. The Boer artillery had got the range so perfectly that the engine could not possibly have run within a couple of hundred yards of the gun-truck without being

smashed; in fact, she could scarcely show her buffers outside
Vredeburg Station.

Then the Major had to watch a gruesome thing through his
glasses. The last spurt of fire came from his beloved gun, and the
next moment Lieutenant Sangate and his men swarmed over the
side of the truck and started running back for dear life. First one
bit the dust with a Mauser bullet through the brain, then another
stumbled, and a comrade caught him in his arms and hurried on.
Then the Lieutenant began to limp on his left leg and had to be
supported, and finally eight men reached Vredeburg Station, five
of them wounded, leaving three motionless in the truck, beside the
abandoned gun, and two more lying by the side of the line.

So the gun was lost, and Major Finch's reflections on the
subject of armoured trains had better not be reported.

But the gun, though lost, was not in the hands of the enemy.
Before they could actually take it they would have to cross the river,
and very soon the sharp eye of Major Finch detected a movement
of this nature some quarter of a mile up stream, where apparently
there was a drift. But half-a-dozen well-aimed shells from his battery soon put an end to this little game, and they had to beat a
retreat.

"Umph," growled the Major, "I suppose we'll try and bring it in
after sundown. But if the beggars have search-lights it won't be
much use. Fortunately, we've got ours, and the Colonel is sure to
fix it up so that they won't be able to show themselves anywhere
within range of our little beauties here. By George, I wish we could
get that gun back!"

Lifting his glasses once more he gazed long and earnestly at
the abandoned truck and its surroundings. As he did so a curious
expression stole over his face.

"She's pulled up close to that distant signal," he murmured;
"and that signal's worked from the station. Well, it's a tough job,
but it might be done, I should think. It's worth trying, too."

As the Major anticipated, when it was dark both sides began to
play on the abandoned gun with their search-lights, and it soon became evident that a night attack to rescue it was out of the question.

The Colonel was very gloomy at the rough-and-tumble mess that evening.

"Well, gentlemen," he said to the officers present, "it's been an unlucky day. But we must get that gun back somehow, even if we have to pay heavily for doing so."

"We've paid pretty heavily for sending it there," growled the Major.

The Colonel bit his lip. Then he began discussing a plan of operations. It was his custom to consult the senior officers individually on such occasions, and presently he turned to the Major and said:—

"Well, Finch, what is your opinion?"

"It's a risky plan, sir, that's what I think. I don't see the use of employing the handful of cavalry we've got over this business, and I'm sorry to say I don't agree with you."

"Perhaps you've got a better suggestion?" retorted the Colonel, who was beginning to get angry.

"Well," drawled Finch, who had the reputation of being annoyingly cool in discussions when other men lost their tempers, "I think your plan risks too many men."

"And how many do you think would be enough, pray?"

"Um; well, I should say *one* man might tackle the job, and—"

"*One man!*" cried the Colonel. "I don't know whether you're joking, sir, but if you are, all I can say is that it's most ill-timed."

"On the contrary, sir, I meant exactly what I said."

"Then perhaps you'll go and get your precious gun yourself!"

The Colonel had completely lost his temper. The little group of officers started in pained surprise as the Major sprang to his feet.

"Thank you, sir," he exclaimed, quietly, "I will obey your orders. All I stipulate is that you keep that engine in steam till you hear from me. Good-night, all!"

And, to the astonishment of all present, he turned on his heel and walked out of the tent, without another word.

If his brother officers could have followed him they would have been somewhat surprised at his movements. His first action was to divest himself of his sword and to glance at his watch.

"About four hours of darkness left," he said to himself. "Well, I shall want them all." Then he made his way to an armourer's tent and demanded a couple of screw-drivers, a file, and a pair of wire-nippers. Armed with these singular weapons he started along the line in the direction of Vredeburg. Just before he came to the station he was challenged by a couple of vedettes, who allowed him to proceed on giving the password. He paced through the empty station until he was just past the signal-box at the farther end. Then he threw himself motionless on the ground as a blinding flash of light came streaming over the spot.

"They'll scarcely pick out one man in khaki," he muttered, when the light had shifted.

Crawling on his hands and knees to the side of the line, he uttered an exclamation of joy as he found what he had come to seek, the signal wire by which the distant signal near the gun was manipulated from the box. It was carried along the side of the line on small posts about a foot high, and some fifteen yards apart, running over a grooved wheel screwed to the top of each of these posts.

"It's a good thick one," he remarked, as he felt the wire, which was composed of several twisted strands, "and ought to stand a jolly good strain. If it doesn't! But, there, we won't think of 'ifs'; we'll get to work."

First of all he cut the wire through with his file and pliers, then he started crawling along the line, keeping absolutely still every time the light came flashing upon him, until he had passed some five of the little posts. Taking hold of the wire, he commenced to pull it towards him from the direction from which he had come. He thus cleared some seventy yards of wire, which he carefully coiled, from the pulley-wheels.

"The others will have to be taken off," he exclaimed, as he drew out one of his screwdrivers and crawled to the next post. It was the work of some ten minutes to find and extract the two screws which fastened the little grooved wheel through which the wire ran to the post. Then he crawled carefully to the next one, and performed the operation in less time—then to a third—and so on, gradually nearing the gun and freeing the wire from the posts as he did so.

As he could not free the pulleys from the wire without cutting the latter, he had to push them along from post to post, and so they gradually accumulated until he had twenty of them together on the wire in this manner.

"At last!" he exclaimed, as he reached the shadow of the truck, shivering for a moment as he crawled over one of the dead bodies in his path. "It's lucky the signal's *beyond* the gun, or there wouldn't have been enough wire."

Then he cut the wire, strung off the score or so of pulley-wheels, thus clearing it, stole gingerly to the end of the truck, and, sheltered completely from the enemy's view, fastened the end of the wire securely to the broken coupling.

It had taken him the best part of three hours to perform this little operation, and now he commenced his slow, painful journey back. Whether or no the Boers were suspicious he could not tell, but certain it was that their flash-light glanced more repeatedly along the track, and once they threw a desultory shell that burst unpleasantly near.

By-and-by, however, he reached the spot where he had coiled the end of the wire, found it, and continued his journey, uncoiling the wire as he went, until he came to the end of it. Then he twisted the end into a large loop, which he carefully placed between the rails.

"It's lucky it's a dead level," he exclaimed, "and that it's a straight line. If only the wire stands the strain!"

Then he rose to his feet and hurried back to the camp. Day was breaking as he reached the British lines, and one of the first to encounter him was Colonel Baxter.

"Man alive," he began, "where the dickens have you been? You weren't so foolish as to take me at my word last night, surely?"

"I don't know about being foolish, sir," replied Major Finch, very quietly; "that remains to be seen. But I want my gun back again, and if that engine's in steam I'll go and get it at once."

"What on earth are you going to do? You *can't* get to the gun, man. It's impossible!"

"Quite so, but I can get the gun to me, I think."

"How?"

"If you wouldn't mind getting on that little hill, where my three guns are posted, you'll see the gun rescued, if I'm successful, sir. Have I your permission to start now?"

With a grunt of astonishment the Colonel consented, and Finch walked off to the line and found the little locomotive with steam up. Getting on to the foot-plate, he motioned the driver to open the regulator.

"Run her forward as fast as you can, and be prepared to stop and reverse her just the other side of the station," he exclaimed.

The Colonel and a few other officers, who had got wind that something extraordinary was on the move, watched the engine from the top of the kopje. As soon as she drew near the station the Boer guns opened a furious fire, and their shells began to drop about the all-important bit of line in front.

"The fool!" cried the Colonel, "I shouldn't have given him permission to perform such a mad bit of bravado. Ah, I thought so; of course he's had to stop."

For the engine had come to a halt just beyond the station.

"He'll have to come back now," said the Colonel. "Halloa—what's he doing? Why, he's got down! He's gone in front of the engine—He's hit!—No, he's picking something up! Ah, now he's back on the foot-plate! What's his little game, I wonder?"

If the Colonel could have been present on the footplate he would have heard Finch say to the driver:—

"Have you reversed her?"

"Yes, sir."

"Open the regulator slowly then—very slowly mind, or the wire will snap. Do you hear?"

"All right, sir, I understand. We'll get her off, sir."

"Aha!" went on the Colonel. "I told you so. He's beginning to move back. He's precious slow over it, too."

"Look at the truck—look—look!" suddenly shouted the officers by his side.

"By George!" cried the Colonel. "It's moving—it's coming along! How in the name of— Hurrah! Bravo, Finch, bravo! He's got her off!"

For, apparently without any cause, the gun-truck began to move away from the river towards the British lines. Finch was bringing back his own. The wire had held, had stood the strain of starting the truck, and the rest was easy.

Amid a hail of shells that truck came in. The driver increased his speed. He had to stop as he began to round the curve to the south of Vredeburg, but the start and the pace attained had been enough to bring the truck with its precious burden rolling along through the station until the engine was properly coupled to it, and Finch brought his train to the camp in triumph.

"Well done, Finch," exclaimed the Colonel, the first to greet him on his return. "Never mind anything I said."

"I don't, sir," said Finch, with a smile. "I've got my little beauty back."

"Tell you what," shouted another officer, "you deserve—"

"What I hope I'll get," said the Major, "and that's breakfast and a snooze."

The Triumph of Seth P. Tucker

"What! You mean to tell me you've been over in the States and never heard of the 'Grand Rocky Hill and Peak City Railway'! Wal, stranger, you surprise me. I guess you Britishers get in such a habit of stickin' your nose in the air over your foolish notions of the value of your forefathers that when you get to a country like the States, where thar *is* somethin' to be proud of, all you reckon to see is the tops o' the houses or the blue sky. Why, Sir, thar ain't a child o' six years old over thar that don't know the G.R.H. and P.C.R. just as well as he does his triggernometry or any other branch o' book-learnin'.

"You talk about your express trains in England! Why. Sir, you're afraid to get up any speed; and it ain't to be wondered at, con-siderin' your island's so small that if you ran at anythin' like our lightning expresses, the whole train would be in danger of runnin' into the sea before the driver had space to pull her up. But on the G.R.H. and P.C.R. I guess there's a length o' track that would sup-ply metals for the entire British Isles; and as for speed, why, if one of the engineers ran under a mile a minute on an ordinary train, I reckon he'd hand in his checks and enjoin his relatives to bury him in the middle of a prairie, whar no one 'ud ever hear of him.

"Have I got anything to do with the line? Yes, Siree, I guess I have. Not that I'm a big boss on it, but—wal, thar, I don't mind tellin' you that Caleb B. Luker (that's my name, stranger) is known on every inch of the G.R.H. and the P.C.R., and his opinion ain't sneezed at, neither.

"But what I was goin' to tell you ain't anything to do with this child—it's a yarn about two engineers when the Peak City branch o' the railway was bein' constructed; and when you've heered it, you'll say it's one o' the most astoundin' railway tales as was ever known since the creation of the world. But I guess I'd better begin the yarn without any further ramifications.

"When the idea of bringing on the track from Big Pine Junction to Peak City was started, everyone naturally said that the crossin' o' the Buffalo Horn River would be a tarnation awkward job, however it was done, for though it looks friendly enough in the summer, thar's an ugly lot o' torrents and melted snow comin' down it in winter and spring, and a wood pile bridge stood every chance of takin' a journey down stream, with or without a train on top.

"But Seth P. Tucker, the company's engineer in this particular department, warn't a man to be frightened by such or'nary things as circumstances. It's my belief that if there were any talk of the Old World and America bein' joined by a bridge, Seth P. Tucker would ha' put in two specifications within a month—one for the Atlantic and the other for the Pacific. I've heard him say often that Natur' is a coward at heart, and Natur' certainly had to take a back seat whar *he* was concerned. Why, Sir, it was Seth P. Tucker who bust up the big obstruction when the San Felippo Railway was being prospected in South America. Thar was a volcano in the line o' route, and as a tunnel couldn't be made through it the track had to cross a deep valley at the foot. It was calculated that a million dollars wouldn't pay for the cost of a viaduct, but Seth P. Tucker jest had a look round, smiled a knowin' sorter grin, and ordered twenty tons o' blastin' powder and a hundred gallons o' nitro-glycerine. He had these taken to the top o' the mountain and fixed up on an electric affair by the edge o' the crater. Then he jest pressed a button at the other end o' three miles o' wire, and the whole show was precipitated at once into the volcano. Talk about a bust-up and the trump of doom! One half o' that mountain was blown clean down into the valley, fillin' it up completely, and only takin' a bit o' leveling to get it ready for the sleepers—while the lava, when broken up, made the best ballast *I* ever saw.

"But it's about the Buffalo Horn River and the G.R.H. and P.C.R. I was talkin'. Wal, stranger, Seth P. Tucker came down and did a bit of prospectin', and in a few days' time he'd fixed up a plan for a bridge and drawn it on paper, so's you might ha' sworn it must ha' been thar already for him to get so neat a pictur' of it. He sends this plan inter the Company's office at Rocky Hill, calculatin' that in a few days' time he'd get the order for the contract. But thar was a disappointment in store for Seth P. Tucker, one that he hadn't reckoned on either. 'Pears thar was another engineer that owed him a grudge. Ebenezer Finch—that was his name—managed to get hold o' the specifications of the bridge, told the directors he fancied he had a plan in his head for fixin' up the show in a way that 'ud beat it, and asked leave to send in his tender. Then he went down to Buffalo Horn River, sounded the stream a bit, had a shaft sunk on either side, took a few levels and such-like. The end of it was that he sent in a specification for *tunnelling* that 'ere river. He pinted out that the Thames had a tunnel under it, that the Severn was goin' to have one, that thar was a lot o' talk o' jining England to France by the same means, 'and if,' he said, '*that* undertaking can be carried through, why shouldn't you run your cars under Buffalo Horn River? It's safer than torrents and snow and timbers driftin' down stream, and it ain't likely that *you'd* be behind Europe in such an enterprise.'

"When Seth P. Tucker first heard of this plan he laughed fit to break his neck, but when he knew that the directors were givin' serious consideration to it, he used enough language to bridge the Mississippi with solid oaths. The fact was that Ebenezer Finch had impressed the directors with his scheme. They rather liked the idea of havin' the tunnel; they'd not only be able to crow over every other line o' railway in the States, but it would be a big boom for the G.R.H. and P.C.R. Folks would flock to see it, and the Peak City branch would become famous all over the world. It wasn't so much the *necessity* of the tunnel as the unique natur' of the idea that fetched 'em. They liked the thought o' saying, 'Any *other* line would have had a bridge, but not for the G.R.H. and P.C.R.! No, Siree, I guess *we've* got a tunnel.'

"So the end of it was that the directors sent for both engineers and interviewed 'em together. Thar was plenty o' words bandied about at the meetin', specially when the chairman announced that Ebenezer Finch's scheme had come out trumps.

"'Not that we want to say anything against your plans, Mr. Tucker,' he went on, 'but because we think the G.R.H. and P.C.R. ought to have this tunnel.'

"'And so you're all goin' to make fools o' yerselves for the sake of a derned experiment, are ye?' yelled old Tucker. 'Let me tell ye it's as bad as diggin' a grave for the lot o' ye; not but what I wish that Finch 'ud dig one for himself, for it's about all he's fit for.'

"'Go and hang ye'self on one o' yer crazy old bridges, if it'll bear yer weight—which I doubt!' retorted the other engineer, with an amiable sorter grin. Then Seth P. Tucker caught up an inkpot and slung it at him, and in less time than it takes to tell they wos rolling over together on the floor in a lovin' grip and the directors tryin' their best to separate them. The meetin' was talked about for weeks, and was a kinder preliminary advertisement to the great tunnel.

"Wal, Seth P. Tucker swore by some biggish oaths that the tunnel should never be made. He considered it the awfullest insult he'd ever had offered to him, and the doom he wished for himself if the other man ever finished that tunnel and run a train through won't bear repeatin', it was so awful. He hung about the country for a bit, and then he suddenly disappeared. No one knew whar he'd gone to, and as nothin' was heered of him, folks got to reckoning that he'd jumped inter Buffalo Horn River outer sheer disapintment.

"But Ebenezer Finch soon brought along his fixin's, and got to work on the tunnel job. His idea was to commence a cuttin' on each side, about a mile and a quarter away from the river-bank, and to lead the track down by an easy gradient till he got it to a level fit to begin borin' under the water. He began operations pretty well on in the fall o' the year, and by the time spring came round he was about ready with his borin'-machines, and towards the end o' March they had a dinner o' the directors in the cuttin', and began the first stroke o' the tunnellin' work with flags flyin' and an old cannon they'd fished up from somewhere a-bangin' away till it very near got red hot. Finch reckoned he'd have that tunnel bored somewhere along the latter part o' the summer, and things seemed going on pretty merrily all round.

"'Twas a few weeks after this that a stranger appeared on the scenes at the little town called Pine Settlement that had begun to spring up on the south bank o' the river near the tunneling operations. He was a feeble-looking old chap, with a big white bears and long hair—an inoffensive-looking coon, who said he'd come to do some fishin' in Buffalo Horn River. Folks hadn't reckoned as a rule that there was any fishin' worth speaking of in those parts, but the old chap seemed to think otherwise, and nobody took the trouble to contradict him much. So he prospected about the settlement for a bit, and finally fixed on a bit o' land close to the river, for which he paid the Government claim, and commenced running up a shanty right on the edge o' the stream. He was mighty particular about havin' it as close as possible, and he had a sorter little landin'-stage on to it, so's to have a comfortable place for fishin' from or bringing a boat to. He bought a few bits o' furniture at the local store, but a lot o' traps came down in a wagon, and he was so mysterious over 'em that he wouldn't let any o' the boys help him in unloadin' 'em, and folks reckoned he'd brought down some patent fishin' apparatus.

"He 'peared to fish a good deal after this; but, somehow or other, he never had much to show for it. He didn't chum up with anyone much, though now and again he'd answer back when he was spoke to. Once a feller said to him: "Scuse me, stranger, but p'raps you don't know that this 'ere shanty o' yours is peculiarly placed?'

"'How's that?' says the old chap in an innercent kinder way.

"'Why, I reckon it's right over the tunnel they're borin' under the river.'

"'Is it? Wal, 'tain't no consarn o' mine if it is,' says the other, as if he didn't care a red cent about the tunnel.

"Thar was a curious story got afloat just after this. A little girl, comin' home by the river-bank rather late one night as the moon

was getting' up, had a fright that most skeered her to death jest as
she passed the little fishin' shanty. She declared she saw Old Nick
hisself a-comin' up outer the river with an ugly big head and goggle-
eyes. Said he climbed up on the landin'-stage and walked right
inter the old fisherman's shanty. It was a funny tale; thar warn't
many that b'lieved it; but still it made the old chap and his doin's
seem a bit queer, especially as no one could prove he *warn't*
entertainin' the devil.

"But folks soon forgot about the old man and his shanty when
the news began to spread that the tunnel was cut at last, and that a
trial train from Big Pine Junction would run through it in a
fortnight's time. Thar was a powerful lot o' people came along to
see things, and even a smatterin' o' Congressmen along of 'em.

"Wal, to make a long story short, the day of opening the tunnel
came, and thar was a good show o' folks on either side o' the cuttin'
hours before the train was timed to arrive from Big Pine Junction.
Ebenezer Finch was in his glory—struttin' about here, thar, and
everywhar, and showin' himself off among the crowd. He was
standin' near the top o' the cuttin', close to the mouth o' the tunnel, talkin' to someone, when suddenly he felt a hand laid on his
shoulder. He turned round, and thar he saw Seth P. Tucker grinnin'
in his face.

"'Mornin', Finch. I guess this here's a proud day in your existence—ain't it?' he drawled.

"For a moment the other engineer was so taken aback that he
couldn't speak. Tucker went on—

"'So ye've bored this wonderful tunnel o' yours, and completed
it, have ye?'

"'Tucker!' gasps the other; 'why, I heered ye was dead!'

"'Maybe ye did, but I reckon I ain't. Retired inter private life a
bit, that's all. Just strolled round now to have a look at this here
masterpiece of yours!'

"'Wal,' says the other, with a grin, 'I don't say but what I *am*
proud of it. Thar ain't no ill feelin' between us now—eh?'

"'Oh, no, I ain't a bit jealous of ye,' said Tucker very deliberately, and lighting a cigar as he spoke; 'the only thing is that I

reckon you'll never get a train to run through this here tunnel o' yours. It's a pity, o' course, but—'

"'What!' yelled Finch; 'not get a train to run through it! Why, thar's one goin' through in less than an hour's time from now.'

"'I reckon not,' said Tucker, blowin' a whiff o' blue smoke out of his mouth and watchin' it curl up to heaven.

"'*Not!* Why, it's on the track now, comin' along. It's turned half after eleven. At half-past twelve or tharabouts you'll see her run through with your own eyes. You can go aboard her if you like.'

"'Ebenezer Finch,' said Tucker, lookin' at his watch, 'I'll bet you ten thousand dollars that train never runs through your tunnel, the only condition bein' that if it don't you let the matter rest thar.'

"'Done, you denied idiot,' roared Finch; 'are you wantin' to give money away? Done, but on the condition you stop here. I ain't goin' to have you foul the track, or wreck the train, or anything o' that sort.'

"'Oh, I'll stay here,' said Tucker, sittin' down on a bit o' turf. 'You're sure that tunnel's all clear?'

"'Certain. I've been through it twice this mornin'.'

"'And the track's all right, and—'

"'The only thing that's wrong is your silly head. It's cracked!' rejoined Finch.

"'All right,' said the other, with a grin. 'We'll soon see!'

"He went on smoking and gazing at his watch. Presently he pocketed it with an air of triumph, muttering—

"'A quarter to twelve!'

"The words were hardly out of his mouth when there was a dull thud, a roar, and a violent tremor of the earth. An instant afterwards, and two men, who were standing at the mouth of the tunnel, came scrambling up the embankment, yelling—

"'The water's through! Get up—get up for your lives!'

"There was a wild rush up the sides of the cutting, and then a stream of water came out of the tunnel's mouth, a stream that in less than a minute had become a roarin' torrent, sweeping along the cutting like an avalanche, tearin' up the track and swirlin' the gravel about like a sea-beach.

"Ebenezer Finch, who had started to his feet at the moment of the explosion, took a glance round. There was a man close by on horseback, tryin' to quiet the brute. Finch recognised him, and shouted—

"'Quick, George! Ride like fury, and stop the train!'

"The other understood at once and galloped off.

"'Wal, Ebenezer Finch, I guess that pile's mine, ain't it?' drawled Tucker.

"'You skunk!' yelled the other. 'Thar'll be a day o' reckonin' for this.'

"'Likely thar will,' said the other coolly, 'but anyway that train ain't goin' through your tunnel unless you make a divin' dress for it, and what's more, I don't suppose thar ever *will* be a train run through now. It'll be a case o' bridgin' it over, after all!'

"And so it was, but not before thar wos a most tarnation row about it. You see, the whole thing very soon leaked out, and the facts o' the case became known. The old fisherman and Seth P. Tucker were one and the same person, and the mysterious lot o' goods that had come to his shanty were a divin'-dress, some big-gish submarine dynamite mines, and a lot of electrical apparatus. And Seth P. Tucker had actually put on that divin'-suit night arter night, climbed down off his landin'-stage, and got into the bed o' the river, and had worked thar with a pick-axe and a patent exca-vating tool o' his till he'd sunk a little shaft in the riverbed right over Finch's tunnel. He stacked this with his dynamite cartridges, attached electric wires to 'em, filled up the hole, and waited. On the mornin' of the openin' day he set a 'cute little clockwork machine goin' in connection with his battery in the shanty so as to fire the charge at exactly a quarter to twelve. Dynamite havin' a habit of explodin' downwards, the thing worked just as he expected it would, and bust up Finch's tunnel in a brace o' shakes.

"At first the directors were fairly mad, and threatened all sorter things, while Finch said he'd shoot Tucker. But Seth warn't a bit discomforted, havin' reckoned up the whole thing from the beginnin'. He pinted out that there warn't no law to prevent him diggin' holes at the bottom of an unnavigable river and experimentin' with dynamite cartridges if he chose. If other folks chose to lay tunnels under his experimentin'-ground, that was their consarn, not his. After the bust-up there warn't nothin' else to be done but to build a bridge. Wal, they knew very well that he was the only man who could do it. They couldn't afford to do without him, and he was willin' to act liberally towards 'em. Finch had had a fair bet with him, and owed him ten thousand dollars. Wal, he didn't mind takin' on the contract for the bridge at ten thousand dollars under the price.

"The directors finally saw they were caught in a hole and caved in. Ebenezer Finch had to pay up, for the bet was a fair one. He lay around for a while arter, and pot-shotted Tucker occasionally; but he warn't good enough with his weapon to hit him, and when the thing grew monotonous, and Tucker began to shoot back, he left altogether. The line was deviated from the cuttin', the earth that had been dug up from it was used as an embankment to run the train up to the level o' Seth P. Tucker's bridge, which is one o' the finest bits o' engineerin' work on the Buffalo Horn River.

"You want to know more details about how he put the divin'-dress on himself, and why they didn't stop up the hole, and a lot o' other things? No, Sir. If you expec' an American citizen to go inter silly details when he is recountin' veracious hist'ry, you're mistaken. *Good* evenin'!"

A Policy of Silence

Walter Meriton put the question boldly to Mr. David Cartwright, even as he had promised the latter's daughter he would, and now he waited, looking straight at the stern, business-like face of the assistant superintendent of the line for his reply, but already reading a decided negative therein.

"See here, Mr. Meriton," he said presently, "some men in my position would have been highly offended at this. But I don't want to treat you in that way. Understand that I am not in the least angry with you for asking the hand of my daughter, though I must confess you have taken me by surprise. But my answer must be no!"

"May I ask your reasons, sir?"

"You may. In the first place you are both very young—my daughter especially. In the second place I intend that my daughter shall marry a man who is able to support her in the manner to which she has been accustomed, which you are certainly unable to do at present. And in the third place, you will pardon me for saying so, I do not see any special indications that you will rise to such a position. The C. M. & St. P. R. R. Company, as you very well know, makes no promotion by favoritism. Every man must win his way up the ladder, as I have had to do myself."

"It is absolutely final as far as the present is concerned," he said, "and unless you progress up the ladder it will be final in the future. The fact of your being what is called a gentleman makes no difference. The question is how do you stand with us from a business point of view? Your chief merit is your knowledge of German.

There you are useful to us in our correspondence. But do something smart on the line, my lad," he went on kindly. "Do something smart! That's the way to get on."

"I'll try, sir—for Evie—Miss Cartwright's sake."

"Very likely. But understand me that from this moment you must not say another word to her on the subject. She must be left free. Can I trust you?"

"Certainly."

"And now to work. I want you to run down to St. Paul tomorrow, and make thorough investigations as to the working of the staff there. I'm not quite satisfied about things, and I want a full report before I go down myself. There's a slack tone about the station and complaints have reached me. We'll go over them now."

He went through a bundle of documents with the young man, and finally dismissed him with the injunction to take the 9:30 express the next morning.

Then he lay back in his chair a minute or two and pondered.

"I like that fellow," he admitted, "and I know Evie's fond of him. But I haven't seen real grit in him yet. Well, time will prove."

Walter Meriton somehow found an opportunity of seeing the assistant superintendent's daughter before the day was over. Possibly the meeting had been arranged beforehand.

"Well," she asked, "did you see him?"

"Yes."

"What did he say?"

Meriton told her.

"Good old dad!" she replied. "I knew he liked you. Then it's all right, Walter."

"I don't see that it's all right at all, dear," said the young man gloomily. "We've got to break off the engagement, and—"

"You silly boy," she interrupted, "just as if it really matters. It's only for a time. I'll wait for you if—if you don't make my wait too long," she added, roguishly.

"Of course I shall try and win you."

There was a resolute look in Walter Meriton's face when he rose next morning. He noticed it himself in the glass. He meant

business, did this young man. He had sat up half the night going
deeply into the question of the St. Paul station staff, for he intended
this report of his to be the first little rung up the ladder before
him.

Railway men from guards to superintendent are generally the
last to get into a starting train. So, as Walter Meriton walked on to
the platform alongside which stood the St. Paul express, the guard
was just preparing to wave his green flag. Even then, Meriton did
not hurry, but exchanged a word or two with one of the officials.

Then, just as the train began to move, he made a dash at a first-
class compartment. It was locked, but the other hastily produced
his key and opened it, and Meriton swung himself in. As he looked
out of the window to say a last word to the official, he heard a deep
voice behind him in German:

"Ach Gott! Curse him, I thought we had the compartment to
ourselves! I gave the guard five dollars to lock us in."

He was on the point of turning to apologize when he heard another voice say in the same language:

"Bad luck! But we must settle with him if he is troublesome."

Now Walter Meriton was a thorough German scholar.

He looked for a moment carelessly at his companions. They
were two evil-looking men—one short and sandy-haired, with little
gray eyes that never kept still; the other big and sinewy, a very
powerful-looking fellow. They, in turn looked at him closely.
Evidently their suspicions were aroused. So were his, but he never
showed it.

Then the short man leaned over and spoke to him in German,
asking whether he objected to smoking. By no hint did he betray
himself.

He simply shook his head and remarked in English that he did
not understand.

"We want to schmoke," said the German in English.

"Oh, certainly!"

He smiled and nodded. But the other man was not satisfied.
Turning to Meriton he let fly a volley of the foulest abuse in German.

Meriton did not turn a hair, though he understood perfectly. He only shrugged his shoulders and looked bewildered.

Then the short man explained, after a pause: "Mine friend shpeaks not English. He ask you for matches!"

"We may speak," said the short man, "he does not understand."

"No, but he will be in the way."

"What shall we do?"

"Don't worry, my friend. We are a match for him, and we can easily tie him up and put him under the seat."

This cheerful bit of information was duly digested by Walter Meriton, but he appeared quite engrossed in his papers. They glanced at him sideways. It was evident he knew no German.

"And now to business," said the bigger man. "You have brought them?"

"Two of them—in the bag," and he jerked his thumb toward the rack.

"Good! Here is the plan."

He called it *eisenbahn fahrplan* in German, and he pulled a printed paper from his pocket. Meriton gave one little glance toward it, and set himself with a mighty effort to keep his countenance. For he had instantly recognized it as the paper of special working instructions for a train that was to run that morning from St. Paul to Chicago, and which was to carry no less a personage than the Governor of Montana, who, after a visit to the Governor of Minnesota, was on his way to Chicago upon another visit.

He might well recognize it, for he had helped to draw it up himself and had dispatched copies of it to all the principal offices along the line some days before. Somehow or other these men had managed to get hold of a copy, and he guessed it meant mischief.

Just a word or two as to these "special working instructions" which are always issued when any excursions or special trains are run. The train in question is carefully timed from start to finish all along the route, not only the times of running through the stations being put down for the guidance of the driver and station masters, but also the principal signal cabins and other points on the road.

Provision is also made for shunting ordinary trains into "refuge" sidings to allow of the passing of the "special," while instructions are carefully issued as to the number of coaches of which the "special" is to be composed, and in the case of governors, mayors, etc., traveling, the exact position of his *salon* in the train is laid down.

High officials of the line always travel on such a train, and in this case Meriton knew very well that David Cartwright, his own particular "chief," had gone down to St. Paul by an early "special" that morning in order to accompany the governor on his journey to Chicago.

"Now then," said the bigger man, "we must find out the exact time when our train is likely to pass this one," indicating the special. "You see, it is timed to run through Evanston at 10:55. Now, we don't stop at Evanston, but I have found out from the 'Working Timetable' that we are due there at 10:35. So, you see, it will be about ten minutes or so the other side of Evanston. There's a signal cabin called Pine Tree Box that the special passes at 10:42. That will be about the point where we shall cross it."

"We must keep the time carefully."

"Of course. And one of us must be looking out of the window down the line. The Governor travels in the third *salon* from the engine. We must have bombs ready in our hands and throw them in as near as we can guess. It will have to be done in a second. I'll throw from the center window, and you throw from the side one at the same time. We'll have to break it first."

"How about this cursed Englishman?"

"I told you, we must tie him up. As for ourselves, well, we knew the risk when we drew lots at the meeting. If our driver hears the explosion and stops we must make a bolt of it. If not, we'll pull the communication cord before we get to St. Paul—in a tunnel if we can—and get clear as best we may."

Walter Meriton had taken in the whole situation, but his face showed no signs of it. These men were about to make a desperate attempt upon the governor's life by endeavoring to hurl a couple of bombs into his *salon* as the trains passed each other.

Rapidly he reviewed the situation. There was a three-fold reason for action. First, the governor was in danger; secondly, his chief's life was at a like risk, and thirdly, there was the honor of the company at stake.

Suddenly an inspiration struck him. It was more difficult than ever now to appear perfectly oblivious of the other men, but by a great effort he did so. He had his pocket case on his knee, and his hands were holding the papers, upon which he was pretending to take notes, apparently. He took a telegraph blank out of his pocket case, taking care, as he did so, that his traveling companions could not see, and quickly wrote these words:

"From St. Paul Express, 3824, C. Dynamitards in compartment. Mean wreck Governor of Montana special. Stop train at Evanston—Meriton."

Carelessly putting his hands in his pocket he took out four or five coppers, wrapped them up in the telegraph form, held it in his left hand, and prepared for action.

Then he looked out of the window. It was a clean run of six miles to the next station, and the train would pass a signal cabin on that side of the line in half a minute.

Then, as the train neared the box, he waved his arm up and down with a peculiar motion, still keeping it out of the sight of the two men, and glancing at the cabin. To his joy, the man was standing at the open window.

Out flew the weighted bit of paper and fell by the side of the line. The signalman put up his hand with a quick jerk. He had seen it, and understood.

The next moment a violent blow struck upon the young man's head from behind, and he fell senseless.

When he came to himself he found that he was lying on the hard floor of the carriage. His hands and feet were firmly tied with string and handkerchiefs, a bandage was over his eyes, and a gag was fastened into his mouth. The train was still rushing along at full speed.

"Better to have given him a few inches of knife," he heard the shorter man growl.

"Oh, it's all right," said the other. "We've no quarrel against him, and he can't do us any harm. Now, then, we're only a few miles off Evanston, and there isn't any time to lose. Better get that window smashed."

There was a crash of glass as his companion struck at the quarterlight with his stick.

"Now, the bombs. Put them on the seat ready. That's right."

"Are we stopping?"

"Yes—no! The man in the signal box is waving a green flag. We are going on. No—no—we're stopping again. Lucky we gagged the fool. Ah, we're going to step in the station. Curse it! Keep still, my friend!"

Walter Meriton heard, understood and rejoiced. The next moment a voice on the platform exclaimed:

"This is 3824, C!" and the lock clicked.

The villains were completely taken by surprise, as a couple of policemen and a railway official dashed in. They tried to open the other door and escape, but in vain. They were handcuffed before they knew what had happened, and the railway official had opened the bag.

"Bombs!" he exclaimed, "and a broken quarterlight. Going to throw 'em at the special, that's it. Lucky we got the message in time. Where's Mr. Meriton, though? I hope they haven't done for him."

Then a form rolled out from under the seat, and Meriton got his bonds off and his gag out. Directly he had done so he made the captives a mocking speech in excellent German.

"Ach!" shouted the bigger of the two as he shook his handcuffed fists. "I wish I had listened to Heinrich and killed you—you pig!"

Meriton acknowledged the sentiment politely and the train went on, leaving the prisoners behind.

"Meriton," said the assistant superintendent, "the company won't forget this. Neither shall I, for I owe you something personally over it."

"Which I hope you'll pay, sir," said Meriton demurely.

"Eh? No, I told you the other day I make no personal favoritism and I stick to that. But you've shown yourself a smart man, and I'll give you a promise. When you've got your divisional superintendentship you shall marry Evie. There!"

"And meanwhile?"

"Meanwhile? Oh, well, you're on the way to it. The G.M.'s got a post for you over this affair. So—well—you'd better go and make it all right with Evie, my lad. That's what you want, I suppose, eh?"

The Romance of the "Southern Queen": Told by the Fireman

"Good morning, sir!"

"Why, good morning, Harry! I hardly knew you at first, and I certainly didn't expect to see you here. How are you?"

"Very well, sir, thank you. I've just come off duty for a couple of hours."

"I see. Are you a fireman still?"

"Yes, sir. I've passed as driver, but I haven't got an engine yet. But that will come all in good time."

"That's right! I'm glad you're getting on. I hope you've a good mate on the footplate?"

"Rather better than the last, sir, I'm thankful to say."

"Eh? What was the matter with him?"

"Well, it's rather a long story, sir, but if you've got half an hour to spare perhaps you'd like to hear it?"

The above conversation took place on the platform of that exceedingly bustling railway station, Portsmouth Town. The young man who had accosted me was a fireman in the employ of one of our southern railway companies running into that station, as one might easily see by his smart, copper-mounted cap, a distinguishing feature of the men on the footplate on that company's system. I had known him when he was quite a lad, and, being always on the look-out for railway adventures, was only too glad to be able to pick up the following extraordinary story which he proceeded to tell me, and which I relate as far as possible in his own words, taking the liberty, however, of making them a little more presentable to the reader.

300

There have been a few exciting stories from time to time on the footplate, and I've noticed that the driver of an engine generally comes in for the biggest share of the thing; but in the adventure I'm going to tell you I fancy the fireman had the liveliest time of it, and that fireman was myself. Soon after I was promoted to the footplate of an express passenger engine it was my lot to serve with Charles Davis, a driver who knew his work and could make as good running out of his engine as any man I've met. He was a youngish chap, too—not more than thirty-six—a quiet, moody sort of fellow, and as strong as a Sandow. We were running Brighton expresses then, and Davis was always at his best on the down journey, for the simple reason that there was someone at the end of the run for him to see when he chanced to get off duty. A signal against him, or a slow down over a permanent-way operation, would quite annoy Davis, because it meant something more than a few minutes late on his time-sheet. That is to say, there was a certain little personage dwelling at Brighton to whom the driver had given his heart. I never thought very much of her myself. She was too flippant for a man like Charles Davis—a fellow who took things as a rule rather more seriously than he ought. But he simply worshipped that blue-eyed, golden-haired little lass, and when at length the day was fixed his joy knew no bounds.

"Only six weeks, mate," he said to me one day, as we bowled along through the fresh green fields of Sussex, "and then she'll be mine! *Mine*, just as sure as yonder signal shows a clear road ahead!"

It was only a coincidence, but even as he uttered the words the arm of the semaphore rose to danger. Anyhow, his face darkened as he pulled the regulator over and laid hold of the Westinghouse brake-handle. It was nothing—a mere momentary block on the line somewhere ahead—and yet it seemed a nasty omen to his speech.

The next day he was singularly silent on the up journey. Only one or two remarks escaped him.

"Harry, mate, ye've got no girl, have ye?"

"Not yet."

"Take my advice and be careful, then. Woman's a rum machine, and you can't regulate her running like you can a locomotive."

"Anything wrong, mate?" I ventured.

"No—not exactly. Only I shall be right glad when we're married, for sometimes I get a bit jealous."

"Any cause to be?"

"Confound you, no!" he cried, turning sharply. "What makes you think that?"

"Nothing—only what you said."

"Look here, mate, if I thought my girl had played me false— I'd—I'd go mad or die."

And he set his teeth with an ugly look as he gazed ahead through the weather-glass.

Whether he had any suspicions or not I never knew, but when we got back to Brighton that afternoon a terrible thing happened. A permanent-way inspector who happened to be on the platform— a tactless sort of man—came up to the engine, and, putting his head inside the cab, exclaimed:

"This is a bad business about your girl, Davis. I'm downright sorry for you!"

"What do you mean, man?" yelled the driver.

"What! don't you know? Why, she's bolted with Jimmy Sparshot—married at a registry office only this morning. You must have passed the train they went to town in on your way down."

"My God! is this true?" gasped Davis.

"I'm sorry to say it is—here, hold up, man! Catch him, Harry!"

For my mate had sunk all of a heap on the footplate. The shock had been too much for him, and the end of it was a dangerous attack of brain fever. Over three months passed before we stood on the same footplate once more, and those three months had wrought a sad change in poor Davis. He never once alluded to his trouble. He drove his engine as well as ever, but he spoke but rarely, and there was often a fixed expression in his eyes that I did not like at all.

For several months we continued running the Brighton expresses, and then a change came. Our locomotive superintendent had been engaged for some time in planning and producing a new type of engine for our line, and when the first of them was turned out of the sheds there were murmurs of admiration. The new loco-motive was a four-wheel coupled engine with a leading bogie—the first tender engine with a "bogie" that had been built for our line—just the type of locomotive for our heaviest express work.

Charles Davis was envied by many a driver when one of the first of these new engines, named the "Southern Queen," was de-livered over to him, and I was not at all sorry to find myself still his mate on the footplate of our brand-new steed. Our line has a practice that might well be followed by others. The driver of an engine has his name painted up in gilt letters inside the cab over the regulator, and this gives him a pride in the special locomotive that he drives, for there is no such thing as change and change about, every man having his own particular engine.

Our run was altered now. We were detailed to bring the special fast train from Portsmouth up to London Bridge in the morning, returning in the afternoon. The run, which is a difficult one on account of the many curves and gradients, had only one stop either way—at Chichester. Davis and I both transferred our lodgings from Brighton to Portsmouth, and prepared for our new duties.

I really thought that the fine locomotive to which Davis was appointed would be the making of the man, it seemed to rouse him from his lethargy so much. When I went down to the sheds on the morning of the first trip I found him there before me, gazing with admiration at the engine, which was standing over the pit.

"Now, isn't she a beauty, mate?" he asked me. "I've seen some fine engines up on the Northern lines, but I'd rather be on the footplate of this than any other I've come across. She's just fine! And what a name— 'Southern Queen'! It sounds like some beauti-ful woman, doesn't it?"

When we drew up at the terminus after the run Davis was more pleased than ever, declaring he'd never travelled so well before, and talking of the "Southern Queen" with the most extravagant praises.

We hadn't been doing this new running more than seven or eight weeks before a peculiar change came over Charles Davis. I noticed it first one day when we were hauled up for a minute by signals just outside Epsom on the down journey. My mate began muttering. At first I thought he was speaking to me, but it soon appeared he was not. I listened, and caught the following: "I can't help it—it's not my fault. I know you want to go on, my girl, but it won't do till they let us. You'd hurt yourself else, and then what should I do? Yes—ask them to let you go on. Speak to them!"

And he blew the whistle. Another moment and the arm fell, and we went on. I didn't think much more about it, but when we got to our destination he began again.

"You can't help it, girl! I know you wanted to be in time; but never mind! You're a bit tired to-night. Have a good rest, and we'll make it up in the morning."

The next day it began again. I had just finished coaling up somewhere past Amberley when Davis muttered:

"You mustn't mind him feeding you. You've mine, you know, anyway. For don't you carry my name? Of course you do. They think you're only 'Southern Queen,' but we know better—eh, Queenie Davis? And you'll be true to nobody else but me, will you? You're not one of the false ones. If you were, my girl, I'd murder you—as I ought to have done the other! Yes, I'd do for you, though you are my lawful wife and bear my name!"

I began to grasp the situation. Davis was imagining the "Southern Queen" was his wife! I'd heard of men getting fond of their engines before, but never such a thing as this. "Those were rather queer things you were saying, mate," I remarked.

"Eh!" he cried, turning sharply upon me. "I suppose I can talk to myself as much as I please without you interfering, can't I! What does it matter to you?"

Then he broke into a loud laugh, and went on:

"Don't take any notice of me, Harry. I'm all right. If I say silly things sometimes I don't mean 'em."

But I watched him narrowly, nevertheless. He was extremely odd for the next few days, constantly addressing his engine with endearing names, and rowing me up if I let the slightest handful of coal-dust fall on the footplate. He'd be down in the sheds long

before the "Southern Queen" was ready to go out, and he'd watch
the cleaners with a jealous eye, and be loth to give her up to their
charge after a run. Once he complained that the coals were not
good enough for her; another time he bought a bottle of scent and
emptied it into the oil-can, declaring that "Queenie liked to have
something sweet about her"; and once I caught him kissing the
reversing gear, and afterwards caressing the pressure-gauge, which
he declared was "Queenie's pulse."

I thought the matter well over, and came to the conclusion that
I ought to tell those in authority that poor Davis was going mad. I
certainly should have done so, and I often wish I had, only my mate
met with a bit of an accident the very nest day. He was getting off
his engine when he stumbled and fell heavily, hurting his leg. The
result was that he had to go off duty and lay up for a fortnight.
During this period a driver named Simmonds was detailed to run
the "Southern Queen," while I, of course, kept my place on the
footplate. I went round to see Davis two or three times, and to my
surprise he never once alluded to his engine, only to remark one
Saturday night that he was well enough to sign on duty Monday
morning, and that I should see him at the sheds.

If I had hoped that his peculiar madness had come to an end I
was mistaken, for the sight of the "Southern Queen" was like a red
rag to a bull. He walked round her, got underneath her with his
oil-can, mounted the footplate and examined everything, muttering more or less all the time. When we got off he suddenly blurted
out:

"Has she been running while I was laid up?"

"Yes," I answered.

"Who's been driving her?"

"Joe Simmonds."

"How dared he do it? Didn't he see my name before him?"

"Yes, of course he did, but—"

"Then what right had he got to interfere with her, eh?"

"Why, of course, mate, he was—"

"There, don't talk to me!" he cried. "How would you like another chap to run off with your wife? But she didn't go willingly,

I'll be bound—not like you're doing now, eh, Queenie?"—and he took back another notch in the reversing gear. "See! she knows her Charlie's with her! Hark at her! Oh, she's a beauty! Gently, then, my girl, gently!"

When we were getting into London he turned round to me again:

"How's she been running?"

"Splendidly! I never knew her in better trim, and Simmonds understood her down to the ground."

"What do you mean?"

"Why, on Saturday we ran into Chichester over a minute under time, and that after two dead stops for signals. I reckon, too, we worked her on the up journey with a couple of hundredweight less coal than usual."

The next moment I regretted having made these statements, for Davis's face grew livid with rage.

"Is this what you're telling me true?" he yelled.

"Yes," I answered; "but—"

"Oh, the false jade! You've proved unfaithful! Simmonds? How could you—you, with my name on you and nobody's hand on the regulator except mine since the day I married you? You're like the other one—false—false—false!"

"For God's sake, be careful, mate!"

"Ah!" he replied, with a smile. "Yes, it's only a silly bit of foolishness. Have I frightened you, Harry? Don't notice me. We're nearly in now. At any rate, we've run to time. Oh, she's a beauty, ha! ha! ha!"

I confess I felt uncomfortable, and I secretly determined that the afternoon journey should be the last I would take without reporting him—in fact, I made up my mind to do so at Portsmouth that very evening. It would have been well if I had seen someone at the London terminus, but I was foolish enough to wait. Hence the awful experience I am about to explain.

Our train was timed to leave London about five, and to run through with only one stop—at Chichester. We got off punctually enough. Davis was silent, and seemed to settle down to his work

quite steadily. The first intimation I had that anything was wrong
was when we were running round the Mitcham curve. We ought to
have slackened speed to twenty miles an hour, but we went round
at a good forty. I thought my mate had forgotten, and sprang to
the brake-handle; but he pushed me aside, crying:

"Leave her alone! We'll see who she goes best, for! Coal her
up—do you hear? I'll teach her to jilt me!"

We thundered through Sutton pretty safely. Then Davis went
to the tool-box and drew out a chisel.

"You've been false to your name, have you?" he yelled, with an
awful look upon his face. "We'll soon set that to rights, for you
sha'n't end your days with my name on you, you vixen!"

Then he deliberately set to work and scratched out the gold
letters of his name.

"Fire her up!" he shouted, turning to me.

"She doesn't want it yet," I replied.

"Never mind if she does or not! She'll have a good deal more
than she wants before we get to the journey's end, I reckon."

I put a couple of shovelfuls on. Then I opened the damper.

"Leave it alone!" said Davis.

"But the pressure's over 170," I remonstrated. "She ought to
blow off."

"She won't blow off—even if we go up to 200. I've screwed up
the safety-valve! See? We'll burst her or smash her somehow—and
don't you try to interfere, or I'll throw you over! No you don't!"

For I had grasped the regulator and was trying to shut off steam.

"You fool!" I cried; "there's a signal against us!"

"All the better, then! We'll smash up sooner! Curse it, the road's
clear again!"

Davis had gone raving mad! He howled with a wild delight as
we plunged into the Dorking tunnel. In less than a minute we were
in daylight again, and Davis was dancing on the footplate.

"Fire her up, curse you! She played me false, did she? Ha! ha!
ha! we'll all smash together! We'll drive to hell this journey! Did
she get up the incline faster than she's doing now? Have a drop of
tea, mate! Yes, you fool, this is the right sort of tea, eh?"

He had filled his tea-can with neat brandy!

"Hands off, or I'll murder you!" he hissed, as I tried to get hold of the liquor. "Your health, Queenie! Success to your last run! Ha! ha! ha!"

And he drained the contents of the can. This made him madder than ever, of course. I grew sick and dizzy as we gained the incline down to Horsham, but my demon companion kept me well at work with his threats. As we flew through the station I glanced at my watch. We were then just over five minutes before time. I turned the matter over in my mind and thought of what was best to be done. There was only one guard to our train in the rear brake-van, and there was no chance of reaching him—only the possibility that he might perhaps guess something was up and put the brake on. But as Davis was one of our best and steadiest drivers, it was scarcely probable that he would notice the advance in time yet. There was only one way out of it to my mind, and that was to make a desperate effort to master the madman. With this thought in view I made a sudden dash at the regulator. He was too quick for me, and in a moment I had his bony fingers round my throat, and he held me against the side of the cab.

"Look here!" he cried, "I warned you once before not to interfere with me, and now you'll have to take the consequences. Listen! You and me and this wretch are running to destruction, and there's going to be no way out of it. We'll go on till she bursts or there's a smash, but there's no such thing as stopping. And you—you, who could stand by and help Simmonds to run her—curse you, you're as bad as she! You shall go first! Get off, I say, get off!"

And he thrust me off the footplate on to the side-step. At first I tried to get along the tender, but he stopped me.

"No, no, go in front—do you hear, in front! I'll push you off altogether if you don't!"

I moved along the engine till I got in front of the cab, holding on by the hand-rail. Suddenly I felt a stinging blow on my arm. The brute was hurling lumps of coal at me!

"Go in front—right in front, I tell you! Go on, you blackguard!"

There was no way out of it. He simply pelted me with huge lumps of coal till I got round on to the little platform in front of the smoke-box. I'd been there often enough before while she was running, but I never felt as I did now. It was an evening in early spring, and dusk was setting in as we dashed through Pulborough and into the open, level country beyond. Above the roar of the engine I could hear Davis yelling madly as every now and then we seemed to give a fresh spurt forward.

I tried to reflect upon the situation. The road was clear as far as the junction with the Brighton branch at Ford, where there might be a block. Between Arundel and Ford there would be a fearful curve, and it was doubtful .if we should keep the metals with the awful speed we were running at. Even if we did run round safely there was bound to be a smash later on. It was an awful position to be in. Once I tried to get back to the footplate; but Davis was on the look-out, and directly I showed my head a big lump of coal came whizzing by.

I half hoped some signalman might see us from his cabin and do something, but, of course, it is no uncommon thing for a fireman to go in front of the engine for a minute or two; and, even if he had noticed that anything was wrong, he could not have stopped the train. We were midway between Amberley and Arundel now, and it was getting quite dark. I could just discern the outline of the castle looming on the heights on our right, and in another minute we were dashing through the station, in spite of the fact that there was a *red light* flashing in our face from the home signal.

What did it mean? It meant that in all probability there was a block ahead at the junction, and, if so, we were doomed. On we rushed through the level country till I saw by the declining light the rails ahead beginning to curve, and with a swing and a lurch we commenced the dangerous piece of road. Ahead was another red light, and just beyond the junction signal-box I saw with horror the glare on the smoke from the open fire-box of an engine! Yes, there could be no mistake, a goods train had left Ford Station and was proceeding towards Brighton, crossing the very points we should be rushing through in another minute or so. A frightful collision was inevitable!

It was just at this awful moment that a plan of deliverance flashed across me—so suddenly that I found myself acting before I had time to think it out. It was this. Just in front of me in the centre of the buffer-plate was the pipe of the Westinghouse brake, used, of course, only when the engine was running tender first. This pipe was closed by a cock, well within reach. Now, by simply turning this cock the compressed air would be free to act *throughout the train*, and the brake would be applied to every wheel from the cylinders beneath the coaches. This is the simple meaning of the "automatic brake." If the pipe snaps or becomes disconnected the brake is applied at once, the driver having no power to prevent it. I ought to have thought of this before, but even now it was not too late.

Throwing myself down on the narrow platform I grasped the pipe, holding on with all my might, for the motion was frightful. Then I turned the cock. There was a hiss and a jar and a terrible grinding as every wheel throughout the train was suddenly braked. I heard Davis yell with fury. The steam hissed from the cylinders, but its power was mastered. With a fearful rattle and jolt the train slowed down—and then stopped! I shall never forget it! Only three yards from the junction points at the moment when the goods train crossed in front of us—three yards, that was all the distance between safety and death!

I sprang down into the six-foot-way, and the madman was after me in a moment. But it was useless. The guard and half a dozen passengers came rushing along and soon pulled him off me, though it was no easy matter to hold him while I climbed to the footplate and shut the regulator.

"Get off!" he yelled. "She's doomed to die, I tell you! She ran off with another man, and we're both going to hell together. Let me get at her!"

But strong hands carried him along to the guard's van. I brought the train slowly into Ford, and was thankful to find a spare fireman there, who came on with me for the remainder of the journey.

Fortunately, Davis had not damaged the engine, though he had let the water run down very low, and very probably if I hadn't have turned on the injector at once we might have had a bad business.

The end of it all was that Charles Davis was put into an asylum, but the poor fellow died shortly afterwards, mad till the last, and mixing up his first love with the "Southern Queen." I had to go off duty for over a week, for I was quite knocked under after that awful ride with a mad driver and hairbreadth escape from a terrible death.

In a Tight Fix

We were strolling through the Paris Salon. Tired of passing through endless galleries and gazing at the pictures, we had descended into the great central hall devoted to statuary, where it is permissible to smoke, and had lit our cigarettes. My companion was only a passing acquaintance, a fellow-countryman I had met at the *table d'hôte*, and who, like myself, was passing a few weeks in the French metropolis. He was a slight, delicate-looking young man of about five-and-twenty, a well-read and charming companion. As we entered the hall, with its long rows of statues, I noticed that he turned a little pale, but put it down to the heat of the day. Presently we stopped to admire a gracefully-modelled figure by one of the most eminent exhibitors. . . . "A very fine piece of sculpture," said my friend.

"Scarcely that," I replied. "It's made out of an appropriate material—plaster of Paris."

"Plaster of Paris!" he replied, with a nervous start; "how terrible!"

"Why, what's the matter?" I asked, with a laugh.

"Ah!" he replied, "I daresay my exclamation seemed strange to you. But plaster of Paris has an awful meaning to my ears, as you would agree if you heard of an adventure from the effects of which I am only just recovering."

"Have you any objection to telling me?"

"Not the slightest. Come and sit down over yonder, and I'll explain myself; then you'll see why I hate the name of plaster of Paris."

312

So we sat down and he began his story, which I repeat in his own words as far as possible.

Jasper Keen and myself were chums during the year we were together at Oxford, and our friendship continued after he had gone down through the two years I remained. He was my senior—three or four years older than myself; and, as is generally the case in strong friendships, my opposite in many respects. I was a reading man; Keen was more noted for the strength of his arm on the river, and as a desperate "forward" in the footer field. My temper was always one of the mildest; Keen would give vent to paroxysms of anger, and weeks of smothered, revengeful passion. He was a tall, magnificently-built fellow, and the men often called us the "long and short of it," so great was the contrast between us.

I do not say that there was nothing intellectual about Jasper Keen. On the contrary, he was a genius; only, like most of his species, he worked by fits and starts. When he did work, however, it was to some purpose, as the examiners knew. And with all his great strength and passion for sport he had a very marked artistic temperament, which showed itself in his love of sculpture and modelling. His rooms were a curiosity. Very few books—he always sold them the instant he had finished reading them—prize oars and "pots" in profusion, and a collection of clay busts, modelled by himself. There was a row of college Dons on his mantelshelf, clever caricatures, his intimate friends—and his enemies. If he liked a man, he made an excellent little bust of him; on the contrary, one who incurred his hatred was modelled in some eccentric or repulsive manner, but still with strict regard to a correct likeness so that it was impossible to mistake the man.

When Jasper Keen left the 'Varsity he set up a studio in London. He was a man of fairly large private means, and did not care about earning money. He devoted himself still to sport during the intervals when he was not exercising his hobby, and lived a generally easy and comfortable life.

In due time I also went to live in town, and plunged into the vortex of literary work, to which I had determined to devote my life. I constantly saw Keen, and our friendship was as great as ever, until—

Yes, "until"—you guess what I mean. There was a woman in it, as there always is, and she stepped in between us. Jasper Keen loved her madly, jealously. Over and over again he was repulsed, for Ivey Stirling never cared for him. He frightened her with the intensity of his devotion. One day he said to her:—

"The truth is, you care for another man."

"And what if I do?" said Ivey, boldly.

"What if you do! Why, this. If I find the man, even if he were my greatest friend, I'd kill him rather than he should win you!"

He *was* Keen's greatest friend. The man who was accepted by Ivey Stirling was myself, and, in spite of all, I trust she will be my wife before the year is out.

I may well say, "In spite of all." When Keen heard of it, he was furious. I told him myself. I thought it best that he should hear the news first from the lips of his friend, and I hoped from the bottom of my heart that our friendship would not be destroyed. So I went round to his studio and broke the news to him.

He stood for some moments with his whole frame quivering, his nostrils dilated, and his eyes starting forward, like some wild beast held in restraint by a chain. Then he turned to a pedestal on which stood a bust of myself, fashioned by him in the old Oxford days, and dashed it to the ground. The fragments of clay went rattling over the studio.

"Leonard Fendron," he yelled, "as I have broken your bust, so will I break you. You false, traitorous hound, you think you have stolen from me the one object I have to live for. But not yet—do you hear? I could crush you as you stand—I could break every bone in your body with this hand of mine. But that would be too poor a revenge. I will wait—I will make you suffer such agony as you have given me. Go, I say, go, and may the worst of all curses light upon you—the curse of a friend you have wronged."

It was useless to explain, so I went. Ivey was much disturbed when I told her about this interview; but to tell the truth, I thought little of it myself. I had seen Keen in a paroxysm of rage before, and I hoped that in time he would see things sensibly for the sake of our old friendship.

For a year I never saw the man. His studio was shut up, and report said that he had gone abroad. Then I suddenly met him face to face in Fleet Street. I was going to pass him by at first, but he stopped me and shook hands.

"How d'ye do, Fendron?" he said. "Last time I saw you I was in a bit of a temper. But that's all over now, and I can afford to let the past be buried in the past—if you can too."

"Certainly," I replied; "I'm only too delighted to hear our friendship still exists."

"That's right," he said. "And now come and have some lunch with me. There's a restaurant handy where we can talk."

So I went with him. He was most friendly and chatty. He told me he had been abroad, but that the last five months he had spent in England.

"I've been living like a hermit," he said. "The fact is, I'm engaged on a master-piece of work. It will beat anything I've ever done. Oh, it's a grand thing, I can tell you. I fitted up a studio in the country some months ago, and I've hardly stirred out of it since—simply worked and seen no one. But I've had an end in view, as you shall see for yourself. Now, I want you to pay me a visit, and you shall be the first to see my masterpiece. Will you come?"

"Certainly," I said; "what day will suit you?"

"Let me see—it's the 9th to-day. I want a clear fortnight on the work before I finish. Can you come on Friday, the 24th, and stay till Monday? I can easily put you up."

"With pleasure. That will suit me capitally. Only, you haven't told me where to come to yet."

"I hardly think you'd find it if I did," he answered, thoughtfully; "it's not very far from town, but it's a bit awkward to get at for a stranger. So suppose you meet me at Euston at half-past eight on that Friday evening, and I'll take you down. It's rather late, but you shall have a good supper as soon as you get there, I promise you."

To this arrangement I accordingly agreed, and on the 24th I

met Keen at Euston. Telling me that he had purchased my ticket, he took me to a local train. We got out at Sudbury, the station near Wembley Park.

"There's some little distance to walk," he said, "so we'd better step it out briskly."

It must have been a tramp of over two miles that finally brought us to a large house, standing quite alone a little way off the road, somewhere in the direction of Edgware. Although not many miles from London, the country about here is very lonely, and there was not a house near. It was about ten o'clock and quite dark when Keen opened the door with a latch-key.

"Welcome!" he cried. "You must be tired and hungry. We'll have supper at once, it's all ready."

And without further ado he led the way into a good-sized room, lit by a lamp, and revealed a table spread with cold viands.

There was a change in his tone of voice that made me feel rather uneasy as he went on:—

"We're all to ourselves, Fendron. I've let the servants out for the evening. But everything's ready for us, so sit down and begin. We must be our own butlers."

It was an excitable meal. The whole of the time Keen talked and laughed and joked. He ran on about old times and our college days; he laughed long and boisterously—once I expostulated with him for his noise.

"What does it matter?" he shouted. "There's not a soul near. That's the beauty of the country. You might yell yourself hoarse in this shanty of mine, and no one would hear you."

He even touched on my engagement. Leaning across the table, he insisted upon grasping my hand.

"I've never congratulated you yet, old chap, you know. Last time we were on this subject I was in a huff. But it's all right now. May you be happy—ha! ha! ha!—as happy as you deserve!"

Supper over, he took up the lamp.

"Come," he said, "we'll adjourn to the studio and smoke there. I've got to show you my great work. It will surprise you. Come along."

He led the way to the very top of the house, and we entered a large room which he had turned into a studio. Lumps of clay, pieces of stone, tools, and half-finished works were lying about in artistic confusion. On a small table was a box of cigars, several decanters of wine and spirits, siphons and tumblers. In one corner of the room was a large bath, filled with a white powder, while a small shovel and a couple of pails of water stood by it. In the centre of the room was a very large, hollow wooden pedestal, shaped like a cylinder, and quite as high as my shoulders, such as is used sometimes for standing heavy busts upon. The top, however, had been removed from this cylinder, and there was nothing on it. The room was evidently only lighted by a skylight, and a thick curtain hung over the door, and stretched across what was apparently a recess at the farther end of the apartment was another curtain, hanging in black folds.

Keen gave me a cigar and sat me down in a chair.

"Well, what do you think of my workshop?" he asked.

"I've hardly had time to look round, yet," I replied. "What's that huge pedestal for?"

"You'll see later on," he said.

Again that ominous change in his voice.

"And what's in that bath?"

"Oh! plaster of Paris," he answered, with a laugh; "but now, watch! I'm going to draw the curtain!"

First lighting a couple more lamps, he drew the curtain aside with a sudden jerk. The result was electrical. There, standing on a small raised platform, life-size and most exquisitely modelled, was a statue of Ivey Stirling, my betrothed. I sprang to my feet and uttered an exclamation of surprise.

"Yes," shouted Keen, "there stands the image of the woman you love—and the woman I loved once. She whose image was so graven upon my heart that I was able to mould this statue as you see it; to mould it for you, Leonard Fendron, who have won the prize. Did I not tell you it was a master-piece?"

"You did. And so it is," I replied, with an indescribable feeling of terror creeping over me. My companion rushed to the table and filled two glasses. One of them he thrust into my hand.

"A health!" he cried. "Drain it to the dregs. A health to the fair Ivey, your betrothed! Drink it, Fendron!"

"A health to the fair Ivey—my future wife," I said, mechanically, drinking the liquor and gazing at the statue.

"Your future wife!" echoed Keen, with a terrible voice. "Never!" I turned and gazed at him. He was foaming with madness and rage. At the same moment my head grew dizzy, and the room seemed twirling round. I made a wild rush for the door, but fell in a dead faint before I could reach it.

When I came to my senses again there was an awful feeling of cramp all over me. My whole body with my legs and arms seemed to be held in a vice that was pressing upon me at every point. I opened my eyes. The first thing that met my gaze was the statue of Ivey placed opposite me. I was in an upright position, but I could not move. I looked downwards, but not even then did I realize the horrible truth. I was up to my shoulders in the hollow pedestal.

"Halloa! you've come to, have you?" said a mocking voice, and Jasper Keen stood in front of me, the grin of a lunatic on his face.

"For God's sake, what have you done?" I asked.

"I'll very soon tell you," he replied, with a sneer; "I've made a statue of you. Listen. You are up to your shoulders in plaster of Paris. Whilst you were insensible from the effects of that drugged wine you drank I placed you in the pedestal, mixed that bathful of plaster and water, and poured it in with you. It took me some time to do, and it's now four o'clock in the morning. By this time it's thoroughly set, and you cannot move hand or foot."

The terrible situation was dawning upon my mind. My tormentor went on:—

"Did you think, Leonard Fendron, that I had forgotten? Did you expect to get a forgiveness from Jasper Keen? You should have known me better, and not have walked so foolishly into the snare that I set for you. I told you I would have revenge. I have waited and schemed a long time, but now the hour of my vengeance has come. Here, before the image of the woman you love, you shall die, Leonard Fendron—die a slow and an awful death. I shall leave you here, fixed, immovable—a living statue. Don't think to escape, for I have planned it well. My servants were dismissed two days ago; I told them I was going to leave the house for some months. You can shriek and howl as much as you please, but no one will hear you. I've tested that carefully. In short, unless an angel from Heaven comes to set you free, here you'll stay till you starve to death in cramp and agony."

"Have mercy—" I began, but he stopped me.

"Mercy? As soon expect to find it at Satan's hands! Here, I'll put this table with the liquor on it close to you. It will be more tantalizing. And now I must be off. I've planned my escape well. Good-bye, Leonard Fendron. I wish you joy with your bride of clay!"

And the madman, for so he was, I am assured, at that moment struck me a heavy blow in the face, turned on his heel, slammed the door, and I heard his footsteps disappear down the stairs. I was alone and helpless.

I cannot describe the torture as the long hours went by and the light of the lamps slowly faded as the day began to dawn. The cramp in my body and limbs was awful, my throat was parched, and my brain seemed on fire. I yelled and screamed at the top of my voice, listening in anguish for an answering call, but answers came there none. The villain had prepared his plot too well! In my madness I tried to lurch forward and hurl myself to the floor. In vain! The pedestal was fixed! And there, a few feet in front of me, stood the statue of Ivey, so lifelike and beautiful that it seemed at times to my frenzied brain that she was smiling and speaking to me. Then came a time when all was dark. I had fainted. Too soon I returned to the fearful reality, and redoubled my screams. It was fruitless. I was in a mental and bodily agony that was too awful for words. How the hours passed I knew not. It seemed years that I had been fixed there. I seemed never to have lived at all, except in a world of terror.

My God! I cannot describe the anguish. . . .

Suddenly there came a sound. . . . Yes. . . . I was not mistaken. . . . A heavy bang on the roof over-head. I listened with straining ears—ah—a footstep!

"For God's sake, help—help!" I cried.

Then there came a tap at the skylight over-head, and a voice spoke:—

"Excuse me, but may I come in?"

"Come in!" I shrieked; "in Heaven's name yes, come in!"

"You seem in a mighty hurry," replied the voice. "Suppose you open the skylight for me."

"I can't," I answered; "smash it—do what you like—only be quick."

Crash! the glass came spattering down on the floor, a foot came through the window, then another, and in a few seconds the man himself stood before me.

"Well, I'm blowed!" he exclaimed; "what on earth does this mean?"

"For God's sake be quick and set me free," I begged. "It's killing me. Give me something to drink first."

I eagerly drained the tumbler of soda-water he held to my lips. Then he set to work. He was a businesslike man, and there were some stone-chisels and hammers about. In a very few minutes he had split the pedestal down, and was hammering and chipping away at the plaster, which, of course, by this time was quite hard, and came off in flakes and lumps. It seemed ages to me, but he afterwards told me it took him a very short time to get me free, though large lumps of plaster still stuck to my clothes. I was horribly cramped, and could not stir when it was over. He undressed me and gave me a tremendous rubbing, until at length the circulation became partially restored and the agony began to subside, and I was able to talk.

"Well," he exclaimed, "this is the rummiest thing I've ever come across. Goodness only knows what would have happened to you if my parachute hadn't gone wrong."

"Your parachute?"

"Yes—that's how I came here. I'm a professional aeronaut, and I've been making a balloon ascent and a parachute descent at Wembley Park every Saturday afternoon for a couple of months past."

"And you landed on the roof?" I exclaimed.

"Exactly. Something went wrong, and I found myself coming down more quickly than I intended. The wind's a bit high and blew me some distance, and I thought I was going smash against this house, but, as luck had it, I just managed to tumble on the roof, which, luckily, is flat, and here I am. Lucky for you, wasn't it?"

Keen's words had come very nearly true. He had said that only an angel from Heaven could rescue me!

Well, little remains to be told. I was very ill for weeks; in fact, I am only just getting over it now. The only wonder is that I escaped as I did, but as Keen had put me in the pedestal with my clothes on, and had not pressed down the plaster, the pressure was slighter than it might have been, though that was bad enough.

As for Keen himself, he got clean away. You see, he had over twelve hours' start, for it was not until late on Saturday afternoon that the aeronaut found me. I don't know, and I don't much care, what has become of him. I only mean to take good care that he doesn't have another chance of stopping our marriage.

And now, perhaps, you will understand why I feel a little queer at the mention of plaster of Paris.

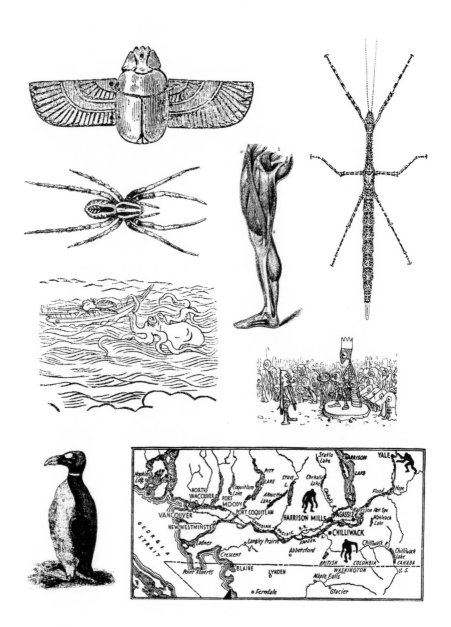

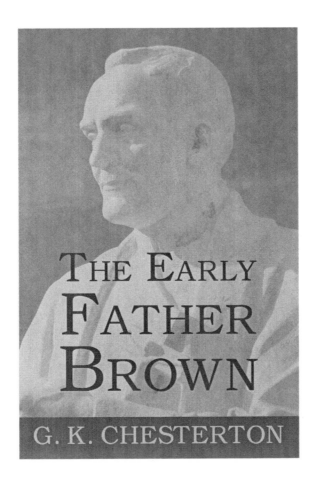

The Early Father Brown
ISBN 1-61646-012-1

Coachwhip Publications

CoachwhipBooks.com

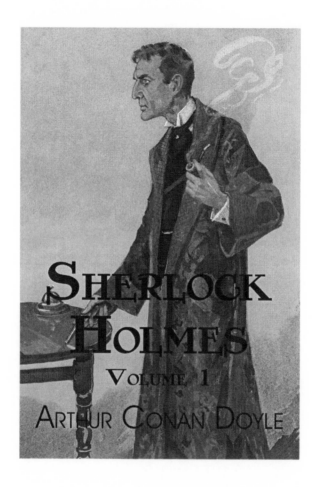

Sherlock Holmes, Vols. 1-3
ISBN 1-61646-006-7
ISBN 1-61646-007-5
ISBN 1-61646-008-3

COACHWHIP PUBLICATIONS

ALSO AVAILABLE

AN
AFRICAN
MILLIONAIRE

Grant Allen

An African Millionaire
ISBN 1-61646-014-8

COACHWHIP PUBLICATIONS

COACHWHIPBOOKS.COM

Mystery and Detection with

THE THINKING MACHINE

Volume

I

JACQUES FUTRELLE

Mystery and Detection with the Thinking Machine, 1-2
ISBN 1-930585-70-5
ISBN 1-930585-71-3

NOVEMBER JOE

DETECTIVE OF THE WOODS

H. HESKETH-PRICHARD

November Joe
ISBN 1-61646-013-X

COACHWHIP PUBLICATIONS

COACHWHIPBOOKS.COM

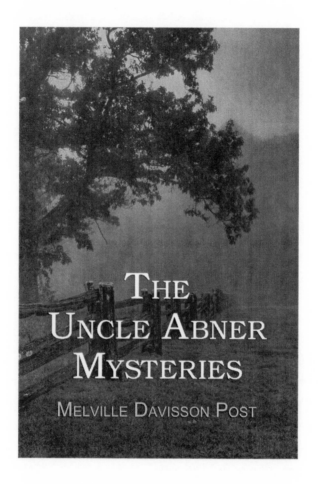

THE
UNCLE ABNER
MYSTERIES
MELVILLE DAVISSON POST

The Uncle Abner Mysteries
ISBN 1-61646-016-4

Coachwhip Publications

Also Available

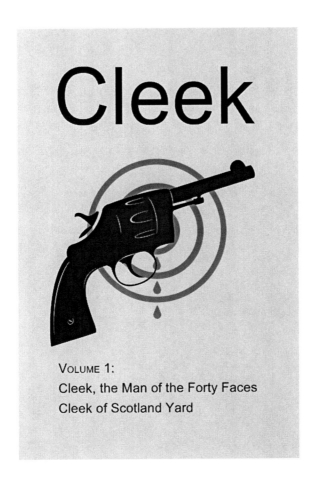

Cleek

VOLUME 1:
Cleek, the Man of the Forty Faces
Cleek of Scotland Yard

Cleek, Volumes 1-3
ISBN 1-930585-97-7
ISBN 1-930585-98-5
ISBN 1-930585-99-3

COACHWHIP PUBLICATIONS

COACHWHIPBOOKS.COM

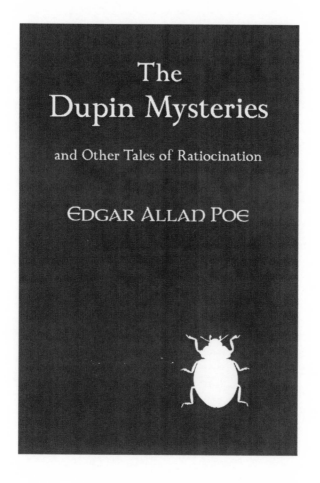

The

Dupin Mysteries

and Other Tales of Ratiocination

EDGAR ALLAN POE

The Dupin Mysteries
ISBN 1-930585-69-1

Coachwhip Publications

Also Available

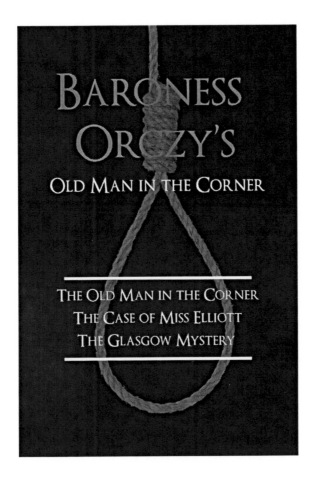

BARONESS ORCZY'S
OLD MAN IN THE CORNER

THE OLD MAN IN THE CORNER
THE CASE OF MISS ELLIOTT
THE GLASGOW MYSTERY

Baroness Orczy's Old Man in the Corner
ISBN 1-61646-015-6